SUNSET

OF

EMPIRE

Stories from the Shahnameh of Ferdowsi

Volume III

TRANSLATED FROM THE PERSIAN BY
Dick Davis

Mage Publishers
Washington, DC
2004

THIS IS A MOHAMMAD AND NAJMIEH BATMANGLIJ BOOK
PUBLISHED BY MAGE

A COMPLETE LIST OF ILLUSTRATIONS, CREDITS AND
ACKNOWLEDGMENTS CAN BE FOUND STARTING ON PAGE 523.

LIBRARY OF CONGRESS CATALOGING-IN-PUBLICATION DATA

Firdawsî.
[Shâhnâmah. English. Selections]
Sunset of empire / translated from the Persian by Dick Davis. -- 1st ed.
p. cm. -- (Stories from the Shahnameh of Ferdowsi ; v. 3)
ISBN 0-934211-68-X
I. Davis, Dick, 1945- II. Title.
PK6456.A13D3813 2004
891'.5511--dc22
2003018801

Printed in Korea

FIRST EDITION
CLOTH BOUND
ISBN 0-934211-68-X

MAGE BOOKS ARE AVAILABLE THROUGH BOOKSTORES
OR DIRECTLY FROM THE PUBLISHER.
VISIT MAGE ON THE WEB AT WWW.mage.com
OR CALL 1-800-962-0922 OR 202-342-1642
TO ORDER BOOKS OR TO RECEIVE OUR CURRENT CATALOG.

❧ CONTENTS ❧

Introduction 7

The Story of Darab and the Fuller 15

Sekandar's Conquest of Persia 33

The Reign of Sekandar 51

The Ashkanians 119

The Reign of Ardeshir 151

The Reign of Shapur, Son of Ardeshir 175

The Reign of Shapur Zu'l Aktaf 179

The Reign of Yazdegerd the Unjust 203

The Reign of Bahram Gur 239

The Story of Mazdak .305

The Reign of Kesra Nushin-Ravan 312

The Reign of Hormozd 353

The Reign of Khosrow Parviz 417

Ferdowsi's Lament for the Death of His Son 441

The Story of Khosrow and Shirin 461

The Reign of Yazdegerd 489

Glossary of Names and Their Pronunciation 514

Credits and Acknowledgments 523

Guide to the Illustrations 523

❧ INTRODUCTION ❧

Fathers and Sons, our second volume of stories from Ferdowsi's *Shahnameh,* ended with the escape to India of Sasan, the eponymous ancestor of the future founder of the Sasanian dynasty. The appearance of his name marks the moment at which the poem begins to move from legend to history. Increasingly, from this point on, many of at least the public figures whose lives are chronicled by Ferdowsi have some correspondence (albeit at first often highly fanciful) to historical characters.

Ferdowsi's record of Iran's pre-Islamic myths, legends, and history culminates in the greatest watershed of the culture, the Arab invasion of the seventh century, which both ended a series of empires and initiated a new, syncretic civilization. Ferdowsi places a similar watershed, the conquest by Sekandar (Alexander), close to the center of his poem, and after this historical crisis nothing in the *Shahnameh* is quite as it was before. The poem's geographical center shifts decisively westward, culminating in the location of the Sasanian capital at Ctesiphon in Mesopotamia, and this shift is reflected in the nature of the enemies the country's kings are forced to fight. If the ancient threat from central Asia is still present (as in the invasion of Saveh Shah, the leader of both Chinese and central Asian Turkish forces), new threats from the west (Greece, Rome, Byzantium) and the southwest (the Arabs) assume decisive importance.

The nature of the stories also changes, and often they seem to be providing a kind of mirror image of the world of myth and legend of the poem's opening half. In the first half of the poem, prominent fathers (Rostam, Kavus, Goshtasp) are directly or indirectly responsible for their sons' deaths (Sohrab, Seyavash, Esfandyar), but in the second half prominent sons (Khosrow Parviz, Shirui) are held to be directly or indirectly responsible for their fathers' deaths (Hormozd, Khosrow Parviz). In the first half, the major champion is Rostam who, despite increasing provocation, attempts to maintain loyalty to the royal families of Iran and emphatically rejects the notion that he might ever be the king of the country. In the second half the major champion is Bahram Chubineh, who rebels against both of his monarchs and attempts to seize the throne for himself.

Most striking perhaps is the way that the role of women, and particularly non-Persian women, is redefined in the poem's second half. Virtually all of the significant women in the poem's mythological and legendary sections are non-Persian in origin (Sindokht, Rudabeh, Sudabeh, Farigis, Manizheh, Katayun) and, with the signal exception of Sudabeh, almost all of them are positively presented. Even Sudabeh, the first time we meet her, is a positive figure like Rudabeh and Manizheh, who defies her non-Persian father to be faithful to the Persian she loves. The most prominent female figure in the poem's second half is certainly Gordyeh, who is not foreign but Iranian, and represents the traditional and deeply Iranian virtue of loyalty to ancient mores. When foreign women do appear in the second half they are much less welcome than they had been in the legendary narratives. In the poem's earlier sections most of the narratives' major heroes have foreign mothers, but this doesn't prevent them from being seen as great exemplars of Persian virtues, and miscegenation is an accepted and generally welcomed fact. Indeed, perhaps the most positively presented king of the whole poem, Kay Khosrow, has only one Iranian grandparent; the other three are all central Asian Turks. But miscegenation is regarded with deep suspicion in the poem's second half, and that Hormozd has a Chinese mother and Shirui a Byzantine mother is seen in each case as a distinct negative. The preference here is for emphatic endogamy, although Ferdowsi is clearly embarrassed by the pre-Islamic laws that encouraged marriages within the immediate family, as is evident from his treatment of the daughter-father/Homay-Bahman relationship, and the way that he glosses over something earlier historians unequivocally recorded, that Gordyeh was married to her brother Bahram Chubineh.

One notable woman who has gone down in Persian legend as foreign in origin, and whose story appears in the present volume, is Shirin. Unlike Nezami (the twelfth-century author of the better known romance version of her tale), Ferdowsi doesn't explicitly tell us that she is not a Persian, but given the suspicion of foreign consorts in the poem's second half, the unexplained scandal that surrounds her in his version of her tale, and the fact that her presence at court needs strenuous justification from her husband and king, Khosrow Parviz, perhaps point to this. This unexplained scandal is also an example of how not only the content of the tales changes in the poem's second half, but also Ferdowsi's method of telling them. In general, when reading the poem's earlier narratives, we have a clear idea of the ethical issues involved, and of where our sympathies are supposed to lie. We know that Seyavash is ethically superior to both Kavus and Sudabeh; that Piran Viseh acts from more morally admirable motives than does his king, Afrasyab; and that Goshtasp is at fault when he sends Esfandyar to bring Rostam to his court in chains. This moral clarity is often much harder to find in Ferdowsi's portraits of the central characters of his poem's later sections, many of whom are presented in a highly ambiguous and ethically unresolved fashion. Are we to approve or disapprove of Shirin? When we first meet her she is an abandoned woman and a figure of pathos; she elicits our sympathy. She is accused of some unspecified moral impurity and the charge is never really denied, merely evaded; we suspend judgment. She secretly murders her husband's favorite wife and assumes her position in the harem; we disapprove. She rejects her odious stepson, Shirui, and has a splendid speech of self-defense and a moving death scene; we approve, and this seems to be the final impression we are meant to bring away from her tale. But the figure she is most similar to from the poem's first half is the generally evil Sudabeh. Like Sudabeh she is a fairly ruthless and (probably) foreign royal consort who combines a dubious ethical reputation with an absolute hold on the king's affections, and at one point she seems to be about to become erotically involved with her stepson. With this comparison in mind we are again tempted to disapprove.

This moral ambiguity is not confined to Ferdowsi's portraits of female characters. Another prime example is that of the reformer Mazdak. We read that he is knowledgeable and that his words are wise, and when there is a famine the analogies he makes to the king concerning the populace's sufferings seem cogent and laudable. But the man who defeats him in argument is sponsored by Nushin-Ravan (Anushirvan), who is presented as one of the most admirable monarchs in the poem, and Ferdowsi explicitly tells us at the end of Mazdak's tale that a wise man would not act as he did. At the opening of his tale we seem meant to admire him; at the end we are virtually told to despise him. Perhaps the poem's most extreme instance of apparent authorial moral ambiguity, in the portrayal of a character, occurs in the account of Sekandar (Alexander), who is presented as both a barbarous conqueror and an ethically motivated searcher for enlightenment.

The reasons for this complexity, and ways in which it affects our experience of reading the tales, can be considered as separate, if related, issues. A major cause of some of the tales' ambiguities seems clear: Ferdowsi had much fuller sources for many of the quasi-historical narratives than he had for the legendary material, and some of these sources seem to have been quite radically contradictory of one another. The fact that he did not, apparently, attempt to resolve these contradictions seems significant. His method sometimes seems analogous to that adopted by a number of medieval Islamic historians (e.g., Tabari) who, when their sources offered differing versions of the same events, put down both versions, and then added, "But God knows best." Ferdowsi doesn't say this, and he doesn't explicitly tell us that he is recording different versions, but he (apparently) simply splices them together and leaves the contradictions intact in the one narrative. What is perhaps especially interesting is that in the pre-Sekandar portion of the poem we can sometimes see him choosing one version over another in the few instances when we know that he had more than one account available for a tale. For example, there were two versions as to why Rostam and Goshtasp quarreled. One was that Rostam despised Goshtasp's family as upstart, and Goshtasp resented this, the other was that Rostam vehemently denounced Goshtasp's adoption of the new religion of Zoroastrianism. The first version, which Ferdowsi follows, is found in Tabari's *History*; the second is in Dinawari's *History*, as well as in a number of works written after Ferdowsi's *Shahnameh*, e.g., the anonymous *History of Sistan*. This second version is wholly ignored by Ferdowsi. Here, for one of the legendary tales, we see him choosing one account over another, but in the historical sections of his poem his method seems to be more one of splicing than of choice and exclusion.

The contradictions are not only moral, but often factual. Sometimes these seem significant (Sasan has two differing lineages), often they seem simply incidental. Who, for example, is responsible for the blinding of King Hormozd? A prophecy says his wife will do it; we are told that members of a mob stirred up by Gostahm do it, unbeknownst to Hormozd's son, Khosrow Parviz. Khosrow Parviz is later accused of either having done it personally or of having instigated it. Ferdowsi apparently favors the second version (the mob), but he still includes the other two in his text.

When we compare the stories included in this third volume to those in the poem's legendary portion we see the truth of A. J. P. Taylor's aphorism, "History gets thicker as it approaches recent times—more people, more events, and more books written about them." One senses Ferdowsi dealing with these accumulating people, events, and books in his presentation of the historical narratives, which are thick with detail in a way that is quite absent from most of the earlier tales. If this multiplicity of detail can occasionally lead to contradictions, and sometimes to outright anachronisms (as in Sekandar's Christianity), it can also, paradoxically, give the tales a quotidian realism that is largely absent from the legendary material, as well as providing for sudden and arresting shifts of tone. Furthermore, the intensity of a number of the psychological portraits in this section (e.g., that of Bahram Chubineh) depends largely on the telling accumulation of such details. This concern with the quotidian brings another advantage; it is in the Sasanian section of the poem that we most often glimpse daily life outside of the court and the realm of the heroic. The occasional vivid vignettes of rural life that we encounter in the reigns of the later Sasanian monarchs contribute a kind of stylized realism that can be charming or sobering, depending on the circumstances recounted. In the same way, much of the humor of the poem also occurs in the Sasanian section, again frequently in moments located outside of the court. A new problem is that when Ferdowsi's sources lack detailed accounts, he must nevertheless give some version of what he believes to have happened. His apologetic and relatively perfunctory account of the Ashkanians (Parthians) was clearly caused by the fact that the Sasanians had fairly efficiently obliterated them from the historical record. Interestingly enough, this is something that Bahram Chubineh threatens to do to the Sasanians themselves. When the government of the Islamic Republic expunged from public life all positive references to the Pahlavis, even changing all the street names in the major cities, they were following ancient precedent.

From the opening of the poem the Persian courts are characterized as centers of both justice and pleasure. The ideal king will administer justice, which includes protecting the frontiers of the country against invasion, and his court will also represent a kind of earthly paradise whose pleasures include feasting, wine-drinking, the giving and receiving of gifts, hunting, and the celebration of the major festivals of the Zoroastrian year. The worst sins, for both the king and his subjects, are greed and excessive ambition. Erotic pleasure is hardly dwelt on in the poem's legendary section, although it is understood that this too is a constituent of the court's function as an earthly paradise.

In the stories that make up the present volume—those from the "historical" section of the poem—erotic pleasure is sometimes brought into the foreground in a way that it had not been in the earlier tales, and the simultaneous association of both justice and pleasure in the person of the ideal king becomes more problematic. The three most positively presented kings of the post-Sekandar section of the poem are Ardeshir (the founder of the Sasanian dynasty), Bahram Gur, and Nushin-Ravan (Anushirvan the Just). Ardeshir is presented as a vigorous reformer who rewrites his country's legal code, energetically puts down internal dissension, and secures the country's borders against invasion. Nushin-Ravan is a man who inherits an empire and strives to administer it justly and according to ancient precepts, while remaining open to wisdom from other sources, especially India. The main difference between them and the more admirable legendary monarchs whom they succeed is the centralization of their administrative and cultural control. The sense of various centers of power (e.g., Sistan) only tangentially under the central government's authority, which is everywhere present in the legendary material, has largely disappeared from the narratives. Nevertheless, both these kings are re-embodiments, in Sasanian terms, of ideals that have been explicit throughout the poem's legendary section.

Bahram Gur, of whom Ferdowsi seems emphatically to approve introduces a relatively new element into the poem, which is the emphasis on pleasure, especially the pleasure of erotic adventure, as the primary, and apparently often sole, activity of a monarch. Bahram Gur is presented as an ideal monarch who is largely preoccupied with sensual, private pleasure, but who is nevertheless just, and widely loved by his subjects, even if his vizier is worried about what he sees as the king's excessive attachment to women. Two stories—one beginning in comedy and ending in tragedy, the other wholly comic, which are placed back to back in his reign—also elaborate on another pleasure that had been taken for granted in the earlier sections of the poem, and this is drinking wine. The first story ends with wine being forbidden, and the second with this prohibition being abrogated as long as one does not drink to excess. It seems more than a coincidence that the outcome of the stories concerning wine in Bahram's reign reverses orthodox interpretation of the Qoranic texts on wine, according to which the prohibition abrogates the implied permission to drink in moderation. At the end of the poem, when Rostam the son of Hormozd prophesies the disasters that will come to Iran as a result of the Arab invasion, Bahram Gur's reign is singled out as emblematic of all that the Arabs will destroy, and we realize that the emphasis on sensual pleasure and its attendant luxuries in his reign was deliberately presented as an alternative to the civilization brought by the Moslem Arab conquerors, which is characterized, by Rostam at least, in wholly negative and dour terms.

But despite Rostam's unequivocally bleak prophecy, the final episodes of the poem are profoundly ambiguous. Hormozd and Khosrow Parviz are complex, weak kings who seem to have inherited Bahram Gur's attachment to pleasure but have none of his panache or instinct for largess, and are unable to command the affection and loyalty of their subjects. They are followed by a virtual rabble. The sense of an empire destroyed as much by the weakness, extravagance, and squalid infighting of its rulers as by outside invasion pervades the poem's closing pages. Although the poet is emphatic in his lament for the civilization that was destroyed by the invasion, his depiction of the negotiations between the Arabs and the Persians seems at times weighted in the Arabs' moral favor. It is difficult to read the scene in which the laconic and almost naked Arab envoy Sho'beh confronts the arrogant Persian commanders, resplendent in their golden armor, as anything but an indictment of the Persians. Despite the undeniable epic grandeur of its best-known passages, the *Shahnameh* is never a simple poem, and the moral complexities it explores throughout its immense length come to a magnificent and unresolved climax in its last pages. If Ferdowsi's final claim is one of pride in his work, an emotion that seems almost as strongly present is that of bewilderment. As he frequently remarks whenever he has to record the untimely death of a character he admires, he cannot understand what the heavens are about, and this sense of a repeatedly frustrated interrogation of God's purposes reaches its apogee in the poem's closing scenes.

A Note on Two Names and on a Game

The geographical term *Rum*, and its adjective *Rumi*, are particularly hard to translate consistently in the stories in this volume. The words refer to the civilizations that lie to the west of Iran, in Asia Minor and in Europe. Thus Sekandar the Macedonian is a Rumi, as are the Roman emperors who fought the early Sasanians, as also are the Byzantine emperors who fought the later Sasanians. For the sake of relative historical veracity I have translated the words in different ways in stories that occur in different epochs. Thus in the time of Sekandar, I have translated Rum and Rumi as Greece and Greek, in the reign of Shapur, I have used the terms Rome and Roman; and for the reigns of the later kings, I have used Byzantium and Byzantine. This has the advantage of reflecting the actual enemies of Iran at the relevant periods, but it does also disguise the way in which, for Ferdowsi, these Western civilizations were one and continuous.

The Sasanian capital was at Ctesiphon, on the River Tigris. In the reigns of the later Sasanian kings, Ferdowsi frequently refers to the city as "Baghdad," and I have kept this usage in most instances, though it sounds and is anachronistic. The Abbassid (751 C.E.–1258 C.E.) capital of Baghdad was deliberately located close to the ruins of Ctesiphon, and materials taken from the ruins were used in its construction. In referring to Ctesiphon by the name of the Arab city that would almost literally take its place as the administrative center of a great empire, Ferdowsi seems to be simultaneously asserting a continuity of civilization across the divide of the conquest and predicting the conquest itself.

The word "*nard*" is usually translated as "backgammon," and it is often said that the story of the importation of chess from India to Iran, and the Persian invention of backgammon in response, comes from the *Shahnameh's* account of the reign of Anushirvan. However, it is fairly clear from Ferdowsi's description of *nard* that the game referred to is almost certainly not backgammon, which does not, for example, involve kings. There were medieval variants of chess, at least one of which involved the use of dice to determine permissible moves, and it seems likely that it is one of these variants that Ferdowsi is describing, rather than backgammon. As we have no names for such variants I have left the word in Persian.

I conclude this brief introduction by recording my sincere thanks to the National Endowment for the Humanities for awarding me a translation grant for the year 2002, during which most of the present volume was translated. I would like to extend my equally sincere thanks to Mohammad and Najmieh Batmanglij of Mage Publishers for their unstinting kindness and support during my work on all three volumes of translations from the *Shahnameh*.

Dick Davis

⁓ THE STORY OF DARAB AND THE FULLER ⁓

Homay Entrusts Her Son to the Euphrates

Bahman, also called Ardeshir, fell sick and died, and the throne became vacant. Homay, his daughter, who was pregnant by him, placed the crown on her own head and began a new reign. She reviewed the army and distributed wealth from her treasury, and as she inaugurated her rule she announced to the world her justice and generosity. Calling down blessings on the crown and throne, she cursed any who wished her ill, promised that she would act benevolently and harm no one, that she would help the poor, and that the rich and powerful had nothing to fear from her. Her wisdom and justice surpassed her father's, and the world flourished beneath her righteous reign.

When the time came for her to give birth, she hid herself away from the army and townsfolk. She enjoyed the fact that the throne was hers, and that the world was in her hands. Her son was born in secret, and she told no one, keeping the boy hidden. Secretly she entrusted the prince to a nobly born wet nurse and told anyone who had got wind of his birth that the boy had died. And so she kept the crown on her own head, victorious and happy in her occupancy of the throne. She sent her armies against powerful enemies wherever they sprang up, and nothing good or bad that happened in the world remained hidden from her. Everywhere, she pursued justice and righteousness and ruled well. The world became safe under her care, and the people of every country praised her.

So eight months passed, but then the young prince began to resemble the dead king. Homay ordered a trustworthy carpenter to choose wood that could be delicately carved. She had him make a small chest, which was smeared outside with pitch, musk, and wax, and lined with soft brocade from Greece. A little mattress sewn with precious pearls was placed inside, and red gold together with rubies and emeralds were lavishly scattered there. A jeweled clasp was fastened to the still unweaned prince's arm.

Then while the unsuspecting baby slept
His nurse embraced him and profusely wept;
She laid the boy to whom she'd fed her milk
Within the chest, beneath a shawl of silk.
The lid was fastened down with pitch and musk;
Now, silently, as night succeeded dusk,
They took the casket to the riverside
And launched it on the quickly flowing tide.
Two men detailed to watch it through the night
Were forced to run to keep the chest in sight—
It bobbed along as if it were a boat.
The broad Euphrates kept the craft afloat
And bore it downstream on its watery way
Until the sunrise brought another day.

A Fuller Brings Up Homay's Son

At dawn the chest bumped against the riverbank. It had reached a place where the river had been deliberately narrowed, and stones had been placed in the channel; fullers worked there, washing and bleaching clothes. One of them caught sight of the little craft and ran over to free it from where it had stuck. When he opened the chest, and drew aside the rich cloths within, he was astonished at what he saw. He wrapped the chest in the clothes he'd been washing and ran home with it, full of hopes that this would mean a change in his fortunes. Meanwhile, the men detailed to watch what happened to the chest quickly went back to the palace and reported to Homay all that had occurred. The queen told them that they must not reveal to anyone else what they had seen.

When the man who had found the chest arrived at his house unexpectedly, his wife said, "What brings you home at this time, with the clothes all wet still? Who's going to pay you for work like that?"

It happened that the couple had had a fine baby boy who had recently died, and the fuller's heart was still grieving for his lost child; his wife too was still weeping and groaning, and had scratched her face with her nails in her grief. The man said to her, "Come on now, pull yourself together, all this crying and moaning isn't doing you any good. Now, promise you'll keep a secret, my dear, and I'll tell you something worth hearing. Next to the boulder where I beat the clothes, where I throw the clean clothes into the water to rinse them, I saw a little chest stuck in the channel, and hidden inside it was a baby. When I opened the lid and saw the little mite

inside I could scarcely believe my eyes. Our own little one died after a short life, but now you've found another son, and there's money with him and all manner of finery."

Then he set the clothes down on the floor, unwrapped them, and opened the chest; his wife stared in astonishment and called down God's blessings on the baby over and over again. She stared at the infant's shining face, which looked like Ardeshir's, nestled in the silk, and at the pearls sewn into the mattress, the rubies and emeralds by his feet, the red gold piled on his left, and the royal jewels to his right. Quickly, overwhelmed with joy, she set the baby to her milk-filled breast; the little child and the wealth that was with him made her forget all her sorrows. Her husband said to her, "We must always protect this child, even at the risk of our own lives. He must be the son of someone important; perhaps he's one of the world's princes." The fuller's wife cared for the child as if he were her own. On the third day they named the child, and because he had been plucked from flowing water [ab], they called him Darab.

One day the fuller's wife, who was a sensible woman, said to him, "What are you going to do about the jewels? What do you think would be the wisest course?" He answered, "My dear, hidden jewels are no more use to me than dirt is. It's better that we leave this town and all our past poverty and difficulties behind. We should go to a town where people don't know whether we're rich or poor." The next morning they packed up their household and quitted their home, and they gave their country no further thought. They carried Darab in their arms and took with them the jewels and gold, and that was all. They traveled for about two hundred miles, and then settled in a town where they were strangers. Here they lived as relatively well-to-do people, being careful to placate the local lord with gifts of jewels, and he sent them cloth and cash in return. The wife, who was always giving her husband advice, said to him, "We don't need to work any more: you're a rich man now, and you needn't worry about looking for a trade to follow." But the fuller answered, "My dear, you're a sensible woman and you give good advice, but what's better than what you call a 'trade'? A trade is the best thing a man can have. And yours is to bring up Darab properly and well, until we see what fate has in store for him." They brought up the child with such care and tenderness that no harsh wind ever harmed him.

In a few years he grew into a fine boy, strong, and with the royal *farr* visible in him. He'd challenge older boys in the street to wrestling matches and none of them were his equals in strength; then they'd rush at him in a group, but he would defeat them all. The fuller became exasperated with him. His own fortunes had declined, and he ordered the boy to beat clothes against the rocks with him, saying there was no shame in this. And when Darab ran away from the work, the man wept tears of rage and grief. He had to spend a good part of each day looking for the boy, either in the town or out on the plain. Once he found him with a bow in his hand and a thumb-stall to protect his thumb as he loosed the arrows. He took the bow from him and coldly said, "You're acting like a vicious, uncontrollable wolf: what business can you have with a bow and arrow? Why have you become such a troublesome young man?"

> And Darab answered, "Father, why must you
> Muddy the stream of everything I do?
> Send me to someone learnèd, one who teaches
> The customs that the Zend-Avesta preaches;
> Then you can put me to a trade. But don't
> Think I'll be settled yet, because I won't."

The fuller remonstrated with him for a long time but finally sent him to a group of teachers, where he learned to be a cultivated young man and stopped being so abusive and stubborn. Nevertheless he told his father, "I'm not cut out to wash clothes; stop worrying about me. The one thing I want in the world is to be a horseman." His father found a fine horseman, a man with a good reputation as a horse-tamer who was also skillful with the bridle. He sent his son to him, and there Darab learned all that pertained to horsemanship: the use of the bridle, lance, and shield, how to control a horse in battle, how to play polo, how to shoot with a bow from the saddle, how to seek honor, and how to evade the enemy's reach.

Darab Questions the Fuller's Wife about Himself and Becomes a Knight

One day Darab said to his father, "There's something I've kept hidden. I don't feel any instinctive love for you, and your face doesn't resemble mine at all. It always surprises me when you call me 'son' and when you make me sit with you at your work." The fuller answered, "These words of yours bring back old sorrows. If you feel your nature is above mine, then go and find your father. Your mother knows the secret of all that business." And when the fuller left one day for the river, Darab locked the house door and came before his mother with a sword in his hand. He said to her, "Don't try any tricks or lies; give me an honest answer to everything I'm going to ask you. How am I related to you? Whose family do I belong to? And why am I living here with someone who washes clothes?"

The man's wife was terrified and begged Darab not to harm her. Invoking God to protect her, she said, "Don't spill my blood; I'll tell you everything you've asked." And then she described without prevarication all that had occurred, telling him about the chest containing the unweaned baby and about the coins and royal jewels. She went on, "We were folk who worked with our hands; we weren't from a wealthy family. All we have in the way of fine clothes and wealth is from you. We served you and brought you up, but it's for you to give the orders. We are yours body and soul, and you must decide what's to be done."

Darab was amazed when he heard all this, and he brooded for a while before saying anything. Then he asked, "Is there any of the wealth left, or has your husband spent it all? We live wretchedly enough these days, but is there enough left to buy me a horse?" The woman answered, "There's more than enough left for that, and besides we've bought profitable woodland, orchards, and pasture." She gave him some money and showed him the jeweled clasp. Darab used the money to buy a fine horse, a cheap saddle, and a lariat.

There was a great lord of the marches living in the neighborhood, a dignified and wise man able to give good guidance. His soul troubled by dark thoughts, Darab presented himself before this man, who took him into his service and saw that he came to no harm. It so happened that an army from the west attacked and began plundering the area. The lord was killed in battle, and his troops were left leaderless. When Homay heard this she sent her general, Reshnavad, to drive the enemy back and to destroy their strongholds. Reshnavad gathered an army and inspected and provisioned it. Darab was overjoyed at the news of the expedition and hurried to register his name as a warrior. Troops poured in from all sides, and when they were amassed Homay and her military chiefs came out of the palace to watch the troops pass by and be counted and to have their names checked. She caught sight of Darab and the *farr* radiating from him. With his great strength and the massive mace on his shoulders, it seemed as though only he were on the plain, and that the ground was there merely to bear his warhorse. And as she stared at his chest and his handsome face, her maternal breasts flowed with milk. She said to one of her entourage, "Where is that knight from? The one who seems to be such a strong, splendid young man? He looks like a nobleman, like a knight who's experienced in warfare, brave, proud, and dignified, but his weapons aren't worthy of him."

The army met with her approval, and she selected an auspicious day for them to begin the campaign. The leaders agreed on their strategy and led the army away. Homay sent her agents with them, so that nothing that transpired would be hidden from her and she would know everything that went on in the army, whether of good or evil, and her worries would be laid to rest. The army set out, filling the plain, marching by stages beneath the moon.

Reshnavad Learns the Truth about Darab

One day a violent wind began to blow; thunder crashed and the sky was filled with rain and lightning. The land was awash with water, and the army fled in all directions, trying to get out of the rain and looking for places to pitch their tents. The commander Reshnavad was worried by this turn of events. Darab too was bewildered by what was happening and tried to escape from the heavy rain. He saw a mass of ruins with an archway that was still standing. High, ancient, and crumbling, it looked as if it had once been part of a royal edifice. Darab had no palace hall or women's quarters at his disposal, not even a tent or a companion or pack animals; he was alone and friendless, and he had no choice but to sleep beneath the crumbling archway.

While Reshnavad was trying to round up his scattered troops he happened to pass by the archway, and he heard a roaring sound coming from the ruins that seemed to say,

> "O ruined arch, be on your guard and keep
> The Persian king you shelter safe in sleep;
> He had no tent or friend, and so he lies
> Beneath you, sheltering from the stormy skies."

Reshnavad said to himself, "Is that the noise of thunder, or is it the howling wind?" And then he heard the roar again,

> "O arch, keep wisdom's eyes awake, take care,
> King Ardeshir's young son lies sleeping there."

And the roar sounded for a third time, at which he turned in astonishment to an advisor and said, "What can this mean? Someone should go and investigate who is sleeping under that arch." A group went and saw a young man lying there; he looked both wise and warrior-like, but his clothes and horse were soaking wet and filthy, and his bed was the black earth. When Reshnavad was told what they had seen, the commander's heart beat faster and he said, "Call him here quickly: who could endure to hear such a roar as we heard?" They went back and called out, "Hey, you lying asleep on the ground, wake up, get on your feet!" As Darab mounted his horse, the arch collapsed. Reshnavad fixed his eyes on Darab, scanning him from head to toe, and said, "This is a marvel among marvels, nothing more wonderful could be imagined." Then he hurried the young man to his pavilion, praising God as they went. He ordered clothes to be brought and a place to be set aside for Darab. They lit a large fire on which they burned sandalwood, musk, and ambergris.

When the sun rose above the mountain top, Reshnavad took a complete set of clothes, a saddled horse with a golden bridle, a bow, and a sword in a golden sheath to Darab. As he presented them, he said to the young man, "You're lionhearted, a fine young man eager for fame, but who are you, what's your lineage, and what country are you from? It would be best for you to tell me the truth." Darab told Reshnavad everything, just as the woman he had thought was his mother had explained it to him. He told him about the chest and the rubies, the jeweled clasp on his arm, the gold coins, the brocade in which he had been wrapped, and his sleep in the casket where he had been concealed. At once Reshnavad said to a messenger, "Go like the wind and bring the fuller and his wife here; bring me this Mars and Venus, both of them."

The army then marched to the frontier with Greece, and Darab was made leader of the advance guard, the tips of whose spears had been dipped in poison. They met with the vanguard of a Greek force patrolling the borderlands. Suddenly the two armies were face to face, and the dust of battle rose into the sky. They fought hand to hand, and blood flowed like a river. Quick as wind-blown dust, Darab urged his horse into the melée and killed so many of the enemy soldiers that it seemed as if heaven itself wielded his sword. It was as if a lion attacked, a lion grasping a monster as a weapon and with a dragon for his mount. The lion pressed on to the Greek camp, guided by his sword's search for victims, till the earth was awash with a sea of Greek blood. Having routed the enemy forces Darab returned in triumph to his commander. Reshnavad showered him with praise and said, "May the royal army never lack your presence. When we get back to civilization from this Greek expedition, you'll be richly rewarded by the queen; she'll give you horses, seal rings, swords, and diadems." All night the army prepared its armor and horses for the coming day, and when the sun rose, illuminating the land like a lamp, the two armies met again and the dust of their encounter darkened the sun. Darab launched his attack, releasing the reins of his charger. He slew all the champions who rode forward from the Greek ranks and like a wolf made for their army's heart, scattering the huge force before him. From there he turned against their right flank, plundering weapons and baggage as he went, with their troops fleeing from him pell-mell. The Persian warriors followed in his wake like lions, killing so many of the Greek troops that the ground turned to a quagmire with their blood. Darab killed forty of their priests and returned to his own lines with a captured cross in his fist. When Reshnavad saw the wonders Darab performed, his heart bounded with joy; again he showered Darab with praise, adding words of affection as well. Then night came on, the world turned black as pitch, and everyone turned back from the battlefield.

Reshnavad made his headquarters in the captured Greek camp; there he rested and loosened his sword belt. When it came to the distribution of plunder, he first sent someone to Darab, telling him to take what he would like and to distribute the rest as he saw fit, as he was a finer warrior than even the great Rostam. Darab chose a fine lance and passed everything else back to Reshnavad, wishing him victory and joy in the days to come.

After sunset, as darkness spread, it was as if a cloth of black brocade had covered the army. The commander made the rounds of the camp guards, and their shouts re-echoed in the darkness like the rumbling of an earthquake, or the roar of a wild lion. When the sun lifted its golden shield again, the sleeping warriors woke, donned their armor once more, and set off in pursuit of the Greek forces. They torched the towns they came on, and the name of Greece was obliterated from the land. Lamenting was heard throughout Greece for the loss of territory: its king felt himself hemmed in by the world's fury, and his noblemen turned pale with shame and fear. His messenger arrived before Reshnavad, saying, "May your queen be just to us: we who desired war are exhausted by it, and Greece's fortunes have declined. If you desire us to pay taxes, we will pay them; let us renew the peace treaty between us." The Greek king also sent gifts of many kinds, in addition to numerous slaves bearing purses of cash. Reshnavad accepted whatever was sent, which included gold coins and uncut jewels.

Homay Recognizes Her Son

Darab and Reshnavad returned in triumph to the ruined arch where Darab had been found sleeping. Filled with fear and foreboding, the man who had found him in the chest, together with his wife, who had brought the jeweled clasp, were waiting for them, and as the two of them were called forward, they entrusted themselves to God's protection. Reshnavad questioned them closely, and they told him all they could remember about the chest and the uncut jewel. Reshnavad said to them,

> *"May you be prosperous now and live in glory,*
> *For no one's ever heard so strange a story,*
> *No priest or chronicler has ever told*
> *A tale like this the two of you unfold."*

Immediately he wrote to Homay, telling her of Darab's sleep in the ruin and of his valor on the battlefield, of how the moment he mounted his horse the arch collapsed, of how a voice had resounded from the arch, and of the dread that he, Reshnavad, had felt on hearing it. Then he added all that the fuller had said concerning the chest, the baby it contained, and the riches. Next, he summoned a messenger, gave him the red jeweled clasp, and said, "Make the wind your partner as you travel." The man brought the jewel to Homay, handed over the letter, and told the queen what he had heard from Reshnavad's lips. And when she saw the jewel and read the letter, tears spilled from her eyelashes. She knew that the tall, splendid young man with a face as fresh as the springtime, the man she had seen that day she reviewed the troops drawn up on the plain, was none other than her own son, a noble shoot of her own stock. Weeping, she said to the messenger, "A master has come to the world. My mind has never been free from care; I have been filled with anxiety for the empire, fearing God and brooding on my ingratitude to him."

Coins were liberally distributed, wine, musk, and jewels were mixed together, and for a week the doors of Homay's treasury stood open to relieve the poor. Wealth was given to all her provinces, and on the tenth day her army commander, together with his officers and Darab, entered the court. But nothing had been divulged concerning Darab's identity.

For a week, by the queen's order, the curtain signifying that the court was closed to outsiders remained in place. She had a golden dais prepared, as well as two thrones studded with turquoise and lapis lazuli, a crown encrusted with royal jewels, two armbands, a jeweled torque, and royal clothes woven with gold and jewels. An astrologer sat before the queen, calculating the most propitious day for what she planned. Then, on the fourth day of the month of Bahman, the queen gave audience to Darab. She filled a bowl with rubies and another with topaz stones. As Darab approached she came forward and made her obeisance before him; she scattered the precious stones before him and, turning aside, wept bitterly. She clasped her son tightly to her breast, kissing him and running her fingers over his face; then she led him to the golden dais and stared at him in wonder. When he had taken his place on the throne,

Homay brought the royal crown and placed it on his head, and in this way proclaimed his coronation to the world. As light flashed from the crown, Homay begged forgiveness for the past, asking him to consider all that had happened as the wind that passes by: her youth and sudden wealth and woman's wiles, his father dead, and her position as a queen bereft of good counsel. She hoped he would pardon her evil deed, and from now on occupy no seat but the throne.

The young prince answered his mother, "You are descended from champions, and it's no surprise that ambition bubbled up in your heart. Why should you weep and wail so much for one bad act? May the Creator be pleased with you, and may the hearts of those who wish you ill be filled with smoke and dust. The things you talk about will ensure that I'm remembered, and my story will never grow old." Then Homay in her splendor called down blessings on his head and said, "May you endure as long as the world endures!"

Then the chief priest was called, and the wise men of every province, together with the army's warlike chieftains: all were commanded to hail Darab as their sovereign, and as they did so, jewels were scattered over the throne. Homay confessed to what she had done in secret, and to the terrible suffering this had caused her. "Know," she said, "that in all the world this prince is the sole heir to King Bahman: everyone must obey him, for he is the shepherd and his warriors are his sheep. Greatness, sovereignty and military might belong to him, and it is your duty to support him." A shout of joy went up from the palace, and men said that they had seen a new shoot of the royal stock. So many gifts were brought from all sides that the young king was almost smothered by them: the world was filled with rejoicing and justice, and old sufferings were forgotten. Homay said to the priests, "I have handed over the empire and all its wealth to him, these things that have caused me such sorrow for thirty-two years. Rejoice and obey him, and take no breath without his advice."

Darab took his place on the throne with pleasure and wore the crown in contentment. Then the fuller and his wife appeared, and cried out, "Young prince, may the royal throne bring you good luck, and may your enemies' heads be severed at the neck!" Darab ordered that ten purses of gold and a goblet of jewels, together with five bolts of various cloths, be given to them for the all they had done and suffered. He said to the man, "Keep to your trade, and stay always alert: it may be that you'll find a chest with a little prince in it!" The couple left the court calling down blessings on the king; the fuller's fate was fulfilled, and he returned to his trade and the alkali ashes with which he cleaned clothes.

The Reign of Darab

When Darab was crowned he prepared himself to be a warrior and a generous benefactor to his people. He addressed his priests, counselors, and chieftains: "I did not scheme and struggle to rule the earth; God placed the crown on my head. No one in the world has ever heard a more remarkable tale than mine, and I know of no greater reward for justice than to be praised after my death. No one must suffer because of my ambition, or because I accumulate wealth. May the land prosper through my justice, and my subjects live in happiness." Representatives came from India and Greece and from every inhabited country, bringing gifts and wishing the new king health and prosperity.

Darab Defeats Sho'ayb

And then a hundred thousand warlike Arabs attacked, under the leadership of a chieftain from the Qotayb tribe, called Sho'ayb. The king of Iran mustered innumerable troops, and when the two armies met, the world was filled with terror and destruction. The earth could hardly bear the weight of such forces, and such was the press of troops that no one could find a way through them. The land was awash with blood from the rain of javelins and arrows; cries resounded from all sides, and everywhere heaps of dead bodies could be seen. The battle lasted for three days and nights, and both sides were hard pressed, but on the fourth night the Arabs turned tail, abandoning the battlefield. Sho'ayb had been killed in the fighting, and the tide of battle had turned against the Arabs. In their flight they left behind many Arab horses with their poplar wood saddles, as well as lances, swords, and helmets. Homay's son distributed the plunder to his soldiers and chose a man from the army who understood Arabic to be lord of the marches. He sent this man to the plains where the Arabs lived, to demand that year's and the previous year's tribute.

Darab Fights against Filqus and Marries His Daughter

After Darab had defeated the Arabs, he marched his army against Greece. The king there was a man called Filqus, who was in league with the king of Susa. This man wrote to Filqus, saying that Homay's son was attacking with an enormous army. When the Greek king heard this, he remembered the ancient feud between the two countries and gathered together an army of experienced warriors from the district of Amourieh. As Darab approached, the Greek nobles abandoned the border areas, while Filqus led his army down from Amourieh. Two fierce battles were fought during three days, but as the sun rose on the fourth day Filqus's army broke ranks and fled, leaving behind even their helmets and Greek headgear. Their women and children were taken prisoner, and a number of men were put to the sword or killed with arrows. Filqus's retreating army had been reduced by a third and the remnant traveled with their lances strapped on their backs. They took refuge in the fortress at Amourieh, and most of them were ready to sue for peace.

A messenger from Filqus arrived before Darab. He was a wise, intelligent man, with the airs and graces of a courtier. He brought slaves, purses of coins, two chests filled with jewels, and the following message:

> *"I ask one thing from God, who is my guide,*
> *That we should look for peace, and put aside*

Our ruinous deceit and enmity;
Come, let us promise mutual amity.
But if you think that in some covert way
You'll take my capital, Amourieh,
There'll be no banquet to confirm our pact.
Honor will make me fight if I'm attacked.
Do what befits a king: your father knew
How kings conduct themselves, and so do you."

When Darab had heard him out he summoned his nobles and laid the matter before them, asking them what they thought of such talk, by which Filqus hoped to save face. They answered, "O perspicacious and pure-hearted king, lord of all lords, whose choice is to do that which is best: this chieftain has a daughter, elegant as a cypress tree, her face as fresh as springtime. No one has ever seen any idol in China as lovely as she is, she outshines all others in her beauty. If the king sees her, she will please him: this cypress would be well placed in his garden."

The king called in the Greek messenger, repeated what he had heard from his advisors, and said, "Go to your king and tell him this: 'There is a young woman in your palace, who is the crown of all princesses; you call her Nahid, and you have assigned her a golden throne. If you want to preserve your honor and keep your country untroubled, give her to me, along with the tribute that Greece owes.'" The messenger traveled like the wind and repeated the message to the Greek king, who was overjoyed that his son-in-law would be the Persian king. There was some discussion about the tribute to be paid, but finally it was agreed that each year Greece would hand over a hundred thousand eggs made of gold, each weighing forty *mesqals*, and studded with jewels.

Filqus gave orders that the roads to the borders of Greece be decorated, and then a magnificent escort bearing gifts set out with his daughter. They had prepared a golden litter and gathered together a group of noble attendants for her. There were ten camels carrying Greek brocade embroidered with jewels and gold, together with three hundred camel loads of carpets and necessities for the journey. The princess remained in her litter, guided by a bishop and a monk. Behind her came sixty maidservants, each of them adorned with a diadem and earrings and carrying a golden goblet filled with jewels. The bishop handed the beautiful princess over to Darab, and the jewels were counted out to his treasurer. After this Darab quit the military camp where he had been waiting and led his army back to Persia. He placed a crown on the princess's head, and they set out happily for Pars.

The Birth of Sekandar

One night this lovely moon, arrayed in jewels and scents, lay sleeping beside the king. Suddenly she sighed deeply, and the king turned his head away, offended by the smell of her breath. This bad odor sickened him, and he frowned, wondering what could be done about it. He sent knowledgeable doctors to her; one who was especially expert was able to find a remedy. There is an herb that burns the palate, which they call "Sekandar" in Greece, and he rubbed this against the roof of her mouth. She wept a few tears and her face turned as red as brocade, because it burned her mouth, but the ugly smell was gone. But although this beautiful woman's breath was now as sweet as musk, the king no longer felt any love for her. His heart had grown cold toward his bride, and he sent her back to Filqus. The princess grieved, because she was pregnant, but she told no one of this.

When nine months had gone by she gave birth to a boy as splendid as the sun. Because of his stature and splendor, and the sweet smell that his flesh exhaled, she named him Sekandar, after the herb that had cured her of her malady. Her father the king told everyone that the boy was his and made no mention of Darab, because he was ashamed to tell people that Darab had rejected his daughter. The same night that Sekandar was born, a cream-colored mare in the royal stables, a huge warlike horse, gave birth to a gray foal with a lion-like chest and short pasterns. Filqus took this as a good omen, raising his hands to the heavens in gratitude. At dawn the next day he had both the newborn child and the mare and her foal brought to him and passed his hands over the foal's eyes and chest, because he was exactly the same age as Sekandar.

So the heavens turned and the years passed. Sekandar grew to have a princely heart, and his speech was that of a warrior. Filqus treated him even more attentively than a son and loved to dress him as a champion. In a little while the boy gained in wisdom; he became adroit, intelligent, grave in his manner, and knowledgeable. He was made the kingdom's crown prince, and Filqus delighted in his presence. Sekandar learned the arts of kingship from his teachers, and it seemed he was born to administer justice, to occupy a throne, and to found an empire.

In Persia, after Nahid had returned to her father, Darab took another wife. She gave birth to a fine, princely son who was a year younger than Sekandar. On the day he was born he was named Dara, and it was hoped that his good fortune would be greater than his father's. Then, after twelve years, Darab's star declined: he grew sick and wasted away and knew he would be called to another place. He summoned his nobles and counselors and spoke to them at length about the business of government and king-ship. Then he added: "Dara, my son, will guide you well. Listen to him and obey him, and may your souls know peace in obedience to his commands. This royal throne is no one's for long, and in the midst of pleasure we are called away. Strive to be kind and just, and rejoice when you remember me." Having said this he heaved a sigh from the depths of his being, and the rosy pomegranate petal turned as pale as fenugreek.

❧ SEKANDAR'S CONQUEST OF PERSIA ❧

The Reign of Dara

Dara grieved for his father's death, and exalted the royal crown of Persia above the sun. He was young, fiery-tempered, quick to take offense, and his heart and tongue were hard enough to blunt a sword. From the throne he addressed his court: "Noblemen and warriors, I do not want my head to be brought down into the pit of servitude, and I will summon no one who is in that pit to approach my throne. Any man who ignores my commands can consider his head as no longer attached to his body, and if anyone so much as murmurs in his heart against me, my sword shall deal with him. No rich man is to use his wealth contrary to my wishes. I need no counselors: I am my own counselor and responsible for my own well-being. The pleasure, treaties, greatness, and sovereignty of the world are mine." He summoned a learned scribe and after some discussion had him write a letter as trenchant as a dagger, in the name of Dara, the son of Darab, the son of Ardeshir, to every other king and independent ruler. The letter read: "Whoever opposes my policies or orders will learn how I can lop off heads. Whether you command souls or your soul is commanded by others, see that you obey my edicts."

Then he opened his father's treasuries, summoned his warriors, and distributed their pay. He raised the stipend of those who had received four coins to eight, paying one man with a goblet full of coins, another with a bowlful. He gave experienced commanders border provinces as gifts and saw that everyone in his army received something of value. Representatives bearing presents and tribute came from all countries and kings, from India, China, Greece, and other lands, since no one felt able to stand against him. He built a city called Noshad—New Happiness—and the province of Ahvaz rejoiced in his reign. He was just to the poor, and he distributed wealth to whoever asked him.

The Death of Filqus: Sekandar Becomes King

It was at about this time that Filqus died, and Greece mourned for him. Sekandar ascended his grandfather's throne and was a man who sought good and impeded the reach of evil. There was a famous man named Arestalis in Greece, in whom the whole country rejoiced: he was a wise, intelligent, and resourceful person. This man came before Sekandar and said, "Fortune smiles on you now my lord, but even you can lose your fame. The royal throne has seen so many kings like you, and it belongs to no one forever. Whenever you say to yourself, 'I have reached my goal, I need no one to guide me in this world,' know that at that moment, when you will not listen to a wise counselor's words, you are the stupidest of men. We are made and born from dust, and we have no choice but to return to dust. If you act well, your name will survive you and you will prosper during your reign; and if you sow evil, you will reap evil, and not sleep easily in this world for a single night."

> King Sekandar approved of what he said
> And instantly decided he'd be led
> In banquets and in battles by this guide,
> And see that he was always at his side.

Then one day an eloquent and courteous messenger arrived from Dara, asking that Greece's tribute be paid. But Sekandar became angry at the thought of this tax he'd inherited and said, "Go and tell Dara that the time for tribute from us is over. The hen that laid those golden eggs has died and there's no more tribute to be had." When he heard such language, the messenger was terrified and scuttled away from Greece. Sekandar, meanwhile, gathered an army together, told them of what had happened, and said, "Not even a good man can escape the turning of the heavens. I must travel the face of the earth, and reckon up what there is of good and evil in the world. And now you must prepare yourselves to bid your country farewell." He opened the doors of his grandfather's treasury and had his army equipped. At dawn an uproar could be heard outside the young king's court: he set out followed by his banner, on which images of the bird of royal fortune, the homa, and the beloved cross were embroidered in red on a turquoise ground.

The Greek army bore down on Egypt, and so thick were their ranks that not a mosquito or an ant could find a way through them. For a week the armies fought, and on the eighth day Sekandar defeated the Egyptian forces. So many prisoners and so much plunder were taken that the victors were at a loss as to what to do with everything: there were maces and horses, warriors' armor and horse armor, Indian swords in golden scabbards, golden belts and golden saddles, brocade and more coins than their pack horses could carry; as well as the innumerable chieftains and horsemen who surrendered to them.

From there this lionhearted warrior stretched out his claws toward Persia. When Dara heard that the Greek army was threatening his country's frontiers he set out toward Greece with an army from Estakhr, and so numerous were its lances that they impeded the winds as they blew. When his men reached the Euphrates, their number was greater than the blades of grass on its shores; the river's water was invisible beyond the press of their armor.

Sekandar Acts as His Own Envoy

Sekandar heard of the Persian troops' approach and set out to meet them. When there were about two parasangs' distance between the two armies, he summoned his counselors. But after a while he tired of their talk and said,

> *"There's only one way forward in this case:*
> *I'll go myself and meet him face to face.*
> *I'll be my own ambassador, and see*
> *The strengths and weakness of my enemy."*

He put on a jeweled belt and a royal cloak worked with gold figures; his mount had a golden saddle, from which hung a golden scabbard. He picked ten Greek advisors who were skilled in languages to accompany him, and he and his chieftains and interpreters set off at dawn.

As he approached Dara he dismounted and greeted the Persian king respectfully. Dara called him forward and motioned him to a seat at a lower level than the throne. Dara's nobles were astonished by the handsome young man's stature and splendor and by his courteous behavior. Silently, to themselves, they called down blessings on his head. He sat where Dara had indicated, then he rose and, as if he were a mere envoy, produced a letter from Sekandar. He began by wishing the king an eternal reign and then continued:

> *"I have no wish to seize your country, nor*
> *To fight against you on the plains of war;*
> *My aim's to travel round the earth, to see*
> *The spacious world in its entirety.*
> *I look for justice, and I understand*
> *That you are sovereign over Persia's land,*
> *But if my progress here is not allowed*
> *I can't go forward like an airborne cloud.*

You've come here with an army, unaware
Of Sekandar's intentions: but beware,
If you desire to fight with me, I'll fight—
I won't retreat in ignominious flight.
Say when you're ready then: you name the day
And see you don't forget or run away:
No overwhelming force will make me yield
When once my army's on the battlefield."

Dara heard him out, and it seemed to him as if this young man were Dara himself, seated on the ivory throne, with the royal torque and armbands, resplendent with *farr*, and with the crown on his head. Dara answered him, "What's your name and lineage? The royal *farr* shines from your forehead as if you were a Kayanid prince. You're too fine a man to be anyone's subject: I think that you are Sekandar himself! With this *farr* and stature and eloquence of yours you seem born to sit on a throne." Sekandar answered, "Neither in peace nor in war has a king ever done what you're suggesting. There are plenty of fine talkers in my monarch's court; they're the crown of all wise men. Sekandar is wise enough to follow his ancestors and not to act as his own envoy. My commander gave me the message as I have delivered it to you, your majesty."

A suitable pavilion was prepared for his stay, and when the evening meal was served Dara had the Greek envoy summoned to eat with him. Once they had eaten, musicians were called and wine was served. As soon as he had drunk his wine, Sekandar secreted the goblet beneath his clothes, and he did this a number of times. The cupbearer went to Dara and said, "Your Greek guest can't be separated from the goblets I serve him." Dara told him to ask why he kept the goblets in this way. "Why, my lion lord," said the cupbearer, "are you keeping the goblets I give you?" Sekandar answered, "And isn't his goblet the envoy's reward? But if the custom is different in Persia, then take them back and place them in your king's treasury." Dara laughed to hear of such a custom, and had a goblet filled with jewels, surmounted by a splendid ruby, handed to him.

Just at that moment the men who had gone to Greece to demand tribute arrived at the gathering. Their leader saw Sekandar's face and as soon as he had made his obeisance before the king he said, "That man is the great Sekandar, whom I saw seated on his throne, crowned and holding the royal mace. As the king had ordered, we went to him and asked for our tribute: he humiliated me and talked insultingly about your majesty. We fled from his realm on horseback, by night. I saw no one like him in all of Greece, and now he has had the audacity to come to this country. He means to deprive you of your army, wealth, throne, and crown." As he listened to the man's words, Dara stared intently at Sekandar, who knew very well what was passing between them. As the sun set in the west he made his way to the tent he had been assigned, then, quickly mounting his horse, he said to his entourage, "Our lives depend on our horses: if they falter, we are finished." The group galloped away and were lost to sight in the darkness. Dara sent someone to Sekandar's tent, and as soon as it became clear that his guest had fled, he sent a thousand warriors after him. They rode like the wind, but in the darkness they lost their way, and when they caught sight of the Greek advance guards they turned back, having achieved nothing for all their pains.

Sekandar reached his own camp, and the Greek nobles crowded round to see their prince return under cover of darkness. He showed them four goblets and the jewels he'd been given, and said, "Give thanks for my good fortune: I earned these cups at the risk of my life, and the stars seconded my attempt. I reckoned up the number of their troops, who are far more numerous than we had heard. Draw your swords for combat. We must march forward across this plain, and if you suffer in the battle, think of the kingdoms and wealth you will win. God is with me, and the stars are favorable to my plans." The nobles congratulated him and wished for world prosperity beneath his reign. They said, "We are ready to sacrifice our lives for you, and we shall never break this promise. Who of all kings could claim to be your equal in manliness, stature, or glory?"

Dara Makes War on Sekandar and Is Defeated

The sun rose over the mountains, and the land glowed like a golden lamp. Dara mustered the ranks of his army, which covered the earth like a pitch-black cloak. He led his men, more numerous than blades of grass, across the Euphrates, and when Sekandar heard of their approach, he had the war drums sounded and his troops prepared. The two hosts could not be counted, but in all the world there was only one Sekandar. Dust loomed over the scene like a mountain, and the whole plain seemed a seething sea of weapons and warriors, of armor and Indian daggers, of war horses and barding. On each side the troops were drawn up, and the sun flashed on their swords. In the vanguard were the war elephants, and behind them the cavalry, men who had renounced all love of life. The very air seemed to cry out for blood, the land to groan with the warriors' battle cries, the mountains to shake with the din of trumpets and Indian chimes. The horses' neighing and the combatants' shouts, the crashing of heavy maces on armor, all seemed to transform the plain to a mountain of warfare, and the air turned black with dust. For seven days the battle raged, and on the eighth a dust storm obscured the sun and blew against the blinded Persians, who fled from the battlefield. Sekandar's men pursued them—the one host full of sorrow, the other of joy—back to the banks of the Euphrates, where innumerable Persians were killed. At first the Greek troops turned back from the river, but Sekandar ordered them across, and they entered the abandoned Persian camp in triumph.

Dara's Second Battle against Sekandar

When Dara fled from Sekandar, he sent mounted messengers in all directions, summoning Iran's chieftains and lords. He distributed money and had the army's quartermasters prepare to provision new troops. By the end of the month he had gathered a new army and renewed his commanders' warlike ambition. Once more he crossed the river and drew up his troops on the wide plain. As soon as Sekandar heard of this, he left his army's impedimenta in their camp and set out to face him. The two armies met and again the land was filled with the din of warfare. For three days they joined battle, until the heaped-up dead hemmed them in. Numberless Persians were slain, and the great king's good fortune deserted him. Full of sorrow, he turned back from the battle, since the lord of the moon gave him no help, but Sekandar pursued him as quickly as wind-blown dust, praising the world creator as he came. He had his heralds cry out to the Persians, "You are subjects who have been misled, but you have no need to fear me, and my army has no desire to meddle with you. Go home safely to your houses and live God-fearing lives. Even though you have washed your hands in Greek blood, you have escaped safe and sound from the Greek army." When the Persians heard they were being granted quarter, they submitted. Sekandar had the plunder heaped up on the battlefield and distributed to his troops, who now found themselves well equipped. He and his army rested in that area for four months.

Dara meanwhile reached Jahrom, where he had access to treasure. Filled with grief and sorrow, his nobles came before him; sons wept for their lost fathers, and fathers for their lost sons. All the land of Iran was filled with the sounds of mourning, and tears stood in all eyes like dew. From Jahrom Dara made his way to the pride of Persian cities, Estakhr. Again messengers were sent out to all quarters, and an army gathered before the king's palace. Dara sat there on a golden throne and his loyal troops paraded before him; then he addressed them:

> *"My wise and warlike warriors, you see*
> *The straits we're in, you know our enemy."*

And as he spoke grief overwhelmed his voice.
He wept, then said, "It is a better choice
To die today as men, than to remain
Alive and subject to an alien reign.
The ancient kings who came before us here
Were paid with foreign tribute every year.
Once we were mighty, and in everything
The Greek realm bowed before the Persian king.
Our luck has turned, and Sekandar alone
Will rule this land, and seize our crown and throne.
Soon he'll be here, too soon, and Persia then
Will be a sea of blood, this country's men,
Its women and its children, will be made
The captives of this conquering renegade.
But if you'll now make common cause with me
We can drive back this pain and misery.
These warriors were our prey once—filled with dread,
When Persia threatened, they turned tail and fled.
Now they're the leopard, we've become the prey,
When battle's joined it's we who run away.
But if we stand together we can still
Crush them and bend their country to our will.
Whoever falters in this war and tries
To save his selfish soul should realize
It is the world that will be lost or freed—
They are Zahhak, and we are now Jamshid."

He wept as he spoke; his heart was filled with pain, his cheeks were yellow, and his lips blue with suffering. His wise, grief-stricken nobles rose and shouted in answer, "We have no desire to live without the king; we are ready for battle, and we shall make the world a harsh place for those who wish you ill. We shall fight together, whether we conquer lands and provinces, or find only the earth of the grave." Dara distributed weapons and money to his army and to his country's chieftains.

The Third Battle between Sekandar and Dara, and Dara's Flight to Kerman

When Sekandar heard of Dara's renewed bid for sovereignty, he led his army out from Iraq, and as he marched he prayed to God in Greek. Sekandar's army had neither center nor limit, and Dara's good fortune had deserted him. Nevertheless Dara led his army out from Estakhr and his troops were so numerous that they seemed to block the turning of the stars in the sky. The armies of the two countries were drawn up in ranks, the men clutching their lances, maces, and daggers. Such a cry went up from both hosts that it seemed to split the ears of the heavens; the warriors' blood transformed the earth to a sea, and headless bodies lay strewn about the battlefield. For the third time Dara suffered defeat; Sekandar pressed forward with his attack, and in fear for his life Dara led his army toward Kerman. Sekandar meanwhile took up residence in Estakhr, the noblest of Persian cities, and from his court a bold proclamation was made:

> "Whoever seeks out God's forgiveness for
> The deeds that he's committed in this war,
> Or looks for my protection, will soon find
> That I've a merciful and generous mind.
> I'll help the wounded, and I will not shed
> The blood of enemies who were misled.
> Since I'm aware the God of victory
> Has given this imperial crown to me,
> My hand won't touch what isn't mine; my soul
> Has chosen light and wisdom as its goal.
> But as for those who'd thwart my wishes, they
> Will find a dragon standing in their way."

Then he distributed the plunder to his army.

By the time Dara reached Kerman, two-thirds of his forces were nowhere to be seen, and wailing was heard among his troops, who were helmetless and dejected. He called together the chieftains who had been with him in battle, all of whom were weeping and bemoaning their fate. Dara addressed them, "There can be no doubt that the heavens have turned against us because of me. No one in the world has ever seen such a defeat, nor have we heard of one like this from those who know the past. Our royal women and children are captives, or they have been murdered with lances and arrows. What can you see that might save us, or that might make those who hate us turn back from their course? No country, no army, no throne or crown, no sovereignty, no heirs, no treasure or forces remain to us. If God does not have pity on us now we are ruined forever."

The nobles wept before the king and said, "Your majesty, we have all been wounded by fate's malevolence. The army is beyond rallying, we are like men over whose helmets floodwaters are rising. Fathers have lost their sons and sons their fathers, and this is now the way of the turning heavens toward us. Our mothers, sisters, and daughters are in Sekandar's hands, and the veiled women of your court who trembled for your life, together with the ancestral treasures you inherited—the noble women of our people and the wealth of our kings—are all in the palm of the Greek conquerors. Your one hope is to conciliate him, for the crown does not stay always with one man. You will have to truckle to him and speak fair words to him, and then we shall see whether all this will end with fate looking more favorably on us. Write him a letter, and try to enlighten his dark soul. The heavens turn above him too, and a wise man will understand this." When he had heard them out, Dara did what seemed best to him and summoned a scribe.

Dara's Letter, Suing for Peace

This is the grief-filled letter he wrote, beginning: "From Dara, the son of Darab, the son of Ardeshir, to the conqueror, Sekandar." His cheeks gaunt with suffering, his eyes filled with tears, first Dara praised God, from whom come the good and evil of our days, then continued, "Certainly a wise man cannot escape the heavens' revolutions, since it is from them that we are fortunate or wretched, that we are sometimes lifted up and sometimes cast down. It wasn't human agency that decided this battle between us, but the dealings of the sun and the moon. Now what was fated has happened, and my heart is left in pain. What is it we can hope for from the blue vault above? Now if you will agree to sign a treaty with me, and repent of your war against Persia, I shall convey from my treasury to yours Goshtasp's and Esfandyar's treasures, including their royal torques and jewel-encrusted crowns, and also the treasures that I have accumulated by my own efforts. I shall be your ally in war, and day and night I shall be prompt in your service. If you will, send me my family members whom you now hold, my women and children—this is what I would expect of you, since a world conqueror is not a man to indulge in petty revenge, and great kings who enslave women receive nothing but reproaches. When my lord reads this letter, may he in his wisdom vouchsafe me an answer."

Quickly a messenger took the letter from Kerman to Sekandar, who was still hostile to Dara. But when he read it he said in answer, "May wisdom always be the companion of Dara's soul! Anyone who stretches out his hand toward your family, either against your womenfolk or your children, will

find that the only throne he will see will be his bier as he is laid in the grave, or he will be hanged from a tree limb. Your family is safe and comfortable in Esfahan, and God forbid that I should demand their wealth from them. If you come to Pars, all the sovereignty of this land is yours; I shall never swerve aside from what you say, and I shall not so much as breathe without asking your advice." Like a skiff over the waves the messenger sped back to his king, whose eyes were filled with tears, his heart with grief.

Dara Is Killed by His Entourage

When Dara read this answer he saw the straits that the world had brought him to and was struck dumb. At last he said, "This is worse than death, that I should stand before Sekandar as his servant; a tomb will be better for me than such shame. Everyone turned to me for help in warfare, but now that it is I who need help, I see that I have no friend in all the world. God is now my only hope." Since there was no one to come to his aid he wrote a humble letter begging for help to the Indian prince, Foor. He began by praising God, and then continued, "Lord of the Indian peoples, wise, knowledge-able, and clear-spirited, you will have heard of the calamity the stars have dealt me: Sekandar brought his army from Greece and has taken from me my coun-try, family, children, throne, crown, treasuries, and army. If you can help me now, I shall send you from what I have left enough jewels and treasure that you shall never want for wealth in the future, and by this act you will also find fame in the world, and noble men will praise you." He dispatched his messenger, who rode as quickly as the wind to Foor.

But Sekandar learned of his plan and had the tucket sounded, and the noise of kettle drums and Indian chimes filled the camp. His army set out from Estakhr, and their dust was so thick that the sun in the heavens lost its way. A great cry went up when the two armies met, and the Greek warriors were impatient for the battle to begin. Sekandar drew up his army's ranks, the air turned black with dust, and the earth could not be seen beneath the mass of men. But when Dara led out his men, they had no longing for battle: their hearts were weary and they were sick of warfare. Fortune had deserted the Persians. They hardly resisted the Greek onslaught; the once-savage lions fled like foxes. Dara's commanders surrendered, and the crest of their glory was humbled in the dust. Seeing this, Dara turned tail and fled, lamenting as he did so, and about three hundred of his cavalry followed him. Two of his closest advisors were also with him on the battlefield that day; one was a Zoroastrian priest called Mahyar, and the other's name was Janushyar. When these two saw that Dara's situation was hopeless, one said to the other,

"This wretch is now deserted and alone,
He's lost the glory of his crown and throne.
A dagger in his chest and he'll be dead,
A single sword blow could cut off his head,
Then Sekandar will honor us and we
Shall have a share in Persia's sovereignty."

The two rode with him, one on each side: Janushyar, who was his chief counselor, on the left, and Mahyar, who was his treasurer, on the right. And as they did so Janushyar plunged a dagger into the king's chest. Dara slumped forward and his head hung down; as one man his remaining warriors fled from him.

Dara's Dying Words to Sekandar

Dara's counselors made their way to Sekandar and said, "Wise and victorious lord, we have killed your enemy: his days as king are over." When Sekandar heard Janushyar's words, he said to him and to Mahyar, "Where is this enemy of mine whom you've cast aside in this way? Take me to him." The two led Sekandar, whose heart was bursting with rage, to where Dara lay with his chest covered in gore, and his face as pale as fenugreek. Sekandar gave orders that no one else should approach, and that Dara's two counselors be detained. Quick as the wind he dismounted and laid the wounded man's head on his thigh. He rubbed both his hands against Dara's face until he began to revive and speak. Then Sekandar removed the royal diadem from Dara's head and loosened his armor. No doctor was nearby, and when he saw Dara's wounds, a few tears dropped from Sekandar's eyes. "May this pass easily from you," he said, "and may the hearts of those who wish you ill tremble in terror! Get up, and let me lay you in a golden litter, or if you have the strength, sit yourself in the saddle. I will bring doctors from India and Greece, and I shall weep tears of blood for your pain. I shall restore your kingdom to you, and when you have recovered, we shall swear friendship. This instant I shall hang from a gibbet those who have injured you. When I heard last night what had happened, my heart filled with sorrow, my soul with anger. We are from the same stock, the same root, the same people: why should we destroy one another for ambition's sake?"

When he heard Sekandar, Dara said, "May wisdom always be your companion! I think that you will find the reward for what you have said from God himself. You said that Iran is mine, and that the crown and the throne of the brave are mine; but death is closer to me than the throne. The throne is over for me, and my luck has run out. So the high heavens revolve; their turning is toward sorrow, and their profit is pain. Look at me before you say 'I am exalted above all this great company of heroes.' Know that evil and good both come from God, and see that you remain grateful to him for as long as you live. My own state shows you the truth of what I say. Look how I, who had such sovereignty and glory and wealth, am now despised by everyone. I who never injured anyone, who had such armor and such armies, such splendid horses, such crowns and thrones, who had such sons and relatives, and so many allies whose hearts bore my brand. Earth and time were my slaves, and

remained so while my luck held. But now I am separated from good fortune, and have fallen into the hands of murderers. I despair of my sons and family; the earth has turned dark for me, and my eyes are white like the eyes of a blind man. Our own people cannot help us; my one hope is in God the Creator. I lie here wounded on the earth, fallen into the trap of death, but this is the way of the heavens whether we are kings or heroes. Greatness too must pass: it is the prey, and its hunter is death."

Sekandar's pity made his face turn pale, and he wept for the wounded king, lying there stretched out on the earth. Dara said to him, "Do not weep, there is no profit in it. My part in the fires of life is now merely smoke. This was my fate from him who apportions our fates. This is the goal toward which the splendor of my earthly days has led me. Listen to the advice I shall give you, accept it into your heart, and remember it." Sekandar said, "It is for you to order me: I give you my word." Then Dara spoke quickly, going over his wishes and omitting nothing. He began by saying, "You have achieved fame, but see that you fear the world's Creator, who has made the heavens and the earth and time, and the strong and the weak. Look after my children and my family, and my veiled wise women. Ask for my daughter's hand in marriage, and keep her gently and in comfort in the court. Her mother named her Roshanak and saw that the world was always a place of happiness and delight for her. Do not despise my daughter, or let malevolent men speak badly of her. She has been brought up as a princess, and at our feasts she has always been the loveliest person present. It may be that you shall have a son with her, and that the name of Esfandyar will be renewed in him, that he will preserve the fires of Zoroastrianism and live by the Zend-Avesta, keeping the Feasts of Sadeh and No-Ruz and preserving our fire temples. Such a son will honor Hormozd and the sun and moon, and wash his soul and face in the waters of wisdom; he will renew the ways of Lohrasp and Goshtasp, treating men according to their station whether it be high or low; he will make our faith flourish and his days will be fortunate."

Sekandar answered him, "Your heart is pure and your words are wise, O king. I accept all that you have said, and I shall not stray from your words while I am within the borders of your kingdom. I shall accomplish the good deeds you recommend, and your wisdom will be my guide." The master of the world grasped Sekandar's hand and began to weep bitterly.

> He kissed Sekandar's palm and said, "I pray
> That God will keep and guide you on your way.
> I give my flesh to dust, to God my spirit,
> My sovereignty is yours now to inherit."

He spoke, and his soul rose up from his body. All those gathered nearby began to weep, and Sekandar rent his clothes and poured dust on the royal diadem. Sekandar made a splendid tomb for him according to local custom and, now that the time for Dara's eternal sleep had come, the blood was washed from his body with clear rosewater. His body was wrapped in brocade woven with gold and sewn with jewels; it was then covered with camphor, even his face, so that no one could see it. As Dara's corpse was placed within its golden coffin the bystanders wept, and then it was carried in procession, passed hand to hand by the mourners, with Sekandar leading the cortege on foot, and as he approached the tomb, it seemed as if his skin would split with sorrow. The king's coffin was placed within the tomb according to the ancient royal rites, and the huge doors of the building were sealed. Then Sekandar had two gibbets built, one bearing the name Janushyar and the other Mahyar, and the two regicides were strung up on them. The soldiers who were there took rocks in their fists and stoned them to death, as a warning to those who would kill a king. When the Persians saw how Sekandar honored Dara and mourned for him, they offered the young king their homage and loyalty.

Sekandar Writes Letters to the Persians

From Kerman a noble messenger traveled to Esfahan, bringing Sekandar's good wishes to Dara's womenfolk. He described Dara's last days to them and said in Sekandar's name, "It is not right for either friends or enemies to rejoice when just kings die. You are to consider me as Dara now; if he has gone from the earth I have appeared before you. The privileges and pleasures of your life will be increased, and there is no need to claw your faces in fear and grief. King and soldier, we are all destined for death, though to some it comes soon and to others later. Go to the city of Estakhr and prepare to celebrate our alliance with all pomp and splendor. Persia is as she always was, and you should rejoice and keep body and soul in good spirits."

Then a letter was sent, from Sekandar the Great, the son of Filqus, world conqueror and destroyer of those who would oppose him, to every province of Persia, and to every nobleman and chieftain, saying, "May the good will of the Creator who made the world and all things visible and invisible, who turns the heavens above us and who alone can be called mighty and wise, who is able to do all things and whose slaves we are, bless our nobles and augment their prosperity! In victory I have known grief, and sorrow came to me in the midst of rejoicing. I swear by the lord of the sun that I intended no harm to Dara: the man who killed him was from his own household, his slave and not a foreigner. Now that man has received God's punishment; he acted evilly and evil came to him. But you must follow justice and swear allegiance to me, if you desire the blessings of heaven and to receive riches, slaves and high office from my hand. My heart is filled with grief for Dara, and I shall try not to stray from his advice. Whoever comes to my court will receive cash, ivory, and the confirmation of his crown and throne. If he prefers to remain in his own castle, as long as he does not go back on his word, he too will receive the treasures he desires from me. Mint coins in the name of Sekandar and see that you remain faithful to your treaties with me. Maintain your palaces as they have always been, and have the markets overseen as is proper, for such things reflect on my sovereignty. Show me your value by keeping watch on the frontiers so that thieves cannot despoil the countryside, and maintain yourselves in joy and prosperity. From every city send a slave girl, someone who is beautiful, modest, and intelligent, to serve in my women's quarters, but send only those who are willing to come, as slaves should not be forced or abused. See that you treat travelers well, especially those who behave appropriately and speak soberly, who are pure in heart and content with poverty, whom men call Sufis; place them at the head of those to whom you give charity. But if you find that people are oppressed by their overlords, break the hearts and backs of those who are troubling them, destroy them root and branch. I shall seek out those who do evil and have them strung up on a gibbet, and those who ignore my commands will pay dearly in the end for their crimes."

Sekandar presided over his court, welcoming the world in peace. From Kerman he made his way to Estakhr, where he placed the Kayanid crown on his own head.

> Don't ask the world her secrets: she will hide
> Them from your gaze, and turn her face aside.

❧ THE REIGN OF SEKANDAR ❧

Sekandar took his place on the throne and said, "Kings' souls should be imbued with wisdom, since it is God who gives victory in the world, and any king who does not fear him is evil. It is certain that both good and evil will pass, and that there is no escaping the clutches of fate. Whoever comes to my court seeking justice, even if it is against myself, and whether it is during a royal audience or in the middle of the night, will be answered as soon as he speaks. Since he who bestows sovereignty has given me glory and opened the gates of victory to me, I shall collect no taxes from any of my subjects for five years, whether they live in the mountains, the plains, by the sea, or in cities. I will distribute wealth to the poor and ask for nothing from the wealthy." With this fine speech Sekandar showed that he was disposed to rule justly, and a cry of homage went up from his palace. Then the crowd dispersed and the world's ruler sat closeted with his advisors.

Sekandar's Letter to Delaray, the Mother of Roshanak

Sekandar summoned a scribe, who brought a Chinese pen and silk. The scribe dipped his pen in the ink, and Sekandar dictated a letter to Roshanak's mother, Delaray, saying, "May God grant you grace and destroy your enemies. I have already written to you concerning your sorrows. When your husband's good fortune deserted him and he was murdered by one of his own slaves, I buried him according to the royal rites and bade him God speed from this world. Before we fought I tried to make peace with him, but his days were numbered and he refused. Even his enemies felt sorrow when his blood was spilled, and may God conduct him to the blue vault of heaven. None of us can escape the claws of death, which is like the winds of autumn before which we are blown like leaves. The world now waits for your response to Dara's dying wishes, which many witnessed: he gave Roshanak to me, saying that she was a suitable bride. Send her quickly to me, accompanied by serving girls, nurses, and Persian noblewomen, so that she may brighten my darkened soul. Keep Esfahan as your own, as it has been in the past, and see that it is looked after by the same wise, experienced, just, and humble administrators whom Dara appointed. And if you do not wish to reign there, all of Persia is yours to choose from. Fill your heart with civility toward me, and proclaim me before the world as the new Dara."

He sent a similar letter to Roshanak. It began with an invocation to the all-knowing God who maintains the world, and continued, "From royal stock none but noble offspring can come, delightful, wise and modest, well-spoken and soft-voiced. Shortly before he died, taking his glorious name to the grave, your father gave you to me. When you enter my apartments, you will be my chief desire, the first among my women: you will make the crown more splendid, the royal torque and ivory throne more glittering. I have written to your mother, asking her to send you to me in a manner fitting for your station, as a princess, preceded by the chief priest of Esfahan, in a splendid litter, and accompanied by your maidservants and the women who brought you up. Come to me with peace of mind, knowing you will be the first of my women, and may you always live securely and safely in my royal apartments."

When Delaray heard the messenger's words she heaved a cold sigh from the depths of her being and wept bitter tears for Dara, who had been hurried ignominiously beneath the dust. Still weeping, she called in her scribe and dictated a shrewd and dignified reply. She began by invoking the world's Creator, then said, "It was Dara's glory that I sought from heaven, from which come war and peace and mercy, but since his time has passed and he has exchanged the throne for a wooden coffin, I wish you well in the world. I wish you greatness, victory, and sovereignty, and that the world's affairs unfold as you desire, and I hide no secret meaning beneath my words. I have heard your offer of clemency, and may the heavens rejoice in the kindness of your soul. I have heard too of the tomb you made for Dara and the gibbets you made for Mahyar and that malignant slave Janushyar (when someone spills a king's blood, he is not long for this world). I know too that you have desired peace and reconciliation, and that you have spent many days with your counselors pondering this matter. But kings do not beg, and no one expects a crowned head to act as a slave. You are now our sovereign, and since the sun has set, you are the moon for us. May the world know only your happiness, and may your name resound forever in its palaces! And it has made our hearts happy that you have thought in this way of Roshanak. She is your handmaid; we are your slaves, and our heads are bowed awaiting your commands. She sends you greetings and has written you a letter, an answer as lovely as paradise. The Lord of the world has chosen you, and no one can turn aside from his commands. I have written to my nobles and warlike chieftains, telling them that Dara's sovereignty is now yours, and that no one should disobey you." Then she gave the messenger robes of honor, a purse of gold, and all manner of precious objects. He returned to Sekandar's camp and told the king all he had seen and heard concerning the court's pomp and majesty, which was as splendid as when its former king still reigned there.

Sekandar Marries Roshanak

Sekandar sent for his mother, who was then at Amourieh, and told her of Dara's dying words. "Go to Delaray," he said, "and win her over with sweet conversation. See that you meet Roshanak, who lives in purdah there, and convey to her my regards. Take torques, bracelets, and earrings, and a royal throne studded with jewels. Take a hundred camels laden with carpets, and a hundred more laden with gold-worked brocade. Take thirty thousand dinars from my treasury, packed in purses, to be scattered before the bride. Take a hundred thousand Greek serving girls, each one reverently carrying a golden goblet, as is proper before a princess. Take slaves to look after you along the way, and see that your progress is carried out with royal splendor."

The king's mother set out with ten wise and eloquent translators, and as she approached Esfahan the nobles of the city came forward in a throng to meet her. Delaray too came out from her palace, accompanied by her retinue of courtiers, and so many gold coins were scattered in the courtyard that men thought of silver as so much dirt. They sat within the palace, the nobles of the court crowded around them, and Delaray brought out such a dowry that it seemed the markets of the world had been emptied for the purpose. For parasangs there was camel after camel laden with gold, sliver, and colored cloths; there were clothes and carpets, cloths to spread and cloths to drape, Arab horses with golden bridles, Indian swords with golden scabbards, armor, and helmets and barding for horses, maces and Indian daggers; so much uncut cloth and so much cloth cut for clothes that no one had ever seen more in all the world.

Slaves were summoned from the palace and forty golden litters were prepared; her heart filled with happiness, Roshanak took her place in a litter shaded by a parasol and surrounded by servants. The road was a mass of gold and silver and horses and escorts; the streets of the city were hung with banners, and there was laughter on everyone's lips, excitement in

everyone's heart. They poured coins on the brocade parasol as it passed, and scattered musk in the procession's path.

> *Then, lovely as the moon, the princess dazed*
> *Sekandar's wondering sight—he stared amazed*
> *At her as though she were compounded of*
> *Intelligence and beauty mixed with love:*
> *Her stature and her soul-bewitching face*
> *Made his apartments an enchanting place.*
> *He sat his mother on a golden throne,*
> *Then fixed his eyes on Roshanak alone.*
> *For seven days they sat there side by side,*
> *Sekandar talking always to his bride,*
> *And all his manner showed his sovereignty,*
> *His grace and wisdom, charm, and modesty.*

Gifts of gold and silver were distributed throughout Iran, and the whole country, together with the cities of China and Turan, sent their congratulations. All the world was filled with justice, and the places that had lain waste flourished again.

Sekandar Leads His Army against Kayd

Mehran, the vizier of Kayd, the king of Qanuj, counseled his royal master, "Sekandar will come here with an army of chieftains chosen from Greece and Persia: if you wish to preserve your status be wise and do not look for war with him. You have four things the like of which no noble or commoner has ever seen in all the world. The first, which gives such luster to your crown, is your daughter, who is as lovely as paradise itself; the second is the philosopher you keep hidden, who tells you all the world's secrets; the third is your physician, who is renowned for his skill; the fourth is the goblet you possess that can never be emptied whether by fire or the sun, or when someone drinks from it. With these four things you can save your position. When Sekandar comes, rely on these and, if you don't want him to stay here a long time, don't think of resistance; you have not the might to withstand his army, wealth, and glory. Now is the age of Sekandar, who is the crown of

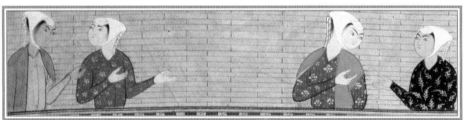

all nobles. When he comes, give him these four things, and I think he will ask for nothing else from you. If you satisfy him in this manner he will go on his way, because he is wise and seeks after knowledge." When Kayd had heard Mehran's words, he felt that the ancient days of his splendor had been renewed.

Having secured Persia Sekandar led out his army, by roads and pathless wastes, toward India and King Kayd. As he went forward the cities opened their gates to welcome him. When his army reached the border city known locally as Milad, Sekandar, as eager as a lion that scents its prey, summoned a scribe and dictated a letter to Kayd. The letter began by praising those who wash their hearts in wisdom, who choose the ways of ease and look to enjoy their wealth, who turn to God for aid, placing their hopes and fears in him. It continued, "They are men who know that the throne derives from my power and that I, Sekandar, am the shadow of the world's victorious Lord. I have written this letter to enlighten your dark soul; when your scribe reads it to you, do not put it aside, thinking to deal with it later. If it comes at night, do not wait till dawn; prepare immediately to obey me. And if you disregard what I say I shall trample your head, crown, and throne beneath my feet."

Kayd welcomed Sekandar's envoy warmly and said, "I am filled with joy at his commands and will not turn aside from them for a moment. But before God, it isn't right to hurry things along in this fashion, and for me to go before him with no preparation." He summoned a scribe, who wrote at his dictation with an Indian pen on Chinese silk. First he

praised the God of victory and fate, who is generous and just, and who rules over manliness, wisdom, and human skill, and then said, "Noble men will not ignore the king's commands, and we should hold nothing back from the master of armies, the crown, and the sword. I have four things that no one else in all the world has, either openly or in secret, and no one else ever will have possessions like them. If the king commands me, I shall send them to him, and his heart will delight in them. And then, when the king orders me to, I shall come like a slave to pay homage to him."

When the messenger told Sekandar what he had heard, and handed over Kayd's letter, Sekandar sent him back again, to ask what these four things were that no one else had. Kayd cleared his court and sat with his advisors. They called Sekandar's envoy in and made much of him, and then Kayd said to him,

> *"I have a daughter here whose lovely face*
> *Would make the sun dark if he glimpsed her grace;*
> *Her lips still smell of milk; her hair, pitch-black,*
> *Hangs like a woven lariat down her back;*
> *The cypress bows before her elegance,*
> *Roses are scattered by her eloquence;*
> *Her speech exceeds her beauty, all she says*
> *Seems taught by wisdom and beyond all praise,*
> *And when she chooses to be silent she*
> *Becomes the soul of gentle modesty:*
> *God-fearing and a princess, chaste and wise,*
> *Her like has not been seen by human eyes.*
> *Then there's the wondrous goblet that is mine*
> *Which, when it's filled with water or with wine,*
> *Stays always full. You and your chosen friends*
> *Could drink ten years, the liquid never ends.*
> *Next there is my physician, who can tell*
> *From one small drop of urine if you're well*
> *And, if not, what is wrong: there's no disease*
> *That can escape his cunning expertise;*
> *With him at court you could dismiss all fears*
> *Of sickness, and survive for countless years.*
> *And lastly there's my court philosopher*
> *Who from the turning heavens can infer*
> *All that will come to pass, and everything*
> *He learns he's prompt to pass on to his king."*

The envoy returned, riding his horse as quickly as the wind, and when he told Sekandar what he had heard, the world conqueror's heart opened like a flower in bloom. He said, "If all he claims is true, the world itself is hardly enough to pay for such things. When he sends these wonders to me, my dark soul will glow with light, and I shall not trample on him as I threatened, but leave his country as his friend."

Sekandar Sends Nine Knowledgeable Men to See the Four Wonders

He chose a number of his advisors, all percipient and knowledgeable men, and sent a letter filled with honorifics and flattery to accompany them. "I am sending nine of my own trusted savants, all wise and reverend men who will not make any difficulties for you. Let the four wonders you mention stay where they are: show them to my envoys, and as soon as I receive a letter from these experienced graybeards saying they have seen these things with their own eyes, and that the world cannot show their like, I shall write a charter such as your heart would desire, confirming you as the king of India."

The nine Greek advisors made their way from Sekandar to Kayd, and the chancellor of Kayd's court made them welcome with questions about their journey and had a suitable place set aside for their stay. On the next day, as the sky turned yellow with dawn and the sun drew its sword for battle, Kayd's daughter was prepared for her audience, although the full moon needs no adornment. A golden throne was placed within the castle, and the room was decorated in the Chinese fashion. Her face as splendid as the sun, the princess sat on the throne, shining more brightly than Venus in the night sky. The nine sages came in, chattering pleasantries and ready to observe carefully. When they saw the princess's face, and the light flashing from her bracelets and throne, they were so astonished that they couldn't move, and their legs felt weak beneath them. The nine of them stood rooted to the spot, giving thanks to God for such loveliness; none of them could tear his eyes from her, or think how to turn away. They stayed so long that the king sent someone to

fetch them, and he said, "What kept you so long? She has a lovely face, but she is human, endowed with her beauty by the stars." The sages answered, "No palace contains a portrait as lovely as she is: each of us will write to our king saying how incomparably beautiful she is."

Then they took pen, ink, and paper and wrote to Sekandar. A messenger took their letters to the king, who was amazed by what he read: each letter described her in the same fashion. The king's answer congratulated them on having seen the loveliness of paradise and continued, "There's no need to inquire any further: return at once and bring these four wonders to me. Assure Kayd that his daughter will be well looked after, and set off with this marvel immediately. Kayd has treated me justly, and from now on no one will be able to harm him."

The Nine Sages Bring Kayd's Four Wonders to Sekandar

The messenger made his way back to the nine sages, who returned to Kayd's audience hall with Sekandar's answers. The Indian king was overjoyed that the threat of an invasion by Sekandar had been lifted. He chose a hundred wise, eloquent Indians as an escort, and from his treasury generously selected bracelets, crowns, jewels, uncut cloth, and other suitable gifts, which were then loaded onto three hundred camels. Another hundred camels carried silver coins, and a hundred more gold. A litter was fashioned from sweet-smelling aloes wood and hung with cloth of gold on which jewels were sewn; ten elephants carried golden howdahs, and the finest of

them bore a splendid saddle. The princess wept bitter tears of farewell and set off together with the philosopher and the doctor. A nobleman carried the famous goblet, and the wine in it kept the accompanying courtiers drunk.

When this beautiful princess, crowned with her musky hair, as elegant as a cypress topped by the moon, entered the inner apartments of Sekandar's castle, no one there felt worthy to look at her. She wore her hair plaited on the top of her head, her eyebrows were arched like a bow, her eyes like paradisal narcissi; she seemed to be fashioned wholly from charm and loveliness. Sekandar took in her stature, her hair, face, head, and feet, and under his breath he praised God that he had created such beauty, saying, "This is indeed the light of the world." He summoned all the wise men and priests of his entourage, and in their presence he asked for her hand in marriage, according to Christian custom. Then he poured over her so many gold coins from his treasury that it was only with difficulty that she could walk through them.

Sekandar Tests the Philosopher, the Physician, and the Goblet

When the lovely cypress had been taken care of and a place fitted out that was suitable for her, Sekandar turned his attention to the philosopher, to see how he would fare in a battle of wits. He sent him a large goblet filled with cow's fat, saying he should rub all his trunk and limbs with it, until his fatigue was quite gone, and then he could come and fill Sekandar's soul and mind with knowledge. But the philosopher looked at the fat and said, "I'm not fooled by this ploy," and he poured a thousand needles into the goblet and sent it back to the king. Sekandar looked at the needles and then had blacksmiths melt them down and make an iron disk from them, which he sent to the philosopher. He in turn looked at the disk and rubbed it for a while, until he transformed the dark metal into a bright mirror. This was taken to Sekandar at night, who kept his own counsel. He placed the mirror outside, so that the dew turned it black, then he sent it back to the philosopher, and so the duel of wits continued. The sage for his part polished the metal again, making it as bright as water, and sent it back to the king, but this time he smeared an unguent on it, so that humidity wouldn't quickly turn it black again.

Sekandar summoned him and had him seated below the throne. He questioned him, beginning with the goblet of fat, to see if the philosopher had understood what was meant. The sage said to the king, "Fat penetrates deeply into the body, and you were saying that your knowledge goes deeper than that of any philosopher. In answer I said, 'O king, the hearts of wise men are like needles that can penetrate feet and bones and split stones open.' You in turn asked, 'How can the subtle arguments of a wise man penetrate a heart that's been darkened by feasting, warfare, bloodshed, and constant fighting against enemies?' And I replied, 'My wise soul and heart know secrets subtler than a hair, but your heart is not darker than iron.' You said that in the passing of the years your heart had rusted with spilled blood, and how was it possible for this to be righted, and for you to frame words in such darkness? I answered that I would work on your heart with divine knowledge, until it became as bright as water and certain of truth."

Sekandar was delighted by the man's ready answers, and he ordered that his treasurer bring him a set of clothes, gold and silver, and a goblet filled with jewels. But when these were given to the sage, he said, "I have a hidden jewel that brings me whatever I wish and provokes no enemies, and unlike wealth, does not bring Ahriman in its train. It has no guards to demand a salary from me, and I fear no bandits when I'm traveling. Wisdom, knowledge, and righteousness are what's needed, and going astray from these will lead a man to knock at ruin's door. The Lord of all that is visible and invisible can provide me with sufficient food and clothing; knowledge is my guardian at night, and wisdom is the crown of my active soul. Why should I rejoice in more than this and worry about guarding such wealth? Tell your servants to take these things somewhere else, and may wisdom be my soul's guide." Sekandar wondered at the sage and thought the matter over. He said, "From now on the Lord of the sun and moon will find no sin in me: I will follow your advice and pay attention to the profitable things you have said."

Sekandar Tests the Indian Physician

Sekandar summoned the Indian physician, who could diagnose a man's health from a drop of urine. He questioned him as to the cause of illnesses that make one weep with pain, and the physician answered, "Whoever overeats, and does not watch what he consumes during meals, will grow ill; a healthy person will not eat too much, and a great man is one who seeks to be healthy. Now I will prepare an ointment for you, from herbs gathered in various places, and by using this you will stay in good health. Your appetites will increase, but if you overeat there will be no harmful results. If you do as I instruct you, your blood and marrow will grow strong and your body more energetic, your heart will feel the happiness of springtime, your cheeks will flush with health, and you will be eager to do noble deeds. And your hair will not turn white (white hair makes one despair of the world)."

Sekandar said, "I have never heard of such a thing, or observed it of any sovereign. If you can bring me this ointment, you will be my guide through this world; my soul will be at your service and your enemies will be unable to harm you." He had a robe of honor and other fine gifts prepared for the physician, and made him the chief of all his doctors.

This eloquent physician then made his way into the mountains, with a few of his own companions. His knowledge of plants was extensive, and he knew both poisons and their antidotes. He gathered a great many mountain herbs, throwing away the useless ones and choosing those that were beneficial; these he used to prepare the ointment. He rubbed Sekandar's body with this concoction, and for years the king's body remained healthy.

Then the king began to devote his nights to carousing rather than to sleep. His mind was filled with the desire for women, and he sought out soft, enticing places to be with them. This way of life weakened the king, but he gave no thought to the harm he was doing his body. One day the physician noted signs of weakness in the king's urine and said to him, "There's no doubt that a young man grows old quickly by sleeping with women. It looks to me as though you haven't slept properly for three nights. Tell me, am I right?" Sekandar answered, "I'm perfectly well, my body has not a trace of weakness in it." But the Indian doctor did not agree with him, and that night he searched his books and prepared a remedy against bodily infirmities. That same night Sekandar slept alone, unaccompanied by any of his beautiful womenfolk. At sunrise the doctor came to examine his urine, and he found that there were no telltale signs in it this time. He threw away the remedy he'd mixed and ordered wine, a feast, and musicians. The king asked him, "Why did you throw away that medicine you'd taken such trouble to prepare?" He replied, "Last night the king of the world gave no thought to finding a companion; he slept through the darkness alone. And since you slept alone, my lord, you need no medicine." Sekandar laughed, pleased to be free of the threat of illness, and said, "May the world never be without India! All the astronomers and great savants of the world seem to live there." Giving the doctor a purse of gold, and a black horse with golden bells attached to its bridle, Sekandar said to him, "May wisdom always guide your noble soul!"

Sekandar Tests Kayd's Goblet

Next he gave orders that the golden goblet be filled with cold water and brought to him. Then everyone drank from the goblet, from dawn to dusk, but the water in it did not decrease. The king said to the wisest philosopher of his time, "You mustn't conceal from me what's happening here: how is it that the water in this cup is always replenished? Is it something to do with the stars, or is it a skill the Indians possess?"

The philosopher replied, "Your majesty, this goblet is not something to make light of. It took the makers many years and a great deal of toil to fashion this. Astrologers from every country gathered at Kayd's court to produce this cup and worked on it through bright days and dark nights, consulting their tables for days on end. Think of what happens here as analogous to magnetism, which attracts iron. In a similar way this cup attracts moisture from the turning heavens, but it does so in such a subtle fashion that human eyes cannot see the process." Sekandar was delighted with the answer, and he said to the elders of Milad, "I shall never break my treaty with Kayd; he is a man whom one must respect, and as he has given me these four wonders I shall demand nothing further from him."

Then Sekandar gathered together two hundred camel loads of precious goods, to which he added a hundred jeweled crowns, as well as uncut jewels and gold coins, and had all this hidden in the mountains.

> *Once all this wealth had been concealed, the men*
> *Who'd done the deed were never seen again—*
> *Only the massive treasure's sovereign lord*
> *Knew where the mountains hid this glittering hoard.*

Sekandar's Letter to Foor

Having hidden his treasure in this way, Sekandar led his army out from Milad and bore down on Qanuj like the wind. He wrote a threatening, bellicose letter, "From Sekandar, the son of Filqus, who lights the flames of prosperity and adversity, to Foor, the lord of India, favored by the heavens, commander of the armies of Sind." The letter opened with praise of God the Creator who is eternal, saying that those to whom he gives victory never want for countries, crowns, and thrones, while those from whom he turns away become wretched, and the sun never shines on them. "You will have heard how God has given me *farr*, victory, good fortune, crowns, thrones, and sovereignty over this dark earth. But none of this will last, and my days draw on; another will come after me to enjoy my conquests. My only ambition is to leave a good name and no disgrace behind me on this sublunar earth. When they bring this letter to you, free your dark soul from sorrow; descend from your throne, do not consult with your priests or advisors, but mount your horse and come to me asking for my protection. Those who try to trick me only prolong matters, and if for one moment you disobey me by choosing arrogance and warfare, I shall descend on your country like a fire, bringing an army of picked warriors, and once you see my cavalry you will regret your delay in submitting to me." The letter was sealed with Sekandar's mark, and a soldier who was eager for fame was chosen to take it. The messenger arrived at the court, and when Foor was told of his arrival he was summoned into the royal presence.

When Foor read Sekandar's letter he started up in rage and immediately wrote a furious reply, planting a tree in the garden of vengeance. "We should fear God, and not use such presumptuous language, because a boastful man will find himself friendless and with no resources. Have you no shame that you summon me like this? Isn't your wisdom disturbed by this kind of talk? If it were Filqus writing thus to Foor, that would be something, but you? You dare to stir up trouble in this way? Your victory over Dara has gone to your head, but the heavens had had enough of him, and fate deals in this way with people who won't listen to good advice. And you found your quarrel with Kayd was like a feast, so now you think all kings are your prey to hunt down. The ancient kings of Iran never addressed us in this way. I am Foor, descended from the family of Foor, and we have never paid any attention to Caesars from the west. When Dara asked for my help, I sent him war elephants to buy time, although I saw that neither his heart nor his fortune were as they should be. When he was murdered by a slave, good fortune deserted the Persians. If evil came to him from an evil counselor, is that any reason for you to lose your good sense? Don't be so eager for battle and so disrespectful toward me; soon enough you'll see my war elephants and armies crowding the way before you. All you think of is your own glory, but inside you are the color of Ahriman. Don't sow these seeds of strife throughout the world; fear misfortune and the harm that will come to you. I mean well by this letter, and may it gratify your heart."

Sekandar Leads His Army against Foor

After reading this letter, Sekandar immediately selected chieftains from his army, men who were worthy of command: old in their understanding but young in years. Then he led his men against Foor, and they were so numerous that the earth was like a heaving sea. They traveled by every pathway, so that there seemed to be no track that they didn't take, over mountains, along the seashores, and through the most difficult terrain. The army grew weary of harsh traveling and fierce battles, and one evening when they pitched camp, a group of them came before the king. They said,

> "Sovereign of Greece and of all Asia too,
> Earth cannot hold the massive armies you
> Lead out against the world: Foor will not fight,
> And China's emperor quails before your might.
> Why should your army's valiant soldiers die
> For worthless lands beneath an alien sky?
> In all our ranks we cannot find one horse
> That's fit for war; if we reverse our course
> The infantry and cavalry will stray
> By unfamiliar paths and lose their way.
> Before, we fought and gained our victories
> Against the strength of human enemies,
> But none of us desires to die in wars
> With mountains and the sea's infertile shores;
> Men do not fight with rocks and ocean tides,
> With barren plains and rugged mountain sides.

Do not convert the glory of our fame
To ignominious and ignoble shame."

Sekandar was angered by their words, and he made short work of their complaints. He said, "In the war with the Persians, no Greek soldier was injured; Dara was killed by his own slaves, and none of you suffered. I shall continue on my way without you, and place my foot on the dragon's heart alone. You will see that the wretched Foor will have no desire for either battles or banquets when I have dealt with him. My help comes from God and the Persian army, and I have no need of Greek goodwill." Frightened by his anger, the army begged him to pardon them and said, "We are all our Caesar's slaves, and we tread the earth only as he wills us to. We shall go on, and when there are no horses left, we shall fight on foot. If the earth becomes a sea with our blood, and the low places become hills of corpses, even if the heavens rain down mountainous rocks, no enemy will ever see our backs in battle. We are your slaves, here for you to command, and how could you suffer any injury from us?"

Sekandar then formed a new battle plan. He chose thirty thousand Persian warriors headed by experienced, well-armored chieftains. Behind them he placed forty thousand Greek cavalry, and behind them his warlike Egyptian cavalry, who fought with swords. Forty thousand of Dara's troops and men from the Persian royal family accompanied them. Sekandar picked out twelve thousand Greek and Egyptian cavalry to bring up the rear and scour the plains and valleys. With his army Sekandar had sixty astrologers and sages to advise him on the most auspicious days for combat.

When Foor became aware of the enemy's approach, he chose a place suitable for battle, and his troops crowded the plain for four miles, with elephants in the van and his warriors behind them. Meanwhile Sekandar's spies told him of the war elephants in Foor's army, and how with their overpowering trunks (that were under the protection of Saturn) they could destroy two miles of cavalry, who would be unable either to defeat them or to get back to their own ranks. The spies drew a picture of an elephant on a piece of paper and showed it to the king, who had a model of the animal made from wax. Then he turned to his advisors and said, "Who can think of some way to defeat this?" The wise men of his court pondered the problem and then gathered together, from Greece, Egypt, and Persia, a group of more than forty times thirty blacksmiths, all of whom were expert at their trade. They made a horse of iron, with an iron saddle and an iron rider; its joints were held together with nails and solder, and then they polished both the rider and his steed. It was mounted on wheels and filled with black oil. They pushed it in front of Sekandar, who was pleased by the device and saw that it would be very useful. He ordered that more than a thousand of these iron horses and riders be made. What king had ever seen an army of dappled, gray, bay, and black horses, all of them made of iron? The devices went forward on wheels, and looked exactly like cavalry prepared for war.

Sekandar's Battle against the Indian Troops; He Kills Foor

As Sekandar approached Foor's forces, the two armies caught sight of each other; amid clouds of dust a great cry went up from each side, and the warriors advanced on each other eager for battle. Then Sekandar's men set fire to oil in the iron horses and routed Foor's forces. Flames flared out from the iron steeds, and as soon as the elephants saw this they plunged precipitately this way and that. Foor's army was in turmoil, and when the elephants wrapped their trunks around the burning horses, they were maddened by their wounds, and their mahouts were bewildered as to what to do. The whole Indian army, including its mighty elephants, began to flee, and Sekandar pursued his malicious enemies like the wind. As the air darkened at nightfall there was nowhere left for the army to fight. Sekandar and the Greeks halted at a place between two mountains and sent out scouts to keep their camp safe from the enemy.

When the sun rose like a gold ingot, making the world as bright as clear crystal, the din of trumpets, bugles, and fifes rang out, and the two armies, thrusting their lances into the heavens, prepared to fight again. Clutching his Greek sword, Sekandar came between the hosts and sent a horseman to shout from a distance to Foor,

> *"Sekandar stands before his troops and seeks*
> *To talk with Foor, and hear the words he speaks."*

When Foor heard this he hurried to the head of his troops. Sekandar said,

> *"Two armies have been shattered on these plains*
> *Where feral scavengers eat human brains,*
> *And horses tread on bones. We're brave and young,*
> *Each of us is a noble champion—*
> *Our warriors have been killed, or they have fled:*
> *Why should they flee, or be left here for dead?*
> *Why should two countries fight when combat can*
> *Decide who is the victor, man to man?*
> *Prepare to face me, one of us alone*
> *Will live to claim these armies and this throne."*

Foor agreed to his proposal, thinking that his own body was like a lion's and that his horse was the equal of any fierce dragon, while Sekandar was as thin as a reed, wore light armor, and rode an exhausted mount. He said,

"This is a noble custom: hand to hand
We will decide who's ruler of this land."

Grasping their swords, they advanced on one another in the space between the two hosts. When Sekandar saw his massive opponent, his fearsome sword in hand and mounted on a huge horse, he was astonished and almost despaired of his life. Nevertheless he went forward, and as he did so Foor was distracted by a cry that went up from the rear of his army and turned toward it. Like the wind then Sekandar bore down on him, and struck the lion-like warrior with a mighty sword blow. The blade sliced through Foor's neck and trunk, and he fell from his horse to the earth.

The Greek commander was overjoyed and his warriors rushed forward; the earth and clouds re-echoed with the thunder of a lion-skin drum, and the blare of trumpets. The Indian warriors looked on Sekandar with fury and were ready to fight, but a voice rang out from the Greek ranks: "Foor's head lies here in the dust, his mammoth body is hacked and torn, who is it you wish to fight for, who will benefit from more sword blows and destruction? Sekandar has become to you as Foor was; it is he you must look to now for battles and banquets." With a roar the Indian warriors called out their agreement, and they came forward to gaze at Foor's hacked and bloody body. A wail of sorrow went up from their ranks, and they threw down

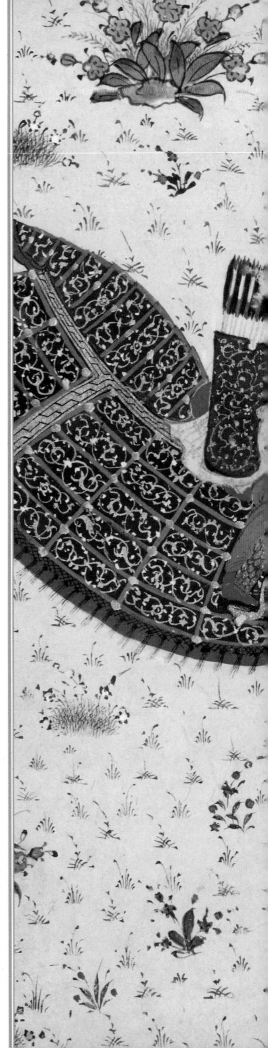

their weapons. Fearfully they went before Sekandar, groaning and heaping dust on their heads, but Sekandar returned their weapons, and his words were welcoming: "One Indian has died here, but you should not grieve. I shall cherish you more than he did and try to drive sorrow from your lives. I will distribute his wealth among you, and make the Indians powerful with crowns and throne." Then he mounted Foor's throne; on the one side there was mourning and on the other feasting. But this is the way of the passing world, which brings sorrow to those who dwell in it.

For two months Sekandar sat on the Indian throne, distributing wealth to the army; then he placed there as his regent an Indian nobleman called Savorg, saying to him, "Don't hide your gold away. Distribute and consume whatever comes to you, and put no faith in this passing world, which sometimes favors Sekandar, sometimes Foor, and sometimes gives us pain and rage, sometimes joy and feasting." Savorg too distributed gold and silver to the Indian warriors.

Sekandar's Pilgrimage to the Ka'abeh

Not long after Sekandar's army had become wealthy in this way, the clatter of drums rang out as dawn broke, and the air became as brilliant as a rooster's eye from the throng of red, yellow, and purple silken banners. Sekandar set out for Mecca, and some of his entourage were pleased by this, some alarmed. With drums rolling and trumpets blaring, he came to the house made with such toil by Abraham, the son of Azar. God named the site the House of Holiness, the goal of all God's roads. He named it his own house, and called you to worship there: the world's God has no need for food or pleasure or rest or comfort, but this has always been his place of worship since any place at all has existed, a place to remember God.

Sekandar approached Qadesiya, laying claim to the land from Jahrom in Fars as he went. Nasr, the son of Qotayb, heard of his approach and went out to welcome him with a group of noble horseman bearing lances. A horseman hurried from Mecca to Sekandar telling him that the man who was coming to greet him had no desire for wealth or power and was a descendant of Esmail, the son of Abraham. When Nasr arrived Sekandar welcomed him, and assigned him a splendid place in his entourage; Nasr was overjoyed, and recounted to Sekandar the secrets of his lineage. The king answered him, "My honest and pure-hearted lord, tell me who is the noblest of your tribe, after yourself?" Nasr replied, "O ruler of the world, Jaza' is the greatest man in this place. When Esmail departed this life, the world conqueror Qahtab appeared from the deserts with a host of savage swordsmen, and by main force took the land of Yemen. Many innocent men were killed at that time, and the fortunes of our tribe declined. But God was not pleased with Qahtab, and the heavens darkened for him. When he died Jaza' took his place, an unjust and troublesome man. From the shrine here to the Yemen is all under his control, and his men fish the Red Sea. He has turned away from justice and gives no thought to the one God; he holds the lands here in his fist, and the tribe of Esmail welters in blood because of him."

When Sekandar heard these words he sought out everyone he could find from the family of Jaza' and had them killed: the children's souls were parted from their bodies, and not one of his race was left alive. With the help of his warriors he freed the Hejaz and the Yemen from their unjust rulers, and exalted the tribe of Esmail. Then he went on foot to the shrine, and the people of Esmail were so overjoyed at his presence that wherever he trod the king's treasurer scattered gold coins before him.

Sekandar Leads His Army to Egypt

When he returned from his pilgrimage he bestowed gold on Nasr, enriching those who had been poor and obliged to find food by their own labors. Then he led his army to Jeddah, where he didn't stay long. The soldiers were set to work making ships and a number of boats, in which the world conqueror and his army set off for Egypt. The Egyptian king at that time was named Qaytun, and he possessed an unimaginably large army; when he heard that a victorious world conqueror was coming with a following wind from the shrine at Mecca, he set out with a large company of soldiers to welcome him and took coins, slaves, and crowns as presents. Sekandar was pleased to see him and stayed in Egypt for a year, until he and his troops were well rested.

Andalusia was ruled over by a woman; she was wise, had innumerable troops at her disposal, and ruled in prosperity and happiness. The name of this generous and ambitious woman was Qaydafeh. She sought out a painter from the ranks of her soldiers, someone who could make an accurate likeness, and said to him, "Go to Sekandar, and see that you make no mention of my country or of me. Look carefully at him, see what his complexion is, examine his face and stature, and then paint me a full-length portrait of him." The painter heard her and immediately mounted his horse, ready to carry out his sovereign's orders. As quick as a royal courier he made his way from Andalusia to Egypt and into the presence of Sekandar. He observed him when he gave audience and when he was in the saddle; then he took paper and Chinese ink, drew his portrait exactly as he was in real life, and returned to Andalusia. Qaydafeh was moved when she saw Sekandar's face and sighed to herself, then hid the portrait away.

Sekandar asked Qaytun, "Who is Qaydafeh's equal in the world?"

> And King Qaytun replied, "In all the earth
> There's no one of her glory and her worth;
> Unless he were to read the muster rolls
> No one could count the soldiers she controls.
> You won't find anyone in any land
> Who has the wealth she's able to command,
> Who has her dignity, her eloquence,
> Her wisdom, goodness, and magnificence.
> She's built from stone a wide and wondrous town
> So strong no leopard's claws could tear it down—
> Four parasangs in length, no man can measure
> Its endless width. And if you ask for treasure,
> Hers is uncountable; for years there's been
> Talk in the world of this exalted queen."

Sekandar's Letter to Qaydafeh

Sekandar summoned a scribe and had a letter written on silk, from Sekandar, the slayer of lions and conqueror of cities, to Qaydafeh the wise, whose name is unequalled in glory. The letter opened by invoking God, who is generous and just and who bestows prosperity on those who merit it, and continued: "I have not rushed into war with you; rather, I have been weighing the reports of the splendor of your court. When they bring you this letter, may it enlighten your dark soul. Send tribute to me, and understand that you do not have the strength to oppose me. You are wise, so act with foresight, as a powerful and religious sovereign should. If you attempt any kind of trick against me, you will see nothing but adverse fortune come your way. You don't have to look far to learn this lesson: consider what happened to Dara and Foor." As soon as the ink had dried the letter was sealed with musk.

A quick messenger took the letter at Sekandar's command, and when Qaydafeh read it she was astonished at its language. Her answer was as follows:

"Praise be to him who created the earth, who has made you victorious over Foor of India, over Dara, and over the nobles of Sind. Your victory over these warriors has made you willful. You have crowned yourself in victory, but how can you put me on their level? I am far greater than they were, in *farr* and in glory, in my armies, and in my royal wealth. How can I submit to a Greek overlord, and how can you expect me to tremble with fear because of your threats? My armies number more than a thousand thousand men, and princes command every one of those armies. Who are you that you should boast in this way? Your defeat of Dara has made you the prince of braggarts!" She placed her gold seal on the letter and dispatched the messenger, who rode like the wind.

The Greeks Capture Qaydafeh's Son

Sekandar read her letter and then he had the trumpets sounded and his army led out. They marched for a month until they reached the borders of Qaydafeh's lands. A king called Faryan reigned there, a man possessed of an army and wealth, and successful in his life. His city was built to withstand war, and its walls were so high that cranes could not overfly them. He and his army occupied this fortress, and Sekandar ordered that balistas and catapults be brought up to batter the walls. After a week of fighting his army entered the town, and the victor gave orders that no blood was to be spilled.

One of Qaydafeh's sons, named Qaydrus, was married to Faryan's daughter, and was in the city, as his father-in-law delighted in his company. Qaydrus and his wife, however, had been captured by a man named Shahrgir; Sekandar knew of this and looked for some way to free them. He summoned his vizier, a wise and reasonable man named Bitqun, and showed him his crown and throne, saying, "Qaydrus and his bride will come before you, and I shall call you Sekandar, the son of Filqus. You will be seated on the throne here like a king, and I will stand ready to serve you. You will give orders that Qaydrus's head is to be severed from his shoulders by the executioner. I will humble myself before you and plead for them; you will clear the audience hall of courtiers, and when I redouble my pleas, you will grant my request." The vizier was very troubled by all this, as he was unsure what it meant. Sekandar continued, "This business must remain secret. Call me in as an envoy and talk a little about Qaydafeh; then cordially send me off to her with ten horsemen, saying, 'Hurry and take this letter and bring me the answer.'" Bitqun replied, "I will do it: I'll carry out this deception according to your orders."

Dawn came, the sun drew its glittering dagger, and night fled away in fear. Bitqun sat on the royal throne, but there was shame in his face and anxiety in his heart. Sekandar stood before him as a servant: he had closed the doors to

the court and opened the doors to deception. When Shahrgir led in Qaydafeh's weeping son as a captive, together with his young and beautiful wife, who was wringing her hands in grief, Bitqun quickly said, "Who is this man, who has cause to weep so much?" The young man answered, "Come to your senses! I am Qaydrus, Qaydafeh's son, and this is Faryan's daughter, my sole wife. I wish to take her home and cherish her like my own soul, but I am a prisoner in Shahrgir's hands, my soul wounded by the stars, my body by arrows." When Bitqun heard him he was distressed and angry. He started up and said to the executioner, "These two must be buried beneath the dust! Cut off their heads with your Indian sword: now, just as they are, in chains here."

Sekandar came forward and kissed the ground, and said, "Great king of royal lineage, if you will free them for my sake, I shall be able to hold my head up in any company. Why should you vengefully cut off the heads of innocent people? The world's Creator will not look well on us for this." Wise Bitqun answered him, "You have freed these two from death," and to Qaydrus he added, "You've kept your head, which was already leaving your shoulders! Now I shall send you and this man who has interceded for you to your mother, and he can explain what has happened. It would be good if she would then send us tribute: this would mean that no one will lose his skin in this quarrel. Look after this vizier of mine, who will offer your mother war with me or prosperity; act well toward him as he has done toward you, since a noble man's heart is moved to repay kindness. When he has received the queen's answer, send him safely back to me." Qaydrus replied,

"I will not take my heart or ears or eyes
From him: how could I treat him otherwise
Since he has here restored to me my wife,
My soul, the living sweetness of my life?"

Sekandar Goes as an Envoy to Qaydafeh

Sekandar selected ten suitable companions from among the Greeks: they
were all privy to his identity and willing to keep his secret. He said to them,
"On this journey address me as Bitqun." Qaydrus led the group, and Sekandar watched him and listened to him attentively. Their splendid horses
galloped forward like fire, until the travelers came to a mountain made all
of crystal, yet with fruit trees and many plants growing on its slopes. They
continued into the queen's realm, and when Qaydafeh heard that her son,
about whom she had been anxiously seeking news, was approaching, she
went out to welcome him with a large escort of nobles. As soon as Qaydrus
saw his mother he dismounted and made his obeisance before her. She told
him to remount, and as they rode on together, she grasped his hand in hers.
Qaydrus told her all that he had seen and heard, and he turned pale as he
described his sufferings in Faryan's city, and how he was now bereft of his
crown, throne, army, and wealth. And he added, "This man who has come
with us saved my and my bride's lives; if he hadn't intervened, Sekandar
would have ordered that my head be cut off and my body burned. Treat him
well, and don't hold back with excuses that would make me break my
promise to him."

Hearing her son's words, Qaydafeh was distraught with grief. She had the
messenger summoned from her palace where he had been installed and
motioned him to a fine throne. She questioned him closely and made much
of him and saw that a special residence was set aside for his stay. There she
sent fine foods, clothes, and carpets.

At dawn the next morning Sekandar made his way to the court to talk with
the queen. Servants drew the curtain aside and let his horse enter. He stared in
wonder at Qaydafeh on her ivory throne, with her crown studded with rubies
and turquoise, wearing a Chinese cloak woven with gold, her many serving
girls with their necklaces and earrings standing around her, her face shining
like the sun, her throne supported on crystal columns, her gold dress woven
with jewels and clasped with a precious black and white Yemeni stone. Under
his breath he called on God repeatedly. He saw that her throne alone surpassed anything that Greece or Persia could provide. He came forward and
kissed the ground, like a man anxious to make a good impression. Qaydafeh
encouraged him by asking a number of questions; then, like the sun passing
from the dome of the sky she declared that the audience for strangers was

over, and summoned a meal, wine, and musicians. Tables made of teak and inlaid with gold on an ivory ground were brought in; various kinds of food were served, and wine was set out for when they had finished eating. Gold and silver trays were put before them; first they drank to Qaydafeh herself, and then, as she drank more deeply, the queen began to look closely at Sekandar. She said to her steward, "Bring me that shining silk with the charming face painted on it; bring it quickly, just as it is. Don't stand there wringing your hands, go!"

The steward brought the cloth and laid it before her. She stared at it for a long time and then looked at Sekandar's face: she saw no difference between them. Qaydafeh knew that her guest was the Greek king and the commander of his armies, that he had made himself his own messenger and bravely come into her presence. She said to him, "You seem a man well favored by fortune. Tell me, what message did Sekandar give to you?" And he replied, "The world's king spoke to me in the presence of our nobles. He said to tell the pure-hearted Qaydafeh, 'Pursue only honesty, pay attention to what I say, and do not turn your head aside from my orders. If your heart harbors any rebellion, I shall bring an army against you that will break it in pieces. I have found evidence of your greatness, and I have not hurried to declare war on you. Wisdom and modesty are yours, and your subtle policies maintain the world in safety. If you willingly pay me tribute, you need have no fear of me; if you refuse to go the way of rebellion and disaster, you will see from me nothing but kindness and righteousness.'"

Qaydafeh was infuriated when she heard this, but she thought that silence was the best policy. She said, "Go to your quarters now, and rest with your companions. When you come to me tomorrow, I shall give you my answer and some good advice for your return journey." Sekandar went to the building that had been assigned to him and spent the night considering what he should do. When the world's lamp appeared above the mountaintops, and the plains and foothills took on the appearance of glittering brocade, Sekandar made his way back to Qaydafeh's court; his lips were full of smiles, his heart of grief and anxiety. The chancellor recognized him as the foreign envoy and, after questioning him, led him into the queen's presence. The audience hall was full of strangers. The queen's throne was crystal patterned with agates and emeralds surrounding gems of royal worth; its base was sandal and aloes wood and it rested on pillars studded with turquoise. Sekandar was astonished at the splendor and glory he saw, and he thought, "This is indeed a throne room, and no God-fearing man ever saw its like." He came forward to the queen and was directed to a subsidiary golden throne. Qaydafeh said to him, "Well, Bitqun, why are you staring in this way? Is it that Greece can't produce the like of what you see here, in my humble country?"

Sekandar replied, "Your majesty, you should not speak contemptuously of this palace. It is far more glorious than the palaces of other kings and seems like a mine of precious stones." Qaydafeh laughed at his reaction, and she felt delight in her heart that she was able to tease him in this way. Then she cleared the court and motioned the envoy to come closer to her. She said to him,

"Filqus's son, I see you're fashioned for
Battles and royal banquets, peace and war!"

Sekandar turned pale at her words, and then blushed violently; his soul was filled with distress. He said, "Wise queen, such words are not worthy of you. I am Bitqun, don't say that I am a son of Filqus. I give thanks to God that there is no one of noble lineage here, because if he reported what you have said to my king my soul would soon be separated from my body." Qaydafeh replied,

"Enough excuses! If with your own eyes
You see yourself, then you must recognize
The truth of what I say, and don't attempt
Either to lie or treat me with contempt."

Then she produced the silk with the charming face painted upon it and laid it before him; if the painted face had moved at all you would have said that it was Sekandar himself. Sekandar saw it and he nervously chewed his lower lip; the day had suddenly turned as dark as night for him. He said, "A man should never go out in the world without a hidden dagger!" Qaydafeh answered, "If you had your sword belt on and stood before me with a dagger, you'd have neither the strength nor an adequate sword nor a place to fight nor a means of escape." Sekandar said, "A noble and ambitious man should not flinch at danger; a low-minded person will never rise in the world. If I had my arms and armor here, all your palace would be a sea of blood; I'd have killed you, or ripped open my own belly in front of those who hate me!"

Qaydafeh Gives Sekandar Some Advice

Qaydafeh laughed at his blustering manliness and his angry words. She said, "O lion-like king, don't let yourself be led astray by your male pride! The Indian king Foor wasn't killed because of your glory, and neither were Dara and the heroes of Sind. Their good fortune was at an end, and yours was in the ascendant; and now you're so full of your manly valor because you've become the greatest man on earth at the moment. But you should know that all good things come from God, and while you live you should be grateful to him. You say the world is yours because of your knowledge, but what you say does not seem true to me. What will knowledge avail you when you go into the maw of the dragon death? Acting as your own envoy is sewing your shroud while you are still young. I am not in the habit of shedding blood, nor of attacking rulers. When a monarch has power and is merciful and just, that is when he becomes knowledgeable. Know that whoever spills a king's blood will see nothing but fire as his reward. Be assured of your safety, and leave here with joy. But when you have gone change your habits: don't go acting as your own messenger again, because even the dust knows that you are Sekandar. And I'm not aware of any great hero whose portrait I don't possess, stored away with a reliable courtier. While you remain here I will call you Bitqun and seat you at court accordingly, so that no one will guess your secret or hear you name. I will send you on your way in safety, but you, my lord, must be reasonable and swear that you will never plot against my son, my country, or any of my people or allies, and that you will refer to me only as your equal, as the ruler of my own country."

Freed from the threat of being killed, Sekandar rejoiced to hear her words. He swore by the just God, by the Christian faith, and by the dust of battle that he would act only kindly and righteously toward her land, her son, and her noble allies, and that he would never plot their destruction. When she had heard his oath, Qaydafeh said, "There is one other piece of advice that should not be kept from you: know then that my son Taynush has little sense and pays scant attention to my knowledge and advice. He is Foor's son-in-law and he must not in any way suspect that you and Sekandar occupy the same skin, or even that you are friends. He is eager to avenge Foor, and to confound the earth and sky in war. Now, go joyfully and safely to your own quarters, and have no fear of the world's sorrows."

Sekandar Takes Precautions against Taynush

When Sekandar left the wise queen Qaydafeh, his grateful heart seemed huge as a mountain; his brow was cleared of furrows, and he had no intention of going back on his promise. At dawn the next morning he went to her again when she was seated on an ivory throne with her commanders ranged about her. On the front of the throne was a design in gold, precious black and white Yemeni stones, surrounded by jewels, and before her there were bunches of musk-scented roses. Her sons Taynush, the breaker of horses, and Qaydrus stood in front of her, listening to her words. Her younger son said to his mother, "Just and fortunate queen, see that Bitqun leaves you well satisfied and with a guide to ensure that no one troubles him along the way or thinks of him as our enemy. I say this because he saved my life, and I think of him as my own soul." His mother said, "I will see that his honors are augmented." Then she turned to Sekandar and said, "Tell us what is hidden; what is it you desire, and what has Sekandar said? What message have you brought us from him?" Sekandar replied, "Noble queen, my stay with you has been lengthy. Sekandar told me to ask for tribute and said that if I delayed my return he would lead his army here and destroy this country together with its crown, its throne, its sovereign, its wealth, and its good fortune."

When Taynush heard Sekandar's words he started up like a wild gust of wind and burst out,

> *"You fool, you nobody, whom no one who*
> *Has sense considers human, who are you?*
> *And don't you realize where it is you're sitting?*
> *Stand, and hide your hands! Don't you know what's fitting*
> *Before a queen? Your stubborn head is full*
> *Of harebrained speeches—you're contemptible!*
> *Who is this king of yours? If you don't bow*
> *Respectfully before our sovereign now*
> *I'll lop your head off here as easily*
> *As I might pick an orange from a tree.*
> *Before our armies I'll display your head*
> *And Foor will be avenged when you are dead!"*

Seeing his bellicose rage, his mother shouted, "These are not his words, his friend sent him to our court and he speaks as his representative!" And she ordered that Taynush be taken out of the court. Then she turned to Sekandar and said to him privately, "This ignorant devil's spawn must not be allowed to think up some plot against you in secret. You're a wise and understanding man, what do you think should be done with him?" Sekandar answered, "This is not how he should be treated; it would be right to call him back." The queen recalled her son and motioned him to his throne again, and Sekandar addressed him, "My lord, if you would accomplish your desires, you should act more calmly. I accept whatever you say and feel no resentment against you. My unfortunate position here is because of Sekandar, who rejoices in his throne and crown. It was he who sent me here to ask for tribute from Queen Qaydafeh, so that I could bear whatever unfortunate consequences there might be. I will soon give him his answer, and I suggest a plan that should have splendid consequences. If I take his hand in mine and bring him to where you're sitting in such a way that you'll see no army with him, and no sword or crown or throne either, what will you give me from your kingdom, if indeed you think well of my friendly offer?"

Taynush responded, "These words of yours should be acted on now. If you're being truthful and can do what you've described, I shall give you treasure and money, horses and faithful retainers, whatever you wish. I shall always be grateful to you and will make you a great lord. You'll be my counselor and treasurer, here in this country." Sekandar stood up and took Taynush's hand in his, to seal the pact. Taynush asked, "But how can you manage this, what magic are you going to use?"

Sekandar said, "When I leave this court you must accompany me, together with a thousand cavalry worthy of warfare. I saw a wooded area on the way here, and I'll hide you and your army there and you can wait in ambush. I'll go on ahead to sound out Sekandar's malevolent soul, and I'll say to him, 'Qaydafeh has sent you so much tribute that you'll never want for wealth again, but their envoy says he's afraid to meet you while you're surrounded by your army. If you and your advisors will come to see Taynush, you will be able to receive the wonderful treasures he has brought. He'll come forward if he sees you without your army, but if he decides to go back, the road is open and we can't stop him.' When he hears these flattering words of mine, it won't cross his mind that I'm deceiving him; he'll come into the shade beneath the trees, asking his treasurer to bring along wine, and his crown and throne. Then you will surround him with your troops and his days will be at an end. My vengeance and your heart's desire will be accomplished together, an enormous amount of wealth will come into your hands, as well as slaves and caparisoned horses, and from then on no one will seek to disturb your peace."

Taynush was overjoyed when he heard all this and lifted up his head like a noble cypress tree. He said, "My hope is that his day will darken while mine grows bright. He will fall suddenly into my trap and pay for the blood he has spilled in the world, the blood of Dara, and of Sind's nobility, and of brave Foor, the king of India." When Qaydafeh heard Sekandar's words, she saw well enough what his plan was; she smiled secretly, hiding her coral lips beneath her muslin veil. As Sekandar left her presence, his darkened soul was filled with anxiety.

Sekandar's Treaty with Qaydafeh, and His Return

All the long night he sought for some solution. When the sun showed the fringe of its Chinese royal robe, raising its golden banner above the mountains, and the purple silken banner of night dipped in submission, Sekandar made his way to the queen. A servant stood to greet him, and the world conqueror dismounted, as was customary, and walked into her presence. He was ushered forward, and the queen cleared the court of strangers. Seeing Qaydafeh on her throne, Sekandar said, "May the planet Jupiter accompany your deliberations. I swear by the Messiah's faith, by his just commands, by God who is a witness to my tongue, by our rites and by our great cross, by the head and soul of your majesty, by our vestments, our clergy, and the Holy Ghost, that the soil of Andalusia will never see me again; that I shall send no army here, that I shall not seek to deceive you, that I shall do no harm to your loved son, neither through my commands or by my own hand. I shall remember in my soul how you kept faith with me and I shall not seek your harm in any way. Anyone who wishes you well is my brother, and your court is as sacred as the cross to me."

Qaydafeh considered his oath, his sincere heart, and his promise. She had golden thrones placed throughout her audience hall, and the front of the hall was hung with splendid Chinese cloths. She summoned her chieftains and assigned them thrones, and then had her two noble sons, as well as her extended family and her allies, called in. She said, "In this fleeting world it is right to avoid sorrow when we can, and I have no desire that the turning heavens should send me vengeance and warfare as my fate. Sekandar's longing for wealth will never be sated, not if he brings the heavens down to the earth. For the sake of wealth he is seeking to harm us, but all the wealth in the world is not worth such pain and sorrow. I have no wish to make war on him, or to bring hardship on this realm. I shall send him a letter full of good advice; I will honor him and offer him good counsel. If then he still looks for war, he will find my advice will be followed by his defeat and imprisonment; if I lead my armies against him, the heavens and the moon will pity his plight. There is no harm in trying this, and it may be that we can remain friends. What do you say to my proposal? Answer me, and give me your counsel."

The assembly raised their heads and spoke in response. They said, "O just and righteous queen, whose like no one can remember having seen before, you say only what is best, and the land over which you rule is indeed fortunate! If this king does become your friend, this is an outcome that all good men would desire: your wealth will not be substantially diminished, and no wealth is worth your distress. If a man like Sekandar, who comes from Greece and turns countries into seas of blood with his sword, can be turned back from your door with a few gifts, we say that all the wealth in the world is not worth one coin if this can be achieved. We too desire only peace between you, and a man who seeks war is unworthy of respect."

Hearing her wise counselors' words, she had her treasury opened and her father's throne, together with his golden armbands and torques, brought out. There was also a crown, inlaid with jewels so splendid that no one in that country could put a value on them. She said to Sekandar's supposed envoy, "This crown is priceless, and it would be wrong for anyone else but your king to have it. Since I see that he is worthy of such a crown I choose him to own it rather than my own sons." The throne had been made in seventy sections, and it could be put together only by the man who had taken it apart, so cunningly were the pieces fitted to one another. Its feet were carved like dragons' heads, and no one could compute the value of the jewels with which it was studded: there were four hundred rubies the color of pomegranate seeds, each weighing two mesqals, and four hundred uncut emeralds, the color of the green in a rainbow. Besides this she gave four hundred huge elephant tusks; the skins of four hundred Barbary leopards; a thousand dappled deer skins, colorfully embroidered with various pictures; a hundred hunting dogs and cheetahs that could see a gazelle quicker than the arrow flies; two hundred water buffalo led by slaves; four hundred ebony stools upholstered in silk brocade; and four hundred more of aloes wood with gold designs on them. A hundred noble and richly caparisoned horses bearing precious goods were led in, besides which there were a thousand Indian and Greek swords to which the queen added suits of armor and twelve hundred helmets. Then she said to her treasurer, "This is the greater part of what I wish to give. Count it out to Bitqun, and tell him that he must be ready to leave at dawn."

Dawn lifted its banner and turned the purple sky as white as camphor; the earth was renewed, the mountains glowed red as juniper dye, and from the royal court the din of drums rang out. Sekandar mounted his horse, ready for the departure Qaydafeh had commanded. Taynush prepared his escort of warriors and made his way to the queen's palace. Those who were to leave bade her farewell, saying, "May your soul and the heavens be as the warp and weft of one cloth."

They traveled stage by stage until they had almost reached the Greek camp. Sekandar made a stop at the place in the woods that he had mentioned, where there was a flowing stream. He said to Taynush, "Rest here, and refresh yourself with wine. I shall go and do as I promised: I'll keep my word in every way." Sekandar traveled on with his men until they reached his army; a great shout of joy went up when he rejoined his troops, since they had despaired of ever seeing his face again. They prepared him a royal crown, congratulating him, and bowing their heads down to the ground in homage. Sekandar selected a thousand armored soldiers bearing ox-headed maces, and in battle order the men surrounded the wood where Taynush and his companions were. Then Sekandar cried out,

"My headstrong lord, consider now and say
Whether you want to fight or run away!"

Taynush trembled in his encampment and regretted his former plans. He said, "Great king, choose kindness over contempt. Act toward me as you did toward my brother, Qaydrus: be magnanimous and just to me. This is not what you promised my mother; didn't you tell her you wouldn't go back on your word?"

> And Sekandar replied to him, "What's made
> You turn so weak, and why are you afraid?
> Your heart should have no fear; you're safe with me,
> As are all members of your family.
> I shall not break my word to Qaydafeh—
> My promise will be kept in every way:
> There is no good in lying kings who make
> Fair promises they then proceed to break."

Taynush quickly dismounted, kissed the ground, and began to weep. The king took his hand in his, just as he had done when they sealed their pact, and said, "Calm yourself, and think no more of this, I bear no grudge against you in my heart. Before your mother on the throne I put my hand in yours and said that in just such a fashion I would place the hand of the king of the world in yours. Now I fulfill my promise, since it is not right for kings to utter empty words. I am Sekandar, and I was Sekandar then, when I spun such tales at your court. Qaydafeh knew on that day that the hand in yours was a king's." Then he said to a servant, "Place a throne beneath that blossoming tree." He commanded that a meal, music, and wine be provided, and gave Greek, Chinese, and Persian robes of honor to Taynush. He gave the prince's companions gold and silver, and to those of appropriate rank he gave crowns and belts. Then he said to Taynush, "You should not stay here, this wood is far from your homeland. Say to Qaydafeh from me, 'Wise, far-sighted, and accomplished queen, while I live I shall keep faith with you, and my soul is filled with kindness toward you.'"

Sekandar Travels to the Land of the Brahmins

Sekandar led his army quickly from that place to the land of the Brahmins, as he wished to learn from the ascetics who lived there of the land's ancient practices. When the Brahmins heard that the king was approaching with his army, these God-fearing men made their way down the mountains and gathered together. They wrote a letter to Sekandar, which began by invoking God's blessings on him, and wishing him victory and increasing knowledge and power. It continued, "O warlike king, God has given you the great world, so why do you come to this worthless land, the dwelling place of those who live in worship? If you have come here looking for wealth, you must be sorely lacking in wisdom: we have only patience and knowledge, and this knowledge fills our souls with contentment. Patience cannot be taken from us, and knowledge never harms anyone. You will see nothing in this place but a troupe of naked ascetics, living scattered here and there in the wind and snow; and if you stay here for long, you will have to live off the seeds of herbs."

A messenger, clothed only in a covering of roots and vegetation about his loins, came to Sekandar, who read their letter and decided to treat the man kindly and well. He left the army where they had halted, while he himself went forward with his Greek philosophers. The ascetics heard of the king's approach and one by one they traveled to greet him. Since they possessed no wealth and had no produce or harvested grain to offer, they brought him small valueless things. One by one they greeted the magnanimous lord of the earth. Sekandar saw their faces, heard their chants, and saw them running with naked feet, bodies, and heads; he saw that their bodies were unprovided for but their souls were filled with the fruits of knowledge; their clothes were of leaves, their diet of seeds, they lived withdrawn from all fighting and warfare, and their food, sleep, and repose were in the plains and mountains.

He questioned them about their food and repose, and their peace in the midst of war. One replied, "We have small need of clothes, carpets, and food: because a man is born naked from his mother and returns naked to the earth, it is wrong for him to fuss about what he should wear. Every place is a place of fear, despair, and terror. The earth is our mattress, the sky our covering, and we watch the road for death to come. An ambitious man struggles to gain something that is not worth the effort he has put forth, and then he passes from the world while his gold and treasure and crown remain here. Only his good deeds will accompany him, and his head and glory will both return to dust."

Sekandar questioned him: "Who is the king of our souls? Who always accompanies us toward evil?" The ascetic answered, "Greed is the king, the ground of vengeance and the place of sin." Sekandar asked, "What is the reality of this thing that makes us weep with longing?" The sage replied, "Greed and need are two demons, wretched and malevolent; one is dry-lipped from longing, the other passes sleepless nights from excess. Time passing hunts down both, and blessed is the man whose mind accepts wisdom." When Sekandar heard these words, his face turned pale as fenugreek; his cheeks became sallow, his eyes filled with tears, and furrows filled his once-smiling face. The great king asked, "What do you need that I can provide? I will not hesitate to give you my wealth, or to undergo suffering for you." The ascetics answered, "Great king, close the door of death and old age for us." The king answered, "But there is no pleading with death: no matter how one hangs back from this sharp-clawed dragon, even if one is made of iron, one cannot escape him. And no matter how long our youth lasts, we cannot evade old age." The Brahmin said, "Wise and puissant king, since you know that there is no recourse against death, and that there is no disaster worse than old age, why do you long for the world in this way, why do you breathe in the scent of this poisonous flower so eagerly? All you will receive is suffering, while your enemies will inherit the wealth you acquire; to make oneself suffer for another's profit is the act of an ignorant man or a fool. White hairs are a message from death, and what makes you hope that you can stay in the world?"

The wise king replied, "Just as by God's will a slave must die, this is my fate too, as the turning heavens direct; neither wise men nor warriors can struggle against fate. And the star of those who were killed fighting against me had declined: they deserved their grief and to have their blood shed, since an unjust man cannot escape his end. They experienced divine punishment, because they had strayed from the way of wisdom. No man can evade the will of God, or explain what fate brings."

Sekandar offered many gifts to the ascetics, but none of them took anything from him: greed was not a part of their natures. He did no harm in that place, and set off toward the west.

Sekandar Reaches the Western Sea and Abyssinia

The army journeyed on, stage by stage, exhausted by their travels, but still determined. After he left the land of the Brahmins, Sekandar saw a deep and boundless ocean. On its shores lived men who veiled themselves like women and dressed in colorful splendid clothes. Their language was not Arabic, Turkish, Chinese, or Persian. Their diet consisted of fish, and their land was cut off from the outside world. Sekandar was astonished to meet such folk, and when he saw the ocean he invoked the name of God. Just at that moment a mountain rose up out of the water; it was in two sections and glittered yellow like the sun. Immediately Sekandar asked for a boat so that he could look at it more closely, but one of his Greek philosophers advised him not to cross the ocean's depths: he said Sekandar should send someone of less importance to look at it. Thirty Greeks and Persians manned the boat, but the yellow mountain was a huge fish and, as soon as the boat approached, it dived quickly beneath the surface, dragging the boat with it. Sekandar's army watched in horror and called on God to protect them. The Greek philosopher said, "Knowledge is the best of all things, and a knowledgeable man is greater than all others. If the king had gone in that boat and been destroyed, all this army would have suffered in their hearts."

Sekandar led his army forward and came to another body of water, surrounded by reeds that were like plane trees, more than fifty cubits high with trunks forty cubits in circumference. All the houses there were made of wood and reeds, and the ground seemed to give beneath their weight. It was inadvisable to stay there long, and the water was so brackish that no one drank it. When they left this place they came to a deep lake. The land there seemed inviting, the soil smelled of musk, and the water was as sweet as honey. They ate and drank and lay down to sleep, but as they did so countless snakes came slithering out of the water, and from the bushes flame-colored scorpions appeared. The world darkened for the sleepers, and many died, both warriors and wise men. Boars attacked them from one side, their tusks glittering like diamonds, and from the other came lions larger than oxen that the soldiers had not the strength to fight against. The army retreated to the reedbeds, which they set fire to, and so killed the lions that made their escape so difficult.

From there Sekandar went to Abyssinia, the land of the Habash. The country was crowded with men whose skin was as black as a raven's feather, and their eyes as bright as lamps. They fielded a redoubtable army of tall, naked soldiers, and when they saw Sekandar's army approaching, their war cries ascended to the clouds. The king's eyes darkened when he saw them advancing in their thousands: they killed many men as they attacked, hurling bones instead of lances. Sekandar ordered his men to prepare their weapons for battle. The naked Habash pressed on with their attack, and many were killed by Sekandar's lion-like forces, until those who survived fled from the battlefield. So much blood was spilled that the land from end to end was like the sea of China, with here and there mounds of the dead piled up. Straw was packed around these heaps of corpses, and Sekandar ordered that they be set on fire.

That night a rhinoceros could be heard, and Sekandar donned his armor and helmet. Then the animal came into view, more massive than an elephant, with a dark horn on his head. He killed a number of soldiers and did not retreat even though he was attacked repeatedly. Finally he was killed by the attackers' arrows, and this conqueror of lions lay there like a huge iron mountain. Sekandar left the area in haste, giving thanks to God as he went.

Sekandar Reaches a Land Where the Men Have Soft Feet and Kills a Dragon

They reached a land where men have soft feet; the host of inhabitants was beyond numbering, and each man was as tall as a cypress tree, but they had neither horses nor armor nor swords nor maces. Their war cry was like the roll of thunder, and they attacked naked, as if they were devils. Against Sekandar's army they hurled a hail of rocks, which rained down like an autumn wind bowing trees before it. But the army advanced with arrows and swords, and the day seemed to turn to night with the dust. When there were only a few of the soft-footed warriors remaining, Sekandar rested, and then led his army forward again.

They quickly reached a city that seemed limitless; the inhabitants courteously and kindly came out to welcome them, bringing with them carpets, clothes, and food as gifts. Sekandar questioned them and treated them respectfully, and a sufficient area for his army's camp was set aside. Tents were set up on the plain, and the army made no attempt to enter the city. Nearby there was an enormous mountain, which seemed almost to touch the skies. The few people on the mountain's slopes didn't stay there at night. Sekandar asked them the best way forward and by which paths he should lead his army. The made their obeisance before him and greeted him as the world's king, and then said:

> "A path exists around this mountainside
> But first you'll have to find a willing guide;
> Beyond the crest there lies a dragon's lair,
> His poison sickens birds that venture there.
> The noxious vapors reach the moon, there's no
> Safe route by which your warriors could go.
> His massive maw breathes fire, and he could snare
> An elephant with his two locks of hair;
> Our city doesn't have the strength to fight.
> We have to take up five cows, every night,
> For him to feed on; and how fearfully
> We place them on the rocks for him to see,
> Afraid that if he finds us he'll come down
> And, piece by piece, destroy us and our town."

Sekandar said, "Tomorrow, see that no one takes him any food." When the time for his meal had passed, the dragon stood on the mountain slope breathing fire, and Sekandar ordered his troops to shoot a storm of arrows against him. The foul dragon exhaled fire and caught a few men in the blast.

Sekandar had the war drums beaten, and the dragon drew back in fear from the echoing drums.

The sun rose in Taurus, and the meadows resounded with the song of larks. When it was again time for the dragon to be fed, the king chose a number of men from his army and gave them money to buy five cows. He killed the cows and skinned them, leaving the hide attached to their heads. The hides were then filled with poison and oil and inflated; prayers were said and the cows were passed from hand to hand up the mountainside. The king approached the dragon and saw that he was like a huge dark cloud: his tongue purple, his eyes blood red, and fire issuing continuously from his maw. The soldiers rolled the cows down toward the dragon, their hearts anxious to see what he would do. Immediately, the dragon descended on the carcasses like the wind. He ate them, and the poison spread throughout his body, bursting his intestines and forcing its way even into his brain and feet. For a long time he beat his head against the rocks in desperation, and the army released a hail of arrows against him. The mountainous monster sank to his feet, and his body finally succumbed to the arrows. Leaving the creature's body where it lay, Sekandar quickly led his troops out of that area.

The adventurous hero led his men to another mountainous area, where he saw an astonishing sight. Perched on a summit sharp as a sword blade, far removed from all humanity, was a golden throne. On the throne was a dead man, and even after death he radiated *farr* and glory. He was wrapped in a brocade cloak, and on his head was a crown encrusted with jewels. So much gold and silver was scattered around him that no one could approach the throne, and anyone who went up the mountain hoping to take some of the dead man's wealth would tremble in terror and die, and eventually rot there. Sekandar ascended the mountain and, as he stared at the man, and at the gold and silver, he heard a great voice that said, "O king, you have lived long enough in the world. You have destroyed so many thrones and raised your head up to the heavens, and you have laid low so many friends and enemies, but now the way of the world has changed." Sekandar's face glowed like a lamp, and he descended the mountain sick at heart.

Sekandar Sees the Marvels of Harum

Sekandar pressed on with his Greek chieftains and reached a city called Harum, a town inhabited only by women, to which no stranger was granted entrance. The right breast of these women was as that of all women, like a pomegranate resting on silk, but on the left their bodies were like that of a warrior who wears armor on the day of battle. As Sekandar drew near the city, he wrote a polite letter to the inhabitants, as was fitting for a wellborn man to do, addressing it from the king of Iran and the West to the sovereign of Harum. He began his letter in the name of the Creator of the heavens, from whom come blessings, justice, and benevolence, and continued, "Whoever possesses wisdom in his soul and lives wisely has heard what I have done in the world, how high I have raised the banner of glory, and how those who oppose my will find that their only resting place is the black earth. I desire that no site in the world be forbidden to my eyes. My coming here is not to make war on you; I wish for only peace and friendship between us. If there is anyone among you who is knowledgeable and wise and able to read this letter, send a person who is honored by you to meet me, and no one will be hurt by such an encounter." He added some more eloquent phrases, and gave the letter to a Greek philosopher to deliver to the city.

When the sage drew near he saw that the city was populated by women, and that no men were there. All those who had the right to express their opinions came out in a body on to the plain, to see the Greek visitor and to hear his message. Once the city scribe had read the letter aloud and they had some notion of Sekandar's intentions, they sat and wrote an answer, as follows: "May you live forever, proud king. We have received your messenger and read through your letter. You speak about kings, victories, and your former battles; if you attack the city of Harum with your army, you will not see the earth for horses' hooves. There are innumerable streets within our town, and a thousand women live within each street. We sleep each night in our armor, cramped together since there are so many of us. And of all these women not one of us has a husband, because we are all veiled virgins. Whichever way you approach our country you will see a deep lake. If a woman decides she wants a husband, she must leave us; in fair weather or foul, she has to cross this deep lake. After taking a husband, if she gives birth to a daughter and the girl is feminine by nature and interested in pretty colors and scents, then she will remain where she was born and breathe the air of that sky. But if she is a manly, confident child, she is sent to Harum. If she gives birth to a son he stays where he is and has nothing to do with us.

"When on the day of battle any of us brings a warrior down from his horse, a golden crown is placed on her head, and she is given a throne more exalted than Gemini. There are thirty thousand women among us who possess a golden crown and earrings, because of such success in battle. You are a great and famous man; don't slam the door on your own reputation, so that men say of you,

'He fought with women on the battlefield,
And when he fought them, he was forced to yield.'

Such a taunt will be shameful for you, and it will last for as long as the world does. If you wish to come with your Greek chieftains and go around our country, and if you act with honesty and chivalry, you will see nothing but kindness and festivities from us. We'll bring so many of our warriors to greet you that you won't see the sun or the moon for the dust."

A woman was chosen to deliver this reply; she wore a crown and royal clothes and was accompanied by ten beautiful outriders. As she approached the king's camp, he sent an escort out a little way to greet her; she handed over the letter to Sekandar and repeated her fellow warriors' message. When Sekandar saw their reply he chose a wise, understanding envoy and sent them an answer: "May men live with wisdom. In all the world there is no king or chieftain who is not my inferior, no matter how great or favored by the heavens he might be. White camphor dust and black earth are as one to me, and so are fighting and feasting. I have not come here to fight with elephants and war drums, and with an army whose horses' hooves trample the mountains and plains to dust. My intention was to see your city, but if you come to me this will be sufficient. When I have seen you I will lead off my army; I shall not stay here for long. I want to find out about your customs and glory, your horsemanship, your beauty, everything about you. I shall ask discreetly about your births here, since how can there be women without men? When death comes, how are your numbers kept up? I want to know what the solution to this problem is."

The envoy delivered his message, and the nobles of the city gathered to give their response: "We have chosen two thousand wise, eloquent women. Each hundred of them will take ten jeweled crowns, making two hundred crowns in all, each of them worthy of a king; with its jewels each crown weighs three *ratl*. When we hear that the king has arrived, we shall go out to meet him one by one, since we have heard of his knowledge and glory." The envoy returned and gave their reply; everyone spoke wisely in this business.

Two thousand women crossed the lake, all of them crowned and wearing earrings. There was a delightful area nearby, filled with trees and streams, and there they spread colorful carpets on the grass and laid out a feast. When Sekandar reached Harum the women ceremoniously welcomed him with the crowns, together with clothes and jewels. Sekandar accepted their presents and made much of them, entertaining them royally. When night gave way to day he entered the city and looked closely at parts of it, searching out information about both big and small things, and staying there till his questions were resolved.

Sekandar Leads His Army to the West

Having asked his fill of questions, and seen the lake, Sekandar led his army toward the western lands. He came to a large town inhabited by a savage population: they had red faces and blond hair, and all of them were fine warriors. Ordered to appear before Sekandar they came in pairs, striking their hands against their heads. When their leaders were asked what marvels there were in that country, one answered, "O king favored by fortune and conqueror of cities, on the other side of our town there is a unique body of water; when the shining sun reaches that place it plunges into the water's depths. Beyond the water the world is dark and the things of the world become hidden. We have heard endless tales about that darkness. A God-fearing and wise man says there is a source of water there, and he calls it the water of life. This wise man says, 'How can anyone die, if he drinks the water of life? The water there comes from heaven, and the man who bathes there washes away all his sins.'"

The king asked, "How can a horse get to this dark place?" The pious man answered, "A man must ride on a young mount to get there." Sekandar ordered that the local herdsmen bring their herds of horses to his camp. He chose ten thousand of them, all four years old and capable of work.

Sekandar Seeks the Water of Life

With happiness in his heart, Sekandar set out, calling his shrewdest chieftains about him. He traveled until he reached a town that seemed to have no center or limit and that was well appointed with gardens, open spaces, palaces, and public buildings. He dismounted, and at dawn he went without his army to the water's edge. He stayed there until the yellow sun descended into the dark blue waters, and saw God's marvel, the sun disappearing from the world. His mind filled with endless speculation, he returned to his camp. In the dark night he was mindful of God, and thought too of the water of life. He chose his most patient warriors to accompany him, packed provisions sufficient for forty days, and then set out impatient to see this wonder.

> He lodged his men within the town, then tried
> To find a capable and willing guide:
> Khezr was preeminent in all that land.
> Sekandar placed himself at his command
> And said to him, "I ask that you incline
> Your heart to this high enterprise of mine;
> If we can find life's water we shall stay
> A long while in the world to watch and pray—

The man who nourishes his soul, who gives
His mind to God's laws, does not die but lives.
I have two seals that in the darkest night,
When water's near, will shine with brilliant light:
Take one, go on ahead of us, and you
Will guide and guard us there in all we do:
The other seal I'll keep with me, to show
My soldiers where it's safe and wise to go,
And so we'll see what God has hidden here."
Then, as the soldiers gradually drew near
The stream of life, the plains rang with a cry
Of "God is Great" that echoed in the sky.
Then, for the next stage, Khezr said that they ought
To leave behind them all the food they'd brought,
And for two days and nights the soldiers went
With mouths that never tasted nourishment;
The road split into two the following day
And in the dark Sekandar lost his way.
Khezr journeyed on; his head reached Saturn's sphere
And when he saw life's glittering stream appear
He bathed his head and body there, and prayed
To God, the only guardian he obeyed:
He drank and rested, then went back again,
And praised God as he crossed the empty plain.

Sekandar Talks with the Birds

But Sekandar emerged into light, and saw a great shining mountain before him, near the top of which were two columns of ebony that reached into the clouds. Each column supported a large nest, on which sat a fierce green bird. The birds spoke in Greek and addressed him as the victorious ruler of the world. When he heard them Sekandar hurried to the foot of the pillars, and one of the birds said to him, "You take pleasure in your pain, but what is it you seek from this fleeting world? If you raise your head to the high heavens, you must return in despair. But now that you are here, tell me, have you ever seen a house made of reeds, or one made of golden bricks?" Sekandar said, "Both these exist." Hearing this reply the bird sat a little lower, and Sekandar, who was a God-fearing man, stared at it in wonder. The bird asked, "Have you heard the sound of lutes in this world, or the noise of drunkenness and singing?" The king answered, "People do not call any man happy who has not had some share of pleasure in the world, no matter how much he pours his heart and soul out to them." The bird hopped down from its ebony column onto the ground and asked, "Is there more knowledge and honesty, or ignorance and lies in the world?" He answered, "Anyone who seeks knowledge raises his head above both groups." The bird hopped back onto its column and cleaned its claws with its beak, then asked the king, "In your country, do God-fearing men live in the mountains?" Sekandar replied, "When a man becomes pure in thought, he goes into the mountains." At that the bird, with an air of authority and independence, sat on its nest again and sharpened its beak with its claws. It told the king that he should climb, without any companions, up to the summit of the mountain, where he would see something that would make any happy man weep.

Sekandar Sees Esrafil

Sekandar made his way to the mountain summit alone. There he saw Esrafil, the angel of death, with a trumpet in his hand, his head raised at the ready, his cheeks filled with breath, his eyes brimming with tears, as he waited for God to order him to blow. Seeing Sekandar on the mountain Esrafil roared with a voice like thunder,

> "Stop struggling, slave of greed! One day, at last,
> Your ears will hear the mighty trumpet's blast—
> Don't worry about crowns and thrones! Prepare
> To pack your bags and journey on elsewhere!"
> Sekandar said, "I see that I'm to be
> Hurried about the world perpetually,
> And that I'll never know another fate
> Than this incessant, wandering, restless state!"

He descended the mountain, weeping and praising God, then set out on the dark road again, following his guides.

Going forward in the darkness, the army heard a voice from a black mountain nearby, which said, "Whoever takes stones from this mountain will be sorry for what he holds in his hand, and whoever takes nothing will be sorry and look for a balm to ease his heart's pain." The soldiers listened to the voice, and wondered what the words could mean, since whether they took stones or didn't, they couldn't see what their future sufferings would be. One said, "The pain will be because of sin, that's the regret for taking stones along the way." Another said, "We should take a little; everyone has to suffer some pain." Some took stones, some took none, some out of laziness took only a few. When they left the land where the water of life was, and found themselves on the plain once more, the road was no longer dark and each man looked at what he'd tucked in his sleeves or his tunic, and so the deceiving riddle was revealed. One found his clothes filled with rubies, another with uncut gems, and they were sorry they had taken so few and hadn't taken emeralds as well. But those who had ignored the precious stones and taken nothing were even more sorry. Sekandar stayed in that area for two weeks, and when he was less fatigued he led his army forward again.

Sekandar Constructs a Wall to Defeat Yajuj and Majuj

Having seen the west, Sekandar turned his attention to the east, choosing to continue his wanderings in the world. He came to a town that seemed as if wind and dust had never blown against it, and when the trumpets were sounded from his elephants' backs and the town's nobility came out to welcome him, the procession stretched for two miles. The world wanderer greeted them warmly and asked, "What is the most astonishing thing about this place?" They began to weep and wail about the revolutions of fate, saying, "We face a difficult task, which we will tell to the victorious king. That mountain, whose summit is in the clouds, has made our hearts grieve and

mourn: we cannot sleep because of Yajuj and Majuj, who live there and whom we have not the strength to resist. When a mob of them comes against our city, we know only pain and sorrow. They have faces like animals, with black tongues and bloodshot eyes; they have black skin and teeth like a boar's. How can anyone stand up to them? Their bodies including the chest are covered with dark hair, and they have huge ears like an elephant's; when they sleep they can fold an ear under them as a pillow, or spread it over them as

a coverlet. All their females give birth to thousands of little brats, so that no one can count how many they are. They flock together like animals, running like wild asses. In spring when the clouds thunder and the green sea churns, the clouds suck up serpents from the waves and the air growls like a lion; then the clouds drop the serpents, and herds of these monsters come to feed on them. They eat them year after year till their chests and shoulders grow big and strong. After that they eat plants, which they collect from everywhere. When it's cold they get very thin, and then their voices are like a dove's, but if you see them in the spring they're like wolves, and they roar like trumpeting elephants. If the king can find some remedy against them, so that our hearts can be freed from this sorrow, all of us will praise him, and our praise will resound in the world for a long time. We ask that you be magnanimous and rid us of our grief, for you too need God's blessings."

Sekandar marveled at what they had told him. He was pensive for a while, then said, "I will provide treasure, your city must provide the labor and effort. With the help of God I will bring them under control." All the townsmen said, "O king, may bad luck never be yours! We are your slaves while we live, ready to offer whatever is necessary. We'll bring whatever you require, as nothing is more important to us than this." Sekandar went out and inspected the mountain and then summoned his sages to him. He called for blacksmiths, together with huge quantities of copper, brass, heavy hammers, plaster, stone, and an immeasurable amount of firewood, as much as would be necessary for the job in hand. When the plans had been well thought out, masons, blacksmiths, and all manner of artisans came from throughout the world to help Sekandar with this project. Craftsmen from every country gathered there, and two walls were constructed on the opposite sides of the mountain, a hundred fathoms wide and stretching from the mountain's base to its summit. One cubit was of charcoal and the next of iron with a little copper mixed into it, then sulfur was poured over it, following the method of the Kayanid craftsmen. Course was laid above course in this way, and then holes were drilled in it from its base to the summit. Next, oil and turpentine were mixed together and poured over the materials. Finally a mass of charcoal was placed on the top of the walls, and the whole construction was set alight. At the king's command a hundred thousand blacksmiths fed the flames with air from bellows; a great roar went up from the mountain, and the stars seemed eclipsed by the fire. The result of all the blacksmiths' labor, the bellows fanning the flames, the materials laid one above another and then melting in the flames, was that the world was freed from Yajuj and Majuj, and the earth was once again a place of peace and pleasure: the famous barrier of Sekandar had delivered the world from strife. The city's nobles thanked him and wished him eternal life; they brought him many presents, but to their astonishment he accepted none of them.

Sekandar Sees a Corpse in the Palace of Topazes

The king and his army marched onward for a month and were sorely tried by their journey. They came to a mountain, where they saw no sign of either wild or domestic animals. The mountain's crest was of lapis lazuli, and a palace stood there, made of topazes. It was filled with crystal chandeliers, and in its midst was a fountain of salt water. Next to this fountain was a throne for two people, on which was stretched a wretched corpse. He had a man's body, but his head was like that of a boar; there was a pillow of camphor beneath his head, and a brocade covering had been drawn up over his body. Instead of a lamp a brilliant red jewel shone there, illuminating the whole area; its rays twinkled like stars in the water, and all the chamber glowed as if in sunlight. Whoever went there to take something, or even simply set foot within the palace, found himself rooted to the spot; his whole body began to tremble, and he started to waste away.

A cry came from the salt water, saying, "O king, still filled with longing and desire, don't play the fool much longer! You have seen many things that no man ever saw, but now it's time to draw rein. Your life has shortened now, and the royal throne is without its king." Sekandar was afraid and hurried back to his camp as fast as wind-blown smoke. Quickly he led his army away, weeping and calling on God's name. From that mountain he headed toward the desert, afflicted with sorrow and concerned for his soul. And so he went forward, at the head of his troops, weeping and in pain.

Sekandar Sees the Speaking Tree

The desert road led to a city, and Sekandar was relieved when he heard human voices there. The whole area was one of gardens and fine buildings and was a place to delight any man. The city's noblemen welcomed him, calling out greetings and showering him with gold and jewels. "It is wonderful that you have come to visit us," they said. "No army has ever entered this town, and no one in it has ever heard the name of 'king.' Now that you have come our souls are yours, and may you live with bodily health and spiritual serenity." Sekandar was pleased by their welcome and rested from the journey across the desert. He said to them, "What is there here that's astonishing, that should be inquired into?" A guide said to him, "Victorious king, there is a marvel here, a tree that has two separate trunks together, one of which is female and the other male, and these splendid tree limbs can speak. At night the female trunk becomes sweet smelling and speaks, and when the daylight comes, the male speaks." Sekandar and his Greek cavalry, with the nobles of the town gathered around, listened and said, "When is it you say that the tree speaks in a loud voice?" The translator replied, "A little after day has disappeared one of the trunks begins to speak, and a lucky man will hear its voice; in the dark night the female speaks, and its leaves then smell like musk."

Sekandar answered, "When we go beyond the tree, what wonders are there on the other side?" The reply was, "When you pass the tree there is little argument about which way to take, as there is no place beyond there;

جنان داد با شیخ بقّت ترجمان

شب تیره کون ماده گویا شود

چنین داد با شیخ گرو بگذری

بیابان و تاریکی آمد به بیش

که از روز چون بگذرد نه زمان

بروبرک چون مشک بویا شود

زرفتن کوته شود داوری

بسیری نیامد کس از جان خویش

که کام ودد و مرغ برن برید

جوآمد بنزدیک گویا درخت

زپوست ددان خاک پیما نند

guides say it is the world's end. A dark desert lies ahead
of you, but no man is so weary of his own soul as to go
there. None of us have ever seen or heard that there
are any animals there, or that birds fly there." Sekandar and his troops went forward, and when they came
near the speaking tree the ground throbbed with heat
and the soil there was covered with the pelts of wild
beasts. He asked his guide what the pelts were, and
who it was that had skinned so many animals in this
way. The man answered, "The tree has many worshippers, and when they come here to worship, they feed
on the flesh of wild animals."

When the sun reached its zenith Sekandar heard a
voice above him, coming from the leaves of the tree; it
was a voice to strike terror and foreboding in a man.
He was afraid and said to the interpreter, "You are wise
and mean well, tell me what the leaves are saying,
which makes my heart dissolve within me." "O king,
favored by fortune, the leaves say, 'However much
Sekandar wanders in the world, he has already seen his
share of blessings: when he has reigned for fourteen
years, he must quit the royal throne.'" At the guide's
words Sekandar's heart filled with pain, and he wept
bitterly. He was sad and silent then, speaking to no
one, until midnight. Then the leaves of the other trunk
began to speak, and Sekandar again asked the inter
preter what they said. He replied, "The female tree
says, 'Do not puff yourself up with greed; why torment
your soul in this way? Greed makes you wander the
wide world, harass mankind, and kill kings. But you
are not long for this earth now; do not darken and
deaden your days like this.'" Then the king said to the
interpreter, "Pure of heart and noble as you are, ask
them one question: Will this fateful day come in
Greece; will my mother see me alive again, before
someone covers my face in death?"

The speaking tree replied, "Few days remain;
You must prepare your final baggage train.
Neither your mother, nor your family,
Nor the veiled women of your land will see

Your face again. Death will come soon: you'll die
In a strange land, with strangers standing by.
The stars and crown and throne and worldly glory
Are sated with Sekandar and his story."

Sekandar left the tree, his heart wounded as if by a sword. When he returned to his camp, his chieftains went into the town to collect the gifts from the town's nobility. Among these was a cuirass that shone like the waters of the Nile and was as huge as an elephant skin: it had two long tusks attached to it and was so heavy it was hard to lift. There was other armor, as well as fine brocade, a hundred golden eggs each weighing sixty *man*, and a rhinoceros made of gold and jewels. Sekandar accepted the gifts and led off his army, weeping bitter tears as he went.

Sekandar Visits the Emperor of China

Now Sekandar led his army toward China. For forty days they traveled, until they reached the sea. There the army made camp and the king pitched his brocade pavilion. He summoned a scribe to write a letter to the Chinese emperor from Sekandar, the seizer of cities. The message was filled with promises and threats, and when it was completed Sekandar himself went as the envoy, taking with him an intelligent companion who was one with him in heart and speech and who could advise him as to what to do and what not to do. He entrusted his troops to the army's commander and chose five Greeks as his escort.

When news reached the Chinese emperor that an envoy was approaching his country, he sent troops out to meet him. Sekandar reached the court and the emperor came forward in welcome, but his heart was filled with suspicious thoughts. Sekandar ran forward and made his obeisance to him, and then was seated in the palace for a long while. The emperor questioned him and made much of him and assigned him noble sleeping quarters. As the sun rose over the mountains, dying their summits gold, the envoy was summoned to court. Sekandar spoke at length, saying what was appropriate, and then handed over the letter. It was addressed from the king of Greece, possessor of the world, lord of every country, on whom other kings call down God's blessings. It continued, "My orders for China are that she remain prosperous, and that she should not prepare for war against me; it was war against me that destroyed Foor, and Dara, who was the lord of the world, and Faryan the Arab, and other sovereigns. From the east to the west no one ignores my commands, the heavens themselves do not know the number of my troops, and Venus and the sun could not count them. If you disobey any command of mine you will bring distress on yourself and your country. When you read my letter, bring me tribute; do not trouble yourself about this, or look for evil allies to make war on me. If you come you will see me in the midst of my troops, and when I see that you are honest and mean well I shall confirm you in the possession of your crown and throne, and no misfortune will come to you. If, however, you are reluctant to come before your king, send me things that are peculiar to China—your country's gold work, horses, swords, seal rings, clothes, cloth, ivory thrones, fine brocade, necklaces, crowns—that is, if you have no wish to be harmed by me. Send my soldiers back to me, and rest assured that your wealth, throne, and crown are safe."

When the emperor of China saw what was in the letter, he started up in fury, but then chose silence as a better course. He laughed and said to the envoy, "May your king be a partner to the heavens! Tell me what you know about him. Tell me about his conversation, his height and appearance, and what kind of a man he is." The envoy said, "Great lord of China, you should understand that there is no one else in the world like Sekandar. In his manliness, policy, good fortune, and wisdom he surpasses all that anyone could imagine. He is as tall as a cypress tree, has an elephant's strength, and is as generous as the waters of the Nile; his tongue can be as cutting as a sword, but he can charm an eagle down from the clouds." When he heard all this, the emperor changed his mind. He ordered that wine and a banquet be laid out in the palace gardens. He drank till evening brought darkness to the world, and the company became tipsy. Then he said to the envoy, "May your king be Jupiter's partner. At first light I'll compose an answer to his letter, and what I write will make the day seem splendid to your eyes." Sekandar was half drunk, and he staggered from the garden to his quarters with an orange in his hand.

When the sun rose in Leo and the heavens dispelled the darkness, Sekandar went to the emperor, and all suspicious thoughts were far from his heart. The emperor asked him, "How did you spend the night? When you left you were quite overcome with wine." Then he summoned a scribe, who brought paper, musk, and ambergris, and dictated a letter. He began with praise of God, the lord of chivalry, justice, and ability, of cultivated behavior, abstinence, and piety, and called down his blessings on the Greek king. Then he continued, "Your eloquent envoy has arrived, bringing the king's letter. I have read through the royal words and discussed its contents with my nobles. As for your claims concerning the wars against Dara, Faryan, and Foor, in which you were victorious, so that you became a shepherd whose flock consists of kings, you should not consider what comes about through the will of the Lord of the Sun and Moon as the result of your own valor and the might of your army. When a great man's days are numbered, what difference does it make whether he dies in battle or at a banquet? If they died in battle with you this is because their fate was fixed for that day, and fate is not to be hurried or delayed. You should not pride yourself so much on your victories over them, because even if you are made of iron there is no doubt that you too will die. Where now are Feraydun, Zahhak, and Jamshid, who came like the wind and left like a breath? I am not afraid of you and I will not make war against you, neither shall I puff myself up with pride as you are doing. It is not my habit to shed blood, and besides it would be unworthy of my faith for me to do evil in this way. You summon me, but to no purpose; I serve God, not kings. I send with this more riches than you have dreamed of, so that there shall be no doubting my munificence."

These words were an arrow in Sekandar's vital organs, and he blushed with shame. In his heart he said, "Never again shall I go somewhere disguised as my own envoy." He returned to his quarters and prepared to leave the Chinese court.

The proud emperor opened his treasuries' doors, since he was not a man who found generosity difficult. First he ordered that fifty crowns and ten ivory thrones encrusted with jewels be brought; then a thousand camel loads of gold and silver goods, and a thousand more of Chinese brocades and silks, of camphor, musk, perfumes, and ambergris. He had little regard for wealth, and it eased his heart to be bountiful in this way. He had ten thousand each of the pelts of gray squirrel, ermine, and sable brought, and as many carpets and crystal goblets, and his wise treasurer saw to their being loaded on pack animals. Then he added three hundred silver saddles and fifty golden ones, together with three hundred red-haired camels loaded with Chinese rarities. He chose as envoy an eloquent and dignified Chinese sage and told him to take his message to the Greek king with all goodwill and splendor, and to say that Sekandar would be warmly welcomed at the Chinese court for as long as he wished to stay there.

The envoy traveled with Sekandar, unaware that he was the Greek king. But when Sekandar's regent came forward and the king told him of his adventures, and the army congratulated him on his safe return and bowed to the ground before him, the envoy realized that he was indeed the Greek king and dismounted in consternation. Sekandar said to him, "There is no need for apologies, but do not tell your emperor of this!" They rested for a night, and the next morning Sekandar sat on the royal throne. He gave gifts to the envoy and said to him, "Go to your emperor and tell him that I say 'You have found honor and respect with me. If you wish to stay where you are, all China is yours, and if you wish to go elsewhere, that too is open to you. I shall rest here for a while, because such a large army as mine cannot be mobilized quickly.'" The envoy returned like the wind, and gave Sekandar's message to the emperor.

Sekandar Leads His Army to Babylon

Sekandar camped there for a month, and then led his army toward Babylon, and the air was darkened with the dust of their march. They pressed on for a month, and no one had any rest during this time. They came to a mountain range so high that its summit was hidden by dark clouds, as if it reached to Saturn. The king and his army could see no way forward but over the mountains and so with difficulty they climbed up toward the crest. The climb exhausted them, but once there they saw a deep lake lying below them. Joyfully and praising God, they began their descent; there was game of all kinds on every side, and for a while the soldiers lived off what they hunted.

Then in the distance a wild man appeared. He was covered in hair, and his body beneath the hair was a dark blue color, and he had huge ears, as big as an elephant's. The soldiers captured him and dragged him to Sekandar, who called on God in his astonishment at being confronted by such a creature. He said, "What kind of a man are you? What is your name? What can you find to live off in this lake, and what do you want from life?" The man replied, "O king, my mother and father call me Pillow-Ears." Then the king asked what it was that he could see in the middle of the lake, over toward where the sun rises. The man answered, "O king, and may you always be renowned in the world, that's a town that is like heaven; you'd say that earth had no part in its making. You won't see a single building there that isn't covered with fish skins and fish bones. On the walls they've painted the face of Afrasyab, and he looks more splendid than the sun itself; and warlike Khosrow's face is there too, and you can see his greatness and generosity by looking at it. They're painted on bones; you won't see one bit of soil in the whole city! The people eat fish there; that's the only thing they have to nourish them. If the king orders me to, I'll go there, but without any of your soldiers." Sekandar said to the man with huge ears, "Go, and bring back someone from the town, so that we can see something new."

Pillow-Ears hurried off to the town and soon came back with some of its inhabitants. Seventy men crossed the water with him; some were young and some old, and they were dressed in various kinds of silks. The older, more dignified men each carried a golden goblet filled with pearls, and the young ones each carried a crown; they came before Sekandar with their heads reverently bowed. They made their obeisance to him, and he talked with them for a long time. The army stayed there that night, and at cock-crow next morning the din of drums rang out from the king's pavilion. Sekandar continued the march to Babylon, and the air was dark with the dust sent up by his soldiers.

Sekandar's Letter to Arestalis, and Arestalis's Reply

The king knew that death was close, and that his days were darkening, and he decided that no one of royal lineage should be left alive in the world: he wanted to ensure that no man would be able to lead an army against Greece. With his mind fixed on this arrogant scheme, he wrote a letter to Arestalis, saying he would invite everyone of royal lineage to his court, where they were to come unsuspecting of what was in store for them. When this letter was delivered to the Greek sage, his heart seemed to break in two. Immediately he wrote a reply, weeping as if his ink were tears. "The king of the world's missive arrived, and he should give up this evil design of his. As for the evil you have already done, think no more of it but distribute goods to the poor. For the future, abstain from evil and give your soul to God; sow nothing but seeds of goodness in the world. From birth we are all marked for death, and we have no choice but to submit. No one who dies takes his sovereignty with him; he leaves, and hands on his greatness to another. Live within limits and do not shed the blood of the great families, which will make you cursed until the resurrection. And if there is no army or king in Persia, armies will sweep in from Turkestan, India, Scythia, and China, and it would be no surprise if whoever took Persia then marched on the west. The descendants of the Persian kings should not be harmed so much as by a breath of wind. Summon them to your court, but be generous to them, feast them, and consult with them. Treat each according to his rank and see that their names are listed in your pension rolls, since it is from them that you took the world, paying nothing for it. Do not give any of them power over another, or refer to any of them as king of the world, but make these royal nobles a shield to protect the west against foreign invasion."

Sekandar changed his mind when he read this letter. He summoned the world's nobly born, all who were chivalrous by nature, to his court, and assigned them suitable places there. He wrote a charter, which designated the portion of each, with the stipulation that none was to encroach on another's power: these nobles he called "kings of the peoples."

That night Sekandar reached Babylon, where he was joyfully greeted by the local nobility. During the same night a woman gave birth to an astonishing child that had a lion's head, a human chest and human shoulders, a cow's tail, and hooves. The baby was stillborn, and it would have been better if the woman had had no offspring at all rather than such a monster. Immediately they brought the child to Sekandar, who took it as an omen, and ordered that it be buried. He told his astrologers of the child, who grew pensive and silent. He demanded their opinion, saying, "If you keep anything back from me I'll cut your heads from your bodies this minute, and your shroud will be a lion's maw." When the king stormed in this way, they said:

"First then, as scribes have written, at your birth
The lion's emblem, Leo, ruled the earth.
You saw the dead child had a lion's head,
Which means your majesty will soon be dead.
The world will be a place of strife until
A new king bends its peoples to his will."
The king grew pensive, then replied, "I see
Death comes, for which there is no remedy.
I'm not long for this world, I know, but I
Refuse to brood on this until I die.
Death comes to us on the appointed day—
We cannot make fate hurry, or delay."

Sekandar's Letter to His Mother

That day, in Babylon, he fell sick, and he knew that his end was approaching. He summoned an experienced scribe and dictated what was in his heart, in a letter to his mother. He said, "The signs of death cannot be hidden; I have lived the life allotted to me in this world, and we cannot hurry or delay our fate. Do not grieve at my death, for this is not a new thing in the world: all who are born must die, be they kings or paupers. I shall tell our chieftains that when they return from this land to Greece they must obey you alone. I have established those Persians who fought against our armies as lords over their realm, so that they shall have no desire to attack Greece; our country will be secure and at peace. See that my body is buried in Egypt, and that you fulfill all that I say here. Every year distribute ten thousand gold coins of my wealth to the peasantry. If Roshanak bears a son, then my name will surely survive; no one but he must become king of Greece, and he will renew the country's prosperity. But if, when her labor pains come to her, she bears a daughter, marry the child to one of Filqus's sons and call him my son, not my son-in-law, so that my name shall be remembered in the world. As for Kayd's innocent daughter, send her back to her father in India, together with the crowns and silver and gold and all the dowry she brought. Now I have completed my affairs and have no choice but to prepare my heart for death. First, see that my coffin is of gold and that my body's shroud is worthy of me; let it be of Chinese silk impregnated with sweet scents, and see that no one neglects the offices due to me. The joints of my coffin should be sealed with pitch, as well as camphor, musk, and ambergris. Honey should be poured into the coffin, then a layer of brocade placed there, on which my body is to be laid; when my face has been covered there is no more to be said. When I have gone, wise mother, remember my words. As for the things that I have sent from India, China,

Turan, Iran, and Makran, keep what you need and distribute the surplus. Dear mother, my desire is that you be sensible and serene in your soul; do not torment yourself on my behalf, since no one who lives in the world lives forever. When your days too draw to a close, my soul shall surely see yours again; patience is a greater virtue than love, and a person blown hither and thither by emotion is contemptible. For months and years you lovingly cared for my body; now pray to God for my soul; with these prayers you will still care for me. And consider, who is there in all the world whose soul is not cast down by death?"

He sealed the letter and ordered that it be taken with all speed from Babylon to Greece, to give news there that the imperial glory had been eclipsed.

Sekandar Dies in Babylon

When the army learned of the king's illness, the world grew dark before them. Their eyes turned toward the throne, and the world was filled with rumors. Knowing that he had few days left to live and hearing of his army's concern, Sekandar gave orders that his sickbed be taken from the palace out to the open plain. His saddened troops saw his face devoid of color, and the plain rang from end to end with lamentations, as if the soldiers were burning in flames; they cried, "It is an evil day when the Greeks lose their king: misfortune triumphs, and now our country will be destroyed. Our enemies have reached their hearts' desire, while for us the world has turned bitter, and we shall mourn publicly and in secret."

> Then in a failing voice their king replied,
> "Live humbly, fearfully, when I have died,
> And if you'd grow and prosper see that you
> Keep my advice henceforth, in all you do.
> This is your duty to me when I'm gone
> Lest time undo the work that I have done."
> He spoke, and then his soul rose from his breast:
> The king who'd shattered armies was at rest.

An earsplitting wail went up from his troops as they heaped dust on their heads and wept bitter tears. They set fire to the royal pavilion, and the very earth seemed to cry out in sorrow. They cut the tails of a thousand horses and set their saddles on them back to front, as a sign of mourning. As they brought the golden coffin their cries resounded in the heavens; a bishop washed the corpse in clear rosewater and scattered pure camphor over it. They shrouded their king in golden brocade, lamenting as they did so, then placed him beneath a covering of Chinese silk, his body soaked from head to toe in honey. The coffin lid was fastened, and the noble tree whose shade had spread so widely was no more.

They passed the coffin from hand to hand across the plain, and as they went forward, two opinions began to be heard. The Persians said, "He should not be buried anywhere but here: this is the land of emperors, what are they doing carrying the coffin about the world like this?" But a Greek guide said, "It would not be right to bury him here; if you hear my view you'll see that I'm right. Sekandar should be buried in the soil that nourished him." A Persian interrupted, "No matter how much you continue this conversation it won't get to the root of the matter. I'll show you a meadow near here that's been preserved since the time of our ancient kings: old folk call it Jorm. There is a wooded area there, and a lake; if you ask it a question, an answer will come from the mountain nearby. Take an old man there, together with the coffin, and ask your question; if the mountain answers, it will give you the best advice." As quickly as mountain sheep they made their way to the thicket called Jorm. And when they asked their question, the answer came, "What are you doing with this royal coffin? The dust of Sekandar belongs in Alexandria, the town he founded while he was alive." As soon as they heard this, the soldiers hurried from the area.

The Mourning for Sekandar

When Sekandar's body reached Alexandria the world was beset with new disputes. The coffin was set down on the plain, and the land was filled with rumor and gossip. As many as a hundred thousand children, men, and women flocked there. The philosopher Arestalis was there, his eyes filled with bitter tears; the world watched as he stretched out his hand to the coffin and said, "Where are your intelligence, knowledge, and foresight, now that a narrow coffin is your resting place? Why in the days of your youth did you choose the earth as your couch?"

The Greek sages crowded round, each speaking in turn, lamenting Sekandar's death. And then his mother came running, and placed her face on his chest, and said,

> "O noble king, world-conqueror, whose state
> Was princely, and whose stars were fortunate,
> You're far away from me and seem so near,
> Far from your kin, far from your soldiers here.
> Would that my soul were your soul's slave, that I
> Might see the hearts of those who hate you die."
> Then Roshanak ran grieving to his side,
> Crying, "Where are those kings now, and their pride?

Where's Dara, who once ruled the world? Where's Foor?
Where's Ashk? Faryan? The sovereign of Sharzoor,
And all those other lords who put their trust
In battle and were dragged down to the dust?
You seemed a storm cloud charged with hail: I said
That you could never die, that you had shed
So much blood, fought so many wars, that there
Must be some secret you would not declare,
Some talisman that fate had given you
To keep you safe whatever you might do.
You cleared the world of petty kings, brought down
Into the dirt an empire's ancient crown,
And when the tree you'd planted was to bear
Its fruits you died, and left me in despair."

When the sky's golden shield descended, the nobles were exhausted by their grief, and they placed the coffin in the ground. There is nothing in the world so terrible and fearful as the fact that one comes like the wind and departs as a breath, and that neither justice nor oppression are apparent in this. Whether you are a king or a pauper you will discover no rhyme or reason to it. But one must act well, with valor and chivalry, and one must eat well and rejoice: I see no other fate for you, whether you are a subject or a prince. This is the way of the ancient world: Sekandar departed, and what remains of him now is the words we say about him. He killed thirty-six kings, but look how much of the world remained in his grasp when he died. He founded ten prosperous cities, and those cities are now reed beds. He sought things that no man has ever sought, and what remains of him within the circle of the horizon is words, nothing more. Words are the better portion, since they do not decay as an old building decays in the snow and rain. I have finished with Sekandar now, and with the barrier that he built; may our days be fortunate and prosperous.

❧ THE ASHKANIANS ❧

What was said in that *Book of the Righteous,* concerning ancient times? What does it say about the period after Sekandar had gone? Who occupied the throne then? A knowledgeable landowner from Chach put it like this: no one occupied the ivory throne. The chieftains who claimed descent from Arash, who were a valiant, impulsive, and stubborn clan, were scattered about in different corners of the world, each of them cheerfully ruling a petty kingdom. Collectively they were called the "kings of the peoples."

> *And so two hundred years went by: you'd say*
> *That monarchy itself had passed away.*
> *The local chiefs were happy to ignore*
> *Each other, and the earth was cleansed of war.*
> *Sekandar had foreseen and planned this peace*
> *To safeguard the prosperity of Greece.*

The first among the new kings was Ashk, of the family of Qobad; others included Shapur who was of equally noble birth, the Ashkanian prince Gudarz, the Kayanid prince Bizhan, Nersi, the mighty Hormozd, and Arash, who was a fearsome warrior. After him there was Ardavan, a wise, clear-sighted man. When the Ashkanian Bahram became king he distributed wealth among the deserving and was called Ardavan the Great because he was a man who protected his flock from the wolves' claws. He held the area from Shiraz to Esfahan, which discerning men have called the seat of nobility, and by his authority Estakhr was ruled by Babak, a man whose snares terrified dragons. But all these ruled for such a short time and had so little influence that the chronicler did not record their lives in detail; I have heard nothing but their names, and seen nothing about them in royal records. All this was as the dying Sekandar had planned: Greece would remain safe and prosperous while the Eastern princes were preoccupied with local affairs, and so paid no attention to her. When a wise man becomes king, his knowledge ensures that such plans come to fruition.

Babak Sees Sasan in a Dream

When Dara was killed in battle and his family fell upon dark times, a wise, brave son, who was called Sasan, survived him. When he saw that his father had been murdered, and that the Persians' fortunes were in ruins, he fled before the Greek army and escaped from the general disaster. He died obscurely in India, but left behind him a son who bore his name, which continued in the family for four generations. They lived as shepherds, sometimes as camel drivers, and all their years passed in poverty and hard labor. The last, while still a child, presented himself before Babak's chief shepherd and said, "Do you need a laborer, someone who can live out his wretched life here?" The shepherd hired Sasan, who worked hard day and night and pleased his masters, so that when he grew up he became chief shepherd in his turn. He was a man who lived in sadness, by the sweat of his brow.

One night as Babak slept, his bright soul dreamt that Sasan was riding a war elephant, and in his hand was an Indian sword. Everyone who came before him bowed down to him; he made the earth flourish, and drove sorrow from men's hearts. The next night Babak dreamed that a fire worshipper lit three fires on the plain; they were just like the fires in the temples of Azar-Goshasp, Khorad, and Mehr, and they shone like the turning heavens. All three burned before Sasan, who fed them with aloes wood. Babak woke in consternation from his dream and summoned oneiromancers. They gathered at his court and when Babak told them what he'd seen, they grew pensive. Finally the most senior among them said, "Great king, we must consider what this means. Anyone who is seen in this way by others, in a dream, is destined to raise his head above the sun in sovereignty; and if the dream does not refer to him it will be fulfilled by his son."

Babak was overjoyed when he heard this, and rewarded each of those present according to his rank. Then he gave orders for his chief shepherd to appear before him. It was a bitterly cold day, and the man appeared dressed in coarse clothes, his sheepskin coat covered in snow, and his heart almost split in two with anxiety. Babak commanded that the court be cleared, and the servants and counselors left the two alone. He questioned Sasan, and was cordial to him, seating him beside himself. He asked him about his family and lineage, but the shepherd was terrified at first and made no answer. Finally Sasan said, "Your majesty, if you will take pity on your shepherd, swear with your hand in mine that no matter what my lineage might be you will not seek to harm me, either openly or in secret." Babak swore by merciful God that he would not harm him in any way; his intention was only to make him happy and treat him with respect.

Then the young man said, "I am the son of Sasan, a descendant of king Ardeshir, who is remembered under the name Bahman, and who was the son of the great Esfandyar, the son of Goshtasp." When he heard this, Babak wept that he had seen such dreams. He had splendid clothes and a royally accoutered horse assigned to Sasan and said to him, "Go to the hot baths while they prepare your court clothes." He had a palace built for this man who had once been his chief shepherd, and when he was installed there Babak gave him slaves and attendants and every kind of necessity for life. He gave him more wealth than he could need, and lastly Babak gave him in marriage the crown of his life, his lovely daughter.

The Birth of Ardeshir Babakan

When nine months had gone by, this beautiful princess gave birth to a boy as splendid as the sun. He looked like Ardeshir, and he grew quickly into a brave, formidable child. His father called him Ardeshir, and his grandfather rejoiced to see him and was always cradling him in his arms. So time passed, and perceptive men referred to the boy as Ardeshir Babakan. He was taught all the skills a prince should acquire, and they made his kingly nature even more splendid: his face and manner were such that you'd say the heavens themselves shone with their borrowed light.

News of the knowledge and courtly accomplishments of this young man, who was said to be a raging lion in battle and as gracious as the goddess Nahid at banquets, came to Ardavan, who wrote a letter to Babak. It said, "Wise, prudent, eloquent, and renowned chieftain, I have heard that your grandson Ardeshir is a fine horseman, an eloquent boy, and a quick study. As soon as you read this letter, send him to me and I shall treat him well. I'll give him all that he requires, and make him the first of my warriors. When he is with my sons I shall make no distinction between him and them."

Babak wept when he read this letter, and had Ardeshir and a scribe brought to him. He said to the young man, "Read Ardavan's message and pay close attention to it. I shall write an answer to the king now and send it with a trusted servant. I shall say, 'I send you this brave, fine, young man who is my heart, the apple of my eye; I have advised him on how to act when he reaches your exalted court. Act toward him as befits a king, and do not let even the winds of heaven blow against him.'" Then Babak quickly opened his treasury doors and made the young man's heart happy with his gifts. He presented him with golden saddles, maces and swords, gold coins and brocade, horses and slaves, Chinese cloths and imperial textiles. He laid his wealth before him, holding back nothing from the boy who was to serve Ardavan. He also sent gifts with Ardeshir for the king—brocade and gold coins, musk and ambergris. And so the promising young man left his grandfather and set off for Ardavan's court at Rey.

Ardeshir Arrives at Ardavan's Court

Word was sent to the king as soon as Ardeshir arrived at the court, and Ardavan had him brought in. He talked with him for a while about Babak, seated him near the throne, and had quarters in the palace assigned to him. He also saw that food, clothes, and furnishings were provided for the young man. Ardeshir, and his companions, who had made the journey with him, went to the lodgings they had been given.

When the sun placed its throne in the heavens, and the world turned as pale as a Greek's face, Ardeshir called one of his servants and had him take to King Ardavan the presents that Babak had sent. Ardavan was delighted by them, and the young man who had brought them seemed to him to be a fine addition to the court. He treated him as his child and for a while saw that nothing disturbed the youth's happiness. Whether they were drinking wine or at banquets or out hunting, Ardavan kept him always nearby, and there was no difference between Ardeshir and Ardavan's own sons.

And so it was that one day a group of courtiers and the king's four sons, all fine young princes, had scattered across the plain in a hunting expedition; Ardeshir rode next to Ardavan, who was delighted to have the young man with him. Then in the distance a wild ass appeared, and cries went up from the hunters; everyone gave chase, and the company was covered in dust and sweat. Ardeshir outstripped the rest, and as he neared the prey he notched an arrow to his bow. When he loosed the shaft, it struck the animal in the flank, and the whole arrow, head, feathers, and all, passed right through the body. Just at that moment King Ardavan rode up; he saw the arrow fly and the wild ass lying dead, and exclaimed, "Bravo, whoever shot that arrow!" Ardeshir said, "I killed this wild ass, with my arrow." But one of Ardavan's sons said, "I killed this beast, and I'd like to see anyone else manage such a feat!" Ardeshir turned to him and said, "The plain is wide, and there are asses and arrows in abundance; let's see you bring another one down in the same way. To a man with any pride, a lie is a sin!" But Ardavan was enraged by this remark and shouted, "This is my fault, since it was me who brought you up. Why should I have you at my banquets and take you hunting with me if you're going to push ahead of my sons and lord it over everyone? Go and look after my Arab horses, and sleep in the stables with them. You can act the master there and be everyone's boy for every job that's to be done!"

Ardeshir's eyes filled with tears, but he had no choice other than to go and live in the stables. He wrote a letter to his grandfather Babak, and as he did so his heart was filled with sorrow, his head with wild schemes. He wrote of how Ardavan had acted toward him and added that he hoped the man would endure bodily pains and mental distress. He went over everything that had happened, and where and why Ardavan had erupted in rage. When this message reached Babak, he kept its contents to himself. He was upset, and he sent the young man ten thousand dinars from his treasury. Then he called in a scribe and dictated a letter to Ardeshir: "You're a callow young man, and you haven't much wisdom as yet. When you went hunting with Ardavan, what business had you attacking his son like that? You're a servant there, not one of the family! You are your own worst enemy, and you've grown used to acting foolishly. Now you must try to please him and keep him satisfied with you: don't deviate from his orders even for a moment. I've sent you some money, and here I'm sending you some advice. When you use the one remember the other, until this business is over."

An old experienced messenger quickly brought the letter to Ardeshir, who was pleased when he read it. His heart began to weave plots and plans. He chose a house near the stables and filled it with carpets, fine clothes, and good food, so that it was hardly suitable for the work he was supposed to be doing. He spent his days and nights eating and drinking; wine and entertainers were his companions.

Golnar Sees Ardeshir; the Death of Babak

> King Ardavan possessed a slave whose face
> Lit up his palace with bewitching grace:
> She seemed a painting, lovely and bejeweled.
> Her name was Golnar, and this slave girl ruled
> The palace as her monarch's counselor—
> His first advisor, and his treasurer.
> He loved her more than life itself: the sight
> Of Golnar filled the king's heart with delight.

One day Golnar went up onto the palace roof and glimpsed the merrymaking in Ardeshir's courtyard. She was charmed by it, and when she saw Ardeshir's smiling face, the young man slipped into her heart. That night, toward dawn,

she knotted a rope and let it down from the battlements. Boldly, invoking God's benevolence as she did so, she made her way to the ground. Wearing her jewels and scented with musk, she appeared before Ardeshir; he raised his head from his brocade pillow, emerging from sleep, and took her in his arms. The young man stared at the beautiful girl before him, at her hair and face and splendor, and said, "Where have you come from, to delight my sorrow-stricken heart in this way?" She answered, "I am a slave, and I live to see you alone, in all the world: I am King Ardavan's treasurer, and the chief pleasure and solace of his soul. But if you accept me, I shall be your slave and fill my heart and soul with adoration for you. I shall come to you whenever you wish, and change the darkness of your days to splendor."

A little later Babak, who had brought up Ardeshir, died, and left his place in this world to others. When news of this reached Ardeshir his soul was darkened and he grieved for his protector. All the nobles vied to be appointed governor of Pars, but the king entrusted the post to his eldest son: he gave orders that the drums were to be sounded, and the army set off across the plain. Ardeshir's heart was dark with grief for the benevolent old man who had guided and cherished him, and he took no pleasure in Ardavan's rule or his army. The news made him look for another course; his heart was filled with resentment, and he looked for some means of escape.

At that time King Ardavan, seeking to know who would be favored by the heavens, summoned astrologers to his court. He sent them up to Golnar's quarters, whence they could observe the stars. For three days they worked there, casting the king's horoscope. The treasurer overheard their conversation

about the stars, and for three days and nights, through the third watch of each night, she eavesdropped on them, her heart filled with hope, her lips with sighs. On the fourth day the sages took their astrological tables from Golnar's quarters to the king, and put before him what they had discovered. They told him in detail how the secrets of high heaven affected him, and said that in the near future something would happen that would bring anguish to the king's heart. A servant who was valiant and of noble birth would flee from his court, and this man would become a great king, a ruler of the world, powerful and blessed by the stars. Ardavan's heart was deeply troubled by their words.

Ardeshir Flees with Golnar

The land turned pitch black and the slave girl made her way to Ardeshir. He was a sea of anger and resentment, unable to have a single day's peace because of his preoccupation with Ardavan. Golnar told him what the astrologers had told the king, and when he heard this he calmed down and was silent for a while. Her words concentrated his mind, and he decided on flight. He said to her,

> "If I'm to get to Pars, if I'm to see
> That land again where men are brave and free,
> I must know if you'll come with me, or stay
> Behind here with King Ardavan in Rey.
> If you accompany me you'll be the crown
> Of Persia, which will fill with your renown."
> And she replied, between expressive sighs
> While flowing tears fell from her lovely eyes,
> "I am your slave, I have one life to give
> And it is yours entirely, while I live."

Ardeshir said to the beautiful girl, "We have no choice but to do this tomorrow." She returned to her own quarters, determined to take her life in her hands and risk everything.

When dark night withdrew and the world turned gold with the rising sun, Golnar opened the treasury doors and began to choose among the jewels there. She selected rubies and other royal gems, as well as a sufficient number of gold coins for their purposes, then returned to her room. There she waited till night came up over the mountains, and Ardavan's sleeping palace was deserted. Quick as an arrow then, clutching the jewels and cash she had taken, she came to the valiant Ardeshir; he stood with a wine goblet in his hand, the stable guards asleep at his feet. He had made them drunk so that they would not impede the escape, and he'd picked out and saddled two fine horses. When he saw Golnar's face and the jewels and red gold she'd brought, he immediately set down the goblet and put the bridles over the horses' heads. Armored, and with a glittering sword in his hand, he mounted one horse and helped Golnar on to the other; together they fled from the palace buildings and took the road to Pars, their hearts filled with joy and ambition.

Ardavan Learns of What Golnar and Ardeshir Have Done

It was Ardavan's habit never to rise from his brocade bed, until he had first seen Golnar's face as a good omen for the day. But when the time came for him to get up and to have his throne spread with brocade, and the slave girl still had not come to his pillow, he exploded with fury against her. The guards stood before his door; his throne, crown, and audience hall were ready for him, and his chamberlain came in saying, "Your warriors and the country's nobility are waiting at the door." The king said to his servants, "See what is the matter with Golnar; it never happens that she doesn't come to my pillow; she knows what my habits are." At that moment the chief scribe came in and said, "Some time last night Ardeshir fled; he's taken from the stables a black horse and a gray, both of them mounts favored by the king. And at the same time the king lost his beloved companion, since it is clear that your treasurer has fled with Ardeshir."

Ardavan's warlike heart was enraged and he set off with a large group of horsemen in pursuit of the fugitives. You'd have said that their horses trod on fire, so swiftly did they gallop. At the roadside they saw a well-populated settlement with a number of animals and asked if before sunrise anyone had heard the sound of galloping. A man volunteered that two figures on two horses, one gray and the other black, had galloped across the plain, closely followed by a pristine mountain sheep, which kicked up as much dust as the horses did. Ardavan asked his advisor why a mountain sheep should be running behind them, and the man replied, "That is his *farr*, an earnest of his good fortune and sovereignty. If this sheep sticks with him, do not struggle against the fact, or this will turn into a lengthy business for us." Ardavan dismounted at the settlement, ate, and rested for a while, and then renewed the chase. With Ardavan and his advisor leading them, the group pressed on in pursuit of Ardeshir.

Meanwhile the young man and the slave girl rode like the wind, without resting for a moment; and whoever is favored by the high heavens cannot be harmed by enemies. When they were tired out by their efforts, Ardeshir caught sight of a lake beneath them as they crested a hill, and he turned to

Golnar and said, "Now that we are both exhausted by the journey, we should ride down to that water; both we and our horses are weak and worn out. We can stay by the water and eat something, and ride on when we've rested." But as they approached the lake, with their faces as yellow and sickly as the sun, Ardeshir saw two young men standing there, who shouted to him,

> *"Stay in your stirrups now, shake out your reins,*
> *Continue on your ride across the plains—*
> *You have escaped the dragon's deadly breath*
> *But if you drink here you'll encounter death."*

Ardeshir said to Golnar, "Remember their words." Their stirrups became heavy, their reins light; Ardeshir lifted his glittering lance to his shoulders and on they rode.

Tired and with darkness in his soul, Ardavan still rode after them like the wind, until at midday, when the sun had traversed half the sky, he saw a fine town. A number of its inhabitants came out to meet him, and he called out to their priests, "When did you last see a young man ride this way?" One of them answered, "Your majesty, benevolent and blessed by heaven, at the time when the sun sets and night spreads its dark veil over the land, two people rode through this town; they were covered in dust and their lips were dry with thirst. A mountain sheep followed one of them, and she was more splendid than any I've ever seen in a painting on a palace wall." Ardavan's advisor said to him, "The situation has changed; you should turn back here, muster an army, and prepare for war. His good fortune follows him, and our chasing after him like this is mere clutching at the wind. Write a letter to your son, telling him of the whole business; perhaps he can find some trace of Ardeshir. He must not be allowed to drink this sheep's milk!" When Ardavan heard these words, he knew that his days were numbered and that his glory was fading. He dismounted at the town, and prayed to God from whom all blessings come.

At dawn the following morning he gave orders for the return journey. He entered Rey at nightfall, his cheeks as pale as reeds. There he wrote a letter to his son, saying, "In our orchard, a twisted root has born fruit. Ardeshir has fled from my hearth quicker than any arrow. He has gone to Pars; find him, but do it discreetly, and tell no one in the world of this."

Ardeshir Gathers an Army

For his part, Ardeshir reached the shore of a wide body of water, where he prayed, "Sole source of help, who has made me safe from my malevolent enemy, I pray that his body may never know health again." Then he rested

and talked with a ferryman there for a long time about the past. The ferryman, who was a wise old man, stared at Ardeshir's face and stature and realized that he must be descended from the Kayanid kings; the prince's *farr* and glory delighted him. Quickly he ferried Ardeshir across the water, and when the young man reached the other side and news of his coming spread, an army of supporters gathered there. Babak's men from Estakhr came, overjoyed at the news of their new king, and all of Dara's descendants came to him from the various provinces where they ruled. Joy at King Ardeshir's presence made old men's hearts young again, and band by band men poured in from the river valleys and mountains. Wise counselors came from every city and gathered about the ambitious youth. He addressed his followers: "Illustrious and righteous as you are, there is no one here who has not heard what the malevolent Sekandar, out of the baseness of his heart, did on this earth. One by one he killed my ancestors and unjustly grasped the world in his fist. Since I am descended from Esfandyar, it is right that I cannot recognize Ardavan as king here. If you are with me in this, I shall not let anyone usurp the title and throne that should be mine. What do you say? What's your answer? Tell me clearly!"

Everyone there, whether a warrior or a counselor, rose to his feet, and together they spoke from their hearts: "Those of us who are from Babak's tribe rejoice to see your face, and those of us who are Sasanians will bind on our sword belts to serve you in war. Our souls and bodies belong to you, our joys and sorrows depend on you. Your lineage on both sides is nobler than anyone's; kingship and heroism are your birthright. If you give the order, we shall make mountains level with the plains, and with our swords we shall make the ocean's water into blood." At such an answer Ardeshir's mind out-soared the spheres of Venus and Mercury. He thanked the nobles gathered there and meditated war in his heart.

At the edge of the water he built a city, which became the site of his preparations for war. A priest there said to him, "O fortunate and inspiring king, renewer of the monarchy, you must cleanse the province of Pars and then make war on Ardavan, because you are a young king and your star is still young. Of all those they call the 'kings of the peoples,' he is the richest, and besides, he has harassed and harried you. Once you have removed him from power, no one will have the strength to offer you any resistance." This was what had to be said, and Ardeshir was happy to hear such words. As the sun rose above the mountain peak he left the shore and set off toward Estakhr. But when the news reached Bahman, Ardavan's son, his soul darkened and his heart filled with pain; he did not sit idly on the royal throne but at once mustered his troops and prepared for war.

Ardeshir's Victory over Bahman

There was a nobleman called Sabak, a just and well-meaning man in charge
of armaments and troops, who ruled over the town of Jahrom. He had
seven fine sons. When he heard what was afoot he defected from Bahman's
side and ceremoniously brought his army, with its war drums beating, to
join forces with Ardeshir. As was customary, he dismounted and ran forward to kiss Ardeshir's feet. The ambitious young king made much of him
and acknowledged the value of his prompt defection. But he was suspicious
of Sabak, and in his heart he feared him. He was guarded with him as they
marched, aware of the might of Sabak's large army. But Sabak was old and
experienced, and he realized what Ardeshir was thinking. He came to the
commander with the Zend-Avesta in his hand and said, "I swear by almighty
God that Sabak's life is worthless if my heart is not blameless toward you.
When I learned King Ardeshir was gathering troops on that shore, I became
disgusted with Ardavan, just as a young man will be disgusted by an old
woman. Consider me as a kind, patient, trustworthy slave, who will bring
you good luck." Hearing this, Ardeshir changed his mind about Sabak; he
thought of him henceforth as his father, and placed him in command of his
other officers.

With his heart freed from this anxiety, Ardeshir paused at the fire-temple
of Ram-Khorad; there he prayed earnestly for God to guide him, to give him
victory in all his undertakings, and to allow the tree of greatness to flourish
for him. Then he returned to his pavilion, where his officers and men
awaited him. He distributed cash to his troops, invoking God as he did so.
His army was now like a valiant leopard, and he advanced against Bahman,
the son of Ardavan, to give battle.

As the two armies approached on one another, each side formed ranks
ready for battle, with lances and Indian swords grasped in their hands. Then
they fell on one another like warring lions, and blood was spilled in rivers.
So they fought until the sun turned pale, and the air was filled with dust,
the ground with corpses. At dawn the next morning, when the sky's veil
turned the color of turquoise, Sabak's troops entered the fray. A wind
sprang up, and the dust made the air like pitch. Ardeshir attacked from the

چو شیران جنگی بر آویختند
همی خاک با خون بر آمیختند

center, and such was his might and the strength of his *farr* that he slew many men with his mace. Bahman fled before him, his body wounded with arrows and his soul shrouded in darkness. King Ardeshir pursued him relentlessly, with trumpets sounding and arrows raining down, until they reached the city of Estakhr, the seat of Bahman's power. At the the sound of Ardeshir's voice a vast number of troops defected to him. He distributed to them the wealth that Bahman had toiled to accumulate, scattering the hoarded coins. Strong and confident, he led his armies out of Pars.

Ardeshir's War against Ardavan; Ardavan Is Killed

The news of Bahman's defeat brought terror to Ardavan's heart and his soul darkened. He said, "A man who knew the secrets of the turning heavens once said to me that whenever an evil surpasses our imagination, our efforts can have no effect on our fate. I would not have thought that Ardeshir could become so ambitious or turn into a conqueror of cities." He opened his treasury's doors, distributed provisions, mustered his army, and set off. He led his men through Gilan and Daylam, and the dust they sent up ascended to the moon. On the other side, Ardeshir too pressed forward; his men were so numerous that they stopped the wind in its tracks, and the columns resounded with the blare of trumpets and bugles, the jangling of bells, and the clashing of Indian cymbals. The armies were now two bow-shots from one another, and the very snakes in the ground cowered away in terror. With a roar the columns attacked, their banners bravely fluttering, their swords lopping off heads, empurpled with blood.

The fighting lasted for forty days. The common soldiers were hard pressed, their provisions ran out, and it was difficult to resupply them. So many corpses were piled there that the plain seemed like a mountain, and the wounded despaired of life. Finally a fierce wind sprang up, and a black cloud that made it impossible to fight spread over the armies; the mountain-side groaned, the ground shook, and the noise re-echoed in the heavens. Ardavan's army was terrified; they all believed that this was a sign from God against their king, and that there was nothing to do for their forces now but weep. On that day, the tide of battle turned against them and they all surrendered. Ardeshir advanced from the center of his troops, through the clash of weapons and a hail of arrows. Ardavan, who had devoted his sweet soul to the crown, was captured by a man named Kharrad who seized his bridle and dragged him before the king. Ardavan dismounted before Ardeshir, wounded and in despair. Ardeshir turned to his executioner and said, "Take that enemy of the king and split him open with a sword: fill the hearts of those who plot against us with terror." The man came forward and did as he had been ordered, and so this illustrious ruler was lost to the world.

پیاده بر ش بهمن اردوان   مرا و را پی سپاهی زپهر و جوان

سپاه از دو رویه کشیده صف   همه نیزه و تیغ هندی بکف

The ancient heavens turn; kings disappear,
Now Ardavan is gone, now Ardeshir,
And though their heads reach to the stars they must
At last be humbled in the lowly dust.

The humiliation of the family of Arash was increased by the capture of two of Ardavan's sons. Their legs were bound, and the king gave orders that they be imprisoned. The two eldest sons fled from the battlefield and escaped capture; weeping they fled to India, and theirs is a story worth recounting. The whole battlefield was strewn with horse gear, baldrics, weapons, and gold and silver objects; the king had all this collected, and then distributed it to his soldiers. Sabak left the other chieftains and cleansed Ardavan's body of blood. Weeping, he wiped away the grime of battle, and made him a tomb suitable for a king. He wrapped the wounded body in brocade and placed a pillow of camphor beneath his head. But when the soldiers went on to Rey they trampled the dust of Ardavan's palace beneath their feet.

Then Sabak came before Ardeshir and said, "Wise king, demand Ardavan's daughter in marriage: she has splendor and beauty and the dignity of her station. The crown and wealth that Ardavan took such trouble to accumulate will be in your hands." Ardeshir accepted this advice, and immediately demanded the girl in marriage. He stayed two months in her apartments; he was now a mighty commander, and a mighty king. Then he made his way from Rey to Pars, having rested from battle and the world's strife. He built a town there filled with palaces and gardens, streams, open spaces, and mountain slopes: a wise old local dignitary still refers to that place as Khurreh-ye Ardeshir—"The Glory of Ardeshir." From an inexhaustible spring of water within the town, he led off streams and irrigation channels. Near the spring he built a fire-temple, and there he celebrated the Zoroastrian festivals of Mehregan and Sadeh. Around the temple there were gardens, open spaces, and palaces; he made it into a splendid place. When later this wise and powerful king had died, the lord of the marches there called the place the city of Gur. Ardeshir built villages around it and settled the area. Although there was a deep lake nearby, it was separated from the town by a mountain. Ardeshir had laborers hack a hundred channels through the rock with picks, so that the water from the lake irrigated Gur, which became filled with buildings and livestock.

Ardeshir's War with the Kurds

Ardeshir led a huge army out from Estakhr, to fight against the Kurds. He sought aid from God in his expedition to spill the blood of these thieves, but when he entered Kurdish territory, a numberless host welcomed him with war. An expedition that should have been a minor matter became difficult, because the whole countryside supported the Kurds, so that they outnumbered the king's men thirty to one. They fought a whole day till nightfall, when the king's army fled and the battlefield was crowded with so many corpses that one could hardly move. Only a few soldiers remained behind with their king, and they were tormented with thirst because of the dust and the heat of the sun. Then night spread its banner and put an end to the fighting and tumult.

Ardeshir saw a fire on the mountainside; he and his companions made their way up to it, and as they drew nearer they saw a few shepherds there, watching their sheep and goats. He and his soldiers dismounted, and as their mouths were filled with the dust of battle, Ardeshir immediately asked for water, which the shepherds gave him, together with some yogurt. He rested and ate a little of what was before him: then he spread out his armor to sleep on, and his pillow was his royal helmet.

Dawn broke over the lake, and the king of Persia lifted his head from sleep. The chief of the shepherds came to his pillow saying, "I wish you lucky days and nights. How is it that you've come here, as this is no place for someone like you to sleep?" The king questioned him about the way, and where he could find a place to rest. The shepherd answered, "You won't find any houses unless you have a guide. But about four parasangs from here there is a place where you could rest, and from there you could go from village to village until you reach the one where the local headman lives." Ardeshir took a few of the older men there as guides and made his way to the village where the headman was. From there he sent horsemen, young and old, to Khurreh-ye Ardeshir, and when the army heard of his escape, they were overjoyed and set out to come to his aid. Meanwhile Ardeshir posted spies, who quickly reported back that the Kurds were reveling in their success and giving no thought at all to the king. They thought that his luck had grown old and feeble, and that he had gone back to Estakhr. The king was happy to hear this, and soon forgot his recent reverses. He selected thirty thousand cavalry from the army that had joined him, as well as a thousand archers.

As the sun grew yellow in the west he led his army out, leaving behind those unfit for the march. By the time half the night had passed, and it was pitch dark, Ardeshir was close to the Kurds. The whole plain was filled with sleeping men, lying here and there, careless of their safety. He drew his sword, slackened his grip on the reins, and charged the Kurds' camp. The grass was crowned with their blood, the plain was filled with their severed heads and limbs, and the heaps of dead were dreadful to see. A huge number of them were taken prisoner: their violence and stupidity had been humbled. Ardeshir turned the country over to his soldiers for plunder, and distributed purses of gold and crowns to them. The country-side there became so secure because of Ardeshir's rule that an old man could have walked across the plain with a salver of gold coins on his head, and no one would have so much as looked at him. Ardeshir did not stay to enjoy the fruits of war but hurried back to Estakhr, where he gave orders that the men's horses were to be tended to and their armor was to be repaired. He told his soldiers to rest and enjoy themselves, since the time for warfare would come again quickly enough. His warriors feasted and rested, while Ardeshir's thoughts were of war.

The Story of the Worm of Haftvad

Consider this strange story, revealed by a local dignitary, telling old obscure tales. There was a poor but populous town called Kajaran near the Persian Gulf, where all the inhabitants lived by their own efforts. A number of girls who had to work for their livelihood lived there. To one side of the town was a mountain, where the girls would go together, taking cotton and spindles made of poplar wood. Traveling in a group through the main town gate, they would make their way to the mountain slopes, taking just enough food with them. But there was very little talk of eating or resting, since their sole concern was the cotton they'd brought to spin. Then they would return to their homes at nightfall, bringing the yarn they had spun. In this needy but cheerful place there also lived a man called Haftvad, who had seven sons, as his name indicates. He had a fine daughter, too, but he took no notice of her. One day the group of girls was sitting on the mountainside with their spindles, which they had put aside for a moment while they were eating.

> Just at that moment Haftvad's daughter found
> A windfall apple lying on the ground
> And picked it up—now listen carefully
> Because this story's quite extraordinary:
> She bit the apple then, but as she tried it
> She saw a little worm there, coiled inside it;
> She scooped it out, and gently found a place
> For this small worm inside her spindlecase.
> And as she took her cotton up she said,
> "By God I swear, today I'll spin such thread,

Helped by this apple's lucky worm, that you
Will be amazed at all that I can do!"
The girls began to laugh—in their delight,
Their faces glowed, their teeth shone silver-white.

But that day she spun twice as much as she normally did; she marked the amount on the ground and ran like wind-borne smoke to show her mother how much she had completed. He mother smiled and congratulated her and said, "You've done well by your mother, my pretty one." The next morning the girl took twice as much cotton as usual, and when she had joined her friends she put her heart into her work and said, "I'm going to spin so much thread, by the grace of this worm, that I'll never be poor again!" She spun what she had brought, and if she had had more with her, she could have spun that, too. She took the thread home, and her mother was so pleased with her daughter that she felt she was in heaven. Every morning the girl fed the worm a piece of apple, and however much cotton there was, the girl magically spun it into thread.

This went on until one day her mother and father said to their clever daughter, "You spin so much that it seems as though you've taken a fairy as your sister!" But the lovely child quickly answered her mother, "It's from the apple, and the little worm that was hidden in it." Then she showed her parents the marvelous worm and explained everything to them. Haftvad took all this as a good omen, and as his prospects seemed to brighten every day, he stopped worrying about his own work. He talked only about the good fortune brought by the worm, and how the worm had renewed his luck. They didn't neglect to look after the worm but gave it good, nourishing food. The worm grew plump and strong, its head and its back became splendid and formidable. The spindlecase was now too small for its body, and from one end to the other its skin was like black musk with a saffron-colored pattern on it. Haftvad made it a fine black chest to live in.

Now no discussion about civic affairs could go forward in the town without Haftvad: he and his seven sons became powerful, respected citizens. But there was a nobleman in the town, a proud man who had his own followers, and he looked for some excuse to take this commoner's wealth away from him. Haftvad was afraid and stole out of the town, leaving his seven sons there. Wherever he went he complained of their situation, and soon a group of men, young and old, had gathered around them. Haftvad was liberal with his gold, and soon he had an army, which made its way to his sons, determined to fight on their behalf.

The noise of trumpets was heard throughout Kajaran, and the army attacked with lances, swords, and arrows. Haftvad fought bravely at the head of his men, took the town, and killed the nobleman who had been

harassing him; a great deal of wealth and jewels came into his possession. Men flocked to him, and he left Kajaran and went into the mountains. There, on a summit, he built a fortress with an iron door for his followers: it was a place of pleasure and repose, but also a place that could withstand a siege. A stream there flowed into the fortress, and around the whole area he built a wall so high that its summit was invisible.

Meanwhile the worm had grown too big for its chest, and so they made a stone cistern inside the fortress, and when the air had sufficiently warmed the stone and mortar, they very gently placed the worm inside it. Every morning the worm's keeper ran from Haftvad and fed the worm with rice, which its swollen body soon disposed of. After five years of this the worm was as massive as an elephant. The fortunate girl still looked after the worm, while Haftvad commanded their armies. A vizier and a scribe waited on the worm, and now it was fed on milk and honey. Haftvad was in charge of the fortress and decided all matters that came before him. He now had an army, a counselor, a chancellor for his court, everything in fact that pertained to a king, and his armies controlled the land from Kerman to the sea of China. Haftvad's seven sons each commanded ten thousand men, and they had wealth and arms at their disposal. If any king marched against them, as soon as his soldiers heard the tale of the worm they lost heart and the army broke up. Haftvad's fortress became so renowned that even the winds of heaven did not dare blow about it.

Ardeshir Fights against Haftvad and Is Defeated

Ardeshir was not pleased when he heard about Haftvad, and he sent a commander against him, with a fine body of men ready for battle. But Haftvad was not at all alarmed: he set up an ambush in a defile of the mountains and then went against the approaching army at the head of his troops. When the two armies had joined battle and were laying about one another with maces and battleaxes, the hidden soldiers burst out from the ambush, and the earth became a dark place for the invaders. They were so hemmed in that no one knew his hands from his feet, and so many were killed that the victors were stupefied by the number of dead. Anyone from Ardeshir's forces who remained alive quickly fled back to the king.

Ardeshir was angered when he heard about the way his troops had been killed and their baggage plundered. He quickly mustered an army, to whom he distributed arms and cash, and set out against Haftvad immediately, while this commoner was still exalting in his triumph. Haftvad brought treasure and weapons from his fortress and was not at all troubled by Ardeshir's approach. His eldest son was living far away, but when he heard of his father's battles, he gave up his life of lazing and feasting and took ship to return. This ambitious youth was called Shahuy, and he was an ill-made, ill-spoken man. When he disembarked, Haftvad's heart rejoiced to see his son, and he put him in charge of the right wing of the army, while he himself remained the overall commander.

Now face to face, the two armies were both well equipped, eager for war, and backed up by considerable wealth. King Ardeshir looked at them, and his young heart grew old with anxiety. The columns faced one another, and the sun glinted on their swords. Then the din of drums resounded from the elephants' backs, and men two miles away quailed at the noise: the blaring of trumpets began, and the squeal of brazen bugles. The earth quaked beneath the horses' hooves, the air was crimson with chieftains' banners, and so great was the racket of maces against helmets that the sky seemed to bid the earth farewell. Galloping horses tore up the earth, the plain was filled with trunkless heads, and Haftvad's army fought with such fury they seemed like a lake whipped up by the wind. So thick was the press of men on each side that not an ant or a mosquito could have found room there. So the battle went on until the day paled into evening, and then night spread its purple cloak. Ardeshir summoned his scattered soldiers and made camp beside a brackish lake. When the rust-colored waters turned black, each army sent out its scouts and guards. The king's army was badly fed that night, because their malevolent enemy had cut off the road by which they'd been supplied.

Mehrak, the Son of Nushzad, Sacks Ardeshir's Palace

In Jahrom there was a low-born man called Mehrak, the son of Nushzad. When he heard that Ardeshir had left the area and was camped by a lake after a hard-fought battle, and that the army's supply route had been interrupted, he set off for the king's palace with a large group of followers. He looted its treasures and distributed crowns and cash to his men. Ardeshir received news of this at the lakeside and grew pensive, saying to himself, "Why am I fighting against strangers when I haven't secured my own palace?"

He summoned his chieftains and told them at length about Mehrak, and then said, "You are my army commanders, what do you think we should do in this desperate situation? Fate has sent us sorrows enough, and we overlooked Mehrak and his potential for trouble." They answered, "Your majesty, may your eyes never see ill fortune. Since Mehrak has revealed himself as your covert enemy, why should you endure these hardships to conquer the world? But you have greatness and the earth is yours; we are your slaves and you our master."

Ardeshir ordered that a meal be prepared, and asked for wine and entertainers. A few spitted lambs were placed before the men, and they began to eat. Ardeshir had a piece of bread in his hand when an arrow plunged right into the lamb carcass in front of him. Alarmed, the chieftains drew back from the food, while one of them took the arrow out of the meat. There was writing on it, and an officer who was also a scribe read it aloud. The inscription was in Pahlavi, and it said,

> "Listen, wise king: this arrow's from the fort
> Where peace reigns, and the mighty worm holds court:
> If I had aimed the shaft at Ardeshir
> It would have passed right through you. It is clear
> No king like you can hope for victory
> Against the worm's all-powerful sovereignty."

It was two parasangs from the fortress to their camp, and when the inscription was read the chieftains' hearts were horrified; all of them invoked God's blessings on their king and his glory.

Ardeshir brooded on these events all night, and when the sun rose the next morning he struck camp and led the army back from the lake, toward Pars. They marched quickly but the enemy forces harassed them from behind, raiding the columns constantly and killing many of their leaders. The cry pursued them:

"The worm's good fortune shines, and he alone
Illuminates the splendor of the throne."

The soldiers said to one another, "This is a wonder, which everyone should marvel at." They rode on across uneven ground, their hearts filled with anxiety, until they saw a large city, and they bore down on it with the speed of wolves. Nearby, they saw two young men standing in front of a house. The king and his men paused for a moment, and the strangers questioned them, asking how they came to be there so unexpectedly, and where they had arrived from, covered in the dust of the road. The king said, "Ardeshir fled this way, and we were left behind in his flight; he's running from the worm, and from Haftvad, and from their rabble of an army." The two young men started forward, filled with concern on the fugitives' behalf. They had them dismount, welcoming them and making them a place to rest and sleep. The two sat with the king at his meal and entertained him well, saying, "My lord, neither sorrow nor joy last for long. Look at the unjust Zahhak and all he took from the royal throne, and at the malevolent Afrasyab, who tormented the Persian kings, and at Sekandar, who in recent times killed the world's kings; they have all departed. All that remains of them is an evil name, and they will not taste the joys of paradise. This Haftvad will end in the same way; he too will at last writhe in his death agony."

At their words, the king's heart opened like a flower in springtime. He was so comforted by their remarks that he decided to tell them the truth, and said, "I am Ardeshir, the son of Sasan, and I need your advice. How can I fight against this accursed worm, and against Haftvad?" The two young men bowed before him, and both said, "May you always thrive, and may the reach of evil be far from you. Our bodies and souls are your slaves; may your spirit endure forever. As for the worm, some kind of stratagem must be employed against it. You won't be able to defeat it unless you resort to underhand tactics. The worm and his treasure and followers are ensconced on that mountaintop, with a city on one side and the lake on the other, and the way up their fastness is a difficult one. In his essence that worm is Ahriman, the enemy of the Creator of the world. You say he's a worm, but inside that leathery skin he's a devil thirsty for blood."

Ardeshir felt reassured by their kind words and said, "All this is true, and I leave it to you to come up with something against him." They answered, "We are your slaves and will always recommend what is right to you." Cheered by their talk the king went forward, once more assured of victory, taking the two young men with him. And so they proceeded, with clear consciences and confidence, to Khurreh-ye Ardeshir.

There, with his courtiers assembled about him, he rested from war, re-provisioned his army, and then turned to the problem of Mehrak, the son of

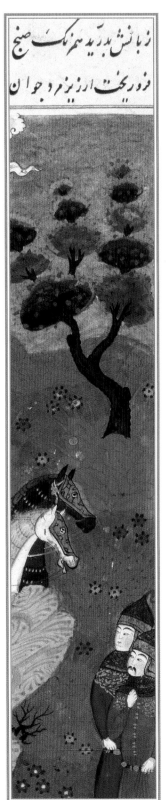

Nushzad. Mehrak was terrified to learn of his approach, and as Ardeshir drew near Jahrom, the traitor hid from him. But the king was determined to hunt him down, and when Mehrak was taken prisoner Ardeshir cut off his head with an Indian sword, and had his headless trunk burned. Then he stabbed to death every member of Mehrak's family who fell into his hands, apart from one of the daughters, who managed to keep herself hidden, even though she was sought for throughout the whole town.

Ardeshir Kills Haftvad's Worm

His next concern was to make war on the worm, and he mustered an army for this purpose. Assembling twelve thousand experienced cavalry, he reunited his scattered troops and brought his reconstituted forces to an area between two mountains. He appointed a shrewd man named Shahrgir as his commander and said to him, "Stay here, and be on your guard; send scouts out day and night, and let them be good, capable horsemen; likewise have sentries and watchmen posted to safeguard the army. Meanwhile I'm going to resort to a trick—Esfandyar's an ancestor of mine, after all. If the watchman sees smoke rise up in the daytime, and then fire at night as bright as the sun, you're to understand that the worm's power is at an end; that I've turned his luck, and rid the world of him."

He chose seven of his best warriors, all brave as lions and men whom he could trust. Not a word was said to anyone else as to what was afoot. He picked out a large number of jewels from his treasury, as well as brocade, gold coins, and other kinds of wealth, his wise eyes carefully selecting the best items. Then he filled two chests with lead and included a brass cauldron, an item that would be crucial for the success of his venture. He wrapped everything in cloth, procured ten large donkeys from the head of his

stables, loaded up his goods, and covered them over with coarse kilims. Impatient to put their plan into action, the little group set off for the worm's fastness. The two young men who had entertained Ardeshir during his flight went with them: they had become friends with Ardeshir, and he valued their advice. The caravan was disguised to look like a merchant's.

When they could see the castle and its city in the distance, a lookout called to them, "What have you got in those chests?" The king shouted back, "All sorts of things for sale: cloth and clothes, gold and silver, gold coins, brocade, pearls and jewels. We're merchants from Khorasan, always traveling, never resting. I've accumulated a fine amount of goods, thanks to the worm's good fortune, so now I've come to pay my respects before his throne. It's his luck that has helped me, and if it is allowable I will offer my homage to him." The worm's servant opened the gates to the castle, and the caravan went inside.

Ardeshir quickly opened up his packages and handed over things worthy of the man's station. He set out a stall before the servants, opened the chests, and filled a goblet with wine. Those whose turn it was to feed the worm with milk and rice turned away from the wine, not wanting to get drunk at this time. Realizing this, Ardeshir stood up and said, "I have a huge amount of rice and milk, and if his keeper will allow it I shall be pleased to feed the worm for three days. This will give me a name in the world, and the worm's lucky star might look kindly on me. Drink wine with me for three days, and on the fourth, when the sun rises to illuminate the world, I'll make a fine shop here, even higher than your palace, and I'll ply my trade of buying and selling. In this way I'll increase my honor in the worm's eyes." With these words he got his wish; the keepers responded, "You can serve the wine." The donkey driver placed everything at their service, and began to serve the wine. Gradually they became drunk; those whom the worm had commanded were now commanded by wine. As soon as their tongues were fuddled, the king and the two young men brought out the cauldron and lead and made a fire. When it was time for the worm to be fed, its food was boiling lead. They saw its vermilion tongue, waiting to lap up the rice as it usually did. The young men poured the lead down its throat, and when its bowels split, its strength oozed away. A loud crack came from its throat, and the cistern where it lived and the whole town round about shook with the force of it. Ardeshir and the two young men attacked like the wind; they snatched up their maces, swords, and bows, and not one of the drunken servitors escaped from them alive. From the roof of the castle they sent up a column of smoke, as a signal to the army commander. Seeing it, a watchman ran to Shahrgir saying, "King Ardeshir is victorious." Immediately he led the army forward to join their king.

Ardeshir Kills Haftvad

When Haftvad heard what had happened he was frightened and confused. He hurried to the castle to retake it, but the king was already on its ramparts. All his efforts were useless: a lion stood on his city's walls. Shahrgir brought up the army like a mighty mountain, but his men hesitated and hung back. Ardeshir shouted down to them, "Come forward and fight, Shahrgir. If Haftvad escapes us, for all your efforts you'll have nothing in your fist but air. I fed the worm hot lead; his power is gone, his anger has melted away." When they heard the king's voice the Persian troops took heart, put on their metal helmets, and prepared for battle. The wind of war turned against the worm's forces: Haftvad was captured, and so was Shahuy, his eldest son and the commander of his troops. King Ardeshir came down from the battlements, and Shahrgir came forward to greet him on foot. He brought a horse caparisoned in gold, on which the triumphant king sat. He gave orders that two gibbets were to be set up on the lake shore, where the two malefactors were strung up alive; the sight of them broke the hearts of Ardeshir's enemies. Then Shahrgir stepped forward from the ranks of soldiers, and Haftvad and his son were killed in a rain of arrows. Ardeshir gave the town over to plunder, and the troops enriched themselves. Servants brought out whatever was valuable in the fortress and took everything to Khurreh-ye Ardeshir. A fire-temple was built in the province, and the festivals of Mehregan and Sadeh were celebrated there; the land was handed over to the two young men who had been Ardeshir's hosts when he fled from the area.

Ardeshir returned in triumph to Pars, and when the populace and flocks were settled again, he led his army to Khurreh-ye Ardeshir. He sent an army to Kerman to keep order in the area, under a man who was worthy to rule. And now that his enemies had been defeated, he took up residence in Ctesiphon.

ستيم جان ورا افريدين که از بد سگالان نشست آمين چو شاپور شاه بود گرد و بلند

سپاریم بدو تاج و تخت و سپاه که پهلوان چنین سبت شاپور شاه

سن این تخت را پایکار رویم همان از پدر یاد کار رویم

❧ THE REIGN OF ARDESHIR ❧

Ardeshir assumed the ivory throne in Baghdad and crowned himself there; with his sword belt, royal mace, and splendid palace, he was indistinguishable from Goshtasp, and from that time on people called him the King of Kings. After he had placed the crown on his head, he gave an address from the throne: "In this world my treasure is justice, and the world prospers through my efforts and good fortune. No one can take this treasure from me, since evil comes to those who do evil; if the world's God approves of my actions, he will not begrudge me mastery of this dark earth. From end to end the world is in my keeping, and my way is the path of justice. No one, whether he be a slave or a free man, must sleep uneasily because of my subordinates, or captains, or cavalry: my court is open to everyone, whether they wish me good or ill." The court called down blessings on him, saying, "May the earth prosper beneath your righteousness!" Then he sent armies in each direction, to persuade whatever chieftains who might oppose him to submit, or face conquest by the sword.

Ardeshir and the Daughter of Ardavan

When Ardeshir killed Ardavan and grasped the world in his fist, everyone, young and old, rejoiced, since Ardavan had acted tyrannically, and Ardeshir's justice would make the world flourish once again. Ardeshir married the dead king's daughter, hoping that she would reveal to him where her father's treasure was hidden. Two of Ardavan's sons were in India, enduring both good and bad fortune together. Two more were in Ardeshir's prisons, their hearts filled with grief, their eyes with tears. The oldest, who was in India, was called Bahman. When he saw that he had lost the whole kingdom, he found a young persuasive messenger, and gave him a package filled with poison. He said, "Go to my sister and say,

> 'Don't look for kindness from an enemy;
> You have two brothers suffering grievously

In India, and two more brothers here
Chained in the dungeons of King Ardeshir—
And can you think that heaven will approve
Of how you're now denying them your love?
But if you would be Persia's queen, and live
Admired by all brave men, contrive to give
—In one dose—this fell poison that I bring
From India, to your husband and your king.'"

The envoy arrived at nightfall and gave his message to the princess. She felt pity for her brothers, and her face glowed with sympathy for their plight. Anxiously she took the precious poison, planning to do what her brother desired.

And so it happened that, when Ardeshir had spent half of one day hunting wild asses with his arrows, he returned to the palace and Ardavan's daughter ran to his side. She brought him a goblet encrusted with topazes in which she had mixed cold water with sugar and wheatmeal and the poison, hoping to bring about the end her brother Bahman desired. But as Ardeshir took the cup from her, it fell from his hand and smashed on the ground. The princess trembled apprehensively and felt her heart fail within her. Her agitation aroused the king's suspicions, and he wondered what fate the turning heavens had in store for him. He had a servant bring four domestic hens and watched them carefully as they pecked up the wheatmeal. When he saw that as soon as they ate the food they fell down dead his suspicions were confirmed. He summoned his chief priest and asked him, "If you were to assign a throne to your enemy, and he became so intoxicated by your kindness that he gratuitously made an attempt on your life, what punishment would you impose on him? What would be the medicine to cure such folly?" The man's answer was, "If a subject stretches out his hand against the king, his head must be severed for this sin; and anyone who advises otherwise should be ignored." The king said, "Take Ardavan's daughter and divide her body from her soul."

Trembling and with guilt in her heart, Ardavan's daughter left the audience chamber with the priest. She said to him, "You are a wise man and know that your days and mine will both come to an end. If you must kill me, know that I am carrying Ardeshir's child. If indeed I'm worthy of the gallows and deserve to have my blood spilled, wait until this child is born, and then do as the king has ordered." The shrewd priest retraced his steps and told Ardeshir what she had said. But the king's answer was, "Don't listen to anything she has to say; take a rope and hang her for her crime."

The Birth of Ardeshir's Son, Shapur

The priest said in his heart, "It's an evil day when the king gives such an order: young and old, we are all destined for death, and Ardeshir has no son to his name. So that even if he lives for many years, when he dies his throne will be inherited by his enemies. It would be best if I were to act chivalrously and make something good come from this sad state of affairs. I will deliver this woman from death, and it may be that I can make the king regret his order. And if not, when her child is born will be the time to attend to his commands. This is not a matter to take lightly, and it is better that I act prudently rather than rashly."

He had a place set aside for the princess in his palace and looked after her as if she were his own flesh and blood. He told his wife, "I shall not be content if even so much as a breath of wind touches her." Then he reflected that there are enemies everywhere, and that all men are thought well of by some and badly by others. He said to himself, "I must arrange matters so that those who'd like to slander me won't be able to pour filthy water into my stream." He went into his house and there cut off his testicles; he then cauterized the wound, applied a salve to it, and bound it up. Pallid and groaning with pain, he quickly put the testicles in salt and placed them in a round jeweler's box, which he immediately sealed. He came into the throne room, carrying the sealed box, and said, "I ask that the king entrust this to his treasurer." The date was written on the box, so that there could be no argument about when this had occurred.

When the time for the princess's confinement came, the priest kept everything secret, so that even the winds of heaven knew nothing of what was happening. Ardavan's daughter gave birth to a splendid son who seemed every inch a royal child. The priest kept visitors away from his house and had the boy named Shapur. He hid him away for seven years, and the boy grew into a fine young prince, endowed with *farr* and a noble stature.

Then one day the priest, who was also Ardeshir's vizier, saw tears in his sovereign's eyes, and said to him, "May the king prosper, and his thoughts nourish his soul! You have achieved your heart's desire in this world and driven your enemies back from the throne: now is a time for rejoicing and to drink wine, not for troublesome thoughts. The seven climes of the earth are yours, and the world flourishes because of your justice." The king answered, "My priest, your heart is sincere and you are privy to all my secrets. My sword has civilized the world; sorrow, pain, and evil have been driven away: But I am now fifty-one years old, my musky hair has turned white as camphor, and the roses of my cheeks are faded. I need a son, standing here in front of me, someone who charms the world, who is strong and a leader of men. A father without a son is like a son without a father: no stranger will embrace him as

his own. After I am gone, my crown and treasure will belong to my enemies; my life's profit will be only dust and sorrow."

The old priest said in his heart, "The day to speak has come," and he addressed the king, "Your majesty, protector of the weak, chivalrous, enlightened, and mighty, if you will now guarantee that my life is safe, I will take this sorrow away from you." The king replied, "You are a wise man; why should you fear for your life? Tell me what you know, speak as much as you wish, what is finer than a wise man's words?" The vizier answered, "You have a jeweler's box in your treasurer's keeping; have it brought to us." The king ordered his treasurer to bring the box and said, "Give it back to him so that we can see what is in it, and whether it will enable me to live freed from anxiety."

The treasurer brought the box and handed it over. The king asked what was hidden under its seal, and the vizier answered, "My own warm blood is there, and my shameful parts, cut cleanly from my body. You gave Ardavan's daughter into my keeping, saying that you wanted her to be a lifeless corpse. I didn't kill her, because she was pregnant, and I feared God's judgment on me if I did. I disobeyed your orders, but at the same time I castrated myself so that no one could speak evilly of me and soak me in a sea of infamy. Now your son Shapur is seven years old: no other king has had such a son, he resembles the moon in the heavens. I named him Shapur, and may the heavens smile on your good fortune. His mother is with him and has brought the young prince up."

The king was astonished and brooded on this child. Finally he said to his vizier, "You have a good heart and pure thoughts; you have suffered much over this, and I would not have your suffering continue. Find a hundred boys of his age, and of the same stature, bearing, and appearance. Dress them all alike, and see there's no difference between them; then send them to the playing fields and have them play polo there. When the plain is filled with these handsome children, we'll see if my soul responds at the sight of my own boy: my heart will bear witness to the truth of what you've said, and acquaint me with my son."

Shapur Plays Polo and His Father Recognizes Him

At dawn the following day the vizier had a bevy of boys assembled on the playing fields, all dressed in the same way, and so similar in face and stature that one could not be told from another. The field was like a festival, and somewhere among the participants was the prince, Shapur. The ball was thrown down, and each of the children strove to outdo the others. As dawn broke Ardeshir arrived at the field, accompanied by his favorite courtiers. He stared at the scene before him and sighed, then pointed to the boys and said, "Is there an Ardeshir among them?" His vizier answered, "Your heart

will tell you which is your son." The king said to one of his servants, "Go and get possession of the ball with your polo stick; stay with the children and hit the ball toward me. Then we'll see which of them is no respecter of persons, which one is brave enough to come forward and strike the ball before my eyes, outrunning the others like a lion surrounded by horsemen. That one will certainly be my son, born of my line and loins."

The servant did as he was told and hit the ball so that it flew in front of the mounted children. They galloped after it as swiftly as arrows, but when it came close to Ardeshir, they hung back, hesitating; all except Shapur, who swept forward and struck the ball away from his father toward the waiting boys. Ardeshir felt his heart fill with happiness, like that of an old man who has regained his youth. The participants lifted Shapur up and passed him from hand to hand till he reached the king, who folded him in his embrace and called down blessings on him, kissing his head and eyes and face and saying,

> "A marvel such as you are cannot stay
> Concealed: I'd never hoped to see this day,
> Since in my heart I thought Shapur was dead
> But even if a man should lift his head
> Above the sun, he cannot turn aside
> The will of God, who humbles all our pride:
> And God has added to my sovereignty
> By giving my young son, Shapur, to me."

He called for jewels, coins, and rubies, and scattered gold, gems, musk, and ambergris over the boy till gold covered the crown of his head and his face was hidden by jewels. Ardeshir also scattered jewels over his vizier, seated him on a golden throne, and gave him beautiful artifacts to adorn his castle. He had Ardavan's daughter come before him, happily and serenely; he pardoned all her past sins and cleansed the stain of guilt from her lovely face. He summoned teachers skilled in the various branches of knowledge to his city, where they taught Shapur how to write in Pahlavi, how to hold a royal audience, how to ride into battle and confront his enemies, the protocols of wine drinking, banquets, and kingly generosity, and how to draw up his army and conduct himself on the day of battle. Ardeshir then had the design of his coins changed, both the gold coins and those of lesser value: on one side was inscribed King Ardeshir, and on the other the name of his vizier, who was honored in this way. The king's letters were signed in the same manner, and the vizier was given the king's seal and authority. Ardeshir distributed wealth to the poor who lived by the labor of their hands, and in a waste place he built the city of Jondeshapur, by which name he always referred to the area.

Ardeshir Asks the Indian Keyd to Predict His Future

When Shapur had grown into a youth as elegant as a tall cypress tree, Ardeshir feared that someone might cast the evil eye on him; the two were never separated, and Shapur was like another advisor and vizier to his father. But Ardeshir was constantly harassed by wars; he could not spend his time in pleasure because as soon as he had dealt with one enemy another would raise his head elsewhere. He said, "I ask God to tell me what is hidden and what is plain, and whether I can rid the world of my enemies." His wise vizier said to him, "I will send someone to Keyd, who is a seeker after knowledge and a help in such matters. He knows the stars in the high heavens, the way to sovereignty, and the path to ruin. If you are to rule the seven climes with no rival, he will be able to foresee this. He can explain things to you one by one, without any difficulty, and he will not ask you for payment for his answers."

Ardeshir chose a fine, intelligent young man as a messenger. He prepared a gift of horses, cash, and silk for the Indian sage, and said to the young envoy, "Go to this knowledgeable man and say to him, 'Fortunate and inquiring as you are, look at the stars and tell me when I can rest from war and bring these provinces under my control. If this is to happen, show me how to plan for such a day, and if it is not to be, I'll give up the struggle and stop spending my wealth needlessly.'" The envoy took the gifts to Keyd and told him the secrets of Ardeshir's heart. Keyd questioned him and grew pensive;

then he applied himself to his science, consulting the stars, his astronomical tables, and his astrolabe, to see what the heavens held of comfort and profit, and of pain and loss. He said to the envoy, "I have consulted the stars, as they affect Iran and the king. If he will join his line to that of Mehrak-e Nushzad, he will rule in peace and there will be no need for him to send out armies everywhere. His wealth will increase and his troubles will decrease. Go now, and ignore the enmity between these families. If he does as I have suggested, Iran will flourish and he will achieve all that he desires." Then Keyd gave the envoy a gift and added, "Don't keep back anything I've said. If he follows what I've said the high heavens will smile on him."

The envoy returned to Ardeshir and reported what he had been told. But Ardeshir heard his words with pain in his heart and his face turned sallow with grief. He said to the envoy, "May I never set eyes on any of Mehrak's family. It would be bringing an enemy off the street into my house, someone intent on destroying me and my people. And then what would my profit be from all the wealth I have spent, all the armies I have dispatched, all the trials I have undergone? Mehrak has one daughter, no more, though no one has ever seen her. I'll have her sought for in Rum, China, India, and Taraz, and when I find her I'll have her burned alive; I'll make the dust itself weep for her sorrows."

He sent horsemen, under the command of an ambitious warrior, to Jahrom, where Mehrak's daughter was living, but when she heard of their approach she escaped from her father's house and hid herself away in a village. There the local headman treated her with respect.

> Now like a lovely cypress tree she grew;
> Wisdom was hers, and royal glory too—
> Her wondrous beauty was beyond compare,
> Unrivaled in that land, or anywhere.

Shapur Marries Mehrak's Daughter

Listen now to what happened between Mehrak's daughter and the valiant warrior Shapur. The king's prosperity flourished, and one day as dawn broke he set out to hunt, taking his son Shapur with him. The horsemen rode forward, clearing the plain of game, and then there came into view a distant village filled with gardens, open spaces, villas, and fine buildings. Shapur rode to the village and dismounted before the headman's house. There was a lovely garden there, and a young woman, splendid as the moon, came into that green courtyard. She let a bucket down into the well and then caught sight of Shapur. She greeted him respectfully, saying, "May the prince live happily for many years, with laughter on his lips, and safe from the world's harm. Your mount must be thirsty, and generally the water in this village is brackish, but the water from this well is cold and sweet; let me draw some for you."

Shapur replied, "Your face is so radiant, why should you be put to such trouble? I have servants enough with me to draw the water." The young woman turned away and sat at a distance, beside the garden's watercourse. Shapur ordered one of his attendants to draw the bucket up from the well; the man ran forward and strained at the rope, but the full bucket was too heavy to raise, and the man's face frowned with the effort. Shapur came forward and muttered impatiently at him, "You haven't half the strength of a woman! Wasn't a woman letting this bucket down into the well and drawing it up, and you're struggling and straining and begging for help?" He snatched the rope from the man's hand and started to raise the bucket himself, but when he saw what an effort it required he congratulated the girl, and said, "Anyone who can lift a bucket this heavy must come from a noble background!" When he had raised the bucket, she came forward and said, "May you live forever, prosperous and guided by wisdom. By the grace of Ardeshir's son, Shapur, the water in this well will surely turn to milk."

Shapur said to this courteous girl, "And how do you know that I'm Shapur?" She replied, "I have heard righteous men say often enough,

> 'Prince Shapur is a noble cypress tree,
> A River Nile of generosity,
> A mammoth in his strength—in everything
> The image of his father and his king.'"

Shapur said to her, "You are a beautiful young woman, now answer my questions truthfully. Tell me what your lineage is, because there are signs of royalty in your face." She replied, "I'm the headman's child, that's why I'm so pretty and so strong." He answered, "A lie to a prince never prospers. No peasant ever had a daughter as lovely and as bewitching as you are." She said, "O prince, when I have a guarantee that my life is not in danger from the anger of the King of Kings, I shall tell you about my lineage." The prince replied, "In a garden like this, anger between friends doesn't spring up from the grass. Tell me what you have to say, and have no fear of me in your heart, nor of our king, who is a just man." She answered, "In all honesty then, I am the daughter of Mehrak-e Nushzad. A wise courtier of his brought me here and gave me to the headman for safekeeping. He is a good man, and out of fear of the king I became his servant and draw water for him."

Shapur scoured the village until the headman stood before him, and said: "Give this beautiful young woman to me in marriage, and may you be our witness." The man did as he was ordered and married them according to the fire worshippers' rites.

Mehrak's Daughter Gives Birth to Hormozd, the Son of Shapur

After nine months this beautiful woman gave birth to a fine son. From his appearance you would have said that he was Esfandyar, or Ardeshir. Shapur named him Hormozd, and the boy stood out like a cypress emerging from a swamp. After seven years Hormozd had no equal, but he was kept hidden from everyone and was not allowed out to play.

King Ardeshir went for a week's hunting, and Shapur accompanied him. Hormozd was tired of his lessons, and he rode out onto the king's main square, a bow in one hand and two arrows in the other, and met up with a group of children who were playing polo there. Just at that moment Ardeshir and his entourage returned from the hunt, and a child struck the ball so hard that it came to rest close to the king; the children hung back, and none of them ran forward to retrieve it. But Hormozd dashed out of the group and snatched up the ball from in front of his grandfather, so that all the soldiers and courtiers began gossiping about him. Then the boy let out a great shout of triumph, which astonished the king, who turned to his chief priest and said, "Find out which family that boy belongs to."

The priest made inquiries, but no one knew anything, or if they did they preferred to remain silent. So the king said, "Pick him up out of the dirt and bring him to me." The priest went and lifted the boy up and brought him to the king, who said, "You're a fine little man, and who are we to say your family is?" The boy felt no fear and said loudly, "My name and family should not be hidden. I'm Shapur's son, as he is your son, and my mother is from Mehrak's family."

The king was astonished at the workings of the world; he laughed and then grew pensive. He gave orders that Shapur appear before him, and he questioned him thoroughly. Shapur was afraid; his heart quaked and his face turned pale. But Ardeshir smiled at his fear and said, "Don't hide your boy away; see that he has everything he's entitled to, so that men say 'He is the prince's son.'" Shapur replied, "May your reign be long and prosperous. He is my child, his name is Hormozd, and he is like a tulip among weeds. I was hiding him from your majesty only until he could show his mettle. He is Mehrak's daughter's boy, and I'm quite certain that he is my son." Then he described the meeting at the well and what had happened there, and during his account the king asked him various questions. The king was happy to hear the tale and went off contentedly to his palace, accompanied by his vizier. He took Hormozd along with him, carrying him in his arms, and in the throne room he had a place prepared for the boy, and gave him a royal torque and a golden crown. They poured gold coins and jewels over the little boy until the pile mounted over his head, and then his grandfather plucked him from the heap, which was distributed to the poor. Ardeshir gave his grandson other valuables, and the fire temple and the rooms in the palace where the New Year's and Sadeh celebrations were held were hung with brocade.

A hall was prepared for festivities; the country's nobility gathered there, and they were entertained by musicians. Then Ardeshir addressed them: "The words of a wise astrologer cannot be gainsaid. The Indian Keyd told me that neither I, nor this country, nor my crown, throne, or army would enjoy good fortune unless my lineage were joined to that of Mehrak-e Nushzad. Now eight years have passed and the heavens have turned as we would wish: that is, since Shapur sought his happiness with Mehrak's daughter, he has seen nothing but what he desires from the world. The world's seven climes are under my command, and my heart has received from the heavens all it has desired." From this time on the king's functionaries referred to him as the King of Kings.

Ardeshir's Reforms

Listen now to Ardeshir's wisdom, and learn of all his reforms one by one. His efforts resulted in new laws, and he made everyone the beneficiary of his benevolence and justice. To assure that the court had sufficient warriors, he sent messengers everywhere to proclaim that whoever had a son should not allow him to grow up without military training: young men should learn how to ride in battle, and how to use the mace and bow. When a young man acquired manliness by such exercises and was skillful in

all areas of warfare, he was to come to the king's court, where his name would be inscribed in a muster roll, and he would be assigned quarters. When war was declared the young warriors would ride out with a seasoned champion, and each thousand of them would be accompanied by someone who would report back to the king on who fought weakly and unsatisfactorily, as well as on who distinguished himself in battle. Then their sovereign would prepare robes of honor and presents for those who had fought well, while those who had been unskillful in battle were dismissed from his service. These reforms increased the size of his army until it was greater than any the stars had ever looked down on. He raised above the mass of men those who were skilled in strategy, and proclaimed, "Let anyone who seeks to satisfy the king, who has soaked the ground in his enemies' blood, come forward and receive a royal robe from me, and his name will be remembered in the world." So his armies subdued the earth; he was the shepherd, and his warriors were his flock.

For the functioning of his government he chose able men and did not entrust work to the ignorant. He chose scribes who paid attention to words and writing and who were skillful in the smallest details of their profession, and when one of them distinguished himself, the king increased his salary. Anyone who was not such a good scribe, or who was lacking in intelligence, could not become a member of Ardeshir's administration. Such men were employed by underlings, while the best scribes were reserved for the king's divan. Ardeshir knew the value of his civil servants, and when he saw a scribe at the court he would say, "A scribe who gathers revenue and diminishes trouble by his efforts is the means by which the country, its needy subjects, and its army prosper; scribes are like the sinews of my soul, they are the unseen rulers of the kingdom."

When an administrator set out for a province, the king advised him, "Despise wealth, and see that you do not sell men for its sake; remember that this fleeting world passes for all men. Seek justice and honor always, and may greed and folly stay far away from you. Take none of your family and dependents with you: the entourage I provide you with will be sufficient. Give money to the poor every month, but give nothing to those who harbor malevolent thoughts. If your justice makes the province flourish, you can remain there and rejoice in your just rule. But if a single poor man sleeps in fear, this means that you have sold a soul for the sake of gold and silver."

Whoever came to the king's court, either on official business or to demand justice, was questioned by the king's officers about the governor of his province. He was asked whether the man administered the province justly or whether he was greedy for wealth, and who lay down in fear because of him. He was also asked about who the wise men of his district were, and whether there were men there who were kept in obscurity by their poverty. He was questioned too as to who was worthy of the king's notice, whether they were old, experienced men, or men distinguished by their honorable behavior. The king would say, "No one should profit from my labors and wealth unless they are knowledgeable men who are willing to learn; what is finer than an old man filled with wisdom?"

When his army set out for war, Ardeshir made wisdom his companion and acted with caution and foresight. He selected a wise and knowledgeable scribe as an envoy and entrusted him with a letter that was polite and conciliatory, so that war would not be declared unjustly. The messenger would go to the enemy to find out his secret intentions, and if the opposing leader seemed to be a wise man who was contemptuous of evil's efforts, he would be rewarded with a royal robe of honor, as well as with a charter and earrings as a sign of his authority. But if his head was filled with rebellion, his heart with hatred, and his entrails with bloodlust, Ardeshir would distribute money to the army, so that there were no malcontents in the ranks. Then he chose a renowned warrior, someone sagacious, alert, and calm, as their commander. He also sent a scribe with his own entourage to accompany the army, to keep an eye on any injustices the soldiers might commit. He had someone whose voice could carry for two miles mounted on an elephant, and this herald would proclaim, "Warriors ready for war, all of you who have any heart, or reputation, or sense of shame: know that neither the poor nor the rich must suffer because of you. At every stage of your journey you must pay for what you eat and show respect to those who serve you; anyone who fears God will not steal others' property. Any man who turns his back on the enemy will suffer a harsh fate: either he will dig his own grave with his nails or chains will wear away his body. His name will be stricken from the muster roll; his food will be dirt and he will crawl in the dust."

To the commander he said, "Do not act feebly, but don't be precipitate and rash either. Keep your elephants in the army's vanguard, and send out scouts to a distance of four miles. When the day for battle comes you must go around the whole army explaining to your soldiers why they are fighting, and tell them that if they can bring down a hundred of the enemy's horses for every one of ours (and even a hundred for one is too few), then they will all, young and old, receive robes of honor from Ardeshir for their service. When the battle begins in earnest and the cavalry charges from both sides, no matter how many men you have, see that the center of the army is not abandoned. Try to manage things so that your left and right flanks attack together, but the center is to remain firm and no one there is to leave his post. After you are victorious, shed no one's blood, because if men have to flee from you, they will hate you the more. If anyone from the enemy's ranks asks for quarter, grant it to him, and put aside any desires for vengeance.

"If you see the enemies' backs, don't dash after them but stay where you are; you shouldn't disregard the possibility of ambush, and your army should remain on the battlefield. When you are safe from the enemy, don't listen to anyone's advice, but distribute booty to those who fought well and who bravely risked their sweet lives. Immediately bring any prisoners you take to my court, and I shall build a town for them in the provinces, on what was formerly thorny wasteland. If you wish to live without pain and trouble, do not deviate from this advice, and in victory see that you turn to God, for he is your only true guide."

If an envoy came from another land, whether from the Turks, the Greeks, or other peoples, the lord of the marches there was informed of his approach and he did not treat this as an unimportant matter. He had places prepared along the envoy's route, and these were stocked with provisions, clothes, and carpets. Once the local governor was apprised of why the envoy was coming to see the king, he dispatched a scribe on a noble mount to Ardeshir, so that an escort could be sent to welcome the envoy. The king prepared a throne for his arrival, and servants stood on either side of the approachway, with their garments embroidered in gold. The king summoned the envoy into his presence and seated him on a throne close by, then he questioned him about himself, the good and bad of his life, and his name and title. He asked him also about the justice and injustice he had witnessed, and about his country, its customs, king, and army. He had the envoy conducted to his quarters with due ceremony, and everything he

could need was provided for. The visitor feasted and drank wine with the king, and he was seated on a golden throne, and the king took him hunting, together with an innumerable entourage. At his departure he was given a fitting farewell, and was presented with a royal robe of honor.

Ardeshir sent wise and benevolent priests about his kingdom, so that they could establish cities and distribute wealth by providing food and shelter for those who had no houses, or were destitute and had fallen on hard times; and in this way the number of his subjects increased.

> *In public and in private his good name*
> *Filled all the world with its illustrious fame;*
> *No king like him had ever ruled, and when*
> *He died his like was never seen again.*
> *I seek to make his name live on—may he*
> *Know happiness for all eternity.*

He talked in secret with many men, and men reported back to him from everywhere. When he heard of someone worthy who had lost his wealth, he helped him as was appropriate, so that the man's days did not remain dark for long: he gave him land and a place to live, servants and subjects, and everything that was fitting. All this was done in secret, without anyone else being aware of it. He gave goods to those who were indigent, and placed children with teachers, caring for them as if they were from his own family; in every street there was a school and a fire-temple. He let no one remain in want, and he kept all this generosity carefully hidden. At dawn he walked in the open spaces of the town, and people came to him asking for justice; in his judgments he tried to harm no one and made no distinction between the least of his subjects and the children of his allies. His justice made the world flourish and rejoiced his subjects' hearts.

Where there were ruins, or where drought had dried up the water-courses, he remitted the taxes of that area; where the peasants were impoverished and faced death, his treasury provided them with animals and tools; he would not allow them to be swept away by disaster.

Ardeshir Bestows the Kingdom on Shapur

When Ardeshir had lived for seventy-eight years he grew sick. He summoned Shapur and gave him extensive advice on how to rule. He knew that he was close to death, and that the green leaves of his life would soon turn yellow. He said to his son, "Pay close attention to what I have to say, and as for those who would oppose you consider their words as so much wind. Act according to my words, since I assume you can distinguish what is valuable from what is worthless. I have ordered the world with the sword of justice, and respected the rank of those who are wellborn. When I had put the world on a sound footing, my territories increased, but my life drew toward its close. And as I have endured countless sorrows, and in the midst of them accumulated my wealth, so there is sorrow and happiness facing you, times of retrenchment and times of triumph. This is the way of the turning world, bringing you sometimes pain and sometimes pleasure. Fortune is sometimes like an unbroken horse, suddenly giving you a harsh ride when you are enjoying yourself; and sometimes she is a well-trained mount, lifting her head proudly, trotting forward as she should. But you should know, my son, that this deceitful world will not give you pleasure without pain, and if you wish your days not to end badly look after both your body and your spirit.

"When a king respects religion, religion and royalty become as brothers: religion has no stability without the royal throne, royalty cannot survive without religion. They are two brocades interwoven with one another by wisdom. Religion cannot do without the king, and the king will not be respected without religion; they are guardians of one another, and you could say that they live together beneath one tent. The former cannot function without the latter, nor the latter without the former; we see them as two companions united in doing good. A religious man is lord of wisdom and sense, and he inherits this world and the world to come; when a king is religion's guardian, you can only call these two brothers. But if a religious man is resentful of the king, you should beware of calling him righteous: any man who speaks against a just king should not be considered as truly religious. As a praiseworthy sage once said, 'When we look closely we see that religion is the pith of justice.'

"The throne is threatened by three things. First if the king is unjust; next, if he promotes worthless men over those who are accomplished; third, if he uses his wealth for his own glory and is always trying to increase his income. Turn toward generosity, and follow religion and wisdom so that no lie can make any headway with you. A lie blackens a king's face, so that his sovereignty lacks all luster. See that you don't hoard your wealth, because this only brings trouble: if a king is greedy for gold, he harms his subjects, since no matter how hard the peasant works, his wealth becomes the king's, whereas a good king is the guardian of his subjects' wealth, so that their efforts bear fruit. Try to control your anger, and when men transgress, be generous and close your eyes. If you are angry, you will regret it; if men repent, have the balm of mercy ready. Whenever a king is quick tempered wise men think of him as a lightweight. It is ugly for a king to have malevolent desires, and you should fill your heart with kindness; and if you ever let fear into your heart, those who wish you ill will confuse all your intentions.

"Don't hold back from being generous, and as far as you can, my son, know what things are worth. You should realize that sovereignty belongs to the king whose generosity encompasses the cosmos. Sometimes the royal office brings sorrow, and then the king should turn to his counselors and priests, asking them what is just and what is unjust, and preserving their answers in his heart. On the days when you go out with your hunting cheetahs, see that you don't play two games at once: riding out and hunting don't mix with wine drinking and banquets, since the body becomes heavy when you drink wine. The nobility know this nostrum. And if an enemy should appear, then both drinking and hunting must be set aside in favor of distributing money, preparing arms, and summoning troops from the provinces. Don't put off until tomorrow what must be done today, and don't promote bad advisors to high office.

"Don't look for righteousness in the hearts of vulgar folk, your search will be a waste of time; and if they speak ill of someone, ignore their calumnies. There's no making head nor tail of someone who loves neither his God nor his king. This is how the common people are, but may you be endowed with wisdom. Beware of those who have an evil nature, and pass your secrets on to no one, for your confidant will have his own friends and confidants, and your words will soon be everywhere. When your secrets are known to the nation, wise men's hearts will lose all respect for you. You'll be angry then, and even if they thought you wise before, people will say you have a trivial nature.

"Don't pay attention to reports of faults in other people, since the person who finds fault in this way will find fault with you too, and if passion overcomes reason, the wise will not think of you as human. A king should be wise and benevolent toward everyone, and God forbid that a quarrelsome man who delights in arguments and confrontation should have any place near you or be your guide. If you wish those who have noble minds to praise you, you must put aside all anger and thoughts of vengeance when you become king. You should not talk too much, and you should not make a show of your goodness. Listen to others' words, consider which you find pleasing, and remember the best of them. Weigh your words well when you speak to educated men, and welcome them politely and with smiles. Don't despise the petitions of the poor, and don't promote to high rank people who have an evil nature. If a man repents of his sins, forgive him and put aside your anger against him. Always be someone who dispenses justice, and who looks after his subjects, since a man who is generous and patient is blessed.

"When your enemies are afraid of you they will flatter you, but you should prepare your army and have the kettle drums made ready. Attack when your enemy is trying to avoid a fight and comes weak to the battlefield.

But when he sues for peace and you can see no deceit in his heart, then demand tribute from him and give up your desire for vengeance: act toward him in such a way that he saves face and honor is satisfied. Adorn your heart with knowledge and act on it as far as you are able to, since a man's value is measured by his knowledge. If you are generous, you will be loved, and your knowledge and justice will make your name illustrious.

"Keep your father's advice in mind, and pass it on to your own son. When I hand over power to my son I do so having injured no one in the world; see that you do not ignore my words or dismiss what I have to say to you. Follow your father's advice, act well, and then you can think of evil as so much wind. Do not make my soul distraught, or plunge my lifeless body into the fire, and do not harm others, my son; do not seek out ways to torment people.

> "The realm that your descendants build will last
> Unharmed until five centuries have passed;
> But then the members of your clan will spurn
> My testament to you; proudly they'll turn
> Their heads away from knowledge, and despise
> The teachings of the just, preferring lies,
> Injustice, exploitation, cruelty
> To wise benevolence and loyalty.
> They will oppress their subjects and condemn
> As foolish simpletons God-fearing men:
> They'll wear the shirt of evil, and exult
> As worshippers of Ahriman's foul cult.
> Whatever I have bound they will release,
> The faith that I have purified will cease.
> My testament will be as naught, and all
> My realm will crumble into ruins then, and fall.

"I pray to God who knows all things visible and invisible that he protect you from all evil, and that all men of good repute be your allies. God and I both bless that man whose warp is justice and whose weft is wisdom, who will not break the testament I give, or try to convert my honey to bitter colocynth. Now forty years and two months have passed since I placed the royal crown on my head. I have founded six cities, which have pleasant air and are well-watered. One I call Khurreh-ye Ardeshir, and its winds would make an old man young again: Khuzestan was revived by founding this city. Now it is a well-watered province, filled with men and business. The name of the next town is Jondeshapur, a place that delights my chief priest. The next is Maysan by the Euphrates, a town filled with streams, livestock, and vegetation. Another is Barkeh-ye Ardeshir, a place of orchards, flower gardens and pools. Another is Ram-e Ardeshir, which I have joined by road to the province of Pars. The last is Hormozd-e Ardeshir, whose air is like musk and whose streams run with milk.

"Keep my soul happy by acting justly, and may your reign be a victorious one. I have borne many sorrows in this world, some known to others some unknown. Now I am ready for the tomb, and you must order my coffin and prepare my bier."

When he finished speaking, his good fortune darkened: alas now for his mind, his crown, and his throne. Happy is he who has not known greatness, and who does not have to leave a throne. You struggle and accumulate all kinds of goods, but neither men nor goods remain. Finally we are partners with the dust, and our cheeks are covered by a shroud.

Come, let us do good with our hands, and not give this unstable world over to evil.

> *That man who lifts a wine glass in his hand*
> *In memory of the kings who ruled this land*
> *Knows happiness: the toasts come thick and fast*
> *Until, content and tired, he sleeps at last.*
> *Tell us of Shapur's banquets now, explain*
> *To us the story of this prince's reign.*

THE REIGN OF SHAPUR, THE SON OF ARDESHIR

When Shapur sat on the throne of justice and placed the royal crown on his head, the priests and nobles of the country gathered before him, and he addressed them: "My wise counselors, I am the son of the illustrious King Ardeshir, hear my commands and do not swerve aside from loyalty to me. Live content with your good name and have nothing to do with malevolent troublemakers. Only those who are lacking in sense will covet others' wealth. My benevolence toward you exceeds that radiated by the stars. I shall keep Ardeshir's ordinances in effect with you, asking for no more than a thirtieth of landowners' incomes, and that only so that I can provide in some small way for my army. Goodness is my eternal treasure, bravery and chivalry are the foundations of my kingdom; I have no need of others' possessions, since this desire is what turns men into enemies. All of you are free to visit me at any time, and I shall treat all who wish me well with affection."

His nobles and subjects stood and acclaimed Shapur as king: they poured emeralds over his crown and called down blessings on his head.

Shapur's War against Rome

News spread that the throne was left idle, that the wise King Ardeshir had died, leaving his wealth and crown to Shapur. Lamentation arose from every quarter, and Qaydafeh, in the Roman provinces, ceased to send tribute. When Shapur heard of this he readied his army, with its drums and banners, for war. Under the leadership of a brave and capable commander they made a quick march, with virtually no baggage, as far as Altouyaneh. The dust of the army that marched out to oppose them from Qaydafeh obscured the sun, and it was joined by a force from Altouyaneh under the leadership of Baranush, a fine horseman who was highly regarded by the Romans.

When the din of drums arose from the opposing camps, Baranush advanced to lead the Roman forces, and from the Persian side a brave warrior called Gorzasp took the offensive. Drums and trumpets were sounded on each side, and the new Persian king, stationed in the center of his troops, felt the thrill of battle. There was such a wailing of trumpets and clashing of Indian bells that the moon and the vault of the heavens shook; there were war drums strapped to the elephants, and their thundering noise carried for two miles. The earth trembled, dust swirled, lances glittered like fire, and the sky seemed to rain down stars. Sick at heart and sorely wounded, Baranush was captured in the midst of his men; three thousand Romans were killed at the Battle of Altouyaneh, and one thousand six hundred were taken prisoner. Their warriors' hearts were filled with despair.

The Roman emperor sent an envoy to Shapur, saying "How much blood will you shed before God, for the sake of money? What excuse can you bring for such behavior on the Day of Judgment? We will send the tribute as before, so that no further ills befall us, and along with the tribute I will also send you a number of hostages, people of my own family. But you should then evacuate Altouyaneh, and if you do I will send whatever further gifts you desire."

Shapur waited until the tribute had been delivered in ten ox skins, together with a thousand Roman young men and women as slaves and innumerable valuable brocades. He stayed for seven days in Altouyaneh, then left Roman territory and returned to Ahvaz. He built a city, with a great deal of effort and at great expense, completing it on the auspicious twenty-fifth of the month. The city was named Shapurgerd; it was a fine flourishing place, and the Roman captives were settled there. It formed the entryway to Khuzestan, and everyone entering the province from that direction had to pass through it. In addition, he built a splendid city in Pars, and another in Sistan, where there are abundant groves of date palms. This latter city had been begun by Ardeshir, and Shapur completed it. He also made the area around Kohandezh into a city, and to this day men say the town was built by Shapur's justice.

Wherever he went he took Baranush with him and paid attention to what he said. There was a river near Shushtar that was so wide no fish could swim across it. Shapur said to Baranush, "If you're an engineer, build a bridge here, so strong that when we pass away it will remain, as a sign to the wise. Make it a thousand cubits long. When you have done this, ask me for whatever treasure you desire. Use the knowledge of Roman savants to build monuments in this country; when you have made the bridge, which will lead to my palace, you can live as my guest, in happiness and safety, secure from evil and the wiles of Ahriman." Baranush set to work and completed the bridge, which was a thousand paces long, and Shapur hastened to cross it in state, passing from Shushtar to his palace.

Shapur's Advice to His Son, Hormozd

After thirty years and two months, the king's splendor and *farr* began to fade. He summoned Hormozd, and said to him,

> "Now you will blossom like an opening flower;
> Be wary as you wield imperial power,
> And pay attention to the words of those
> Who know how worldly fortune comes and goes.
> Don't hope for much from sovereignty; take heed
> Of all the ancient precepts of Jamshid:
> Be just in all your deeds—to nobles be
> Their splendor, to the poor their sanctuary.
> Be kind and openhanded, do not make
> A great noise for a minor setback's sake.
> These are the words I learned from Ardeshir,
> Remember all that I have told you here."

When he had finished speaking his face turned pale in death, and the young man grieved in his heart.

Ferdowsi gives brief accounts, omitted here, of the relatively uneventful reigns of Hormozd, Bahram Hormozd, Bahram Bahram, Bahram Bahramian, Nersi Bahram, Hormozd Nersi.

⚜ THE REIGN OF SHAPUR ZU'L AKTAF ⚜

After Hormozd the son of Nersi had reigned for nine years, the pomegranate color of his cheeks became like a yellow flower. His kingly mind felt the sorrows of death, and he died, leaving behind no son. This exalted and eloquent man passed from the fleeting world with a cry of anguish on his lips.

He was mourned for forty days; during this time the throne remained empty and lost its power and prestige, and the country's nobility were filled with anxiety. Then a priest discovered a beautiful young woman in the king's private quarters: her face was as splendid as the new moon, her cheeks glowed like tulips, her eyelashes were like daggers from Kabol, and her braided hair, gathered in a knot on the top of her head, was as curled and wavy as the script the Mongols use. This lovely young woman was pregnant, and the world rejoiced as soon as this became known. The celebrations, with feasting and music, lasted for forty days, and a royal couch was prepared for her. The crown was suspended above her belly, and gold coins were poured over it. Forty days passed, and a baby as splendid as the sun was born to her. The chief priest named him Shapur, and held festivities in his honor. The boy seemed blessed with wisdom and the royal *farr*. The gold-belted nobility poured gold over the boy's crown; he was suckled till he was satisfied and then wrapped in silk swaddling clothes. For forty days the baby lay on his father's royal throne, beneath the suspended crown.

A learned priest acted as regent; he was humble in his manner and ruled wisely and well. He managed the army and the king's wealth, and was an adornment to the throne and palace. This continued until the little prince was five years old. One evening the boy was sitting in Ctesiphon, and his wise regent was with him. As the sun set and night began to spread its purple cloak, a confused noise rose up from the direction of the river, and the prince asked his regent, "What's that shouting?" The man answered, "Blessed and fortunate king, this is the time when men who have shops or go out to work return home. The bridge over the Tigris is narrow, and the men crossing over it are so cramped for space that they're afraid of being jostled and squeezed, and that's why they shout out as loudly as a drum being beaten." Shapur said to his advisors, "My wise counselors, now you must build another bridge, so that there will be one for coming and one for going, and my subjects and soldiers will be able to pass back and forth without trouble. We must spend a lot of money from the treasury on this." The king's advisors were pleased that the young sapling had so soon produced green leaves. The regent had another bridge built, as the young prince had ordered, and his mother was overjoyed and arranged for tutors to begin teaching him. He learned so quickly that he soon surpassed his teachers in knowledge. When he was seven he learned to ride, both as a warrior and a polo player: at eight he learned the ceremonies of kingship, and he was careful to make his body and appearance worthy of his rank. He fixed his capital at Estakhr, following the example of his illustrious ancestors.

The Arab Tayer Captures Nersi's Daughter, and Shapur Attacks

When Shapur had been king for some time, the lionhearted warrior Tayer, a chieftain of the Ghassanid tribe, gathered a huge army together from Roman territories, Qadesiya, Bahrain, Kurdistan, and Pars, and attacked the outskirts of Ctesiphon. No one could resist his forces, and they plundered the whole area. A daughter of King Nersi, named Nobahar, was living there, and Tayer attacked her palace, while the whole of Ctesiphon waited apprehensively. His ignorant, barbarous troops took her from the palace as a captive. For a year Nobahar lived, wretched and heartsick, with Tayer and then gave birth to his daughter, a lovely child who was the image of her grandfather, King Nersi, and indeed she seemed so worthy to rule that her father named her Malekeh [Queen].

Years passed and Shapur reached the age of twenty-six; he was a noble king, as splendid as the sun. He came out onto the plain, inspected his army, and chose twelve thousand warriors mounted on swift camels. The group set off, led by a hundred guides, with each man riding on a camel and leading a horse, in search of that ravening lion, the Ghassanid chief. When they found the enemy, they killed many of them, and seeing this, Tayer himself turned tail and fled. The din of blows and counterblows rose up;

the Persians captured innumerable prisoners, and the remnant of Tayer's people made their way to the Yemen. There they took refuge in a fortress, which soon filled with the wailing of men, women, and children. Shapur besieged them with such a mass of men that not an ant or a mosquito could have passed between them. The siege lasted for a month, and provisions began to run low in the fortress.

Tayer's Daughter, Malekeh, Falls in Love with Shapur

At dawn Shapur mounted his horse, wearing his black royal armor, and a shining black sash was tied about his helmet; he grasped his bow and rode forward impetuously. Malekeh looked down from the fortress walls and saw the warrior's sash and helmet: his cheeks were as pink as rose petals, his hair as black as musk, his face as ruddy as the sweet smelling blossoms of the Hyrcanian willow tree. All rest and sleep deserted that lovely young woman, and with her heart overflowing with love, she came to her nurse and said:

> *"This king who's come against us here to fight*
> *Shines like the sun itself; how could his might,*
> *His power, be something that I'd fail to see?*
> *I name him World, since he's the world to me.*
> *Take him a message now, and tell Shapur*
> *I welcome him, although he comes for war,*
> *And tell him that through Nersi we are kin,*
> *Descended from a common origin.*
> *Say that my promise to him is, 'If you*
> *Desire me you will have this fortress too.'"*

The nurse said, "I shall do as you have ordered, and bring you news of him." When night took possession of the world, and its army spread from sea to sea, when the plains darkened and the mountains seemed like indigo, and in the empyrean the stars flickered like thirty thousand suspended candles, the nurse set out, trembling with apprehension, her heart filled with anxiety lest Tayer learn of her movements. When she reached the entrance to Shapur's royal pavilion she said to one of the guards, "If you take me to the king I'll reward you with a diadem and a ring." The chamberlain ushered her into the king's presence. She prostrated herself, touching the ground with her eyelashes, and told him the words Malekeh had said to her. The king laughed in response, and in his joy gave the nurse a thousand gold coins, two armbands, a torque, a ring, and brocades from China and Barbary. Then he said, "Speak gently and at length to your lovely mistress. Tell her that I swear by the sun and moon, by the belt our priests wear, by Zoroaster himself, and by the royal crown, that she can have whatever she desires from me, even if to give it will harm my kingdom. Her ears will never hear harsh words from me, and I shall never try to escape her embraces. I swear by God that I will bestow treasures and troops and a crown and throne on her."

As soon as she had heard him out the nurse ran back to the fortress. There she told her mistress, who was as lovely as a silver cypress tree and whose face was as splendid as the shining moon, all she had heard. She said that now Venus would mate with the sun itself, and she described Shapur's stature and appearance, and how the meeting had gone.

Malekeh Delivers Tayer's Fortress to Shapur; Tayer Is Killed

When the sun showed its crown in the east and turned the ground that had been as dark as teak the color of yellow roses, Malekeh took from the castle's treasurer the keys to where the victuals and amphorae of wine were kept. She sent food and wine, together with scents made from narcissi and fenugreek, to the nobles and warriors in the fortress. Then she called the wine steward to her and spoke to him kindly and carefully: "Tonight see that you serve Tayer unmixed wine: keep him and his men plied with wine till they are drunk and fall asleep." The steward replied: "I am your slave; it is by your commands that I live in this world."

When the sun turned yellow in the west, and night was hard on its heels urging it onward, Tayer asked for a bowl of royal wine. First he toasted his Ghassanid kinsfolk and, by the time the first watch of the night was over Tayer was oblivious to the tumult around him. Then the castle's inhabitants made their way to their sleeping quarters, and Malekeh ordered her servants not to speak above a whisper. Secretly they opened the great door to the fortress.

King Shapur was watching, filled with impatience at the sounds of drunkenness that he could hear. Then seeing a candle glimmer through the open door, he said, "Good fortune is with us!" The beautiful Malekeh was spirited away to his tents, where he'd had a fine space prepared for her. A force of picked warriors was ready, together with a few horsemen. They entered the fortress and set about killing the defenders and looting its ancient treasures. More than a thousand sleeping, drunken soldiers were with Tayer in that fortress. Some woke in bewilderment, and in every part of the building they fought back; none turned tail out of fear, and the Persian king killed a number of them. Tayer was caught and pushed before the

king, running and naked, as a captive. The whole fortress and all its goods were now in Shapur's hands, and his enemies were his prisoners.

Night passed, and when the sun raised its golden crown above the horizon, a turquoise studded throne was ceremonially installed in the fortress, and Shapur held court there. Once the formal audience was over, Malekeh, as lovely as a flower that blossoms in the spring, came before him. She wore a crown of red rubies, and her glittering robes were made from Chinese cloth of gold. Then Tayer understood that the trick that had been played on him was her doing, and that his evil fortune was because of her. He said,

> *"You are a noble king, your majesty,*
> *Consider what my child has done to me!*
> *Be careful of her kindness—you should fear her,*
> *And watch for any strangers who come near her."*

But Shapur said to this contemptible man, "When you stole the king's daughter from her apartments, and shamed and humiliated her people, you rekindled old enmities that had died down." He gave orders that the executioner cut off Tayer's head, and that his body be burned. He forbade the Arab prisoners to speak to anyone; he removed their shoulder blades from their bodies, an act which astonished the world. From this time on the Arabs called him Shapur Zu'l Aktaf, which means Shapur, Lord of the Shoulders.

Then he returned to Pars, and all the world bowed down before him. So the heavens smiled on Shapur for a while, but then they showed him a quite different face.

Shapur Travels to Rome and the Emperor of Rome Has Him Sewn in an Ass's Skin

One day, despite his crown and wealth, Shapur felt oppressed by his existence. When three watches of the night had passed, he called for his astrologer, and asked him what would become of the royal throne, and to describe the good and evil days that lay ahead. The man shook off his sleep and brought an astrolabe; he looked in the house of Leo, the harbinger of victory and glory, to see whether misfortune threatened the king, or whether his favor with God would increase. When he had examined the signs he said, "O noble king, who rules the world and is pure of heart, a difficult and painful business lies ahead, and no one has dared warn you of this."

Shapur replied, "You are a knowledgeable man, and able to search out secrets. What can I do so that this will pass from me, and evil stars will not bring me to my knees?" The astrologer answered, "My lord, bravery and knowledge will not enable a man to evade the revolution of the heavens, no matter how wise or warlike he is. What is fated will surely happen, and we cannot fight against the turning of the sky." The king said, "May God be our refuge from all evil, for it is he who created the turning heavens, and all that is powerful or weak."

For a while Shapur ruled justly, and he remained prosperous and without troubles. Under his care all the provinces flourished, and seeing this he conceived a wish to travel to the west, to see whether the Roman emperor was worthy of the position he occupied, and to find out about his armies and wealth. He disclosed this secret plan to his vizier, who was a fine, sensible warrior, but told no one else, and added, "Rule this realm justly in my absence; your justice will bring you happiness."

Then he asked for ten camel caravans, each with its own leader, and loaded up thirty camels with jewels and gold coins. Carefully, he made his way toward Roman territory. Near Rome there was a small town, and he stopped there, at the house of a landowner, and asked for shelter. The owner warmly welcomed him, saying he had never had such a distinguished guest. The king ate and slept there for one night, and when he gave the owner a present, he again received the man's blessings. At dawn he loaded up his camels and set out quickly for the emperor's palace. There he greeted the chamberlain respectfully and gave him a present of cash. The man said, "Tell me who you are. You have the stature and air of a king." Shapur replied, "I'm a free Persian, my lord, and I've come from Jez as a merchant, bringing a caravan of silks and fine textiles. I've come to see if I can gain entrance to the emperor, so that I can present him with something valuable from my merchandise—jewels, or weapons for his army. If he'll accept some token from me, I'll be very happy and hand it over willingly. Then I can sell the rest of my goods for gold and silver, and I'll be under the emperor's protection, so I'll have nothing to fear. And I can buy what I need in Rome and then make my way back to Persia."

The old man got up from his seat by the palace doorway and went and told the emperor what he had heard. The emperor had the curtains drawn aside, and Shapur was brought into his presence. He made a fitting obeisance, and the emperor scrutinized him carefully, taking in his fine appearance and manner. He had wine and food brought, and the court was cleared of all but his counselors. But there was an Iranian there, a cruel, unjust man, who said to the emperor, "My lord, I've some news to tell you, in confidence. Listen: this fine merchant who's here selling silks for cash, I tell you he's none other than Shapur, the Persian King of Kings: he has the king's way of talking, he looks like him, and he has that aura of glory the Persian kings have."

When the emperor heard this, his mind darkened and his eyes clouded over: he signed to a guard to watch Shapur, but told no one else. Shapur became drunk; he stood up, and the emperor continued to stare at him.

Then the guard strode forward and seized hold of him, saying, "You are Sha-pur, Nersi's son; it's a wonder you show yourself here." They took him to the women's quarters, and bound his arms. They lit a candle in front of the drunk king, and by its light they sewed him into an ass's skin, saying as they did so, "This luckless fool gave up his throne for an ass's skin."

There was a small dark room nearby, and they threw the unfortunate man into that tiny space and locked the door. The emperor gave the key to the mistress of the palace and said to her, "Give him a little bread and water, and that should cool his greed. If he lives for a while, he'll realize what my throne and crown are worth, and he'll see that the Roman emperor's throne is no concern of anyone who is not of the imperial family." The emperor's wife locked the doors and retired to her own part of the palace. There was a beautiful serving woman whom she had chosen as her subordinate and

treasurer, who was Persian by descent and who remembered her family's former generations, from father to father. To this woman the empress gave the key to the chamber where Shapur was kept. That same day the emperor led his troops across the border with Persia, while Shapur languished in the ass's skin.

As the Roman troops approached the frontier with Iran, they drew their swords for battle. The Persians had no one to lead them, and the Romans carried off numerous captives. Iran became depopulated and bereft of wealth: neither men, women nor children remained, and the Persian army had no news of whether Shapur was dead or alive. The population fled before the Roman armies, and the land emptied of its inhabitants. Innumerable Persians became Christians, and the land surrendered itself to their bishops.

The Empress's Servant Frees Shapur from the Ass's Skin

So conditions continued for a while, with Persia's army in disarray, and Shapur imprisoned and watched constantly. Because she was of Persian descent, the empress's servant was not happy to see Shapur still sewed in the ass's skin, and day and night she wept for him.

> One day she said to him, "O handsome youth,
> Who are you? Have no fear now, tell the truth.
> Sewn in that skin your slender form can find
> No bodily content or peace of mind:
> You were a cypress in your elegance,
> Your face the full moon in its radiance,
> Your hair a musky crown—and now you've grown
> So bent and thin you seem mere skin and bone.
> My heart's tormented for you, day and night
> My eyes weep tears for your horrific plight.
> What can you hope for now? Why keep from me
> The secret hiding your identity?"

Shapur said to her, "If you feel any love for me, I ask that you will remember my sufferings and hardships, and that you swear that never will the least of what I say to you reach my enemies; then I will tell you truthfully what you have asked." The maidservant swore by the seventy twists in a priest's belt, by the soul of Jesus and his sufferings on the cross, and by the lord of Iran that she would neither tell anyone his secret, nor seek to worsen his situation in any way. Then Shapur told her all that he'd kept from her and added, "If you do what I say and keep my secret in your heart, your head will be lifted above that of all other women, and the world will be at your feet. When it's time to bring me bread, stealthily bring warm milk, and with it macerate this ass's hide, which is going to be notorious throughout the world and will be remembered by the wise long after I'm dead."

Quietly, undetected, the serving girl procured milk and heated it over a fire in a large dish shaped like a ship. Telling no one of what she was up to, she took the milk to Shapur. Two weeks passed, and finally the ass's skin became pliable enough for Shapur to emerge from it, his body covered in blood, his heart filled with pain. He said to the serving girl, "You are a pure-hearted and resourceful woman; now we must think hard and find some way to get away from this accursed city of Rome." She answered, "Tomorrow at dawn all the nobles here are going to gather together for a festival; there's a celebration going on, and everyone will be there—men, women, and children. When the empress leaves the city for the festivities, the palace will be empty and I'll find a way to save us; I'm not afraid of rumormongers. I'll gladly bring you two horses, two maces, a bow, and arrows."

The maid put her mind to the task and chose two fine horses from the stables; then she provided herself with a sword, maces, barding for the horses, armor, and an Indian helmet. She'd thought long and hard and prepared her heart for what had to be done, taking wisdom as her guide. When the sun set in the west, and night drew its dark veil over its head, King Shapur's soul was filled with anxiety, wondering what the maidservant would do the next morning.

Shapur Flees from Rome to Iran

The sun rose in the house of Leo, day dawned, and sleep fled. As the people of the city went to enjoy their festival, the resourceful maidservant put her plan into action. The palace was now empty and in her hands, and she felt her heart was like a lion's, her grip like a leopard's. She brought two noble horses from the stables, fine armor for a knight, as well as a number of gold coins, pearls, rubies, and other valuables. By the time she had everything ready for their flight, night had fallen again. Then the two of them set out joyfully for Iran, riding day and night without pausing either to eat or sleep. When they reached Khuzestan their bodies and horses were weak with exhaustion, and they looked for somewhere they could dismount and rest. They saw a beautiful village before them; it was filled with gardens and open spaces for the inhabitants to gather and enjoy themselves. Tired out by their flight, they knocked at the door of an orchard. The owner, a kind hearted and hospitable man, came running, and as soon as he caught sight of the two, dressed in armor, helmeted, and holding lances, he said, "What kind of a greeting is this? Where have you sprung from at such an hour, and why are you all dressed up for a military expedition?"

Shapur replied, "You seem a good man, but how many questions are you going to ask someone who's lost his way? I'm a Persian, and I've come here fleeing from the Roman emperor and his army, and may I never see his head or crown again! If you can give me shelter tonight and treat me well, as a lord of the marches would, I think this will stand you in good stead one day; the tree you plant will bear you fine fruit." The man answered, "My house is yours and I am at your service; I'll try to provide whatever I can for you, and I'll mention your presence here to no one." King Shapur dismounted from his horse, and the maidservant followed suit. The orchard owner's wife made them a little meal from whatever was available to her, and when they had eaten, they were shown to a place where they could relax and drink wine. Their host passed the wine to Shapur and said, "Drink to whoever is in

your mind now!" Shapur replied, "My fine and eloquent host, the man who brings the wine should drink first, especially if he is older and wiser. You seem a little older than I am, and as you brought the wine, you should drink first." The owner replied, "A sober answer! The man who is more cultivated should drink first, which means you should, as you are old in the grace of your manner, even though you are still a young man. The scent of the crown comes from your hair, and your face glows like ivory."

Shapur laughed and took the wine, and a cold sigh rose from his vitals. He said to his host, "You're a man of the pure faith: what news have you of the fortunes of Iran?" His host answered, "My lord, may evil never touch you, and may our enemies suffer as the Roman emperor has made Iran suffer. Persia's population has scattered, and agriculture here has gone to rack and ruin. There has been so much looting, and so many men and women have been killed, that this great people has hidden itself away. And many have turned Christian and gone over to their bishops." Shapur said, "And where is King Shapur, whose splendor was like that of the full moon, that the Roman emperor has grown so powerful, darkening the bright fortune of Iran?"

The orchard owner said, "My lord, may you be always mighty and prosperous: Iran's nobles have no notion where he is, or whether he's alive or dead; everyone who was of any consequence here is now a prisoner in Rome." And the man began to weep bitterly. He said, "Stay here for three days, and make my house shine like the sun with your presence, for a sage has said that whoever acts inhospitably has no wisdom and will suffer a harsh fate. Stay, rest, drink wine to your heart's content, and then, when it seems appropriate to you, tell me your name." Shapur replied, "I accept, and for now my host is as my king."

The Persians Recognize Shapur and Come to Welcome Him

That night passed in drinking and the back and forth of conversation. When the first light of dawn touched the mountain peaks and spread its golden banner over the foothills, the owner of the orchard came to his guest and said, "May your day be happy, and your head reach higher than the rainy clouds. My house is unworthy of you, it's not a fit place for you to stay. You have to eat like a poor man here, and I have neither clothes to offer you, nor the means to make you comfortable." Shapur said, "You are a lucky man, and I would rather be in your house than crowned and seated on a throne. Bring me the Zend-Avesta, and the barsom, and as we pray I wish to ask you something."

The man brought all the king commanded, and when everything was ready the king asked him in the murmur of prayer, "Tell me truly, where is the chief priest now?" And the answer came, "From where I am sitting now I can see the house of the

chief priest." Then quietly the king said to him, "Ask the headman of this village for clay to make a seal." No sooner had he heard these words than the man ran to bring clay, musk, and wine. The king set his seal ring in the clay, handed the impression over to his host, and said, "Give this clay seal to the chief priest, and pay attention to what he says."

At first light, the man took the impression made by the king's seal to the chief priest. The door to the audience hall was closed and guarded by a number of men, and he shouted out asking to be admitted. When they let him in, the orchard owner went straight to the chief priest, showed him the clay, and made his obeisance. When he looked at the seal's impression, the priest's heart leaped for joy; he wept over the name he saw, and said, "Whose seal is this?" The orchard owner said, "The knight who owns it is sitting in my house; there is a lovely young woman with him, as slender as a cypress tree; she is beautiful, wise, and has a royal dignity about her." The priest said, "Describe this man's face and stature to me."

> The man replied, "In springtime, when you see,
> Beside a stream, a single cypress tree—
> That's how this knight is: he has arms the size
> Of some great horse's noble thighs,
> His chest is like a lion's, and his face
> Is ruddy: there you see such kindly grace
> It makes you blush bright red: it is as though
> His face gave off a crown's imperial glow."

As the orchard owner spoke the priest realized that this lionhearted man could be none other than the king, and that such a face belonged only in the royal court. He sent an envoy to the army's commander saying that the glory of Shapur had been found, and that he should gather forces from every quarter. The priest's messenger hurried to his destination and said, "In the garden of happiness and good fortune, the royal tree has blossomed!" The commander was overjoyed at these words: his lips were filled with sighs, his heart with the longing for warfare. He prayed to God, saying, "O you who holds the world, only you are worthy of praise! Who could have known that Shapur would see the army again, or that the army would see him?"

When night displayed its black flag and the stars appeared around the moon, from every quarter an army of men gathered in the place where the lord of the world was living. Joyfully they crowded about the house belonging to the orchard owner, who came to Shapur and said, "An army has collected outside our door, what do you think we should do?" Although the place was small and humble, Shapur ordered that they be admitted; as they entered one by one, they bowed their faces down to the dust. Shapur embraced each of the nobles and wept to tell them of the evils he had endured. He told them of what he had suffered in the ass's skin, and of the words he had heard from the emperor; he described the beautiful serving girl's nobility of spirit, and all she had done for him, and added,

> "To her and God I owe my life: may she
> Be blessed with happiness eternally!
> A mighty king's the slave of those slaves who
> Show magnanimity in all they do:
> I am the slave of this true-hearted slave
> Who's been so selfless, generous, and brave.

"Now that I resume my kingship and the command of my armies, send messengers and set advance guards on the roads; in particular close the roads to Ctesiphon, as I want no news of this to reach the Roman emperor. If he realizes the glory of Persian sovereignty has awoken again, he will lead an army against us and break the backs of our forces. At the moment we can't equal him in military might, and we shouldn't engage in a struggle with his flourishing good fortune. When our priests have gathered an army so dense that not a mosquito can pass through the ranks, then we shall revise our plans and secretly rid our garden of these noxious weeds. For now we need guards everywhere, watching day and night: no one should take off his armor and lie down to sleep while the Roman threat hangs over us."

Shapur Attacks by Night and Takes the Roman Emperor Prisoner

Not many days passed before the Persian army had grown to six thousand men. Shapur sent spies to Ctesiphon, which had been occupied by the Romans, to report on the emperor and his court there. Stealthily and secretly the spies collected information; they reported to the king and said, "The emperor spends all his time drinking and hunting, and gives no thought to warfare. His army is scattered about the countryside plundering what they can find. They send out no scouts by day, they set no guards at night, they're like a flock without a shepherd. The emperor has no thought of any enemy attacking from anywhere, and is content to live following his fancies."

Shapur was overjoyed to hear this, and his past sorrows dispersed like the wind. He chose three thousand Persian warriors, well equipped and with barding for their horses. They put on their armor in the night's darkness and set off toward Ctesiphon, riding quickly by night and hiding during the day. The king and his men rode through deserts and mountains, by trackless ways, with scouts sent two parasangs ahead of the main body of men. So they went forward, until the scouts came within sight of Ctesiphon. At this time two watches of the night had passed, and the emperor had no suspicion that anything was amiss, until he heard the din of drums and the cries of sentries ringing out like a cockcrow. The whole plain was filled with the Roman tents, but who in all that encampment was aware of the impending attack? The emperor was drunk in his pavilion, and his soldiers were crowded around in disorder. When Shapur saw how things stood, he gave his horse its head, and his men charged the Roman camp, with the king laying about him with a huge mace. The blare of trumpets, the clash of maces, the clanging of Indian bells rose up to the clouds. Cries of combat and the noise of arms crashing against armor came from every side: you'd have said the sky had split open, and that the sun dripped blood down through the air. In the darkness the Kaviani banner glittered and swords flashed, and it seemed that the earth was covered with clouds that rained down weapons. The dust of battle hid the mountains, and the stars veiled their light. Shapur flattened the evil emperor's pavilion; his men set fires on all sides throughout the Roman camp, and the skies seem to come down to the earth. Finally the emperor was taken prisoner, and his fortunate star deserted him. Many of his brave nobles and commanders were hauled from their tents and put in chains.

At dawn, when night drew in her skirts and the sun's banner appeared on the mountain tops, Shapur asked for a scribe to come, bringing a pen, inks, musk, and silk. A letter was written to every chieftain, every king, and every country. The letter began with praise of God, whose slaves we are, since it is he who aids the virtuous and has no need of human aid, who created the world and guides us to righteousness. It continued, "Since the Roman emperor did not take wisdom as his soul's guide, but instead ignored God's commands and sowed nothing but seeds of evil in Iran, he now languishes weeping in chains. God entrusted him with the crown of Iran, but he

لشکر و نامداران او

یران و جنگی سواران او

سرانجام قیصر گرفتار شد
وز و اخترنیک پیراز شد

will take nothing from this world but an evil name. By the power of God who guided us, his court and army have been broken, and any Romans found in the city will be put to the sword. Pursue justice, obey my commands, and willingly renew your oaths of loyalty to me." Swift messengers took the king's letter to every quarter.

Shapur moved his court from the camp to Ctesiphon, and when he placed his ancestors' crown upon his head again, he gave thanks to God. He sent a scribe to the prisons, to write down the names of their captives; the number of Roman nobles held there came to one thousand one hundred and ten, all of whom were relatives or allies of the emperor, and among the first men of their country. The king had the hands and feet of those who had been involved in oppression cut off, then he ordered that the Roman emperor be brought before him. The executioner dragged him by the arm from the prison, and he was like a man who has lost consciousness. When this tyrannical man saw Shapur's face, he wept and prostrated himself, rubbing his face in the dust, and calling down blessings on the throne and crown. His tears soaked the ground, and his face and hair were coated with dust.

The king said to him, "You are entirely evil, a Christian, and an enemy of God. You say that he who has no partner, whose realm has no beginning or end, has a son. You don't know how to speak except in lies, and lies are an evil fire that gives no light. If you are an emperor, where are your shame and good sense, where is your conscience to guide you? Why did you imprison me in an ass's skin and bring my greatness down into the dust? I came as a merchant looking for a fair, I didn't come with drums and an army looking for war. But you shut your guest up in an ass's skin and led your army against Iran. Now you know what war with brave men means, and you won't be looking to fight with Iran again."

The emperor replied, "Who can evade God's will? My royal fortune made wisdom a stranger to me, and my soul became a devil's mercenary. But if you return good for evil, you will be a legend in the world, your name will never grow old, and your chivalry will bring you all that you desire. If I receive my life at your hands, all wealth and gold will be contemptible to me, I shall be a slave at your court, seeking nothing but how to augment its splendor." Shapur answered, "You are an evil, ignorant man. Why did you plunder this country? I want back immediately all the prisoners you took from here to Rome; then you must return all the wealth you took to Rome too, and may you never see that shameful city again! You must provide money to rebuild the parts of Persia you have ruined, where lions and leopards now build their lairs. Further, you must have ten noble Romans handed over for every Persian you killed; I want only members of the imperial family, and they will live here with me as hostages in this happy land. For every tree you cut down in Persia—and a good man does not cut down trees—you must plant another and build walls to protect it, and in this way you may lessen the rage that people feel against you. I have you in chains now, but how can I ever forgive you that ass's skin? If you do not do as I have ordered, your own skin will be cut open from head to foot." They split his ears with a knife, and bored a hole through his nose, in which they put a piece of wood of the kind by which a camel is led; this was done because Shapur remembered the ass's skin. Two heavy shackles were placed on his feet, and the executioner returned him to prison.

Shapur Leads His Army into Roman Territory: His Battle with the Emperor's Brother

Shapur drew up his troops for review, and as the treasuries were opened and he provided his men with provisions and payment, his head filled with thoughts of revenge, his heart with ambition. He led his army into Roman territory; they killed whomever they found there and burned all the buildings, making the world glow with fire.

When news reached Rome from Persia that their land had been devastated and the emperor taken prisoner while fighting at night, all Rome wept and trembled at the name of Shapur. They said, "Who but our emperor, that unchivalrous man, brought this evil on us?" The emperor had a younger brother; their father was dead, but their mother was still alive. This brother's name was Yanus, and he was an ambitious, generous, open-hearted man. The army gathered at the imperial court, and Yanus's mother, who was a bellicose woman, distributed cash to them and said to Yanus, "You must avenge your brother, since you can see an army is attacking us from Iran." Yanus was swept away by anger when he heard this and said, "Revenge for a brother is not something to push aside and forget!" He had the drums sounded and brought a large cross out before his formidable army.

When the armies came face to face, the men on each side were eager for battle. Their ranks were drawn up, the din of battle began, and Yanus led his troops in an attack. But such clouds of dust sprang up that his men lost their way. On one side they were hemmed in by mountains, and on the other by a wide river, and the dust continued until the sun turned yellow in the sunset. So many men were killed that the ground seemed paved with the iron armor of the dead. Shapur was in the center of his forces, calling out to his officers on the right and left; he and his nobles urged their horses forward, the ground shook, and their troops engaged the enemy. They launched an all-out attack against the Romans in which officers and foot soldiers became indistinguishable. Yanus saw that his forces couldn't withstand the king's, and he and his army fled. Shapur pursued them, and the dust dimmed the shining air. Heaps of corpses lay everywhere, and the plants that grew there were smeared with men's brains. The whole plain was filled with trunkless, limbless heads of slaughtered Romans. No army or cross remained on that plain, and no bishops or crosses remained in the castles. The army was astonished at the amount of booty that was gathered on all sides. The king distributed everything to his troops, reserving only the emperor's personal treasure for himself, a treasure that had caused him such pain in the past and that was not enough to cancel that pain. The Roman soldiers gathered round and spoke against their emperor, saying, "May we never have another ruler like him, may the name of emperor disappear from Rome! Away with altars and crosses and vestments; now our priests' belts and crosses have been burned, Rome is like pagan Qanuj for us, and the fame of the Messiah's faith grows weaker."

Baranush Is Crowned Emperor of Rome: His Letter to Shapur

There was a noble Roman, of the emperors' line, called Baranush: he was a wise man, knowledgeable and able to give good advice. The army said to him, "You should be emperor, and the leader of this country and people." They prepared an ivory throne for him, and Baranush placed the crown on his own head. The Romans sat him in the center of power and all of them called down blessings on him.

Baranush sat on his throne and thought of Rome and her battles. He knew that she would be harmed by further confrontations with the great king, and he selected a messenger, a man who was sensible and humble, who could speak wisely and eloquently, and was both a great scribe and someone experienced in the ways of the world. He summoned this man and conferred with him, then dictated a letter to Shapur, beginning with praise of God, who rules the world. It continued:

> "May all the chieftains of the world bow down
> As slaves before your everlasting crown:
> You know that our, and your, nobility condemn
> Oppression visited on guiltless men.
> Whether performed in Rome's or Persia's name,
> Rapine and murder are a source of shame.
> If we may trace this warfare to the time
> Iraj died, Manuchehr avenged that crime—
> Both Tur and Salm are dust now. And if you're
> Remembering Dara's and Sekandar's war,
> Dara was murdered by his ministers
> And plucked from power by his opposing stars.
> And if you hate our emperor, he remains
> A captive in your dungeons, bound in chains.

But Rome, which has no equal anywhere,
Should not be prey to ruin and despair.
If you attack us we cannot withstand
The force of your assault against our land,
Our wives and children are already yours,
Made captive, or left wounded by your wars.
It's time to close your eyes to what is past,
To lay aside your warlike plans at last.
Day follows day, and every day in turn
Sees yet another of our cities burn!
Let joy into your heart—it cannot be
That God looks kindly on such tyranny.
God keep Your Highness—may your star arise,
And crown the moon, and dominate the skies."

The letter was sealed with the emperor's seal, and the messenger set off for Shapur's court. When the letter with its fine sentiments was read to Shapur, he frowned, his eyes filled with tears, and he forgave the Romans. He immediately wrote an answer, going over the good and bad of the past, and adding, "Who was it who sewed his guest in an ass's skin and rekindled ancient enmities? But if you are wise come before me, bringing philosophers from your country. Since I have decided on peace, I shall not prepare for war. I shall let you go free from this narrow pass in which you find yourself." The messenger returned and took the king's answer; word by word he reported everything that had been said.

Baranush Visits Shapur and They Conclude a Treaty

Baranush was overjoyed when he saw the answer to his letter. He ordered that a hundred Roman nobles travel with him to Shapur's court, and took sixty donkey loads of silver, together with jewels and textiles, and thirty thousand gold coins as a present. The nobles entered Shapur's presence bareheaded and scattered the gold before him. Shapur welcomed them warmly, then turned to Baranush and said, "Many shameless, unjust men came here from Rome and turned our cities into waste reed beds. I want compensation for these ruined places that are now the haunts of lions and leopards." Baranush replied, "Tell us what must be done; do not turn your face from us now that you have granted us peace." The great king answered, "If you wish me to cancel your sins against us, three times a year Rome must send us a million gold coins; and if you wish to curtail my anger you will grant me the town of Nasibin, in Mesopotamia." Baranush replied, "Iran is yours, and Nasibin and its plains and warriors are yours; we accept your terms and the tribute we must pay, since we have not the power to oppose your anger." In the treaty between them, Shapur promised never to lead an army into Roman territory, unless it was done in a fitting, ceremonial manner that did nothing to diminish Rome's dignity. Then Shapur made much of his guests, treating them more kindly than his own nobles.

When the embassy had gone, Shapur gave many thanks to the world's Creator and set off joyfully for Estakhr, the most splendid site in Pars. But when news of the treaty reached Nasibin, its inhabitants prepared for war, saying, "Shapur should not own Nasibin or bring an army here, since he has no respect for Christianity; all his concern is for the Zend-Avesta and the faith of Zoroaster. He won't listen to us when he comes, and we have no interest in his scriptures or his faith." The common people took over the city, and its citizens sat in the saddle ready for war. When news arrived that the way to Nasibin had been blocked, Shapur burst out in rage against the Christian faith and sent a huge army against the town. He said, "It's ridiculous to respect a religion whose prophet was killed by the Jews." The army traveled as quickly as wind-borne dust; for a week its cavalry and lion-hearted warriors fought, and the city's inhabitants were hard pressed. The Persians killed many of their leaders and put those who remained alive in chains. Then the citizens sued for quarter, sending a letter to Shapur, who granted their request and ordered his army home.

Shapur was now famous throughout the world, and his power was acknowledged everywhere; he was referred to as "the victorious king." As for the young serving girl who had released him from captivity, and helped him to this power, he named her Delafruz-e Farrokhpay—the heart's delight who brings good luck—and she was his favorite among his womenfolk. He gave the orchard owner considerable wealth and sent him happy on his way. The Roman emperor remained in his prison, wretched and in chains, with his flesh eaten away by shackles. His wealth in Rome was gathered together and sent to Persia, and he lived a little longer, with sighs always on his lips. Finally he died while still chained and imprisoned, and his crown passed to another man. Shapur sent his corpse to Rome, in a coffin, with his head crowned with musk, and said, "This is the end of all of us, and I do not know where our peace is to be found. One man acts with cruelty and stupidity, another with wisdom and glory; but for each of them his time here passes in the same way. Blessed is the man who commits no evil in the world!"

Then Shapur built a city for the prisoners he'd taken, in Khuzestan, which he called Khorramabad—The City of Joy—and he settled there the men whose hands he'd cut off; the whole area was given over to them and each New Year they received a robe of honor from the king. He built another city in Syria, which he named Piruz-e Shapur—Shapur's Victory— and he built a third city, which had a castle and a hospital in it, near Ahvaz. He called this city Kenam-e Asiran—The Captives' Dwelling—and his prisoners found peace and contentment there.

The Coming of Mani: His Claim to Be a Prophet

Shapur had reigned for fifty years, and there was no one to equal him at that time. An eloquent man arrived from China, and the world will never see his like again. His abilities had stood him in good stead, and he had become a powerful man: his name was Mani. He said, "I am a prophet and a painter, and I am the first of those who introduce new religions into the world." He asked for an audience with Shapur, hoping to persuade the king to support his claim to be a prophet. He spoke fluently, but the king remained unconvinced by his talk. Shapur's mind was troubled by his words, and he summoned his priests and spoke to them at length about Mani. He said, "This man from China talks very well, but I have doubts about the religion he proposes. Talk to him and listen to what he has to say; it may be you'll be won over by him." They answered, "This painter will be no match for the chief priest. Listen to Mani by all means, but summon our chief priest, and when Mani sees him he won't be in such a hurry to talk."

Shapur sent for the chief priest, who spoke for a long time with Mani, and Mani was left speechless in the middle of his discourse, unable to answer the chief priest's remarks about the ancient faith of Zoroaster. The chief priest said to him, "You love images; why do you foolishly strive with God in this way, God who created the high heavens and made time and space in which darkness and light are manifest, whose essence is beyond all other essences, and who fashioned the heavens to turn by night and day? Your refuge is with him, all you suffer is from him. Why do you put such trust in images, ignoring the advice of the prophets? Images are multiple, but God is one, and you have no choice but to submit to him. If you could make your images move, then you could say that this is a demonstration of the truth of what you say. But don't you see that such a demonstration would fail? No one is going to believe your claims. If Ahriman were God's equal, dark night would be like smiling daylight; in all the years that have gone by, night and day have kept their places, and the heavens' turning has neither increased nor diminished. God cannot be contained by our thoughts, for he is beyond all time and place. You talk as madmen do, and that is all there is to it: no one should support you." He said much more beside this, and Mani was unable to answer his words. Mani's credibility, which had seemed so flourishing, withered away. The turning of the heavens was against Mani. The king was enraged by him and had him ignominiously dragged from the court. He said, "The world is no place for this image maker; he has disturbed the peace long enough. Let him be flayed and his skin stuffed with straw so that no one will be tempted to follow his example." They hung his body from the city gates, and then later from the wall in front of the hospital. The world praised Shapur, and men flung dirt on Mani's corpse.

Shapur Makes His Brother, Ardeshir, His Regent

Shapur's life became a garden within which grew roses without thorns. His justice and good sense, his actions, his wars and his policies were such that he had no enemies anywhere, and evil had no refuge in all the world. When he was more than seventy years old and had little hope of living longer, he summoned a scribe, together with the chief priest, Ardeshir, a wise and just man who was Shapur's own younger brother. Shapur had a son who was still very young and had little experience of the world.

The king said to Ardeshir, "You are a champion among men, and a fine, brave horseman. If you will swear truthfully to me, giving your word, that when my son reaches his majority and has grown into a brave youth, you will hand over to him the throne, the royal treasuries, and command of the army, and that you will be his benevolent guide until then, I shall hand over this royal crown to you, together with our treasuries and the army." Before the scribe and the nobles who were there, Ardeshir accepted Shapur's words, promising that when the boy reached manhood and was worthy of the royal crown, he would hand over the authority of kingship to him and would strive only to advance his interests.

Then Shapur handed him the crown and royal seal, in front of the nobles, and gave him lengthy advice on the duties of a just king. When he had heard Shapur out, his brother wept. The king lived for one more year after he made Ardeshir his regent.

Ferdowsi's accounts of the brief reigns of Ardeshir Niku Kar, Shapur III and Bahram Shapur are omitted

⚜ THE REIGN OF YAZDEGERD THE UNJUST ⚜

Yazdegerd rejoiced at his brother's unhappy death, taking his crown and placing it on his own head. All those who had lived by the sword and mace trembled like willow trees; Yazdegerd's rule over the world became more secure, and his benevolence faded away as his authority increased. Wise men meant nothing to him, and his royal obligations were forgotten; lords of the marches, champions, scholars, and learned priests—all were like so much wind to him, and his dark soul gave itself over to tyranny. Justice and kindness were cancelled from his heart, and he granted no man his requests. He respected no one's rank, and faults were elaborately punished. His ministers, whose task was to increase his power and glory, agreed among themselves never to tell the king of the country's true condition; they all shrank from him in terror and lived in fear for their lives. As soon as the chamberlain heard that envoys had come to see the king, or that subordinates had arrived at court seeking help, he hurried to reassure them with kind and gentle words. Later he said, "The king is not in the mood for work, and you cannot have an audience with him. I have told him of your requests, and he will act appropriately."

The Birth of Yazdegerd's Son, Bahram

Seven years went by, during which time the country's priests lived in fear and torment because of Yazdegerd's cruelty. Then, at the beginning of the eighth year of his reign, at the spring equinox, a son was born to him under an auspicious star. Delighted with his little son, Yazdegerd named him Bahram. Two renowned astrologers were summoned before the king: Sorush was the best of Indian astrologers, a man of great glory and intelligence; Hoshyar was a Persian, and his knowledge was such that he could put a bridle on the heavens. They used their astrolabes and Greek astrological tables to uncover the happy fortune that Bahram would be a great prince in the world, and that he would rule over the seven climes. Still grasping their instruments and tables, they ran into the king's presence and said, "We have brought together all we know, and it is clear from the stars that the heavens look kindly on this baby: he will rule the seven climes, and be a great and glorious king." Yazdegerd was overjoyed to hear this and rewarded them with royal jewels.

Once the astrologers had left the court, the priests and ministers sat together and discussed what should be done. They believed that if the new prince did not take after his father he could be a great and just king, but if his character turned out like his father's, he would ruin the whole country, and neither the priests, nor the country's warriors, nor the young prince himself would have an auspicious future. With good intentions in their hearts, they went to the king and said, "This splendid child is beyond any reproach or blame; all the world is his to rule, every country will pay him tribute. Look for a place where wisdom has ensured the country's peace and prosperity, and choose someone noble from there to bring him up. Then this fine prince will learn the skills he needs, and the world will rejoice in his rule."

Accordingly, the king summoned envoys from every country, and at the same time he sent his own men to Rome, India, China, and other civilized regions. One man went among the Arabs to study the nature of their life, and he searched for someone eloquent and wise who could bring Bahram up. Experienced sages came from every country and gathered at the Persian court. The king questioned them at length, made much of them, and assigned them living quarters. One night two Arab princes, No'man and his father Monzer, arrived with their entourage. When all these visitors had assembled in Pars, they presented themselves before Yazdegerd and said, "We are your slaves and will the obey the words we hear from you. Who among us will be fortunate enough to take the king's son in his arms, to teach him the ways of knowledge and to cleanse his heart of darkness?" Then each of these eloquent, experienced men, whether he was from Rome or India or Persia,

whether an astrologer, a mathematician, or a philosopher, said humbly, "O just, wise, and honorable king, we are all as the dust beneath your feet, and stand ready to act as your guide to knowledge. Look at us, and decide which of us pleases you, which of us will be useful to you." But Monzer said, "We are your slaves, and our lives in this world are the king's. The king knows of our qualities, since he is as a shepherd to us and we are his flock. We are riders, warriors, tamers of horses, and we have no tolerance of so-called wise men. We are not astrologers or mathematicians: our souls are filled with love of the king, and we trust in the quick Arab horses we ride. We are all your son's slaves, and we laud his glory."

Yazdegerd Entrusts His Son Bahram to Monzer and No'man

When Yazdegerd heard these words, he gathered his thoughts together, came to a decision, and handed over Bahram into Monzer's keeping. He had a robe of honor made for Monzer and exalted his head to the skies; the king of the Yemen's horse was called for at the door to the court, and all the plain in front of the palace was filled with camels, horses, litters, servants, and nurses for the baby. The whole area from the city gates to the court was decorated in royal fashion for the prince's departure.

When Monzer arrived back in the Yemen, all the men and women of the country came out to greet him, and as soon as he reached his home he began to search for worthy, wellborn women to suckle the child. From among the noble Persians and Arabs there he chose four accomplished women: two were Arabs, and two were Persians of royal descent, and these four prepared themselves to act as the baby's wet nurses.

They suckled him for four years, and he grew satisfied and stout on their milk; they weaned him with difficulty, but still they continued to cuddle and caress him. When he was seven the wise child said to Monzer, "My lord, don't treat me like a baby at the breast! Send me to teachers; there's work to be done, don't leave me idle and useless like this!" Monzer replied, "You don't need teachers yet, my lord. When it's time for you to be taught your lessons, I won't leave you to play in the palace and boast about your games." But Bahram answered him, "Stop thinking of me as an idle good-for-nothing. It's true I'm young in years, and my chest and shoulders aren't like a hero's, but I have some knowledge. You're old in years, but you don't have much wisdom, and my nature isn't what you think it is. Don't you know that when someone is ready to seek things out, he chooses what he has to do first and concentrates on that? If you're going to be always waiting for the right time, your heart will lose everything good, everything will be out of place, and nothing will come out right. It's the head that matters for a human being! Teach me everything that a king should know: the beginning of righteousness is a knowledge of God, and blessed is the man who is wise and has knowledge!"

Monzer stared at him in astonishment and murmured the name of God to himself. He immediately sent a messenger to Shurestan, who sought out three teachers who were highly respected there. One was to teach the boy how to write, and so to cleanse his heart of darkness. Another was to instruct him in the management of hawks and hunting cheetahs, which delights the heart. Another would teach him how to play polo, shoot with a bow, fight in combat against enemies, and tug his reins to right and left and so control his horse on the battlefield. These learned men presented themselves to Monzer and described to him the things they could teach. Monzer handed the young prince over to them for instruction, and he learned so quickly that his abilities were soon those of a grown man. His intellect grasped whatever they said to him, and by the time he was eighteen he had grown into a brave youth as splendid as the sun. He no longer needed his instructors to tell him anything about hunting with hawks and cheetahs, or about how to ride and attack on the battlefield. He said to Monzer, "My pure-hearted protector, you can send these teachers back to where they came from." Each of the men was given a number of presents, and they left Monzer's court in good spirits.

Later Bahram said to Monzer, "Have the Arabs bring their horses before me, and make them tug on the reins and flourish their lances. Then they can put a price on whichever horse pleases me, and I'll pay more for it than they ask." Monzer replied, "You're an ambitious young prince, and the herder of my horses is at your service, as his lord is too. I have no objection if you want to buy an Arab horse." Bahram said, "You have a noble reputation, and may you live prosperously for many years. I'll choose a horse I don't have to rein in when going down a slope, one I can make sure-footed at a gallop, and then I'll have him outstrip the winds of spring. But before he's properly trained, it's not right to force a horse to gallop too fast."

Monzer said to No'man, "Choose a number of horses, and as they're driven across the plain, watch out for a good mount for a warrior." No'man quickly brought a hundred horses, of which he chose a number suitable to be ridden in battle. Bahram wandered among them, but whenever he mounted one that had the speed of the wind, it could not bear his weight. This continued until finally he settled on a chestnut horse that was both swift and broad chested. He also chose a bay horse with a black mane and tail that was as big as a sea monster, and Monzer paid a just price for the two of them. They were both from the woods near Kufah. Bahram accepted the horses as a gift from him, and they glowed like the fires of Azar-Goshasp. Monzer looked after the young prince as if he were the apple of his eye, and did not let even the wind disturb him.

One day Bahram said to Monzer, "You are a noble, well-intentioned man, but you hem me in with your excessive care and constant worry. Everyone we see has some secret sorrow that turns his face yellow with grief, and a free man's health is revived by pleasure, so allow me this one further pleasure then, the pleasure that cures all pains. Whether he's a prince or a warrior, a young man finds comfort and happiness with women. They are the foundation of our faith, and they guide young men toward goodness. Have five or six beautiful slave girls, as splendid as the sun, brought here, so that I can pick one or two of them. I've been thinking too that I should have children: if I had a child that would bring me some comfort. The king would be pleased, and men would praise me for it."

The old man congratulated the young prince on his words and had a broker hurry to the slave-seller's depot.

> He brought back forty western slaves, each one
> A heart-delighting girl, a radiant sun.
> Bahram chose two of them, who seemed to be
> Fashioned from roses and pale ivory;
> Tall in their elegance, and cypress slim,
> Their grace and loveliness delighted him.
> One played the harp, one seemed to Bahram's eyes
> Bright as Canopus in the Yemen's skies.

Monzer bought both of them and Bahram laughed, then blushed like a ruby from Badakhshan.

The Story of Bahram and the Harp-Player

For a while Bahram occupied himself solely with playing polo and hunting. And so it was that one day he went out hunting without any of his companions, taking with him only his harp-playing slave girl. Her name was Azadeh, and her cheeks were as red as wine: she sat with him on his mount, her harp in her hand. She was his heart's delight and desire, and his name was always on her lips. That day, Bahram had asked for a brocade cloth to be draped across his camel's back, and that it be provided with four gem-studded stirrups, two of which were silver and two of gold. Beneath his quiver he had a slingshot, as he was adept at all forms of hunting. Two pairs of deer appeared in front of them and the young prince turned smiling to Azadeh and said, "When I draw back the bowstring, which of these two do you want my arrow to strike? There is a young female, and she has an old male companion." Azadeh replied, "You are a lion of a man, and a warrior doesn't fight against deer! But turn that doe to a buck with an arrow, and with another arrow make the buck into a doe. Then urge your camel forward, and as they flee from you, use your slingshot, and strike one of the deer on the ear, so that she will rub it against her shoulder and lift up her foot to scratch the spot, and when she does that—if you want me to call you the light of the world— pin her foot, ear and head together with one shaft."

Bahram readied his bow and broke the silence of the plain with his cry. He had a double-headed arrow in his quiver, and as the buck fled before him, he shot this arrow so that it severed the buck's antlers; instantly, now that its antlers were gone, the buck looked like a doe, and Azadeh stared at Bahram in astonishment. Then he shot two arrows into the doe's head, so that they protruded like antlers, while the blood ran down over her muzzle. Next he urged his camel toward the other pair; he fitted a pellet in the fold of his slingshot and loosed it at the ear of one of them. He was rightly pleased with his skill, because the deer immediately scratched at its ear, and Bahram notched an arrow to his bow. The shaft pinned foot, ear, and head

نمودست بهرام واورا زبن آمکو نشاہ پرزورو روی نہ مین

together, and Azadeh's heart was wrung for the animal. Bahram pushed her from the saddle and she fell headlong to the ground. He said, "You're nothing but a stupid harp-player. What do you mean by setting me such a task? If I had missed, I'd have brought shame on my lineage." He trampled her beneath his camel's hooves, and blood spurted from her breast and arms. After this, he never took a slave girl hunting with him again.

Bahram Shows His Prowess as a Hunter

Another time, Bahram went out to the hunting grounds with a large group of companions, taking his hawks and hunting cheetahs with him. On a mountainside he saw a lion clawing apart the back of a wild ass. He notched an arrow with three raven plumes to his bow string and pinned the wild ass's heart and the lion's back to one another. The lion lay drenched in blood atop the ass, and their hunter returned in triumph to the palace, his sword in his fist. Another time he went hunting with No'man and Monzer, together with a number of noble Arabs who had been his advisors for good and ill, and Monzer was eager for Bahram Gur to display his horsemanship and hunting skills to them. They saw a flock of ostriches running about like a herd of camels, and Bahram Gur sped forward like the wind. He laughed as he took his bow in hand and thrust four poplar wood arrows into his belt. One by one he notched them to the bowstring, and as each found its mark each one split the feathers of the former arrow; there was not a needle's width between where they struck. The nobles went forward and examined the prey and found not a hair's breadth of space from arrow to arrow. Monzer cried out his congratulations to him, as did their companions. Monzer continued,

> "You fill my heart with such intense delight,
> You're like a rosebush blossoming in my sight—
> And may your moonlike glory never wane,
> Your back remain unbent and free from pain!"

And as soon as they reached the palace Monzer, whose thoughts elevated Bahram to Saturn's sphere, sought out painters from the Yemen. A number of them gathered at the court, and Monzer gave orders that they were to represent Bahram mounted on a camel, together with the ostrich wounded by his arrows. His slingshot was also to be there, as well as the lions, deer, and wild asses he'd brought down by his massive strength and skill. The ostrich's wound, Bahram's arrows, and the surrounding plain all lived again in black ink brushed on silk. The picture was sent by a mounted messenger to King Yazdegerd, and there the whole court crowded around to see his missive. They were astonished at what they saw and called down blessings on Bahram and his skill.

Bahram Returns with No'man to His Father, Yazdegerd

His father longed to see Bahram again, who seemed less a man than the glorious sun itself. The lion prince said to Monzer, "The longer I stay with you the more I wish to see my father. My heart tells me that I'll be safe with

him." Monzer collected together appropriate royal presents from his country: Arab horses with gold-worked bridles, valuable objects, Yemeni textiles and swords, as well as whatever precious stones the mines of Aden could provide. Bahram traveled with No'man, who was highly regarded by the king, until they reached the city of Estakhr. As soon as the king learned that his son and No'man were approaching, he and his courtiers went out to meet them, and when he saw his son's glory, his fine body and shoulders, his stature and noble bearing, he was sunk in amazement. He questioned him closely and made much of him, and kept him nearby. He chose lodgings for No'man and an appropriate palace for Bahram. Day and night Bahram was with his father, and he was treated with such attentive kindness that he scarcely had to lift a finger.

After No'man had been with the king for a month, he was ready to return home. Yazdegerd summoned him one night, sat him down beside him on the royal dais, and said, "Monzer took great pains to bring Bahram up, and I shall reward him well: he has been like an angel of good fortune to me. I delight in his intelligence and opinions, and I see his aim has always been wisdom. You have been with us for some time now, and your father must be watching the roads for your return." From the treasury he was given fifty thousand gold dinars, together with royal clothes; from the stables ten fine horses with gold and silver trappings. To these were added beautiful carpets, as well as other splendid gifts that were brought one by one and handed over to No'man. Yazdegerd was happy to open the doors of generosity and to reward No'man's entourage with gifts too, according to their rank. He then wrote a letter worthy of his royal state to Monzer,

thanking him for the guidance and friendship he had shown to Bahram, and saying that he now lifted up his head in pride because of his son and would attempt to repay the debt he owed.

Bahram Gur also wrote a letter to Monzer, saying, "My life here is hard and bitter: I didn't expect my father to treat his inferiors in the way he does. I'm not like a son here or a servant, and I'm not like one of his subjects who's happy simply to be at the court." He told No'man what he had seen in private of the king's evil ways. No'man returned to Monzer and gave him the king's letter. Monzer kissed it and touched it to his forehead: he was overjoyed to see the gifts that had been sent and repeatedly expressed his wonder and gratitude.

Then in private No'man told Monzer of Bahram's complaints, and when a scribe read out his letter, Monzer's face turned pale. He immediately wrote Bahram a careful answer, saying, "My noble lord, see that you don't oppose your father. Be content with what he does, whether for good or ill; obey him and be prudent. Noble men escape evils through patience, and a man must be wise in such cases. To some the heavens send a heart filled with kindness, to others a vengeful heart and a frowning face: this is how God has made the world, and we must walk as he directs us to walk. I'm sending you whatever you might need by way of gold and royal jewels; my wealth is not worth your suffering. See that you keep your heart free from pain. I'm sending ten thousand dinars as a gift, and also the slave girl who delighted you so much and who was like a guide to you, so that she may lighten your soul's darkness. Whenever you need money, don't burden the king with your requests; I can send you much more than I have done, and other kinds of wealth from our kingdom too. Strive to be ever more obedient and humble: you can't privately separate the king from his evil ways." Monzer sent ten eloquent and loyal Arab horsemen, and they reached Bahram with the money and Bahram's favorite slave. Bahram was pleased at this, and his sorrows disappeared; wisely he followed the Arab king's advice and served his father obediently by night and day.

Yazdegerd Has Bahram Confined in His Palace; Bahram Returns to Monzer

One day, when Bahram had been standing before the king at a banquet, for a long time, he was overcome by the need for sleep. When his father saw Bahram's eyes closing, he shouted in his fury,

> "Take him away! He can't act as he ought,
> Never again will he appear at court.
> Lock him in his palace. He's unfit for
> The royal throne and leadership in war."

For a year Bahram stayed in his palace sick at heart, and never saw his father's face, except during the festivals of No-Ruz and Sadeh, when he was simply one of the crush of people who appeared before the throne. This was the situation when the Roman envoy Taynush arrived at court with the cash and slaves that had been sent as tribute. The King of Kings welcomed him and assigned him suitable living quarters. Bahram sent him a message: "You are a noble and successful man; something has made the king angry with me, and I've been excluded from his presence, even though I've done nothing wrong. If you intercede on my behalf, the king might look kindly on me, so that my fortunes will flourish again. He might send me to the people who brought me up, because Monzer means much more to me than my own mother and father do."

Taynush agreed to help him, and Bahram, whose heart had been so troubled, was overjoyed. He was freed from his miserable confinement and, after distributing many goods to the poor, made preparations to leave. He gathered his people together and in the darkness of the night they set off like the wind. He said to his friends, "Thanks be to God that we've managed to get away, and are safe from fear." When he arrived in the Yemen, men, women, and children came to greet him. No'man and Monzer and an escort of riders bearing lances set out, and the crush of people around Bahram was so great that the world grew dark with the dust they sent up. The two of them dismounted, and Bahram told them of his sorrows and hardships. Monzer wept to hear his words, and then asked after the fortunes of the king. Bahram replied, "May he never realize how evil his star is!" They took him to his former quarters and added new kindnesses to the old. Bahram spent his time in festivities and on the playing field, in largess and training for combat.

Yazdegerd Travels to Tus and Is Killed by a White Horse

And so for a time the father was in Iran while his splendid son lived in the desert. Yazdegerd grew concerned for his sovereignty and summoned advisors from every province. He told his astrologers to look at the stars and tell him when his death would come, and where his head and helmet would be darkened, how and when the flower of his life would wither. The astrologers said, "It is wrong for the king to think on the day of his death. When the fortune of the King of Kings declines, he will travel from here to the fountain of Su; he will gather his men together and go accompanied by the noise of drums and trumpets to Tus, and it is there that death will come to him." The king swore an oath by the fire-temple of Khorad-Borzin and by the golden sun, saying, "My eyes will never see the fountain of Su, neither in times of joy nor in distress."

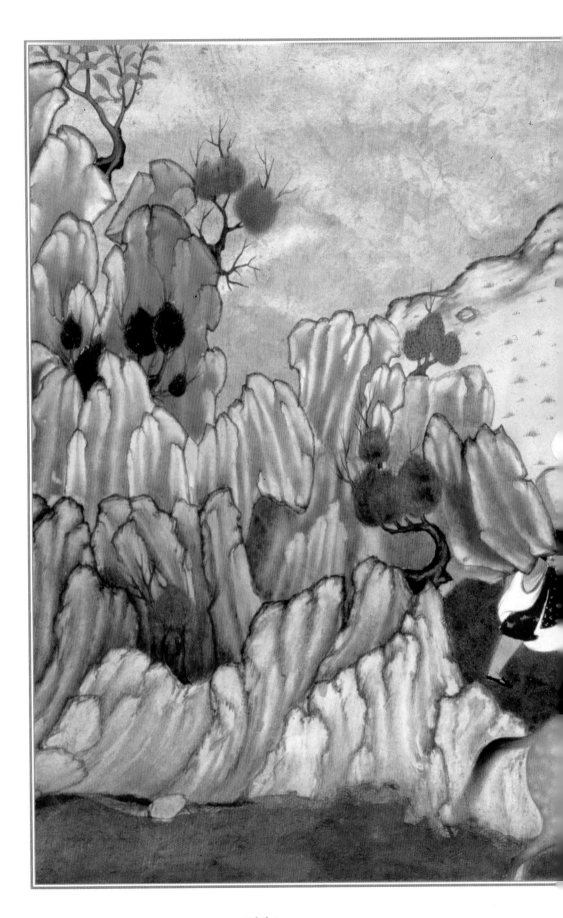

دمان همچو شیر ژیان نیزه خشم | بلند و سیه خایه و لاغ چشم

So three months passed, and then the world was thrown into turmoil by a rumor about the king's blood, causing men to say that he had been an unjust shepherd to his flock, and now all his sins were returning to him. Blood began to flow from Yazdegerd's nose one day, and doctors came to him from every quarter. They stopped the flow for a week with their medicines, but then it began again, coursing down like tears. His priest said to him, "Your majesty, you strayed from God's path when you said you would escape the clutch of death, which is like the autumn wind that tears the leaves from the tree. You must go in a litter, by way of Shahd, to the fountain of Su. Pray to God and make your way, weeping and penitent, to that scorching land. Say 'I am a help-less slave who trapped his own soul by an oath, and now I come before you, O just and righteous Lord, to know when my time will be fulfilled.'"

The king accepted his advice, and with a caravan of three hundred litters he set off for Shahd. He stayed in his litter day and night, and still from time to time blood flowed from his nose. When he reached the fountain of Su, he came out of his litter and saw the lake there. He dabbed a little of its water on his head and prayed for God's benevolence. In a short time the flow of blood from his nose stopped, and he and his advisors rested in relief. But then his pride and complacence took over and he said, "I've done what I was supposed to, so why should we sit here any longer?" Because of the king's arrogance in ascribing everything good to himself, a white horse emerged from the lake. He had a round rump, like a wild ass, and short pasterns. He was tall and had black testicles and eyes like a crow's; his tail reached to his black hooves, and he had a full mane. He galloped forward, raging like an angry lion, with foam flying from his mouth. Yazdegerd told his courtiers to have the horse brought to him. A herdsman and ten men experienced at breaking horses set off with a saddle and a long looped lariat.

But what did Yazdegerd know of the secrets of God, who had set this monster in his path? The herdsman and his assistants were helpless to control the
animal, and in his fury the king snatched the lariat and saddle from them and
confidently approached the horse, who then stopped stock still, and stirred
neither his forelegs nor his hind legs. He let the king fasten the bridle on
him and stayed quiet as the saddle was put in place. The king pulled the saddle straps tight, and still the horse did not stir. Then the king went behind
him to loop the crupper under his tail, and the stony-hoofed horse neighed
loudly and kicked him so hard in the chest that his head and crown struck
the dust. Yazdegerd had come from dust, and now he returned to the dust.
When the king was dead, the horse galloped to the lake, which was the color
of lapis lazuli, and he disappeared beneath its surface; in all the world no
one had ever seen such a marvel.

A cry like a roll of drums went up from the army: "O king, it was your
fate that brought you to Tus." Everyone present ripped their clothes and
heaped dust on their bodies. Then a priest removed the dead king's brain
and the vital organs from the body cavity; filling the space with camphor
and musk, he wrapped the body in brocade to keep it dry. The king's corpse
was conveyed to Pars in a golden coffin within a litter made of teak. So
turns this world, and it is when you feel secure that you should fear its evil.
Though you might rest, the world will not, and when you eat your bread,
wine is the best comfort. While a man lives in this world, it is better to follow the faith than to act sinfully.

The Nobles Set Khosrow on the Throne

After the king of the world had been placed in his tomb, the Persian nobles gathered together and wept. The lords of the marches, the priests and great warriors, the wise counselors, all came to Pars and gathered at Yazdegerd's tomb. Gostahm who had killed an elephant while he was mounted on a horse; Qaren, who was Goshasp's son; Milad, the lord of Pars and a breaker of horses; Piruz, famous for his exploits with his mace; and all the other great lords whom Yazdegerd had treated with such contempt came together in Pars. Goshasp, an eloquent and literate man, addressed them:

> "My noble lords, no man has ever seen
> A king as wicked as this king has been:
> He hoarded all he'd stolen from the poor,
> His reign was murder, rapine, grief, and war.
> No one has heard of any former reign
> That was so evil, or that caused such pain.
> We do not want his seed here on the throne
> And from his dust we turn to God alone.
> Proud Bahram is his son, and we'll soon find
> He has his father's heart, and will, and mind;
> Besides, he talks of Monzer all the time.
> We can't accept a king who's steeped in crime!"

All the Persian lords swore a solemn oath that they did not want anyone of the seed of Yazdegerd to assume the crown and throne. Then they rose, determined to find some other king.

When news of Yazdegerd's death spread among the nobility, various chieftains, such as Alan Shah, Bivard, and Shegnan with his golden diadem, each thought, "Sovereignty is now mine, from the earth to the moon's sphere." And since there was no king occupying the throne, the world was filled with discord. The priests and champions of Iran gathered in Pars and discussed the situation, wondering who was worthy of the throne and of such a task. They wanted a just and generous man to quell the disorder in the land, since without a king the world was like an uncultivated meadow. There was an old, chivalrous man from a wealthy and noble family, who lived in the borderlands. His name was Khosrow; he was benevolent and had been successful in his life. Iran's chieftains bestowed the crown and throne on him, and an army of men from every quarter came to him.

Bahram Gur Learns of His Father's Death

They told Bahram Gur of the bitter fortune that had come to the throne, saying, "Your father, illustrious among kings, has died, and in dying he took the good name of the kings with him. An assembly of nobles has sworn that they want no seed of his to be king, that Bahram, his son, is as he was, and that in both appearance and substance he takes after his father. They have placed a man named Khosrow on the throne."

Bahram scored his cheeks with his nails; he seemed desperate with sorrow at his father's death, and for two weeks the wailing of men, women, and children could be heard throughout the Yemen. At the new moon, after he had mourned for his father for a month, he gave audience again. Monzer and No'man and a crowd of Arabs came weeping into his presence, burned by their sorrow. Monzer spoke: "Great prince, all of us arrive in this world destined for dust, and we come with no hope of a remedy for this. Whoever is born from his mother dies; I see man's life as injustice, and it is death that is justice."

Bahram Gur said, "If the name of king passes from my family, a great glory will depart. These usurpers will attack your plains, and the land of the Arabs will become like a pit of death. Mourn for my father, then think how you can help me." Monzer chivalrously replied, "This land is mine, and I pass my days hunting in these plains. You should mount the throne and govern the land, and may your reign last forever!" All the nobles supported what he had said and rose up before the young ambitious prince, ready for war. Monzer said to No'man, "Bring together an army of ten thousand young lions from the Shayban and Qaysian tribes, then I will show these Persians who is king!"

No'man gathered together a mighty army of warriors armed with swords and lances and ordered them to begin their attacks and to subdue the land. They trampled all the marshy country beneath their horses' hooves, as far as Ctesiphon; the people had no protector, and men, women, and children were taken captive. The throne was powerless and the world became a place of plunder and burning; news reached Rome, China, India, Makran, and the land of the Turks that there was no worthy candidate to be king. All these peoples prepared to attack, stretching out their hands toward Iran, and each thinking to make their own lord the King of Kings.

The Persians Write to Monzer: His Response

When the Persians became aware of this, they scrambled to find some remedy for their plight. They chose an eloquent and perceptive priest named Javanui as their messenger; he was to go to Monzer and say to him, "Protector of Iran and support of the valiant; when our throne became vacant our country turned as red with blood as a francolin's wing, and we asked you to be our lord, since we thought our land worthy of you. But now you are plundering us, shedding our blood, and spreading rapine and warfare through our land, although previously you were not an evil ruler. Fear men's curses and reproaches. You are an old man—take heed of what we say, and may it please and benefit you. There is another judge besides you, one who is above the understanding of the highest of men."

Javanui traveled to the land of the Arabs, where he spoke to Monzer and gave him the letter with which he had been entrusted, repeating all the Persians had said to him. The Arab king heard him out but did not reply to the charges. Instead he said, "You are a wise man, seeking a way out of misfortune; tell the King of Kings what you have said. If you want a response, tell King Bahram what you have told me; he will show you what must be done." He sent a courtier to take Javanui to the prince. When he saw him, Javanui was astonished at the might of Bahram's chest and shoulders, at his strength and stature, and called down God's blessings on his head. The prince's cheeks were the color of red wine, and his hair exhaled the scent of musk. The learned messenger lost all his dignity of rank; he became confused, and his message went completely out of his head. Bahram saw that the man was bewildered, and questioned him at length, gently and kindly, and sat him on a throne. When Javanui had come back to himself, Bahram asked him why he had made the arduous journey from Persia.

He sent Javanui back to Monzer, with a courtier, saying that Monzer was to write a suitable answer to the letter. Monzer smiled, his face opening like a blossoming flower when he heard this reply. He set about writing his answer, and said to Javanui, "You're a wise man, and you know that whoever does evil will suffer punishment. I heard your message and the greetings you brought from Iran's chieftains. Say to them, 'Who began this? Who was senseless enough to start this war? Bahram Gur, the King of Kings, is here, splendid, powerful, and possessed of an army, and if you drag a serpent from its hole, you're likely to see your skirts dragged through blood. If I had been the Persians' advisor, they wouldn't have been overrun in this way.'" Javanui had seen Bahram's face and talked with him, and he pondered whether Bahram was worthy of the throne. As he listened to Monzer, he had an idea and said: "You are a noble lord who needs no one else's advice. Since the Persians lost their wisdom, many of their leaders have been killed. I'm an old man looking to save my reputation, and if you will hear me out, I will put a plan to you. You and Bahram Gur, as King of Kings, must come to Iran without warfare or strife. Come with your hawks and hunting cheetahs, as befits a splendid king. You have heard what the Persians said, and no harm will come to you there. You are a sensible man, far from all foolishness, and you will know what must be said in such circumstances." Monzer gave him gifts and sent him happily on his way back to Iran.

Bahram Gur Travels to Jahrom, and the Persians Come to Meet Him

Monzer, Bahram, and an advisor discussed the situation in private. They agreed that, together with a group of warriors, they would travel to Iran. Monzer chose thirty thousand Arabs armed with lances and daggers, paid them in gold, and filled their leaders' heads with ambitious hopes for the expedition. News of this reached the Persians as Javanui arrived at the assembly of their chieftains. The leaders were apprehensive as to what would happen, and they gathered in the fire-temple of Borzin to pray, asking God to convert their state of warfare to one of peace and happiness.

Monzer approached Jahrom, traveling across the waterless plain. King Bahram pitched his pavilion and the army gathered about him. He said to Monzer, "You've traveled from the Yemen to Jahrom, and now their armies and ours are face to face. What should we do now? Fight, or negotiate?" Monzer replied, "Call their chieftains here and prepare a table for them. Talk with them and listen to what they have to say, and if anyone gets angry, you must stay calm. We shall see what they are hiding and who they want to nominate as the world's king. When we know what they intend, we can take appropriate measures. If things go easily, we can put aside thoughts of war, and if they want to fight, if they won't fall in with our plans and show themselves like leopards eager for prey, then I'll convert this plain of Jahrom into a sea of blood. But I think that when they see your face and stature and goodness, and how wise, cultivated, patient, knowledgeable and dignified you are, they won't want anyone else for their crown and throne but you. And if they make a mistake and think they can deprive you of your position, then I and these cavalry will use our swords to bring the Day of Judgment down on their heads. When they see our innumerable army and our dignity and discipline, and when they reflect that kingship is your inheritance, passed down from father to son as is right, and when they consider that bloodshed is our trade and that God is our support, then they are not going to want anyone but you as their king." Bahram's heart was filled with joy at these words, and he laughed aloud.

As the sun rose above the mountain peaks the Persian nobles prepared to welcome Bahram. Meanwhile, Bahram was seated on an ivory throne, and he wore a crown of great value. He held court according to the protocol of a King of Kings: on one side of him Monzer sat, and on the other No'man, his sword in his hand. Around his pavilion, circle upon circle, stood Arab chieftains. A number of the noblest of the Iranians approached the pavilion threshold; Bahram gave orders that the flap be drawn back, and their arrival was announced in a loud voice. They called down blessings on the king's head and wept as they did so. When they came into King Bahram's presence and saw the splendor of his crown and throne, they said with one voice,

"May you prosper, and may evil be far from you!" The king of kings questioned them kindly, then motioned them to places according to their rank.

He said, "My noble lords, you have seen the world and are experienced in its ways; from father to son, sovereignty has passed to me; why then is the choice now up to you?" The Persians answered, "Do not prolong our sufferings. None of us want you as king; even if you have an army to back up your claim, this land is ours. The seed you're from has brought us grief and sorrow, filling our days and nights with sighs and torment." Bahram answered, "It is true that everyone will wish to be a king. But even if you did not want me, why did you put someone in my place without consulting me?" A priest replied, "If you will join us in choosing a king, everyone will praise the process."

Three days passed while they searched for a king among the Persians. Then they wrote down the names of a hundred nobles worthy of the crown, throne, and royal belt. One of these hundred was Bahram, whose royal charm won many hearts. The hundred were reduced to fifty, and the debate grew long and earnest. Bahram was the first contender among the fifty, and this was so irrespective of the fact that it was his father's place he was seeking. From fifty they came to thirty, and from this thirty the wise priest reduced the number to four, of whom Bahram was still the first. But when the discussion seemed close to a conclusion, all the older Persians said, "We don't want Bahram; he is brave, foolhardy, and arrogant." Shouting broke out among the chieftains, and men's hearts seethed with anger.

Monzer said to the Iranians, "I want to know for good or ill why you are so troubled about this young prince." In answer the nobles summoned many Persians who had suffered under Yazdegerd. One by one they presented themselves: one had had both his hands and feet cut off; another's body was in one place but his mind in another; one had lost both hands, both ears, and his tongue, and he was like a body that had no soul; another had had his shoulder blades removed; another his eyes gouged out. Monzer stared at these men in bewilderment, and rage swept through him. Bahram was deeply affected by what he saw, and he cried out to his father's dust, "If you shut your eyes to human happiness, did you have to steep your soul in the fires of hell as well?" Monzer said to Bahram, "This evil is not something that can be pushed aside for them. You heard what they had to say, now you must give your answer. Anger does not become a prince."

Bahram Speaks to the Persians about His Qualifications to Be King

Bahram said, "My noble lords, you know the world's ways, and you have spoken truly. There are even worse things still unsaid, and it is right that I

بیک دست بهرام اندر نشست
دگر دست نعمان و یغمی بدست

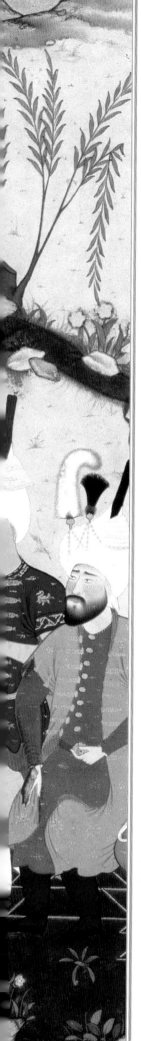

reproach my father. All this is bitter in my mouth and has darkened my soul. His palace was my prison, and it was God who saved me; Taynush freed me from his snare. I fled to Monzer for refuge because the king had never shown me any kindness. May men never have his nature; if that were to happen, all trace of humanity would disappear. I thank God that I have wisdom, and that my soul is nourished on wisdom. I have prayed to God that he guide me, so that I can cleanse men's souls and hearts of all the evil this king did. I am a God-fearing man, and I live for my subjects' well-being: I shall be a shepherd and my subjects, my flock. I will seek only peace and justice. I am magnanimous, cultivated, and careful in my judgments. An unjust king has no sound judgment: his wretchedness makes him vile and perverse, and one should weep for such a tyrant. Sovereignty passes to me from father to son, and I am wise and benevolent. On my mother's side I am descended from King Shemiran, and my wisdom equals that of my ancestors. I have wisdom, good judgment and greatness; I ride well, I am humane, and I am strong. I consider no one my equal in manliness, not in fighting or feasting or any other matter. I have a hidden treasure, which is those illustrious men who are loyal to their sovereign. I will make the world flourish from end to end with justice, and may all of you flourish and live happily! I will rebuild those lands the king's injustice destroyed, and make them prosperous again.

"Now I will make a pact with you, which I will swear before God to keep. Let us bring the ivory throne of the King of Kings and set the crown upon it. And then bring two savage lions from the wilderness and set them on either side of the crown. We'll tie them one on each side, and whoever desires to be king will go between them, take the crown, and place it on his own head. Then he will sit as king between the two lions: the king in the middle, the crown above him, the throne beneath him. We'll have no one but that man as our king, even if other candidates are just and nobly born. And if you reject my plan and choose some ambitious contender in place of me as your king, you will have horsemen's spears to prick and goad you. I and Monzer and our maces and swords will be there; Arab warriors have never learned how to flee from the battlefield, and we'll raise the dust of warfare over your kingdom and its provinces. Now, reply to what I have said, and use your best judgment as you decide." Then he retreated into his tent, and the world was astonished by his words.

The Persian priests and nobles who heard his speech said, "He possesses the divine *farr;* this is not said out of perversity or folly. He speaks about nothing but justice and we should rejoice in this. And as for his talk of wild lions and placing the crown and throne between them, God will not question us if the lions tear him in pieces, because it was his idea. Not that we would be pleased if he were to die; and if he does gain the crown, his glory will surpass Feraydun's. We want only him as our king and agree to what he has proposed."

Bahram Takes the Crown from between the Lions

The next day at dawn Bahram sat on his throne and summoned the Persians to him. They talked about the previous day's discussions and then the priests said:

> *"We see you are the wisest of the wise:*
> *If, by your skill and bravery, you rise*
> *To be the King of Kings, what will you do*
> *To further justice? How will you renew*
> *The ways of righteousness, and set us free*
> *From fears of theft and royal tyranny?"*

Bahram replied, "My actions will be greater than my words. I shall avoid injustice and ambition, and I shall distribute territories to those who are fit to rule. I will hold the world by justice, and this will be my happiness and security. I will relieve the sufferings of the poor. If a man sins I shall admonish him, and if he sins again, I shall imprison him. I shall pay the army at the appointed times and make the wise rejoice. My heart is as I speak, and I will turn my soul aside from all perversity and darkness. If a man dies without heirs, I shall distribute his goods to the poor, keeping nothing for my own treasury, since my heart is not set on the pleasures of this fleeting world. I will consult with the wise, and by their advice break the back of foolish desires. If I want to embark on any new venture I'll consult the priests first. If a man comes to me seeking justice, I shall not dismiss the assembly, but dispense justice to whoever desires it, saying nothing but what is right, and punishing evil, as a king must. All this I swear by God, as wisdom guides my tongue."

When the assembled nobles and priests heard his answer, they regretted what they had said before. Those who had sinned sought to remedy their wrongdoing and said, "Who is more worthy to rule than he is? In chivalry, eloquence, wisdom, and lineage, no one has ever been born who equals him. God has created him from justice, and may evil never touch him!"

They addressed Bahram, "You possess the divine *farr*, and our souls accept you as our king. None of us knew of your abilities and knowledge, or of your soul's purity. But Persia has sworn allegiance to Khosrow, who is descended from Pashin; we are bound by our oath to him, and you could say we are at his mercy. If he were to remain as Persia's king, all our country will be rent apart by lions' claws, with one side supporting Bahram and the other rallying to Khosrow. But it would be just for you to be king and for the world from now on to be beneath your command. We could use your proposed combat with lions as a pretext, and then no one would put himself forward as a candidate." Bahram agreed to this, as it was he who had originally suggested it.

The custom of that time was that when a new king was to be crowned the chief priest and three wise advisors went before him and placed him on the throne. They called down blessings on the crown, which was placed on his head in the name of the Kayanid kings; then the chief priest placed his cheeks in joy against the king's chest. Lastly the king distributed largess to the needy, using the goods that had been brought to him in homage, and a throne and crown were presented to the chief priest, who returned to his home in the plains.

The warrior Gostahm kept two savage lions in chains, and handed these over to a priest. They dragged the animals to the foot of the ivory throne and secured them there: the men who handled the chains almost fainted from fear. Placed on the throne, in one corner, was the royal crown. The world watched, wondering what would happen to the prince, who seemed so blessed by fortune.

Bahram and Khosrow, their hearts filled with apprehension confronted the lions. When Khosrow saw the two savage beasts and the crown placed between them, he turned to the priests and said,

> *"Only a prince ambitious for renown*
> *Deserves to reign and to possess the crown;*
> *And then I'm old, while he is young and strong—*
> *I can't fight lions' claws, I've lived too long.*
> *Let him display his prowess, let us see*
> *His youth and health enjoy their victory."*

Bahram said, "What you say is true, and there is no reason to hide the truth." At that, he seized his ox-headed mace while the world looked on in wonder. A priest said to him, "My lord, you are wise, knowledgeable, and nobly born; who has ordered you into this combat against lions? What more can you desire than the crown? Don't lose your life seeking sovereignty and pointlessly feed your body to the fishes. We are innocent of this, it is your doing; there's no need for it, all the world is with you." Bahram replied, "You're a seeker of religious truth, and you and everyone else are innocent in this affair. I will face these lions in combat, and it is I who desire to fight against them!" The priest said, "Before you go further in this, cleanse your soul of sin, before God." Bahram did as he advised, repenting of his sins and purifying his heart.

Then he strode forward with his mace. As soon as they saw him the lions were eager to attack, and one of them broke free of his chains and bounded toward the prince, who struck him on the head with his mace, so that the light faded from the animal's eyes. Then he turned to the other one and struck him too a mighty blow on the head, so that the blood flowed down from his eyes onto his chest.

The world conqueror sat on the ivory throne, placed the splendid crown on his head, and prayed to God, who shows the right way to the lost, as his refuge. Khosrow came before him and paid homage to him, saying, "Great king, may your reign be glorious, and may the world's heroes stand before you as your slaves. You are our king, and we are your slaves who wish you well." The nobles poured jewels over him and called down blessings on the new wearer of the crown. The world rang with acclamations, and all this happened in the month of Azar, on the day called Sorush.

پامد بر سرتهر یار لبند
رخ چشم شب می روشنایی میبرد

فرو ریخت از دیده خون بر سرش

᪥ THE REIGN OF BAHRAM GUR ᪥

When Bahram became king he rewarded Monzer and No'man with splendid gifts, and at Monzer's intercession forgave those who had opposed his becoming king. He also treated the interim king Khosrow well and compensated everyone who had suffered under Yazdegerd. He made his own younger brother, Nersi, the commander of his armies. Then he declared a tax amnesty and burned the tax records, an act which caused rejoicing throughout the country.

> Once Bahram was established in his reign
> Grief fled, and pleasure flourished once again;
> Horses were his delight, and he would play
> At polo or go hunting every day.

The Story of Bahram Gur and Mehrbandad

Bahram enjoyed hunting with cheetahs, and one day when he was occupied in this manner, with a swift horse under him and with his hawk on his wrist, he came on a well-wooded place that looked like the home of people who'd been blessed by good fortune. The green pastures and foliage were like a paradise, but Bahram could see neither men nor flocks there. He said, "There must be lions around: this is somewhere for brave men to show their mettle." He readied his bow, and as he did so a male lion appeared and gave a mighty roar. The king's arrow pierced its side and entered its heart. Seeing this, the female lion's heart was wrung, and she roared and sprang at Bahram, so that her claws scored his body. He struck at her with his sword, and the valiant beast sank back defeated.

An old man emerged from the trees and spoke sweetly to Bahram. His name was Mehrbandad, and he was overjoyed at the king's sword-stroke. He was a farmer, a God-fearing man, and the wooded area was his home. He came forward and congratulated the king and bowed before him.

He said, "My lord, may heaven favor you
And make you prosperous in all you do!
My noble lord, I farm these fields—I own
The land here, both the waste tracts and the sown,
As well as donkeys, cows, and flocks of sheep.
These lions' attacks have made me curse and weep,
But now through you I'm free of them—God sent
Your strength and prowess as their punishment!
Stay with me for a while, and when you dine
I'll set before you honey, milk, and wine:
I've plenty of good lamb, and there's a glade
Whose trees will give us fruit and ample shade."

Bahram dismounted and saw that the green landscape filled with streams was a delightful place for a young man to spend time. Mehrbandad went to the nearby village and returned with the village elders and a group of musicians. He slaughtered a number of plump sheep and came to Bahram with a golden goblet in his hand. After their meal, cups were placed before them, surrounded by roses and wild saffron flowers. When Mehrbandad had grown tipsy with the wine, he said to Bahram, "You're a fine, fortunate fighter, and you should know that you look just like a king and deserve a golden throne and all its pomp and ceremony!" Bahram replied, "You're right, and he who limns our faces has created them as he wishes them to be, and chooses whomever he wishes to choose. If I look just like a king, I bestow on you as a gift all the area here, the forest and the surrounding land."

Then he mounted his horse, rode back to his beautiful palace quite drunk, and slept that night in his orchard.

The Story of Kebrui;
Bahram Forbids the Drinking of Wine

At dawn the next morning Bahram called for wine, and his courtiers began another round of merry-making. At that moment the headman of a village entered with a present of fruit: he brought camel-loads of pomegranates, apples and quinces, and also bouquets of flowers fit for the royal presence. The king welcomed this man, who had the ancient, noble name of Kebrui, and motioned him to a place among the young men there. He handed him a large goblet of wine, that held two maund. The visitor was pleased at the king's and his courtiers' attention, and when he had drained the cup, he caught sight of another and felt a craving for it in his heart. In front of all the nobles there he reached out and seized it. He stood and toasted the king, and said, "I'm a wine-drinker, and Kebrui is my name. This goblet holds five maund of wine, and I'm going to drain it seven times in front of this assembly. Then I'll go back to my village, and no one will hear any drunken shouts from me." And to the astonishment of the other drinkers there he drained the huge cup seven times.

With the king's permission he left the court, to see how the wine would work in him. As he started back on his journey across the plain, the wine began to take effect. He urged his horse forward, leaving the crowd who were accompanying him behind, and rode to the foothills of a mountain. He dismounted in a sheltered place and went to sleep in the mountain's shadow. A black raven flew down from the mountain and pecked out his eyes as he slept. The group that had been following along behind found him lying dead at the foot of the mountain, with his eyes pecked away and his horse standing nearby at the roadside. His servants, who were part of the group, began wailing and cursed the assembly and the wine.

When Bahram awoke from sleep, one of his companions came to him and said, "Kebrui's bright eyes were pecked out by a raven while he was drunk at the foot of a mountain." The king's face turned pale, and he grieved for Kebrui's fate. Immediately he sent a herald to the palace door to announce: "My lords, all who have glory and intelligence! Wine is forbidden to everyone throughout the world, both noblemen and commoners alike."

The Story of the Cobbler's Son and the Lion: Wine Is Declared Permissible

A year passed, and wine remained forbidden. No wine was drunk when Bahram assembled his court, or when he asked for readings from the books that told of ancient times. And so it was, until a shoemaker's son married a rich, wellborn, and respectable woman. But the shoemaker's boy's awl was not hard enough for its task, and his mother wept bitterly. She had a little wine hidden away; she brought her son back to her house and said to him,

> "Drink seven glasses of this wine, and when
> You feel you're ready, go to her again:
> You'll break her seal once you two are alone—
> A pickax made of felt can't split a stone."

The boy drank seven glasses down, and then an eighth, and the fire of passion flared up in him immediately. The glasses made him bold, and he went home and was able to open the recalcitrant door; then he went back to his parents' house well pleased with himself. It happened that a lion had escaped from the king's lion-house and was wandering in the roads. The cobbler's son was so drunk that he couldn't distinguish one thing properly from another; he ran out and sat himself on the roaring lion's back, and hung on by grasping hold of the animal's ears. The lion keeper came running with a chain in one hand and a lariat in the other and saw the cobbler's son sitting on the lion as unconcernedly as if he were astride a donkey. He ran to the court and told the king what he had seen, which was a sight no one had ever heard of before. The king was astonished and summoned his advisors. He said to them, "Inquire as to what kind of a man this cobbler is." While they were talking, the boy's mother ran in and told the king what had happened.

She said to him, "May you live happily
As long as time endures, your majesty!
This boy of mine's just starting out on life—
He'd found himself a satisfactory wife.
But when the time came . . . well, his implement
Was just too soft, and he was impotent.
So then I gave the boy (but privately,
To make him father of a family)
Three glasses of good wine; at once his face
Shone with a splendid ruby's radiant grace,
The floppy felt stirred, lifted up its head,
And turned into a strong, hard bone instead.
Three drafts of wine gave him his strength and glory
Who would have thought the king would hear the story?"

The king laughed at the old woman's words and said, "This story is not one to hide!" He turned to his chief priest and said, "From now on wine is allowed again. When a man drinks he must choose to drink enough so that he can sit astride a lion without the lion trampling him, but not so much that when he leaves the king's presence a raven will peck his eyes out." Immediately a herald announced at the palace door, "My lords who wear belts made of gold! A man may drink wine as long as he looks to how the matter will end and is

aware of his own capacity. When wine leads you to pleasure, see that it does not leave your body weak and incapable."

Bahram Gur's Priest Ruins and Revives a Village

Another day Bahram went out hunting at dawn with a group of companions. His vizier Hormozd rode on his left, and a priest on his right, and the two told him tales of Jamshid and Feraydun. They took dogs, cheetahs, and hawks with them and searched through the morning, but by noon they'd found no trace of either onager or deer, and when the sun shone in the heavens like a bright coin, Bahram irritatedly made his way back from his expedition. A green area, filled with men and flocks, appeared, and many people gathered round to stare at the hunters. Bahram was weary and feeling short-tempered; he'd hoped to dismount and rest in the village, but no one came forward to greet him, and the place seemed inhabited by donkeys. He grew angry with the people there and looked askance at them, saying to his priest,

> "May this green, prosperous village be a den
> Of beasts—a wild, uncultivated fen—
> And may the water dry in every ditch
> And turn to stagnant mud as black as pitch!"

The priest knew how to fulfill Bahram's command and he turned aside from the road and entered the village. He said, "This green area, filled with

houses, people, and flocks, has pleased King Bahram and he has a new plan for you. Rejoice in your hearts, you are all masters now and can make this a splendid place. Here women and children are masters too, and no one has to obey anyone else. Laborer and headman are equal: men, women, and children, you are all headmen of the village!" A cry of joy went up from the inhabitants; in their minds men and women were the same, and laborers and

servants were equal to the village headman. Since the young men now felt
no fear of authority, they cut off the heads of the village elders: everyone
became muddled up with everyone else, and bloodshed became common-
place. The area became as confused and horrifying as the Day of Judgment,
and the inhabitants fled. A few weak, old men stayed there, but every sign
of activity or prosperity had gone. The whole village took on a rundown
look: trees withered, irrigation ditches dried up, houses were in ruins, fields
were uncultivated, men and their flocks were nowhere to be seen.

A year passed, and the following spring Bahram again went hunting in that
area. He reached the place that had seemed so pleasant and prosperous, but

the village he remembered was not there. All the trees were dead, the houses in ruins, the fields empty of flocks and people. Bahram's heart was wrung to see this; he feared God and wished to act justly. He said to his priest, "Ruzbeh, it hurts me to see this lovely place in ruins: go quickly and provide them with money from my treasury, so that they won't suffer any more."

The priest left his king's side and rode into the ruins. He went from house to house and finally found an old man who had no work. He dismounted, greeted him politely, and invited the man to sit with him. He said, "Old man, who ruined this prosperous place?"

> The old man answered him, "By chance one day
> The king and his companions came this way.
> A foolish priest with no sense in his head,
> One of those noble idiots, born and bred,
> Declared to us, 'You're all the masters here,
> Social distinctions are to disappear.
> The ranks of those who rule and those who serve
> Are niceties that no one need observe.'
> As soon as he'd said that our little village
> Was filled with fights and plundering and pillage:
> May God reward that man's stupidity
> And fill his days with grief and misery!"

Grieved to hear this, Ruzbeh asked, "Who is your village headman?" The man replied,

> "A headman's for a place where grain is grown,
> And men can reap the harvest they have sown."

Ruzbeh said, "You are to be the headman here, you're to rule over these ruins. Ask the king for cash, seed, cows, and donkeys, and bring back to your village whomever you can find who is destitute. You are to be the headman and they're to do as you tell them. And don't curse that priest who came here before, as he didn't want to say what he did. If you need help from the king's court, I'll send you whatever you need. All you have to do is ask."

The old man was pleased to hear this and forgot his former sorrows. He immediately went from house to house to find men to work on the irrigation channels and to start cultivating the land again. They asked neighboring villages for donkeys and cows and set to work making the plain productive. The headman and his villagers worked hard at planting trees everywhere, and their hearts were filled with happiness each time they saw a house had been rebuilt. All those who had fled from the place weeping and wailing came back one by one when they heard of the success of the old headman's efforts. The watercourses in the streets were rebuilt, the stocks of hens, cows, donkeys, and sheep multiplied in the pastures, and the trees that people planted everywhere made the former ruins look like a paradise.

By the following year the village had responded to the old man's efforts and was as he wished. Once again, at spring time, the king went hunting with his priest, Ruzbeh, and for a third time they came to the village. Bahram Gur saw the land under cultivation, the herds of animals, the fine buildings, the plains and mountain slopes covered with sheep and lambs, the water courses coming down from the foothills, and the village filled with handsome men. He turned to his priest and said, "Ruzbeh, what have you done? This fine village was in ruins, its people and animals had fled. What did you give them so that they were able to make it flourish again?"

Ruzbeh answered, "One speech was enough to bring this ancient village to its knees, and one idea was enough to make it prosperous again, and so rejoice the heart of Persia's king. You had ordered me to destroy the village using money from your treasury, but I was afraid of God's judgment and the reproaches of noblemen and commoners. I saw the strife that results when one heart has two thoughts, and knew that when a town has two masters it cannot survive. I told the village elders that there was no master over them, that women were masters now, and children too, as were servants and laborers. When the commoners became masters, the masters' heads were brought down to the dust. This lovely place was destroyed by a speech, and I escaped reproach and did not fear God's judgment. But then the king forgave them, so I went to them and suggested another course of action. I set a wise old man over them as their headman, someone who was eloquent and knowledgeable. Through his efforts he restored the village's prosperity and made his inferiors' hearts happy. Once one man was put in charge of the rest, things went well again: goodness increased and evil decreased. I showed them the way of evil and then I opened the door to God for them. If a man uses speech in the right place, it is worth more than fine jewels. If you want your soul to have no troubles, wisdom must be your king, and language your champion. May the king's heart be eternally happy, triumphing over all evil and ruin."

The king responded, "Ruzbeh, you are worthy of a crown!" He gave this clever and perspicacious man a purse of gold coins and a royal robe of honor, raising his head to the clouds in glory.

The Story of Bahram Gur and the Four Sisters

One week the king went out hunting with his priests and advisors, and they stayed for a month drinking wine and hunting game in the mountains and plains. When they had had their fill of this, the king set off in good spirits to the city again, but night overtook them on the way and the world turned black before them. The group pushed on through the darkness, telling stories of the ancient kings. Then Bahram saw a fire in the distance, like those the king lights during the winter festival. He stared at the fire and made out a pleasant village to one side of it. In front of the village there was a mill, where the village elders were sitting, scattered in little groups. On the other side of the fire were some young women wearing chaplets of flowers in their hair, and musicians were sitting all round them. They were singing songs about the king's exploits, and as one song ended they started another. Their

faces shone like the moon, their musky hair was arranged in ringlets, and there were jewels sewn onto their clothes. They were lined up on the grass in front of the mill door: each of them held a bouquet of flowers, and they were half-drunk with wine and happiness. Loudly their song rang out:

> *"Long live King Bahram, glorious and brave,*
> *To whom the turning heavens are a slave,*
> *Whose hair is musky, and whose handsome face*
> *Is red as wine and filled with kindly grace—*
> *They call him Bahram Gur, and every day*
> *Wild onagers and lions are his prey!"*

Hearing their song, the king tugged on his rein and went over toward them. As he approached he saw that the plain was filled from end to end with young women, each of whom was as lovely as the full moon, and he realized that he was in no hurry to reach the city. He ordered the wine servers to bring him some wine and invite a few of the women who were drinking there to come to him. A servant put a crystal goblet in Bahram's hand, and the four leaders of the young women stepped forward. There names were Moshk, Sisanak, Naz, and Susanak. Tall, and as lovely as the spring, they held hands as they approached the king. They sang a song to Bahram, the wise and famous King of Kings, and his heart was charmed by them. He said to the four of them, "Your faces are like roses; whose daughters are you, and why have you lit this fire?" One answered him, "And you, a horseman tall as a cypress tree, the image of a king in every way, know that our father is an old miller who is out hunting in these mountains with his bow. He should return soon, now the night has grown dark and he finds it hard to see in the darkness."

And at that moment the miller returned from the mountain, bringing the game he had killed. When he saw Bahram, the good old man bowed his face down to the dust, and Bahram ordered that a golden goblet be handed to him. He said, "Why do you keep these four, whose faces are as lovely as the sun? It's time they were married." The old man called down blessings on him and said, "There are no husbands for these four girls of mine. They've reached the right age, and they have lived modestly, but they have no wealth; I don't want to say any more than this now." Bahram said to him, "Give these four to me, and see you don't have any more daughters!" The old man replied, "My lord, don't say such things. We've no land or income, no gold, no house, no cows or donkeys." Bahram replied, "Then they will suit me; I must have them just as they are, with no dowry." The old man said, "All four are your wives then, to serve you in the privacy of your home: you've seen their good and bad qualities, and you liked what you saw." Bahram answered him, "I accept all four, from the hand of the good man who raised them."

Having said this he jumped up, and the sound of his escort's galloping horses was heard on the plain. He had his eunuchs take the four young women to the king's harem. One by one his escort came forward, and it took the whole night for them all to pass by. The miller was astonished at this and spent the night brooding on what it could mean. He said to his wife, "How did this nobleman, a man as radiant as the moon, and with such an entourage, come to our mill in the darkness of the night?" His wife replied, "He saw the fire from far away and heard the girls singing." Then the miller said, "Tell me wife, is this going to end well or badly?" She answered, "It's God's doing; when he saw them he didn't ask about their family, and he wasn't concerned about their wealth. He was searching the world for a woman as lovely as the moon, and he didn't care about money or royal rank. If idol worshippers in China saw girls as lovely as ours, they'd forget about their idols!" And so the two talked all night about evil men and good, until the sun shone on the mountain slopes and the world glowed like a lamp.

When night had turned to day, a local landowner came to the old miller and said, "Luck came to your pillow in the dark night, and the green branch of your tree has borne fruit. In last night's darkness King Bahram was returning from a hunting trip. He saw your celebration and the fire, tugged at his reins, and came to this spot. Now your daughters are his wives and live in comfort and security in his harem. Their faces, hair, and elegance made them fit for a king; Bahram, the King of Kings, is your son-in-law, and in every country from now on men will remember you. He has given you this entire province; grieve no more, you can live free from sorrow and fear. Give us your orders, we are all yours to command. We are your subjects; no, more, we are your slaves!"

The miller and his wife stared at him in wonder, repeating the name of God over and over again. The landowner said, "Those faces and that hair brought a husband down from the sun's sphere."

Bahram Gur Finds Jamshid's Treasure

Bahram Gur was out hunting with his priests and companions another time when one of his devoted subjects approached the group, running like the wind and carrying a spade. He asked where he could find King Bahram. Everyone said to him, "What do you want the king for? Can't you tell us?" He answered, "I'm saying nothing until I see the king's face." A priest said, "What do you know about the king's face? Tell me what you have to say." When finally they took him to the king, the man said, "I have something to tell you in private." Bahram gave a tug to his reins and rode apart from his companions, and then the man told him, "You're a king who's seen the world, but listen to what I have to say. I'm the landowner here; the crops this area produces and its buildings are all mine. I was channeling water to irrigate the land so that I could get the best yield from it, and at one point the force of the water undermined the earth and a hole appeared. Then I heard a terrifying cry, followed by the clash of cymbals; that noise indicates there's a treasure there." Bahram rode over to the area the man indicated and saw a green landscape with irrigation channels in it. He summoned a number of workmen with spades who had to be brought from far away; then he dismounted, and a tent was pitched for him in the pastures. Night fell, the soldiers in his entourage lit candles, and fires burned throughout the camp.

When the sun rose above the sea and its blue surface glittered with light, workmen gathered from every quarter. They started to dig, and soon the whole plain was covered with ditches. Just as they were getting tired a structure like a mountain appeared in the ground. It was a building made of baked brick and covered with splendid plaster work. The workmen excavated all round it, until a door appeared. A priest and a companion entered and saw a long, wide room several cubits high. Two bulls made of gold were standing in front of a feeding trough, also made of gold, in which there were emeralds mixed with rubies. The bulls were like two signs of Taurus; their bellies were hollowed out and filled with artificial pomegranates, apples, and quinces. In the midst of the quinces were splendid pearls, each as clear as a drop of water. The bulls were represented as old, with wrinkled foreheads, and their eyes were made of rubies. All around them were lions and wild asses with eyes made of rubies or crystal, and there were golden pheasants and peacocks whose breasts and eyes were made of jewels.

The priest returned to the king, and said to him politely, "Come, your majesty; we have found a treasure to eclipse all others. There is a room full of jewels, to which the heavens hid the key." Bahram replied, "See if anyone has written his name on this treasure, saying it is his. See whose it is, or in whose reign it was collected here." The priest went back and saw the seal of Jamshid on the bulls. He reported to the king, "I looked, and on the bulls there is written 'King Jamshid.'"

> "O wisest of the wise," King Bahram said,
> "Why should I claim the treasures of the dead?
> As Jamshid put together this rich hoard,
> I'll win my wealth with justice and my sword.
> God keep me from defeat and poverty!
> Distribute all you've found in charity,
> Don't give it to my soldiers, I have land
> And gold enough for those whom I command.
> Sell all the jewels for cash, and so relieve
> Our widows and our orphans, those who grieve

Because they're poor despite a noble name,
Living their lives in indigence and shame.
Bring them from every ruin, every town,
And one by one write all their details down;
Give them this wealth, and may your actions bring
Peace to the soul of Persia's ancient king.
That man the soldiers tried to keep from me,
Who showed us where the treasure ought to be,
Should get a tenth of everything we found.
But I'm still young, my body's strong and sound,
So why should I have Jamshid's gold? I'll fight
With China and with Rome—my army's might,
My horse Shabdiz, my sword will win me fame,
And royal treasure, and a glorious name."

Then he went to his own treasury, whose contents he had accumulated by the sweat of his brow, and summoned all the country's warriors and gave them a year's pay. He decreed festivities, like those held at spring, and his audience hall, encrusted with gems, was prepared for this. Bahram Gur held a crystal goblet filled with ruby wine, and in his happiness he said to his companions, "My noble lords, who have heard tell of the great men who have reigned here, from Hushang to the famous Nozar, who was a descendant of Feraydun, and so to Kay Qobad who placed the crown of Feraydun on his head; you see what has remained of these great men, who speaks anything but good of them? When their days were cut short, speech remained to remind us of them, saying that this one had magnanimity and that one did not, that one was reproached and another praised. One by one we too shall depart, and it would be well for us not to act evilly in the world. Why should we covet the wealth of the dead, or give our hearts to the greed for gold? I shall not tie my heart to this fleeting world, or glory in the crown, or seek for treasure. If our days can pass in happiness, why should a wise man grieve? I want neither the crown nor my wealth if any of my subjects, any farmer or courtier, complains of being harmed by me."

Bahram Gur and the Jeweler's Daughter

Bahram, Ruzbeh, and a thousand horsemen went hunting and came on a plain filled with wild asses. It was spring and the males were searching for females and fighting with one another; they bit one another's hides so viciously that the ground was stained ruby red with their blood. Bahram watched one such combat, until the animals separated in their fury, and the victorious male mounted a female. Bahram smiled to see the animal's pleasure and drew back his bow. The arrow entered the male's back and the whole

shaft sank in, up to the feathers, pinning the male and female together. Those in his entourage who had seen the shot congratulated the king and said, "May the evil eye be far from you, and all your days be like a festival: you have no equal in the world, you are a king, an emperor, and a hero!"

Bahram was riding Shabrang and urged him forward to a thicket, where he saw a pair of lions. He drew back his bow, and the arrow entered the male lion's chest, which it passed right through, and then plunged into the ground. He then loosed an arrow at the female, which pinned her thigh to the earth. He said, "That last arrow had no feathers, and its point was blunt." His soldiers all congratulated him and said, "No one has ever seen a king like you; if you can subdue a lion with a flightless arrow, you can overturn a granite mountain."

Bahram and his companions rode in the meadows. They saw a grove of trees where there were many sheep, but the shepherds were fleeing as if in fear of some danger. The head shepherd ran toward Bahram, who asked, "Who has brought these sheep to such a dangerous place?" The man replied, "In all the world I'm the only man brave enough to come here. These sheep belong to a jeweler, and I brought them down from the mountain yesterday. The owner of the flock is rich, and he's always worried about danger. He has donkey loads of fine jewels, as well as gold and silver. He has just one daughter, who plays the harp and whose hair is a mass of ringlets. He'll only take his wine from her hand: no one's ever seen an old man like him. And if it weren't for King Bahram's just rule, how would he be able to keep his wealth? The King of Kings isn't greedy for gold, and his chief priest isn't an unjust man either. Won't you tell me who killed these two savage beasts, may God preserve him?"

Bahram replied, "These two lions were killed by a brave warrior, and then he left; he rode away with seven companions. But where's this jeweler's house? Tell me how to get there, don't hide anything." The head shepherd answered him, "Go straight ahead and you'll come to a recently built village. The fame of this place has reached the town and even King Bahram's palace. When the heavens spread their black silk over the world, the jeweler starts his merry-making. If you wait there a while, you'll hear toasts and the sound of a harp." Bahram asked for a pack horse and royal clothes: then he left his vizier and the soldiers and went off with his head full of high hopes.

Ruzbeh said to the priests and courtiers, "Now the king is going to that village. He'll sit down in the jeweler's house, and you mark my words, he'll ask her father for that young woman's hand. There's no doubt he'll put a golden crown on her head. He can never get enough of sleeping with women, and in the darkness of the night his sleeping partners run away from him. He keeps more than a hundred at a time there; whoever heard of such a king? The chief eunuch has counted nine hundred and thirty nobly born women in his harem, and all of them have their diadems and jewels and crowns and bracelets and golden thrones and bejeweled Byzantine brocade. None of them are left without their own wealth. He keeps demanding tribute from every country and province, and every year the tribute from Rome is spent on them. I grieve for our king's strength and stature, for that face of his with which he commands the court: no one's ever seen a man who could pin two wild asses together with one arrow. All this sleeping with women will destroy him; he'll soon be as soft as silk. His eyes will darken, his cheeks turn yellow, his body will become weak, his lips will turn blue; his hair will turn white from the scent of women, and white hair means you must despair of the world. His back will become bent while he's still young. So many evils come from associating with women! Once a month is sufficient for sex; if it's more often than that a man is just pouring his blood away. A wise young man should stick to once a month, and that's for the sake of having children. If you do it more often it weakens you, and when a man gets soft like that his body becomes bloodless." And so the conversation went on as they made their way back to the palace till one man said, "The sun has lost its way."

Meanwhile Bahram rode through the darkness, accompanied only by a groom. Hearing the sound of a harp, he directed his horse toward it and quickly reached the jeweler's house. He lifted the knocker on the door and asked for hospitality. One of the jeweler's maids, a kind woman, said, "Who's knocking at our door in the darkness of the night, and why?"

Bahram answered, "This morning the king went hunting, and my horse was lamed under me and I had no choice but to turn back. With a horse like this, and with its gold-worked bridle, I'm afraid I'll be set on by thieves, so I'm looking for shelter." The maid told her master, "There's a man who wants to stay with us. He says that people will steal his fine horse and its golden trappings, and that if he goes any further he'll be in difficulties." Her master said, "Open the door," and to Bahram he called out, "Come on in, boy!"

When Bahram entered he saw a fine hallway with servants standing ready. He said to himself, "O God of justice, guide me now. May all my acts be just, and may I not follow the ways of pride and greed. Make me just, so that my subjects rejoice in my existence. If my justice and knowledge increase, my memory will remain bright after my death. May all my subjects live as this jeweler does, with wine and the sound of the harp." As he went further he saw his host's daughter through a doorway. When the jeweler saw Bahram he stood, came forward, and bowed his tall, straight body before him. He said, "May this night bring you good fortune and make those who wish you ill your slaves." He spread a carpet and placed a cushion on it, and then quickly had a table laden with various kinds of food brought in. He told a servant to see to Bahram's horse, and Bahram's groom was given a separate table and a place to sleep. They brought a seat for the host and he sat himself down next to the king. Then he made excuses for his hospitality and said, "You seem to be a lord of the marches; while you are a guest in my house, my body and soul are at your service."

Bahram replied, "Who can find such a welcoming host in the darkness of the night? When we've eaten, we must drink wine and refresh ourselves with sleep. And we must not be ungrateful to God, because a man who forgets God lives in fear." A maid brought water in a bowl for them to wash their hands, and she stared at their guest in astonishment. The host called for the comforts of wine and music, and the maid brought red wine, roses, and wild saffron flowers. The host drank first, then he washed the cup, which was very beautiful, in musk and rosewater, passed it to Bahram, and said, "And what's our wine-drinker's name? I want to make a pact of friendship with you now, and seal it in the name of King Bahram." The king laughed long and loud and said, "My name is Goshasp, and I'm a knight; I came here because I heard the sounds of a harp, not for somewhere to rest."

His host replied, "This daughter of mine makes me so proud I feel my head's in the heavens! She serves wine, plays the harp, and sings better than anyone. Her name is Arezu." Then he called to Arezu, who was as elegant as a cypress tree, "Bring your harp and show Goshasp what you can do." The harp-player came before Bahram, moving as beautifully as if she were a Hindu idol, and said to him, "You are a fine knight, and in everything you are like a prince. You should understand that this house is here for your pleasure, and that my father is both your host and your treasurer. May the dark nights bring you good fortune and lift your head above the clouds!" Bahram replied, "Sit down, and take your harp: I want a song now."

Arezu lifted her harp and sang first a song in praise of the Zoroastrian priests. Then she sang in praise of her father; the harp itself seemed to weep in her hands, and as the silken strings began to speak, all her house was filled with the scent of jasmine. This was the song she sang for her father:

> "Mahyar, a noble cypress tree that grows
> Beside a bank where limpid water flows,
> Your musky hair's grown camphor-white, your mind
> Is gentle and your voice is warm and kind—
> May wisdom nourish your good soul, and may
> Confusion sweep your enemies away!
> You are like Feraydun, that noble king
> Who valued freedom above everything,
> And your obedient daughter Arezu
> Lives only to devote her life to you.
> Now you've a guest, I'm like a king who sees
> His armies conquer all his enemies."

When she had finished her song she turned toward their guest; again she took up her harp and sang to him:

> "And you are like a prince, whose heart's sincere,
> Who's fortunate in war, who knows no fear,
> And any man who hasn't seen our king,
> Great Bahram of whom all musicians sing,
> Should look upon your face without delay,
> Since you resemble him in every way.
> You're cypress-tall, reed-slim, your walk's a stride
> That's like a strutting pheasant's in its pride;
> Your heart is like a lion's, and your face
> Shines with a pomegranate blossom's grace,
> As though a rose were washed in wine. You stand,
> And like a mountain dominate the land:
> No one has seen, no one will ever see,
> A man like you for war and victory.
> May Arezu live all her years for you,
> The dust beneath your feet in all you do!"

The king was so overcome by her song and her playing, by her beauty, her bearing, and her voice that his heart was thrown into a tumult. When the wine had begun to affect Mahyar, Bahram said to him, "If you want to be well thought of, give me your daughter in marriage." Mahyar turned to Arezu and said, "Do you want this lion-hearted guest to pay court to you? Look at him well and see if he pleases you, and if you think you would like to live with him." Arezu said, "My kind and noble father, if you wish to give me to anyone, let if be to none but this knight Goshasp, who so resembles Bahram: simply to sit with him for a while is like life itself." But Mahyar did not accept his daughter's words, and he said to Bahram, "Look at her carefully, from head to foot; consider her knowledge, diligence, and intelligence. See if she pleases you, and if she measures up to her reputation. She is a fine woman, and she is not poor. I'm not one to compare my wealth with others', but if you count up Mahyar's jewels, they come to more than you'd find in a king's purse. Even if you still want her, drink another cup of wine; there's no hurry, you should rest tonight. Men of standing don't enter into agreements when they're drunk, especially if they have any sense. Stay here till sunrise and our elders have woken up, and then we can call together those who have patient hearts and are literate. It's against our customs to do these things in the darkness of the night; King Feraydun would not have done it like this. And it's not auspicious to ask for a woman's hand, or to start on any new undertaking, when one is drunk."

Bahram replied, "There's no point in saying this, and it's a bad idea to start predicting what might happen. This harp-player pleases me tonight, so you should stop all this talk about the future." Mahyar turned to his daughter Arezu and said, "Does his character please you, and what he says?" She answered, "Yes, they please me; my heart and soul have been his since I set eyes on him. Do it, and leave the rest to God; the heavens are not at war with Mahyar." Her father replied, "Then you are now his wife, and you should understand that you now live for him." And he gave her to Bahram, who took her as his wife.

As night began to turn to day all had happened as it should, and Arezu went through the sleeping household to her own room. In another part of the house Mahyar was preparing everything for his guest, the knight Goshasp. He said to a servant, "Lock the doors, and send someone quickly to the shepherds: we can't have a meal without lamb, and it must be the best lamb too. When he wakes up take him some beer and some ice, and see that someone is there to serve him. And set a bowl of camphor mixed with rosewater in his bedchamber, so that it smells sweet. Despite the wine I drank, I feel as fresh as I did yesterday: wine's not going to overcome this old jeweler!" Having said this he pulled the coverlet over his head and sank into an untroubled sleep.

When the sun lifted its glowing crown into the sky and the world glowed like a sea of ivory, Bahram's servant hung his master's whip on the door at the front of Mahyar's house. The king's men were looking for some sign of their master, and as soon as they saw the whip they began to gather in front of the house, as they would in front of the king's court, and everyone who recognized the whip went forward and greeted it respectfully. When Mahyar's doorman saw this huge crowd, with so many of them wearing nobles' belts and boots, he ran to his sleeping master and woke the old man. He said, "Get up and quickly, this is no time for sleep or rest. Your guest is the king of the world, and he's staying in this humble little house of yours!" Bit by bit the old jeweler took in what his doorman was saying, and then his heart was in a turmoil. He said to him, "What are you telling me? What's this about the king?" He was still drunk, but when at last he realized what he was being told, he leaped up and shouted, "A wise old man like you doesn't say things like this." To which his doorman responded, "Since you're so experienced, tell me who has made you the king of Iran? At dawn, before the sun came up, your guest's groom hung a golden whip covered in jewels on our door, right where people pass by our house."

When he had heard his doorman out, the old man woke up completely and said, "And I got drunk last night in front of the King of Kings, and had my daughter serve him wine?" He went to Arezu's room and said to her, "My dear, you've always loved your freedom: well, that was Bahram, the King of Kings, who came to our house last night. He had been hunting and turned aside from the road to Kohandezh. Now get up and put on your Chinese silk gown, and put on that diadem you were wearing last night. Make him a present of some of our best jewels, give him three red rubies worthy of a king. When you see his sun-like face, bow before him and cross your hands over your breast, and don't look him in the eye. You're to think of him as your own body and soul. If he questions you, speak gently, humbly, and respectfully. I won't put in an appearance unless he calls me and places me among his servants. To think that I sat at the table with him last night as an equal, it makes me want to smash every bone in my body! How could I be so forward with the king? Wine leads young and old alike astray!" At that moment a slave ran in and said, "His serene highness the king has woken up."

Bahram woke feeling healthy and happy and went into the garden where he washed his head and body. He prayed before the sun, and his heart was filled with hopes of God's favor. Then he went and sat down and called for someone to serve him wine. When he heard about his subjects gathered at the door waiting for him, he ordered them to go back to the court. He asked that Arezu be sent to him, as he had a strong desire to see her. Arezu went to him with wine and her gifts, wearing her diadem and earrings. She bowed low and kissed the ground before him: the king smiled at her and said, "You made me drunk and then disappeared. Where have you been keeping these? But taking gifts from a woman is for others; all I want from you is your songs. Sing me those songs you told me about, the ones about hunting and battles and lances and the king's blows." Then he added, "Where's the jeweler I got drunk with last night?" The young woman called her father; she was astonished at the king's kindly manner. The jeweler came in, his arms crossed over his chest, and stood before his sun-like king.

He said, "Your majesty, how wise, how noble, how great, how brave, how heroic, and how learned you are. Before you, a person with any sense can only choose to be silent. My sin came from ignorance: you must think I am crazy. It would be fitting for you to forgive my sin, because I am a foolish slave at your door, and the King of Kings cannot consider me as someone possessed of intelligence."

The king replied, "Wise men don't take offense at anything done by someone who is drunk. If a man is made surly by drinking wine, then he should leave it alone, but I saw nothing bad in you when you were drunk. But now we'll listen to Arezu, and you can consider her song about tulips and jasmine as your excuse. As she sings we'll have some wine and give no thought to the days that are to come." Mahyar kissed the ground, brought in a table, and made everything ready, and then invited in the nobles who were standing outside the door. Arezu went to her own room, frowning at the appearance of these strangers, and stayed there until the heavens put on their black veil and stars came out around the moon.

When they had eaten, Arezu was summoned and seated on a throne worked in gold. Mahyar told her to take up her harp and sing the song that the king had mentioned. Arezu sang:

> "Brave king, at whose name lions disappear,
> Leaving their dens to slink away in fear;
> Destroyer of your foes, victorious king,
> Whose face is like a tulip in the spring:
> No king is tall like you, the moon at night
> Does not possess your beauty or your light,
> When your victorious armies take the field
> Your enemies disperse, their forces yield,
> Their hearts break with despair, in headlong flight
> Their ranks are broken and they cannot fight."

As they grew happy and tipsy with the wine, they progressed from small cups to large. Ruzbeh joined them and lodgings were found for him in the village. Bahram summoned forty charming servants; their Byzantine faces were as beautiful as Byzantine brocade and they escorted Arezu to the king's harem, where they placed a jeweled crown on her head. The King of Kings and Ruzbeh returned cheerfully to the palace, and Bahram made his way to his jasmine-scented beloved.

Bahram Gur, the Landowner Farshidvard, and the Gatherer of Thorns

The next morning Bahram returned to his hunting grounds, and for a month he and his entourage stayed on the plain, both following the paths and going by unfamiliar ways. They camped in tents and pavilions and emptied the area of game. There was no sleeping on that plain while they were there, only hunting, wine, and the sounds of music, and fires burning both dry and green wood lit up the landscape. People looking for a profit came out of the city to trade with the hunters; a lively market was set up and the waste places bustled with activity. Anyone could find game and ducks to buy, to take home to their children and guests by the donkey-load.

After a month Bahram was overcome with a desire to sleep in his harem again; he and his men began their return, and the dust they sent up obscured the roads. They rode quickly until the day turned purple with dusk, when they saw a little town filled with houses, streets, and shops ahead of them. Bahram ordered his men to continue on their way with the baggage, while he would stay there alone that night. He asked who the local landowner was and made straight for his house. He saw a wide, deep, broken-down doorway; the owner appeared and bowed before him. Bahram said, "Whose is this ruin, and what is a ruin doing in the middle of the village?" The owner replied, "This house is mine, and you can see what a pass bad luck has brought me to. I've no cows, no clothes, no donkeys, no knowledge, no courage, and no strength. You've seen me, now come and see my house, which is more deserving of curses than praise."

Bahram's limbs were weak with fatigue; he dismounted and looked about the house. The floors were covered in sheep droppings, but it was a fine building, large and spacious. Bahram said, "You seem a hospitable man; bring me something to rest on."

> The man replied, "Why are you mocking me?
> There are no carpets here, as you can see,
> And there's no food here either—you had best
> Look for another place to eat and rest."

Bahram said, "At least bring me a cushion, so that I can sit for a while."

> The man replied, "A cushion! That's absurd,
> You might as well expect milk from a bird!"

"Well," Bahram said, "just bring me some warm milk then; and, if you can find it, some bread that's not stale."

"Pretend I gave it you," the man replied,
"And that you ate it and felt satisfied:
If there was bread to eat, then I assure you
You'd see a healthier host standing here before you."

Bahram asked, "If you have no sheep, how is it your house is full of their droppings?"

"It's dark already, look!" the owner said,
"This talk of yours has muddled up my head.
Go choose a house where they can entertain you
And where the owner will be happy to detain you:
Why stay with some unhappy wretch who grieves
For his bad luck, and has to sleep on leaves?
You have a gold sword, and gold stirrups too,
You don't want thieves to come and frighten you.
A house like this attracts such dangerous men,
And lions might well choose it as their den."

Bahram said, "If thieves take my sword, I won't hold you responsible."

The man replied, "Enough of all this chatter;
No one stays in this house; that ends the matter!"

But Bahram persisted, "Why should a wise old man like you be so troubled by my presence? But I think you will have the magnanimity at least to give me a drink of cold water."

He said, "Go back two bow shots and you'll see
A pond—drink all you want. Stop bothering me,
It's obvious I'm old, worn out, and poor,
Too weak to earn my living anymore."

Bahram replied, "If you've no nobility about you, at least don't quarrel with people. What's your name?"

He said, "My name is Farshidvard, and I've
No clothes or food to keep myself alive."

Bahram asked, " Why don't you make some effort to earn your daily bread?"

He said, "I pray for my release; I pray
You'll leave my ruin and be on your way.

What's brought you to this empty house? It's clear
There's never any wealth or welcome here!"

And as soon as he'd finished talking he began to weep and wail so loudly that the king fled from the noise. Laughing at the old man, he left the town, and his entourage rejoined him. They came to a waste area covered with thorn bushes, which a man was chopping down with an ax. Bahram left his men and said to him, "You're a real enemy to those thorns! Who would you say is the most powerful man in these parts?" He answered, "That's Farshid-vard, a man who for years has hardly let himself eat or sleep, even though he owns a hundred thousand sheep and about as many horses and camels. The ground is full of the gold he's hidden there, and may he have neither marrow in his bones nor skin on his body! His belly's hungry, his body's naked, he's no children, relatives, or friends. If he sold the farmland he owns, he could fill his house with jewels. His shepherds boil their meat in milk, while he eats a measly bit of bread and cheese. He's never owned two sets of clothes at the same time; he's his body's own worst enemy."

Bahram said to the thorn cutter, "If you don't know how many sheep he has, is there someone who does know?" The man replied, "My lord, no one knows how rich he is." Bahram gave the man some gold coins and said to him, "Now you've become someone to reckon with." He ordered one of his entourage to come forward, a man also named Bahram: he was a brave knight who charmed those who met him. The king also chose thirty horsemen, selected for their suitability for the work he planned for them, together with a scribe who was a good accountant. Then he said to the thorn cutter, "Off you go now; you've cut thorns and now you're going to harvest gold. Show these men the way to Farshidvard's wealth, and you will get to keep a tenth of it."

The thorn cutter's name was Delafruz; he was strong, and a fine figure of a man. Giving him a splendid horse, Bahram said, "You must make the wind your partner." Delafruz took the group to the mountains and plains, and there they found innumerable sheep. In the mountains were ten caravans of camels, each one with its own camel driver. There were draft oxen and milk cows, as well as wool, oil, buttermilk, and cheese; the whole plain was churned up with hoof prints. They found jars of butter kept in caves, and three hundred thousand cheeses stored in camel-loads next to a stream. Bahram the knight wrote to Bahram the king, beginning his letter with praise of God, who rules and nourishes all things, and invoking blessings on the king, who makes evil customs wither away. Then he continued, "King of the world, nobles and commoners rejoice in your reign. This Farshidvard, whom no one's ever seen at either a banquet or a battle, whose name is unknown to both nobles and commoners, who is loyal neither to his king nor his God, and who does not know what gratitude is, has untold wealth scattered throughout the world, while he sits hidden away, empty-handed and bent with grief. His injustice is—and do not take what I am saying as a sin—as extensive as the king's justice. You can make a great treasury of his wealth, and three years will not be enough to reckon it all up. I've summoned scribes and installed them in the mountains here; their backs are bent with the work, but I've been told that he has hidden under the earth more gold and jewels than we have already found, and the extent of his riches is not apparent yet. I wait in the mountains for your orders. Greetings from me to the king of Iran, and may his fame live forever!" He sent a swift messenger to the king with his letter.

When Bahram Gur read this missive through, he was saddened; his eyes were wet with tears and his warlike eyebrows frowned. He summoned a scribe, who brought a Byzantine pen and Chinese silk, and began his letter with praise of God, who confers victory and well-being, who is the Lord of knowledge and glory and of the imperial crown. Then he wrote: "If I am to be just, I should not harass this man. He didn't amass his wealth by theft and bloodshed, nor did he lead anyone else into evil ways. His sin is his ingratitude, the lack of any fear of God in his heart. He has been a guardian of this wealth, and the more he accumulated, the more his heart and soul withered away. What's the difference between having wolves or sheep on the plain if his sheep are not to be used for anything? What does it matter if one has jewels or gravel hidden underground if the jewels are not to procure anyone food and clothing? I won't make a treasury of my own out of his wealth, because I won't tie my heart to this fleeting world. Feraydun has disappeared from the world, and Iraj, Salm, and Tur have gone from our nobility, as have Jamshid, Kavus, Kay Qobad, and the other great men whom we remember. My father too, who grieved so many hearts and who was neither just nor chivalrous, has gone from this earth. None of these great men are here now, and we cannot quarrel with God because of this. Gather Farshidvard's wealth together, distribute it, and don't keep back one item from it. Give it to those who have concealed their needs and who are unable to escape their poverty, to those who are old and unable to work and are despised by the powerful, to those who have consumed their wealth and who are now left only with sorrow and heavy sighs, to those who still have a reputation but no money and who have no one to help them among the merchants, to orphans whose fathers have died and left them without money, to women who have no husbands or no clothes and who have no skill or energy to earn their living. Give these people all this wealth, and rejoice the hearts and souls of those who have suffered. Although you have gone in search of Farshidvard's riches, be just and temperate. Leave him the money and jewels he has hidden away, so that he won't live in want, even though they are like so much dirt to him that he has buried them in the earth. May the turning heavens be favorable to you, and may you act with justice and sobriety." They placed the king's seal on the letter, and the messenger returned with it.

The Emperor of China Invades Persia

Word reached India, the western kingdoms, the Turks, and China that Bahram was a pleasure-loving king who gave no thought to anyone or anything, who sent out no lookouts or spies, and who did not trouble to place good warriors at his frontiers. It was said that he passed his time in entertainments and had no notion of what was going on, either openly or covertly.

When the emperor of China heard this, he gathered an army from China and Khotan, distributed gold, and set off for Iran, believing that no one paid any attention to Bahram. And on the western frontier the Byzantine emperor also raised an army to threaten the country. Hearing that the Byzantine and Chinese emperors had mobilized armies against their country, the Persian nobles, both old and young, came before Bahram Gur. They were angry and filled with bitterness and spoke harshly to him, saying, "Your splendid good fortune has abandoned you. A military leader spends his time fighting with his army, but your heart is taken up with pleasure and banquets. In your eyes the army and treasury are of no account, and neither are the crown and throne of Iran." The king replied to them, "The just God of this world, who is beyond the knowledge of the greatest of men, is my support, and I shall preserve Iran from the wolf's claws. With my fortune, army, sword, and wealth I shall drive this threat back from Iran."

He went on with the pleasures of his life as before, and the country's leaders wept bitter tears. Each of them said, "The hearts of honorable men are abandoning this king." Bahram was aware of this, and troubled by it. In secret he built up his army, and no one knew of his preparations. The whole country was afraid because of the way he was living, and men's hearts were riven with anxiety. Everyone despaired of the king, despising both him and his rule. When news reached the king that the emperor of China's forces were menacing the frontier, he summoned Gostahm, who was a wise counselor and a fine warrior, and discussed the situation with him. He also summoned Behzad's son Mehr-Piruz, and Khorad's son Mehr-Borzin, as well as Bahram Piruz, Khazravan, Andian, the king of Gilan, the king of Rey, Dad-Borzin who governed Zavolestan, and Borzmehr's son Qaren. He gathered a force of thirty thousand Persian warriors, men who were prudent and ready for combat. Next he handed over the crown and throne to his brother Nersi, a wise man, just, God-fearing, and possessed of the divine *farr*, enjoining him to watch over the country's wealth and army. Then he led the forces he had gathered to Azerbaijan. Because he was taking so many troops from Pars, everyone, nobles and commoners alike, believed that he was fleeing from the war.

While Bahram was on the march, a messenger arrived from the emperor of Rome, and Nersi assigned him suitable quarters in the palace. Advisors sat with Nersi and their talk was all concerning the king. They said, "He has given all he has achieved to the wind." Meanwhile representatives of the army came to the chief priest and said, "He has scattered gold everywhere and doesn't know what behavior is appropriate for a youth. The country and the army are in turmoil, and everyone is trying to push his way to the top. Now we have no news of him, and we don't know whether to expect good or evil." After a long discussion, they agreed to send someone to the emperor of China to try to prevent an attack, so that the land of Iran would survive, even though its leader had fled. But Nersi said, "This is not what we should do, there's no channel in all the world for such waters to flow in! We have arms, wealth, and fine warriors who are able to fight with fire and sword. Bahram has left with a few soldiers; is that any reason for despair? If you think evil, evil will come to you; why have your thoughts become so gloomy?"

The Persians heard him out but disagreed: "Bahram has taken his army, and it is right that our hearts are filled with melancholy. If the emperor of China makes war on Iran, this country will forfeit all its splendor and glory; neither the army nor Nersi will survive, and the invaders will trample us beneath their feet." The Persians chose a wise and knowledgeable priest called Homay as the man best suited to represent them. Then they wrote a letter from Iran to the emperor. Saying that they were his slaves, and that their heads were bowed awaiting his commands, they wrote, "We will send what we can in the way of gifts and tribute from Iran to the emperor of China, since we do not have the strength to resist the armies of central Asia." Homay and a group of noble companions took the Persian nobles' letter and presented it to the emperor, whose heart rejoiced to see it. Homay also told him of Bahram's hasty flight with his army, and the emperor's heart and soul opened like a blossoming flower. He said to his Turkish companions,

> "What sovereign has subdued Iran before,
> By policy and plans, without a war?"

He showered gifts on the Persian envoy and gave him Chinese gold and silver coins. He composed his answer: "May wisdom be the companion of well-meaning men. I agree with all the messenger has said. I shall travel with my army as far as Marv and make the countryside there as resplendent as a pheasant's feathers. We shall wait for the Persian tribute, and the gifts from her warriors. I shall halt at Marv and go no further, since I do not wish to inflict suffering on you with my armies." The messenger hurried back to Iran and reported all he had seen and heard.

The emperor came to Marv, and the world turned black with the dust sent up by his cavalry. When he had rested he occupied himself with feasting, and no one there gave any thought to Bahram. So loud were the sounds of harps and lutes in Marv that no one could sleep, and the army wandered across the plain in no order, without posting sentries or sending out bands of scouts. The emperor's time, day and night, was taken up with hunting, drinking wine, feasting, and the music of harps, and he gave no thought to war. He was watching for the tribute from Iran to arrive, and his heart grew angry that it was taking so long.

Bahram Gur Attacks the Emperor of China

But for his part Bahram stayed alert and preserved his army from the enemy. Day and night he sent out spies, and his own troops' whereabouts remained unknown. When he learned that the emperor and his forces were in Marv, he brought his men from the environs of Azar-Goshasp; each soldier traveled with two horses, his armor, and a Byzantine helmet. Like a flood rushing down a mountain, they marched from Ardebil to Amol and thence to Gorgan, and as their leader, Bahram bore all the expedition's anxieties. They pushed on to Nisa, following a skillful guide through trackless mountains and deserts, traveling by both day and night. In the daytime they sent out scouts, and at night posted sentries. And so they came to Marv more swiftly than a pheasant can fly. His spies informed Bahram that the emperor spent his days and nights carelessly hunting at Keshmihan, or closeted with his advisor, who was of the spawn of Ahriman. Bahram rejoiced to hear this, and the pain of all his efforts dispersed like the wind.

He rested for a day, and when both he and his army were refreshed, Bahram made his way to Keshmihan as the sun rose above the mountains. Suddenly all ears were filled with the blare of trumpets, all eyes with the colors of banners. The sounds of men's cries and the clash of arms rose up from the hunting grounds, splitting the ears of the king and his men. The emperor had been asleep, worn out by the hunt, and he woke to find that he had been captured by Khazravan. The earth of the battlefield was so soaked in blood that it seemed to have rained down from the moon. Three hundred Chinese noblemen were captured and slung across saddles, and the captured emperor's dream was shattered. Bahram marched from Keshmihan to Marv; he had ridden so long and so hard that he was as thin as a reed. Few of the Chinese troops had remained in the city; those who were still there were killed, and Bahram went in pursuit of those who had fled. He followed them for thirty leagues, with Qaren bringing up the rear. When he returned, he went to the hunting grounds and distributed plunder to his men. He lifted up his head in pride at his victory over China and acknowledged that all power comes from God, who gives strength to both the good and the evil, and who is Lord of the Sun and Moon.

Bahram Gur Erects a Column to Mark the Border Between Iran and Turan

Bahram Gur rested for a week, and when he and his horses were refreshed he decided to make war on Bokhara. Princely ambition, rather than hunting and pleasure, preoccupied him, and in a day and a night he reached Amui. From there, in one watch of the night, he reached the sands of the River Oxus and crossed at the town of Farab. When the sun turned the air yellow and cast aside night's black cloak, the dust of his armies made the world as dark as a black hawk's feathers. He pressed on through Mai and Margh, overwhelming the Turkish forces and setting fire to the countryside as he went. The stars clung to the moon's skirts for comfort, and fathers fled to their

children for safety. The leaders of the Turks, both the elders and young warriors, came to Bahram on foot, as abject suppliants, saying,

> "Great king, whose star has brought you victory,
> Lord of the earth and its nobility,
> If China's mighty emperor betrayed you
> And went back on the promises he'd made you,
> You conquered him in war; the renegade
> Is now your prisoner and his debt is paid.
> Do not then shed the blood of innocents,
> Such cruelty mars a king's magnificence;
> If you want tribute, this is just—but why
> Should guiltless people be condemned to die?
> Our men and women are your slaves, we bow—
> Defeated by your strength—before you now."

Bahram's heart was wrung for them, and with the hand of wisdom he sewed shut the eyes of anger. The God-fearing king became thoughtful and forbade his warriors to shed any more blood. When it was clear that mercy had prevailed with the king, the suppliants' hearts grew calm again. Their leader agreed to send a large tribute, to be paid annually, and Bahram also imposed a fine on them. Smiling and content, he then made his way back to Farab, where he rested for a week. He summoned the Chinese nobles and erected a column of stones and mortar. He said that no one from the land of the Turks was to pass this column into Persia except with the king's permission, and that the River Oxus was to be the frontier between the two peoples.

There was a man in the army named Shemr, who was wise, powerful, and from a fine family. Bahram made him king over Turan. A gold crown was placed on his head, and all the land of Turan rejoiced in his reign.

Bahram Gur wrote to his brother Nersi describing his victory over the emperor. The nobles who had been in touch with the emperor asked Nersi to write to Bahram and intercede for them. Nersi did this, and Bahram forgave them. Before returning to his capital Ctesiphon, he went to Azerbaijan, where he prayed in the great fire-temple there and refurbished it, and distributed wealth to the poor. In Ctesiphon he made a proclamation to his people remitting taxes for seven years and promising to relieve the sufferings of the poor. He sent his brother Nersi to rule Khorasan.

The Ambassador from Byzantium

One day Bahram said to his chief priest, "That messenger the emperor of Byzantium sent has been here a long time now; what kind of a man is he, and how wise is he?" The chief priest answered, "May the king of the world flourish, blessed by divine glory. He is an old man, intelligent, and humble; he's a persuasive speaker and has a soft voice. He was a student of Plato; he's wise, knowledgeable, and from a good family. When he came from Rome he was very confident, but now he seems lost in our country, withered away like a tulip in winter; his body has grown emaciated and his face has turned the color of dry reeds. His entourage are like sheep when a hunting dog confronts them. He regards us with neither anger nor lethargy; he takes no account of anyone in this country."

Bahram said, "God has made me victorious and turned night to day for me, and I should remember that Feraydun placed a crown on the head of Salm, from whom the present Byzantine emperor is descended. He has acted with nobility and chivalry and has not taken leave of his senses like the emperor of China. I will summon his ambassador when I give audience, and see if he has anything useful to say. Then I will send him back in a friendly manner, since I'm not someone who doesn't care what others in the world think of him. Some seek for war and muster armies, others bring a golden crown and look for peace; I must distinguish the one from the other. It takes greatness to deal with these leaders." The priest blessed him and said, "May you enjoy happiness for as long as the heavens continue to turn."

The Ambassador's Questions

Bahram summoned the messenger to his court, and the old man, who had seen the world and was eloquent and wise, entered the audience hall. His arms were crossed over his chest, and his head bowed: he knelt before the throne. Bahram questioned him kindly and motioned him to a turquoise-studded seat. "You have been here a long time," he said, "and must be tired of this country. My war with China was like a constant companion and kept me away from you. Seeing you now has refreshed my life, but your stay here has gone on for too long. Whatever you say we will respond to, and your voice will distinguish this day for us."

The old man praised the king, saying, "May time and place never be without you. You are the most magnificent of the world's kings, because you have greatness as well as sovereignty; you have knowledge, good sense, justice, and glory, and you act as a victorious king should act. You have wisdom and morality, and you are the lord of the learned. I wish long life to your body and noble soul; may the heavens never see you grow weak. Your speech is as balanced as a scale, and your words are like jewels, jewels that can never be weighed in gold. Although I am the Byzantine emperor's messenger, I am also the servant of your majesty's servants. I bring greetings from the emperor to the king, who wishes long life to you, your crown, and your authority. He has also commanded me to ask your wise men seven things."

The king said, "Say what these seven things are: a fine speaker is highly honored." He called the chief priest forward, together with other distinguished advisors, and the messenger revealed what the emperor had told him to say. Addressing the chief priest, he said, "Guide us then: what is that thing which you call 'within,' and then what is that thing which you call 'outside,' because you know no other name for it? What is 'above' and what is 'below,' what is 'limitless,' and what is 'contemptible'? What is that thing which has many names and which rules everywhere?" The chief priest answered him, "Be in no hurry, and do not turn aside from the path of knowledge. There is one answer to each of your questions; that concerning 'within' and 'outside' is a small matter. 'Outside' is the sky, and 'within' is the air, by the glory of God who orders all things. That which is 'limitless' in the world is God, and it is evil to turn from him. 'Above' is paradise, and hell is 'below'; and anyone who opposes God, he too is evil. That which has many names and rules everywhere is wisdom that, old man, has many names; it is wisdom that enables a king to fulfill his desires. Some call it 'kindness,' others 'fidelity'; when wisdom leaves, pain remains, and oppression. The eloquent call it 'righteousness,' the fortunate call it 'cleverness.' Sometimes it is called 'the patient one,' sometimes 'the keeper of secrets,' since speech is safe with it. Wisdom has innumerable names; you know nothing that is higher than wisdom, since it is the best of everything that is good. Wisdom seeks out the secrets that the world contains, those hidden things our eyes cannot see. As for what is 'contemptible,' this refers to a branch of knowledge of the works of God. The man who sees the shining stars in the high heavens and claims to know their number, who says he can distinguish the rays of Mercury, when the heavens cannot be measured in leagues and no one has access to their depths—such a man will astonish those with understanding. What is more contemptible than someone who numbers the stars in the heavens?"

When the emperor's representative heard these answers, he kissed the ground and acknowledged defeat. He turned to Bahram and said, "You rule the earth, your majesty; ask for no more than you already have from God, since all the world is under your command and the heads of the haughty obey your orders. The world cannot recall another king like you, and your priestly advisor is more knowledgeable than other wise men. Philosophers are his slaves and bow their heads before his knowledge." Bahram's heart lit up at these words, and he showed his pleasure. He rewarded his chief priest with gold, fine clothes, a horse, and other goods. Having demonstrated his wisdom, the chief priest left the court in state, and the ambassador returned to his quarters.

Bahram Gur Bids Farewell to the Byzantine Ambassador

When the sun touched the heavens the king sat on his golden throne, and the ambassador and chief priest presented themselves at court again. They talked happily about various matters, and then the priest said to the ambassador, "You are unique in your intelligence; tell me, what is the most harmful thing in the world, whose actions make one weep; and what is the most profitable, whose actions raise a man up to glory?" The ambassador said, "A man who is knowledgeable will always be great and powerful, while the body of an ignorant man is more contemptible than mud and suitable for nothing good. Your question refers to ignorance and knowledge, and you have received, I think, a just answer. It is good to talk about knowledge. If you would put the matter differently, tell me, since knowledge increases honor." The priest answered, "Think, then, for speech grows beautiful from thought. The less a man hurts others, the greater an evil you should consider his death to be; but it's right to rejoice in the death of evil men, since both the good and evil are born for death. One is profitable, the other harmful, and you must make your wisdom distinguish between them."

The ambassador approved of this answer; he smiled and congratulated the king, saying, "Happy the land of Iran, that has such a king and such a chief priest! It is right that you demand tribute from the emperor of Byzantium, since your advisor is a king of the world." Bahram was pleased by his words, and his heart opened like a rose in springtime. The ambassador left the court. Night came with its black banner and its musky cloak, darkening the face of the sun. But the turning heavens did not pause and soon roused the sleepers again. The sun raised its banner, and the world's king woke lightly from sleep. His chamberlain opened the door to the audience hall, and Bahram seated himself on his throne. He ordered that a robe of honor be prepared and delivered to the ambassador, and to this he added unimaginable quantities of silver, gold, horses and their trappings, gold coins stamped with kings' names, jewels, musk, and ambergris.

Bahram Addresses His Court

After Bahram had dealt with Byzantium, he became concerned for his armies. Calling his chief priest and the leaders of the country before him, he gave his warriors grants of land, together with cash, horses, seal rings, and diadems; to the greatest of them he gave provinces and crowns. He filled the world with justice, and both nobles and commoners rejoiced in his reign. He sent away the unjust, without gifts and with cold words, and then he addressed his priestly advisors: "You are wise, capable, and pure of heart; you know all the ways of the world, and the acts of just and unjust kings. How many kings were left empty-handed and worn out for lack of rest, because of greed and injustice! The world lived in fear because of their malevolence, and good men's hearts were broken; everyone strove to do evil and no one battled for God. Women and children had no king as their protector, and the hearts of the righteous were filled with grief. Demons stretched out their hands everywhere, and men's hearts forgot the fear of God. The source of good, the hand of evil, the door to knowledge, the struggle for wisdom—all these come from the king, from whom all things come, whether righteous or perverse. If my father stretched out his hand toward injustice, if he was neither pure, knowledgeable, nor God-fearing, if the colors of fire overcame his bright heart, this should not surprise you. Look at what Jamshid and King Kavus did when they followed demons' ways. My father sought the same ways they had sought and did not wash his dark soul in the waters of wisdom. All his subjects trembled for their lives, and many lost their lives because of his anger. Now he has gone and left an evil name behind him, and there is no more to say: no one blesses his memory. But I bless his memory, for I would not have his soul be tormented by our rancor. Now that I am seated on his throne, surely he travels toward the celestial regions.

"I ask the Creator to give me strength to act with probity toward my subjects, in private and in public, and to turn the common earth into pure musk for them, so that when I become one with the dust again, the oppressed will not grasp at my skirts in reproach. May you veil yourselves in righteousness, and wash all evil from your hearts; for all men—Persian, Arab and Roman alike—are born from their mothers marked for death, whose attack is like a lion's, and from whose claws no man can turn aside his neck. The ravening lion himself is death's prey, and death humbles the dragon in the dust. Where are the heads and crowns of our kings, the nobles and splendid courtiers? Where are the proud knights, of whom we see no trace in the world? Where are the women, whose beautiful faces delighted the hearts of our nobles? Know that all those who once veiled their faces are now partnered with the dust."

Bahram Gur Writes a Letter to Shangal, the King of India

One day the king's vizier rose and said, "King of justice and righteousness, the world has no fear of malevolence now, and within our borders suffering and hardship have disappeared; but the soul of Shangal, the lord of India, turns away from justice. From India to the border with China the land is overrun with bandits. He has designs on Iran, and it would be appropriate to do something about this. You are the king, and Shangal is only the guardian of India, so why does he demand tribute from China and Sind?

Consider this, and look for a way to remedy the situation; evil should not be allowed to flourish."

The king became thoughtful, and the world appeared as a thicket before his eyes. He said,

> "I'll act in secret; I shall go alone
> To see this Indian Shangal on his throne.
> I'll see the customs of his court, his land,
> And all the forces under his command.
> I'll be my own ambassador—no one
> In Persia is to know where I have gone."

His vizier, a scribe, and other indispensable courtiers discussed the matter, then wrote a letter to Shangal. Beginning with praise of God, of wisdom, and of those who act wisely, it continued, "But you do not know your own limits, and your soul wallows in blood. Since I, Bahram, am now king, and good and evil emanate from me, how is it right for you to act as a king? Discord springs up on all sides, and it is not a kingly custom to attack others, or to consort with troublemakers. Your grandfather was our subject, your father stood as a slave before our kings, and none of us ever allowed the tribute from India to come late. Look at what happened to the emperor of China when he marched on Iran: all he had brought was looted, and he regretted the evil he had done. I see your preparations, your distribution of largess, and your glory. But I am ready for war; I have wealth and a united and determined army. You don't have the strength to resist my warriors, and there is no one in India who knows how to lead an army. You're mistaken in your assessment of your power; you're opposing your little stream against an ocean. I am sending you an eloquent, knowledgeable, and noble envoy; remit to us the tribute you owe, or if you ignorantly decide on war, see that you are well prepared for our response. I give my greetings to any man whose warp and weft are justice and wisdom." When the ink had dried, they scattered musk on the letter, which was addressed, "In the name of Bahram, whose justice resolves all evils, who received the Kayanid crown from Yazdegerd on the day of Ard in the month of Khordad, lord of the marches and protector of his country, to whom the Romans and Slavs pay tribute, to Shangal, guardian of India from the Lake of Qanuj to the frontier with Sind."

Bahram Gur Travels to India with His Own Letter

When the royal seal had been placed on the letter, Bahram made preparations as if for a hunting expedition. None of his courtiers knew where he was going, except the nobles who accompanied him as an escort. He traveled to

India, crossed the magicians' river, and saw before him Shangal's palace. Its roof reached into the sky, and in front of it there were armed men, cavalry, and elephants, and the air rang with the din of bells and trumpets. Bahram was astonished at the sight and grew thoughtful. He said to the doorkeepers and other servants there, "A messenger has come to this court from the victorious king Bahram." Immediately the chamberlain went behind the curtain to the king, ordered that the curtain be drawn back and that Bahram be conducted to the audience hall with appropriate ceremony.

The ceiling of the room Bahram entered was made of crystal, and there he saw Shangal seated on a throne of crystal and gold, wearing his crown, and dressed in cloth of silver embroidered with gold and sewn with jewels. His advisor stood behind him, and his brother was seated on another throne and wore a crown studded with precious stones. Bahram approached Shangal's throne and made his obeisance; he waited for a long time, and then said, "I bring a letter, written in Pahlavi on silk, to the king of India, from the great King Bahram, lord of the world and servant of God." When the king heard Bahram speak, he had a golden seat brought for him, and his companions were invited forward from the doorway. As soon as he was seated, Bahram began his speech: "Great king, as you command me, I shall speak, and may virtue and power never forsake you." King Shangal said, "Well, speak then; the heavens look well on a good speaker."

Bahram said, "I bring a letter to the king of India, written in Pahlavi on silk, from my king, born of kings, the like of whom no mother ever bore, who lifts up his head in glory, whose justice turns poison to its antidote; to whom the great of the world pay tribute, whose prey is lions, whose sword in battle turns the desert to a sea of blood, whose generosity is like a cloud that rains down pearls, and who has contempt for gold treasures."

Shangal's Answer to Bahram's Letter

Shangal asked for the letter and looked at the envoy in astonishment. When his scribe read the letter aloud, Shangal's face turned as yellow as bile. He said to Bahram, "You speak well, but don't be in a hurry to talk now, and control your emotions. Your king has shown us his greatness, and so have you by coming here. But I cannot agree with anyone who asks for tribute from India. This letter talks about armies and treasure and trampling countries underfoot, but you must understand that kings are like herons, and I am an eagle compared to them; or they are like dust, and I am the ocean. A man does not attack the stars, or vie with the heavens in glory. Virtue is a finer thing than vain talk, which will only make knowledgeable men contemptuous of you. You have no courage, no knowledge, no country, no city; your sovereignty is all in your tongue. My land is filled with hidden treasures untouched by my ancestors, and there is so much barding and armor hidden away that if my treasurer wanted to access it all, he would need elephants simply to bring the keys to the places where it's stored. If you reckoned up my swords and breastplates, they would outnumber the stars. The earth cannot support my armies and war elephants. Multiply thousands upon thousands, and that is the number of people in India who call me their king. Mountains and seas of jewels are mine, and it is I who sustain the world. I own the sources of amber, aloes wood, and musk, unexhausted stores of camphor, medicines enough for everyone in the world who falls sick; my country is filled with all these things, as well as with gold, silver, and jewels. Eighty crowned kings stand ready to serve me, seas and rivers enclose my country, and no devil can conquer our land. From Qanuj to the sea of China, from the land of the Slavs to Iran, all the chieftains are under my control and have no choice but to serve me, and only my name is on the lips of those who guard the borders of India, China, and Khotan. The daughter of the emperor of China lives in my harem and calls down blessings on my head; I have a son by her, a lionhearted boy whose sword can cleave mountains. From the time of Kay Qobad and Kavus, no one has ever thought to demand tribute from this country. Three hundred thousand warriors call me their king; one thousand two hundred allies, each of them related to me by blood, protect me and give no one access to me, and lions bite their nails in terror when they attack. If it were permissible for a nobleman to kill an envoy in anger, I would have severed your head from your body." Bahram replied, "Great king, if you are a nobleman, don't stir up unjust desires. My king told me to say, 'If you are wise, don't follow unjust ways. Produce two knowledgeable and eloquent men from your court and if either of them shows himself superior in wisdom to one of my men I have no claims on your country, because a wise man does not despise language. Or, if you would rather, choose a hundred of your mace-wielding cavalry and let them fight against one of our men. If they can show their worth and courage, I shall not ask for tribute.'"

Bahram Wrestles Before Shangal and Shows His Prowess

Shangal heard him out and said, "You don't think in a chivalrous way. Come down from your arrogance for a while, and be more at ease; there is no point in saying such foolish things." Bahram rested in his quarters until midday, while a splendid banquet was prepared. When the food was set before Shangal, he said to one of his servants, "Bring that envoy of the Persian king. He talks well and he's a novelty for us. Bring his companions too, and sit them with the other envoys." Bahram came quickly; he sat down, reached for the food, and said nothing. Once the main course was over, musicians were called in while the guests reclined on gold-worked embroideries, and the scent of musk rose up from the wine. The courtiers became cheerful from the wine and forgot their anxieties over all that was yet to come.

Shangal summoned two wrestlers, men who could stand against a devil. They put on their wrestling breeches and began their bout, straining and struggling against one another. The wine had taken effect in Bahram's brain; he picked up a crystal goblet, and said to Shangal,

> "Let me put on those breeches! When I fight
> Against a man of comparable might,
> The wine I've drunk has no effect on me—
> I'm not unmanned by feasts and luxury!"

Shangal laughed and said, "Go on then, and if you bring one of them down, shed his blood!" Bahram stood and bent his tall body, crouching in the wrestler's stance. He grasped one of the two around the waist, like a lion leaping on a wild ass, and threw him against the ground with such force that the man's bones were broken, and his face turned pale. Shangal gazed in

astonishment at Bahram's stature, his broad shoulders, and his strong body. In his own language he said the name of God to himself and reflected that Bahram had the strength of more than forty men. When the assembly was drunk, the party broke up and left the jewel-encrusted hall. The sky put on its cloak of Chinese silk, and everyone, young and old, rested from drinking.

When night's musky tent turned gold again, and the sun showed its face in the heavens, the Indian king rode out with a polo stick in his hand. His men had brought his bow and some arrows, and he amused himself with these for a while. Then he ordered Bahram to mount and to take the royal bow in his hand. Bahram said, "Your majesty, I have a number of horsemen with me

who would dearly like to play at polo, or to shoot at the target. What are your orders for them?" Shangal replied, "Skill with the bow is certainly praiseworthy in a knight. You, with your strength and stature, draw this bow back and show us your skill." Bahram gave his horse its head, and as it galloped forward he shot an arrow that shattered the target. All the knights and warriors who were there cried out their congratulations together.

Shangal Is Suspicious of Bahram and Prevents Him from Returning to Persia

Shangal became suspicious of Bahram and thought, "No envoy—neither Indian, Turkish nor Persian—has his strength and glory, or his skill with a bow. If he is himself the king, or a great nobleman, it would be best for me to refer to him as the king's brother." He smiled, and said to Bahram, "You are skilled and have the qualities of a man of authority. With such strength and abilities you must be your king's brother. You have the royal *farr*, and a lion's might, you must be more than just a brave warrior." Bahram replied, "Your majesty, do not mock a simple messenger. I am not of Yazdegerd's family, nor am I the king, and it would be a sin for me to refer to the king as my brother. I am just a stranger from Iran, neither a scholar nor a nobleman. Allow me to return now, since the road is long, and I do not want to incur my king's wrath." Shangal said, "Not so fast; you and I still have things to discuss. You should not be in any hurry to leave; a quick departure would not be appropriate. Stay with us, and put your heart at rest, and if you don't want our strong wines, drink new wine."

Then he called his vizier and talked with him about Bahram for a while. He said, "This is either Bahram, or at least someone more important than a simple warrior. Tell him kindly that he should stay here and not try to leave Qanuj. If I tell him, he will be afraid; you can say whatever's appropriate. Tell him that the best thing he can do is ingratiate himself with the king of India. Say, 'If you stay near the king and follow his advice, he'll give you the choicest province, you'll be the army commander there and recipient of the taxes in a place where it's always spring and the streams give off the scent of spring, where there are jewels and cash enough to keep a man's heart from sorrow. You have won favor with the king and he smiles whenever he sees your face. A man who is fortune's favorite will not leave Qanuj, where the trees bear fruit twice a year.' When you've talked to him in this way, ask him his name, because I'd dearly like to know it. If he is happy to stay here in our country, our glory will be increased by his. I'll quickly make him the leader of our armies and equal to myself in this land."

The vizier said all this to Bahram, and then asked him his name, indicating that his answer would not be complete if he didn't give it. The color in Bahram's face changed, and he wondered how he should respond. Then he said,

> "Don't shame me in two countries in this way!
> For treasure, or from need, I won't betray
> My country's king—our faith says that to rise
> Against our kings is neither good nor wise:
> Since good and evil, all we meet with here,
> Will pass away from us and disappear,
> A wise man does not let ambition lead
> His soul astray, or give his heart to greed.
> Great Feraydun, and Kay Khosrow, and all
> The mighty kings who held the world in thrall,
> Where are they now? And Bahram is a king
> Who won't be disobeyed in anything.
> If I should go against his orders he
> Won't be content when once he's punished me;
> He'll conquer India, and bring this land
> Of ancient magic under his command.
> It's better I return to see once more
> My valiant king, victorious in war.
> As for my name, they call me Borzui,
> This is the name my parents gave to me.
> Tell Shangal all I've said, so that he'll know
> That I've been here too long now and must go."

The vizier went over all he had been told with his king, who frowned and said, "This is pointless chatter; I'm going to arrange something that will bring this splendid warrior's life to its close."

Bahram Fights against a Rhinoceros and Kills It

Roaming in Shangal's territories was a rhinoceros so huge that even lions and vultures fled from it, and the whole country was in a deafening uproar. Shangal said to Bahram, "All men respect you, and this is a task for you: you must approach this rhinoceros and pierce his hide with your arrows. If your glory can rid our land of this danger, I shall seat you next to myself, and your name will live forever in India!" Bahram said, "I shall need a guide, and when I catch sight of this animal, by the strength that God has given me, you'll see his hide soaked in blood."

Shangal gave him a guide who knew the area where the rhinoceros was lurking. As they approached the place the guide described the animal's lair,

and the great size of its body. He pointed out the thicket where the rhinoceros was and withdrew, while Bahram strode forward. A few Persians were
following him, thinking they too would fight against the rhinoceros. But
when they saw its huge snout in the distance, and all the vegetation there
flattened by its weight, they said as one man to Bahram, "Your majesty, this
is beyond any man's courage; no matter how valiant a prince you are, people don't fight with mountains and rocks. Tell Shangal that this can't be
done, and that you don't have your king's permission for such a battle." But
Bahram replied, "If God has given me a grave in India, how can my death
occur somewhere else? It is impossible even to think such a thing!" The
young man grasped his bow, as if careless of his life. He ran forward until
he was close to the rhinoceros, his brain full of fury, his heart ready for
death, and snatched a poplar wood arrow from his quiver. He rained down
arrows like a hail storm, until the rhinoceros started to weaken, and when
he saw that the animal's time had come, he exchanged his bow for a dagger.
He severed the rhinoceros's head and cried, "I do this in the name of the
one God, who has given me this strength and glory, and at whose command
the sun shines in the heavens!"

He ordered that an oxcart be brought, to take the rhinoceros's head out of
the thicket. When Shangal saw them in the distance, bringing the head, he had
his audience hall hung with brocade, and as the great king sat on his throne,

Bahram was ushered into his presence. All the nobles of India and the Chinese knights who were there called down blessings on him, and chieftains went forward with gifts, exclaiming, "No one's feats of bravery can compare with yours." Shangal showed joy outwardly, but his heart was troubled; at times his face was full of smiles, and then a frown would cross his features.

Bahram Gur Kills a Dragon

Also in that country was a dragon that lived both in the water and on dry land, sometimes wallowing in a lake, sometimes sunning itself on land. Its long tail could encompass an elephant, and it made great waves in the lake's waters. Shangal said to his intimate advisors, "This lion-like envoy sometimes delights me and sometimes fills me with anxiety. If he stays here, he'll be a great support to me, and he can lead the armies of Qanuj; but if he goes back to Iran, I fear that Bahram will destroy Qanuj. With a subject like this envoy and a king like Bahram, nothing of value will be safe here. I've pondered this all night, and I've thought of another stratagem: tomorrow I'll send him

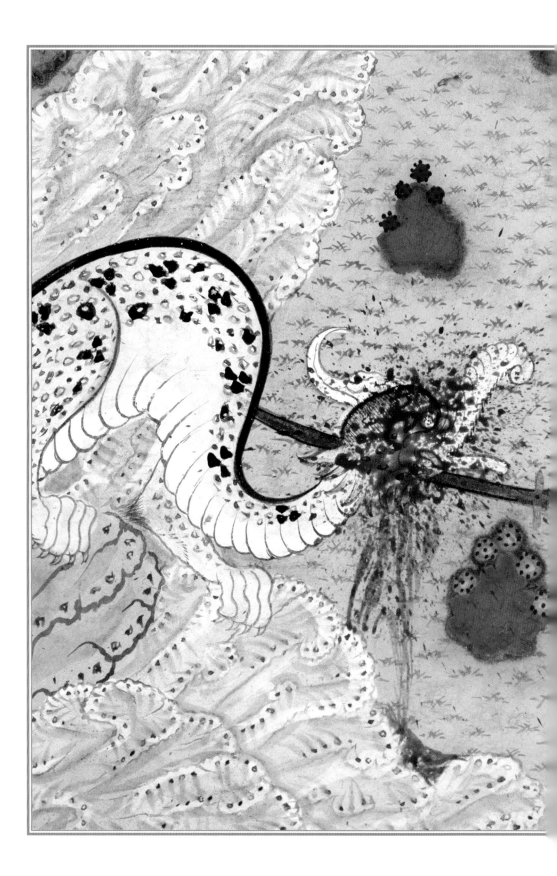

against that dragon, from which he certainly won't escape unharmed. I won't be blamed for this because he'll be only too eager to fight it."

He summoned Bahram and talked with him at length about the deeds of brave warriors. Then he said, "God brought you from Persia to India so that you could cleanse our country of evil, as is the custom of great men. There's something that has to be done, and it is a difficult and dangerous task, but it could end with your becoming wealthy. When you have completed this task you are free to go with my blessings." Bahram replied, "The heavens will change their courses before I disobey your orders." Shangal continued, "The disaster we're faced with is a dragon; he lives both on dry land and in the water, and he can kill a gaping crocodile. If you can rid India of this monster, then you can take India's tribute back to Iran, and everyone in our country will agree to this. You will also take presents from India, like aloes wood and ambergris and all sorts of other things." Bahram said, "Your majesty, great lord of India, as God is my witness I will eradicate all trace of this dragon. But I don't know where he lives, someone must show me the way to him."

Shangal sent a guide with him to point out the dragon. Thirty Persian knights rode with him too, as far as the lake. They saw the dragon looming in the darkness, and the Persian nobles were so alarmed at the sight that they cried to Bahram, "My lord, you shouldn't think of this monster as being like the rhinoceros." Bahram replied, "We must leave the outcome to God. If I am to die fighting this dragon that will neither increase nor decrease my courage." He readied his bow and selected arrows whose tips had been dipped in poison and milk; then he showered the dragon with arrows, shooting on horseback, striking it right and left. The steel arrow-heads pinned its mouth shut, and the surrounding thorns were burned by the poison it shed. Then Bahram struck its head, and mingled blood and poison coursed down its chest. The dragon's body was weakening, and the ground was awash with blood and poison; Bahram drew his glittering sword and split open the monster's heart. With his sword and an ax he hacked off the head and flung the lifeless body to the ground.

He had the head dragged to Shangal on a cart, and when Shangal saw it all India called down God's blessings on Persia that had produced such a strong and splendid knight who was worthy of combat with a dragon, and whose only equal was his own king.

Bahram Marries the Daughter of the King of India

But Shangal's heart was heavy with worry, and his face turned yellow at the thought of Bahram's feats. When night fell he called his advisors to him, men of his own family and others to whom he was not related, and said to them, "This man of King Bahram's, with that strength and power and authority he has, says that nothing will keep him here, although I have

offered him all kinds of glory and splendor. But if he returns to Iran and goes to his courageous king, he'll say our army is weak and that there are no knights in India. My enemy will be contemptuous of me. To prevent this I shall cut off his envoy's head. I want to do away with him in secret; what do you say to my plan, and how should I proceed?"

His advisors said, "Your majesty, do not torment yourself in this fashion. To kill a king's messenger would be a foolish act; no one has ever thought like this or followed such a path. Your name would be despised, and a king should be dear to his people. And then an army would come from Iran, and a king like Bahram wouldn't leave a single one of us alive; you must not wash your hands of righteousness in this way. He delivered us from the dragon, and his reward for his troubles should not be that he is killed. In our land he killed both the dragon and the rhinoceros, and he deserves a long life, not death." Shangal's soul was darkened, and he was unsure what to do.

At dawn the following morning he sent for Bahram and talked with him alone, with neither his vizier nor his advisors present. He said, "You charm everyone, and you've become very powerful, but don't be too ambitious. I'm going to give you my daughter in marriage, and I shall do more than I have promised. But when I have done this, you must forget about leaving here. I shall make you commander of the army, and you will rule over India." Bahram was silent, and he thought of his throne, his lineage, and his battles. To himself he said, "There's no arguing with him. It would not be shameful to be related to Shangal, and besides I shall save my life in this way, and perhaps one day see Persia again. I have been here a long time now: the lion has fallen into the fox's trap." He answered, "I shall do as you say, and your words will be my soul's guide. Choose one of your three daughters, and when I see her I shall call God's blessings down on her."

The king was delighted at his response and had his audience hall decorated in Chinese silk. His three daughters came forward in their gorgeous clothes, their scent, and their beauty. Shangal said to Bahram, "Go, and delight your heart with something you've never seen before." Bahram hurried to them, and chose one, as lovely as the spring. Her name was Sepinoud, and she seemed compounded of modesty and grace, good sense and desire. Shangal gave him Sepinoud, who was as elegant as a cypress, and as pure as a candle that burns without smoke. He then selected a rich treasury and gave his daughter the key to it. Next he gave gold and silver coins and other goods such as aloes wood, ambergris, and camphor to the splendid knights in Bahram's entourage. His jewel-studded chamber was decorated for a feast, and all the nobility of Qanuj came to the festivities, which were presided over by the king. For a week they sat there, carousing happily with wine, and Sepinoud, as lovely as wine in a crystal goblet, was seated at Bahram's side.

Bahram Gur Flees from India with Shangal's Daughter

When Bahram had lived with Shangal's daughter for a while, she realized that he was the king of the world. Day and night she wept with love for him, and her eyes were always fixed on his face. And when Shangal learned of their mutual love, he ceased to be suspicious of Bahram.

Bahram and Sepinoud were seated together one day happily talking of this and that, when he said to her, "I know that you want what is best for me. I want to tell you a secret, but you must see that it remains unknown to anyone else. I want to leave India: can you agree to this? I'm telling only you about it, and nobody else must know. My situation in Persia, where I am under God's protection, is much better than here. If you wish to go too, your good sense will guide us and you will be recognized as a queen everywhere; your father will kneel before your throne."

Sepinoud said, "You are a proud man; see that you don't wander from wisdom's path. But the best of all women in the world is the one who makes her husband smile continually; my soul will deserve your contempt if it deviates from your intentions." Bahram said to her, "Then find some way to carry out this plan, and speak not a word to anyone." Sepinoud replied, "Truly you are worthy of the throne: I will find a way, if luck helps me. There is a place in the forest not far from here, where my father holds religious festivals. It's about twenty leagues away, and is believed to be sacred; it's customary to weep in front of the idols there. Good hunting for wild asses can be found there, and aloes wood for burning in Qanuj grows in that area. The king and his entourage are going, and there will be such a crush the roads will be blocked. If you want to leave for Iran, wait for five days, and be ready to set off when the king leaves the city."

Bahram was overjoyed to hear her suggestion, and that night he did not sleep till dawn for thinking about it. The next day, when the sun touched the morning sky, and like a stranger night prepared to depart, Bahram went out hunting for wild asses. As he left he said to his wife, "Make everything ready for our departure, but tell no one." All the Persians in his escort went with him, and they reached the shores of a river, where they saw merchants' baggage piled up. They were Persian merchants, men who braved the seas and the deserts, and when they saw Bahram's face the king bit his lip and ordered them not to bow down before him. Wanting to keep his identity hidden, he said to the merchants, "Keep your mouths shut; this situation can be profitable but also dangerous. If the secret of who I am is known in India, Persia's soil will be drenched in blood. A man who can keep his mouth shut can help me; he needs his lips closed and his hands ready for action. Swear silence, till Fortune favors us. Swear that if you ever betray King Bahram, you have broken with God and made a pact with the devil!" When they had sworn to this, Bahram's heart ceased to worry about their loyalty. He said, "If you would turn my words to diadems, guard my secret as you guard your souls. If the throne loses me, armies will attack Iran from all sides, and there will be no merchants or king there, no landowners, no army, no throne, and no crown."

They wept at his words and said, "May our merchants' souls be sacrificed for you, and youth and sovereignty be yours!" The king called down blessings on them, and then, entrusting his soul to God, he returned anxiously to his quarters. There he said to his wife, "When King Shangal goes to the sacred grove, a messenger is sure to come from him asking for me. Arrange things with your mother, but in such a way that she doesn't realize your secret. Tell her that Borzui is sick, and may the king excuse his absence." Sepinoud told her mother this, and when Shangal was ready to set out for the grove his wife said to him, "Borzui is ill; he asks to be excused, your majesty, and says that you are not to worry about him. A sick man will only be depressed by such observances, as the king knows." Shangal agreed: "A sick man should not be thinking of ceremonies."

At dawn the following day Shangal set off from Qanuj with his entourage. When night came Bahram said to his wife, "My dearest partner, it's time for us to leave." Invoking God's name, he placed Sepinoud in the saddle; then he put on his armor and mounted his horse. His lariat was tied to the saddle, and he grasped his mace in his fist. They rode until they came to the river, where they saw the group of Persians asleep. Bahram commandeered a boat for his companions and placed Sepinoud in a little skiff; they reached the far shore just as dawn was breaking.

Shangal Pursues Bahram and Learns Who He Is

A horseman rode out from Qanuj with the news that Borzui and his Persian entourage had left, taking the king's daughter with them. When Shangal heard this, he came from the hunting grounds like a raging fire. With a group of soldiers he pursued Bahram until he reached the banks of the river and saw Bahram and Sepinoud on the other shore. In his fury, he crossed the river in the twinkling of an eye. He said to his daughter,

> "May no king ever have a child like you!
> This man deceived you, and away you flew
> To cross this river without telling me—
> You're leaving our celestial sanctuary
> For what? A ruined and impoverished land!
> You'll know the force of this spear in my hand
> If you think you can simply leave my side
> And, without warning, run away and hide!"

Bahram said to him, "You wretch, why have you ridden here like a fool? You've put me to the test and you know that I'm as much of a man on the battlefield as I am at banquets and wine drinking. You know that a hundred thousand Indians against me count for less than one knight. If I and my thirty companions are armored and have our Persian swords, we can fill the land of India with blood, and leave not one person alive."

Shangal knew that he spoke the truth, because there was no denying his courage and fighting ability. Shangal said to him, "You were dearer to me than my own eyes, I preferred you to my children and to all my family. I put a crown on your head and gave you the bride you wanted. I acted justly toward you, and you acted deceitfully. You chose treachery instead of loyalty, and when has it ever been right to return loyalty with treachery? What can I say of a man whom I treated as my own son, whom I believed to be wise, and who now acts like a belligerent knight, or as though he were the king himself? When was a Persian ever loyal? When a Persian says 'yes' he's thinking 'no.' This is just how a lion cub acts; its keeper cares for it and soaks it in tears, but when it cuts its teeth and its claws become sharp, all it wants is to fight with whoever brought it up."

Bahram replied,

> "When you know who I am, you will not blame
> Me for my acts, or slander my good name.
> I am the King of Kings, and my commands
> Are absolute throughout the warlike lands
> Of Persia and Turan. From now on you
> Will reap the benefits of all I do.
> You'll be my father here, and I won't say
> 'Where is the tax your country has to pay?'
> Your daughter is the eastern candle flame
> Who crowns all other women with her fame."

Shangal was astonished at his words. He tore his Indian turban from his head and urged his horse forward, so that he left his troops and stood before the king. In his happiness he embraced Bahram, asked pardon for what he had said, and commanded that a meal and wine be prepared. Bahram explained everything that had been hidden from him, telling him all the details of what had happened. They drank a quantity of wine and then rose; each asked pardon of the other, and the two brave, God-fearing kings clasped hands in promises of mutual devotion, saying,

> "Our hearts will never break this loyalty,
> And we'll uproot the tree of treachery;

The friendship that we swear to will abide
Forever now, with wisdom as our guide."

Shangal bade farewell to Sepinoud, embracing her as though his own chest were the warp and hers the weft of one cloth. Then the two kings quickly turned from one another, having abandoned all the rancor that was in their hearts. Happily and in haste they set out, one over dry land and the other over water.

The Persians Come to Welcome Bahram Gur

When news reached Iran that the king and his entourage had returned from Qanuj, all the streets and towns along the way were decorated to welcome him, and everyone took part in this, scattering gold and silver coins, musk and saffron. Bahram's son Yazdegerd called the scattered troops together to form a welcoming party, and Nersi and the chief priest accompanied him. When Bahram's son saw his father, he went forward and pressed his face against the dust, as did Bahram's brother Nersi and the chief priest, and though their faces were dusty, their hearts were filled with happiness. And so the king progressed toward his palace, entrusting his body and soul to God. The world turned dark, and he rested; the moon was like a silver shield in the sky.

When day tore night's dark shirt, and the candle that lights the world appeared in the sky, the King of Kings sat on his golden throne. The doors to his audience hall were opened, and his lips were closed. The nobles, wise men, and client rulers of his realm came before him. Bahram rose and addressed them with words of advice and wisdom: his nobles responded with congratulations, and by calling down blessings on his head.

Then the king mounted his horse, and he and his courtiers rode to the fire-temple of Azar-Goshasp. There he distributed a great quantity of gold and silver to the poor, giving more to those who tried to conceal their need from him. The keepers of the flame of Zarathustra came to him with gifts and the sacred barsom, and Bahram presented Sepinoud to them. They taught her the principles of the faith and bathed her in pure water, so that she was cleansed of all corruption, dust, and dirt. Bahram opened the prison gates, freeing the prisoners, and gave money liberally to the needy.

Shangal and Seven Kings Visit Bahram

After Sepinoud had been Bahram's wife for some time and had told her father of Bahram's exploits, Shangal desired to go to Iran. He sent an eloquent and noble Indian messenger to request that a new treaty be drawn up between him and Bahram, one that he could keep in his palace as evidence of their friendship. Bahram responded with a new treaty that was as fair as the sun shining over a celestial garden. He also wrote a letter in Pahlavi script that the messenger took to Shangal. The king of India then made preparations to travel to Iran, but hid all this from his Chinese father-in-law.

Seven kings came to Shangal's court to accompany him on his journey, including the king of Kabol; Sandal who came with his entourage; the noble Mandal; and the powerful Jandal. All were great kings, eager for fame; they wore torques and earrings and were resplendent in jewels, gold, and silver. Parasols of peacocks' feathers were held over their heads, and their elephants were draped in brocade. The caravan's splendor could be seen for miles as they traveled taking gifts for Bahram, even though he despised such wealth. They went forward, stage by stage, and when Bahram heard of their approach, nobles from every town went out to welcome them. The King of Kings traveled as far as Nahravan, and there the two great monarchs met and dismounted, each offering greetings and apologies for the trouble the other had taken. These two crowned, glorious kings embraced one another, while their escorts dismounted and the world was filled with the hubbub of greetings. The two kings traveled on horseback, side by side, gossiping of this and that, until they reached Bahram's palace, where a golden throne was placed ready for Shangal, and imperial robes were given to him. The tables spread for the feast stretched for a bowshot and were piled with lamb and spit-roasted chicken. Musicians sang and wine was brought, so that from one end of the feast to the other all the glasses were full. A splendid space for talk and relaxation, with attentive servants, had been prepared for after the meal, and the whole palace and its grounds seemed like a paradise. The wine flasks were all of crystal and set out on golden trays, and other trays were piled with musk, while the stewards wore golden diadems and jewel-encrusted slippers.

Shangal was astonished by the palace, and as he drank his wine he thought to himself, "Is this paradise, or a garden where all one's companions exhale the scent of musk?" In private he said to Bahram that he would like to see his daughter, and the king gave orders that eunuchs from his entourage escort him to her. As Shangal went with them he saw other parts of the palace that were as beautiful as the spring. And then

> He saw his daughter, gloriously gowned,
> Calm on her ivory throne, and nobly crowned;
> He kissed her forehead then, and bent to place
> His face against her radiant, moonlike face:
> They wept in one another's arms, and he
> Caressed her hands with his continually.
> He said, "You live in paradise, my dear;
> The palace that you left, compared to here,

Is ugliness itself—a noisome lair,
Impoverished, idolatrous, and bare!"

He gave her the presents he had brought—purses of gold, crowns, and slaves—and they made her apartments look like a garden in springtime. Then he returned to Bahram but saw that the festivities were breaking up; the nobles were tipsy with wine and calling for all kinds of bedding, ready to go to their sleeping quarters. Shangal too decided to sleep. The musky cloak of night, spotted with stars like a leopard's hide, was spread, and all the wine drinkers slept until that golden goblet that we call the sun appeared. Night's cloak was pushed aside, and the plains glistened like yellow topaz. Bahram took the king of India hunting, and when they returned they sat to feasting again. Whether they were engaged in conversation, hunting, or feasting, Shangal was almost never absent from Bahram's side.

Shangal Returns to India

Shangal went to his daughter and there asked for a pen, paper, and ink made from black musk. He wrote a proclamation, beginning with blessings on him who had cleansed the world of sorrow, spreading righteousness and justice so that evil and vice had become only the devil's portion. Then, "I gave Sepinoud to the famous King Bahram as his bride; may the King of Kings live forever, with all other nobles as his slaves. When I leave this fleeting world I entrust Qanuj to King Bahram. Commit my dead body to the flames, and do not disobey Bahram. Hand my treasures over to him, and hand over to him too our country, its crown, its throne, and its armies." He gave this proclamation, written in Devanagari script on silk, to Sepinoud.

Shangal stayed for two months in Persia; then he sent a messenger to Bahram, asking that he and his entourage be allowed to return home. Bahram agreed to his return to India and ordered his chief priest to select some Persian goods as presents: there were gold coins and royal jewels, innumerable swords, helmets and belts, and more brocades and uncut cloth than one could reckon. According to their rank, the men of his entourage were given horses caparisoned in Chinese brocades. Then the king cheerfully bade them farewell and went with them for three stages of the journey. Not content with what he had already bestowed on them, he gave them enough fodder for their animals to last until they reached the border with India.

Bahram Remits the Taxes Paid by Landowners

When Bahram returned, he sat quietly on his throne and thought of the evil day of death; his heart was filled with pain, and his face turned pale. He summoned his vizier and commanded him to inspect his treasuries and count the gold, jewels, and cloth he possessed. He did this because the words of his astrologer were troubling him. He had said, "You will live for three score years, and during the fourth must weep for death." Bahram had replied, "I shall enjoy myself for twenty years, with partners for my journey through the world; during the next twenty I shall act righteously and justly in private and in public; and during the third twenty I shall stand before God asking for his guidance." The astrologer had said sixty-three years, but the number three was obscure. It was his words that had made him think of his treasury, even though he usually paid little attention to wealth. Blessed is the man who lives without trouble or self-indulgence, especially if he is a king.

His vizier spent many difficult days reckoning up his wealth, and when he arrived at a figure he returned thoughtfully to the king. He said, "You have sufficient wealth to last for twenty-three years. I have taken into account provisions, the pay for your splendid army, and the expenses of messengers who come to your court from client kings and the provinces.

Your treasury is full of gold and silver and other wealth, and will last for twenty-three years." When Bahram heard this and reflected on it, he stopped worrying about those things that were to come.

> He said, "My reign is coming to a close.
> Consider: we've three days here, and of those
> Tomorrow has not come, while yesterday
> Has gone forever now, and passed away:
> I won't be bent down by anxiety
> During the one day that is left to me."

He gave orders that taxes, on both the nobility and the commoners, were to be remitted throughout the world. Then he established a priest in each town to wake up those who were asleep and act as a mediator in all disputes. He gave these men a stipend for food, clothes, and furnishings and said to them, "Neither good nor evil must be hidden from me; arbitrate among men and tell me of both the good and the bad so that I can lay my fears of evil to rest."

The priests went out into the world, and nothing, whether good or evil, remained hidden from them. They did as they were ordered, but letters came in from every province saying that wisdom was deserting men's minds, that the world was full of battles and bloodshed. The young did not respect their elders; their hearts were puffed up with wealth and they had no regard for the king or his priests. As the letters arrived, one after another, the king's heart became tired of bloodshed. He chose an administrator for each province, a man who was just, knowledgeable, and well qualified. These functionaries were given a stipend from the treasury and told to collect silver in the form of taxes from the area's subjects for six months. They sat in state and were crowned; for six months they collected taxes, and for six months distributed revenue, but they themselves were not to profit from the silver they collected. The intention was to stop the bloodshed caused by men being led astray, but the king's agents wrote to him that justice and security were disappearing from the world: the rich paid no taxes, but in their arrogance thought only of squabbles and arguments.

When Bahram read these letters, his heart became bitter. He chose lords of the marches, righteous men such as the situation required, gave them financial support for a year, and ordered them to apply God's law against those who were shedding blood, so that men should be at peace again. When some days had passed he wrote to his agents, who were scattered throughout the country, asking them to identify those things that were harmful to his kingdom. They answered, "The king's liberality has meant that no one cares for the old and true ways. Agriculture is neglected, we see draft oxen wandering at will, and plants are growing indiscriminately in the fields and plains." He answered, "Men are not to rest from agricultural labor till midday, when the sun is high in the sky. But don't expect to get anything out of men who have nothing. When men don't work, it's from ignorance, and ignorance is something we should weep over. A man in that condition should be given a few coins to stave off hunger. If a man has neither seed nor livestock, don't act harshly with him; help him with money, to relieve his sufferings. Do likewise when disaster strikes from the sky, since no man can rule the sky; if the ground is covered with locusts that eat all the crops, give the farmers a grant from the treasury, and have this proclaimed throughout the province. And if there is an uncultivable or sterile area, as there is in all provinces, on the lands of both nobles and commoners, if any man tries to collect taxes on such an area, even if he were my own guardian, I'll bury him alive and curse his house!" They set the king's seal on this letter, and a messenger took it to all quarters of the land.

Bahram Gur Brings the Luris from India

Where there were poor men he clothed them, and he wrote a letter to the provinces asking who lived well, and who were destitute. "Tell me," he wrote, "what is happening in the world, and lead my heart toward the light." Answers came from the nobles in all provinces saying, "We see that the land is flourishing, and everywhere blessings are called down upon you, but the poor complain about the king and about their bad luck. They say, 'When the rich drink their wine they have chaplets of flowers on their heads, and they drink to the accompaniment of musicians' songs. They don't consider us as people at all, which is unwise of them: we have to drink our wine without music and without any flowers.'"

The king laughed aloud at this letter, and he sent a hard-riding messenger to Shangal saying, "You must help me out now: choose ten thousand of those Luris, men and women both, who know how to play the lute. Send them to Persia so that they can entertain the poor here." Shangal read the letter, chose the Luris, and sent them to the king, just as he had asked. When the Luris arrived at court, the king admitted them and gave an ox and a donkey to each of them, hoping to make farmers of them. He also donated a thousand ass-loads of wheat, so that they could use the animals to plough the land, sow the wheat, and so bring it to harvest. They were also to be musicians for the poor, so that commoners would be like the nobility. Off the Luris went, but they ate the oxen and the wheat, and by the end of the year their faces were pale with hunger. The king said to them, "You weren't supposed to waste the seed like this, and forget about seed time and harvest! Well, you still have the donkeys; load up your goods and put silk strings on your lutes!" And now, because of his words, the Luris wander the world trying to make a living, traveling and stealing by day and night.

Bahram Gur's Life Comes to an End

And so sixty-three years passed, and the king was unequaled in the world. At the new year, the wise priest who was his vizier came to him and said, "The great king's treasury is empty, and I have come to hear your commands." The king replied, "Do not trouble yourself, we no longer need such things. Abandon the world to its Creator, who established the turning heavens. The heavens turn and God remains, guiding both you and me toward the good." He slept that night and at dawn the following morning a large crowd came to the court. All who should be there had come, among them the king's son Yazdegerd. In front of the assembled nobles Bahram gave him the crown, the royal torque, the diadem, and the ivory throne. He wished to devote his thoughts to God, and so gave away the crown and throne. He was tired of the world's affairs, and when the dark night came he tried to sleep.

When the sun raised its hand in the sky, the king's vizier became anxious because the king had not risen, and he was afraid that Bahram had fled from the world. Yazdegerd went to his father's side, and when he saw him the saliva froze in his mouth. The king's cheeks had the withered color of death; wrapped in golden brocade, he had given up his soul. So this world is, and always has been. Do not torment your soul with greed and ambition: even a heart of stone or iron fears death, and there is nothing you can do against it. You must act with humanity, troubling no one, if you want your past not to harm you. Here I remind men of Bahram's justice and generosity, and may no one think ill of his memory!

They made him a royal tomb, and his people mourned his death.

⚜ THE STORY OF MAZDAK ⚜

*B*ahram *Gur was succeeded by his son Yazdegerd, who ruled for eighteen years. He was succeeded by two of his sons—Hormozd, who reigned for only a year, and Piruz, who ruled for eleven years. Piruz was succeeded by his sons Balash, who ruled for five years, and Qobad. During Qobad's reign a man called Mazdak, who claimed to be a prophet, appeared.*

A man named Mazdak, who was eloquent and knowledgeable and possessed of great abilities, came to the court. Qobad listened to his wise words and made him the king's chief minister and treasurer.

There was a drought, and food became scarce throughout the world, for both the common people and the nobility. No clouds appeared in the sky, and throughout Iran no one saw either rain or snow. The great men of the land appeared at Qobad's door, demanding bread and water, and Mazdak said to them, "The king will be able to give you hope." Then he ran to the king and said, "Your majesty, there is one question I wish to ask you, in hopes that you will give me an answer." Qobad replied, "Speak, refresh my mind with your words." Mazdak said,

> "Suppose there's someone who's been bitten by
> A poisonous snake, and he's about to die:
> What do you say, my lord, should happen to
> A man who has the antidote but who
> Insists on hoarding it, and will not give
> The bitten man the means to help him live?"

The king replied, "The man who has the antidote is a murderer. He should be hanged at the gates as punishment for the dead man's blood, as one hangs an enemy one has captured." Mazdak left the king's presence and returned to the crowd that was seeking relief. He said to them, "I have talked with the king about your demands. Wait until dawn tomorrow, and then I shall show you the path of justice."

The crowd came back the next morning, weeping and with their faces gaunt with sorrow. When Mazdak saw them from the doorway, he hurried to the king and said, "You majesty, victorious, eloquent, and wise, I asked you a question and you answered, opening a door that had been closed to me. If you will allow it, your councilor wishes to ask you one more thing." The king said, "Speak, don't hesitate; let me profit from your conversation." Mazdak said,

> *"Picture a man in chains; for want of bread*
> *He wastes away and soon he will be dead:*
> *Now he's denied bread by a passerby*
> *Who lets the miserable captive die.*
> *Should this man suffer punishment? Or would*
> *You say that what he did was just and good?"*

The king replied, "Destroy the wretch; by not acting he has another man's blood on his hands."

Mazdak kissed the ground before the king and left his presence. At the court gates he addressed the crowd, "Take the grain that has been hoarded and hidden away; put it at men's disposal in the streets and throughout the town; let each man take his share!" The hungry mob ran to loot the granaries, and soon there wasn't a single grain left in either the city's or the king's warehouses. When they saw this the overseers went to the king and said, "The king's granaries have been plundered, and Mazdak is responsible for this!"

Qobad summoned Mazdak and demanded that he account for the looting of the warehouses. Mazdak replied, "I told the suffering citizens what I'd heard from the king. I talked to the king of the world about the poisonous snake, and about the man who had the antidote. The king told me that the man who had the antidote had committed a sin, and that if someone shed his blood there would be nothing wrong in this. For a hungry man bread is the antidote to his sufferings, one that he won't need when he's well fed again. If you are a just ruler, your majesty, you won't hoard grain in your granaries. How many hungry men have died with empty bellies because of those granaries!"

The king's heart was hurt by his words, and they stayed in his mind. He questioned Mazdak and listened to the answers, and saw that Mazdak's heart and soul were full of such ideas. Mazdak talked of what the prophets and just religious leaders had said, but his arguments went beyond all boundaries. Crowds collected about him and were led astray by his talk. He said that those who had nothing were equal with the powerful, and that one man should not own more than another, since the rich were the weft and the poor the warp. Men should be equal in the world, and why should one man seek to have more than another? Women, houses, and possessions were to be distributed, so that the poor would have as much as the rich. "By the power of the pure faith I proclaim equality," Mazdak said, "and what is noble will be distinguished from what is base; any man who follows any faith but this will be cursed by God."

Young and old, the poor flocked to him; he confiscated wealth from this man and gave it to that, and the wise were deeply troubled by his talk. But Qobad rejoiced in his words and followed his teachings. Mazdak sat at his right hand, and the court had no notion of where the chief priest was. The poor and anyone who lived by the sweat of his brow were with him; his faith spread throughout the world, and no one dared to stand against him. The nobility faced ruin and gave what they had to the poor.

Kesra Opposes Mazdak and Kills Him

One morning Mazdak came from his house to the king and said, "A great number of my disciples and the leaders of my faith have gathered at your door; will you see them, or should they be sent away?" Qobad told his chamberlain to grant them audience, but Mazdak said, "This hall is too small to accommodate such a large number, it would be better if the king went out onto the plain." The king gave orders that his throne be taken from the palace to the plain. A hundred thousand of Mazdak's followers were gathered there, and they came confidently before the king.

Mazdak said to the king, "Your majesty, you are above all wisdom, but you should know that your son Kesra is not of our faith, and who has the right to oppose us? He must promise in writing to abandon his evil ways. There are five things that lead us away from justice, and the wise cannot add another to them. These five are envy, the longing for vengeance, anger, desire, and the fifth, which becomes a man's master, greed. If you can conquer these five demons, the way to God lies open to you. It is these five that make women and wealth the ruin of the true faith throughout the world. If women and wealth are not to harm the true faith, they must be held in common. It is these two that generate envy, greed, and desire, and secretly they link up with anger and a longing for vengeance. Then demons corrupt the wise, and to prevent this these two must be held in common." As he finished speaking he seized Kesra's arm, and the king of Iran stared at him in astonishment. Angrily Kesra pulled his arm away and indignantly turned his eyes from Mazdak.

Qobad laughed and said, "Why are you so concerned about what Kesra believes?" Mazdak said, "He secretly denies the true faith; he's not of our religion." Qobad said to Kesra, "This is not the right way, to deny the true faith." Kesra replied, "If you give me time, I can show you how false and dangerous all this is, and then the truth will be plain to you." Mazdak said to him, "How many days are you asking the king, whose splendor fills the world, to grant you?" Kesra replied, "Give me five months, and in the sixth I will answer the king." This was agreed to, and the king returned to his palace.

Kesra sent messengers to find knowledgeable men to help him in his cause. One went to Khurreh-ye Ardeshir where the wise sage Hormozd lived, and another to Estakhr to summon Mehr-Azad, who came with thirty of his companions. These venerable seekers after wisdom sat together and discussed all manner of things, then they made their report to Kesra. When he had heard them out, Kesra went to Qobad and talked with him about Mazdak. "The time has come for me to learn which is the true religion," Kesra said. "If Mazdak is right, then Zoroaster's faith will disappear. I will accept his faith as true and choose in my soul as he has chosen. If the way of Feraydun, of Esdras and Jesus and the Zend-Avesta, is mistaken, then Mazdak's words are to be believed and no one in the world should be our guide but him. But if all he says is perverse, and he does not follow the way of God, hand him over to me, together with his followers, and I shall separate their skins and the marrow in their bones from their bodies." He swore this before Zarmehr, Khordad, Farayin, Banduy, and Behzad, and then returned to his palace determined to keep his oath.

When the sun displayed its crown on the following morning, and the ground became like a sea of ivory, the king's son and the priests and sages he had summoned arrived at the king's palace, talking matters over as they came. Mazdak delighted Qobad's heart with his words, and then a Zoroastrian priest addressed Mazdak in front of the assembly and said, "You are a seeker after knowledge, but the new religion you have made is a pernicious one. If women and wealth are to be held in common, how will a son know his father, or a father his son? If men are to be equal in the world, social distinctions will be unclear; who will want to be a commoner, and how will nobility be recognized? If a laboring slave and the king are the same, when a man dies, who is to inherit his goods? This talk of yours will ruin the world, and such an evil doctrine should not flourish in Iran. If everyone is a master, who is he to command? Everyone will have a treasure, and who is to be its treasurer? None of those who established religions have talked in this way. You have secretly put together a demonic faith; you are leading everyone to hell, and you don't see your evil acts for what they are."

When Qobad heard the priest's words, he sprang up and shouted his approval. Kesra added his support, and Mazdak's impious heart was filled with apprehension. The assembly rang with voices saying, "Mazdak should not sit next to the king, he is destroying our religion, he has no place in this court!" The king turned away from Mazdak's teachings in disgust, and his mind was filled with regret for what he had done. He handed Mazdak and his followers, who included a hundred thousand men of good standing, over to Kesra, and said, "Do with these men as you will, and never mention Mazdak to me again."

In Kesra's palace there was a garden with a high wall around it. It was dug up from end to end, and Mazdak's followers were planted there head down, with their feet in the air, like trees. Kesra said to Mazdak, "Go to my garden and see there trees of a kind no one has ever seen or heard tell of before." Mazdak went to the garden expecting to see fruit trees, but when he saw what was there, he gave a cry of despair and fainted. Kesra had a tall gallows built, and the impious Mazdak was strung up alive and head down. He was killed with a shower of arrows. If you have any sense, you will not follow Mazdak's way.

The nobility were once more assured of their wealth, their women folk, children, and splendid gardens. For a while Qobad was ashamed of what he had done and cursed Mazdak's memory. He distributed large amounts of wealth to the poor, and gave gifts to the country's fire-temples.

بشد مرد و باغ بکشاد در
کپید هی برجمن بارور
بران درختان بد

پند

خیش

از روت

Kesra Is Made Qobad's Heir and Is Named Nushin-Ravan

The king was so pleased with Kesra for showing such wisdom that from then on he always consulted with him and listened to his advice. When he had ruled for forty years, the fear of death entered his heart, and he wrote a document on silk, acting as his own scribe. He began with praise of God from whom faith and ability come, whose commands are always fulfilled secretly or openly, whose sovereignty no one has fathomed, and whose followers are never cast down. He continued, "Whoever sees Qobad's handwriting here should listen only to Kesra's advice. I have bestowed the glorious throne on Kesra, and may he flourish after my death. May God be pleased with my son, and may the hearts of his enemies be confounded. Never swerve from his commands; rejoice and grow wealthy beneath his rule." He placed his golden seal on the letter, and entrusted it to Ram-Borzin.

Qobad was in his eightieth year, but he was not content to die. The splendor faded from his face and eyes; death came to him, and the world felt his absence. His body was wrapped in brocade and prepared with roses, musk, camphor, and wine. They built an imperial tomb for him and placed a royal couch and crown there. They laid the king on the golden couch and closed the tomb forever.

When the chief priest had ended the period of mourning, he made the king's letter public. It was read before the court, and the crown prince was seated on the throne amid the court's acclamations. Taking his place there, Kesra was hailed as the new king; jewels were poured over his head, and he was given the name Nushin-Ravan. So ends the reign of Qobad; now I shall set before you the reign of Kesra, who ruled with justice and glory, and who became renowned for his righteousness and generosity.

⁓ THE REIGN OF KESRA NUSHIN-RAVAN ⁓

Kesra Nushin-Ravan promised a just administration and set about making the tax system more equitable. He toured his country's provinces, and secured the border areas against invasion. In particular, he built a wall between Iran and central Asia, to keep out attacks from that direction. Skirmishes across the western frontier with the Roman empire, in which Kesra was mostly the victor, led to a treaty, which included the provision that Kesra marry the Roman emperor's daughter.

The Story of Nushzad

You should understand that both king and subject need a partner, clothes, food, and somewhere to sleep. If this partner is a noble and sensible woman, she will be a treasure to her husband, especially if she is tall and has musky hair that reaches to her feet, and if she is wise and modest, with a soft and eloquent voice. Such was the king's wife: as tall as a cypress tree and as lovely as the moon. She was a Christian, and the whole town was filled with talk of her beauty.

She gave birth to a boy, with a face as radiant as the sun, more splendid than Venus shining in the night sky. Kesra called him Nushzad, and the child was protected from the strong winds of heaven. He grew to be like an elegant cypress, an accomplished young man, and an ornament to the kingdom. When he learned about hell and the way to heaven, Esdras, Jesus, and the path of Zoroaster, he rejected the Zend-Avesta and washed his face with the waters of Christianity. He chose his mother's beliefs over his father's faith, and the world was astonished at this. The king grieved that this rose had produced only thorns; the doors to the young man's palace were closed, and it became his prison. He was confined to Jonde-shapur, far from both the Persian capital and the west, and his companions were criminals in chains.

به پیش سپه پیله کنده بساخت

کنده به پیش شد بر شاه راه

It happened that when the king was returning from an expedition to the west he complained of fatigue and the pains of travel, and he became so weak that he halted at the River Jordan. Someone took the news to Nushzad that the imperial splendor was shrouded in darkness, that the great king Kesra was dead and had entrusted the world to another. Nushzad rejoiced to hear of his father's death, and may his name be cursed for this. As a wise man once said, "If you rejoice at someone's death, make sure that you never die!"

Kesra Nushin-Ravan's Illness and Nushzad's Rebellion

When Kesra's son heard that the throne was vacant, he threw open the doors of his palace, and a crowd of senseless criminals who had been imprisoned by Kesra flocked to him. Nushzad freed them all, and the town was in an uproar. All the Christians there, priests and bishops alike, joined him, and soon he had a force of thirty thousand men, armed and ready for war. The Roman emperor wrote him a letter, as murky as his behavior, recognizing him as the lord of Jondeshapur and as the emperor's ally and co-religionist. Nushzad's fortunes had been at a low ebb, but now they revived and he filled the town with evil men.

News of what Kesra's son was up to reached Ctesiphon. The commander in charge of the city's defenses sent a horseman to Kesra, passing on all the secret reports he had heard. Kesra was saddened by the news and his mind grew dark with apprehension. Talking privately with his chief priest about the matter, he finally came to a decision. He summoned a scribe, and with a frown on his face and cold sighs on his lips, he dictated a letter filled with anger and sorrow to Ram-Borzin.

He began with praise of God who created the world and time, who maintains the sun and Saturn and the moon in their places, who bestows glory and sovereignty on men, whose rule is limitless and cannot be diminished, beneath whose rule everything exists from the least straw to elephants and lions, from the dust beneath an ant's feet to the River Nile. He continued, "I knew of the emperor's letter, of the evils my son has instigated, and of the criminals who have broken out from the prisons and rallied to his cause. It would be better for a man to leave the world than to see such a day. And we are all of us born for death, including Kesra and Nushzad. No one, neither the ant and the mosquito nor the lion and the hippopotamus, escapes Death's beak and talons. If the earth were to open and reveal what is hidden within her, we'd see her lap filled with past kings and with the blood of warriors, and the pockets of her skirts stuffed with wise men and beautiful women. Whether you wear a crown or a helmet, the point of Death's lance will pierce it. If those men who have gathered around Nushzad at the rumor of my death can escape death themselves, then there is sense in what they do, but it is only evil men who rejoice at a just king's death.

"Nushzad has taken leave of his senses and is in league with some devil: he flared up when he thought his desires had come to fruition, but he cannot destroy my power on the strength of a rumor. If the throne were vacant, he would be its new occupant; his conduct is worthy of his faith and his malignant soul. But if my son's faith is impure, this is no cause for fear, and I care nothing for the wealth he has squandered, or for those who have rallied to his cause. They are an idle, low-born, malignant rabble, unworthy to be my subjects. Talk of what they've done doesn't interest me, and you should not be concerned by it. I fear only God, who is beyond all knowledge, and to whom we must not be ungrateful: it is he who has given me victory and glory, power and the imperial crown, and if my praises had been equal to his gifts my power would have been even greater. Would that the seed of my body had found another womb in which to sleep; when it woke my enemy appeared, and I fear that I have brought these sorrows on myself. But if God is not angry with me, I am not concerned about the outcome of all this. As for the men who have flocked to his cause, I despise them. It is the emperor's letter that has muddied the waters in this way; they think that because he is a co-religionist and an ally, he will support them. A man loses his

senses and pays no attention to the faith of his ancestors; but when this fool turns his head away from justice I shouldn't curse him since he is from my blood and body, and to curse him is to curse myself.

"You are to equip an army to fight them, but proceed cautiously and slowly, and if matters deteriorate and you have to fight, do so without rashness. It would be better to capture him than to kill him; it may be that he will repent of his sins. But if he is intractable and stoops to low tricks, don't hesitate to use your sword and mace against him. When someone we love is drawn to contemptible things, it is useless to try to separate him from his desires, and a noble man who rebels against the world's king deserves a wretched death. Don't be afraid to kill him; he has rebelled against our crown and embraced the Roman emperor's religion.

"As for the rebels who make up Nushzad's army, think of them as so much wind; they're malcontents, like gossiping women. The Christians among them will give up if you shout at them loudly enough, that's their way, and in the end they'll renounce that cross of theirs. The rest are slaves and malignant fools with not a noble thought in their heads, blown hither and thither by every wind. But if you capture Nushzad in battle, don't say these things to him. His womenfolk support him, so make his palace his prison and let him live with those who are happy to obey him. Give him free access to his wealth, women, food, and palace furnishings; he mustn't

be in need of anything. But when you're victorious, don't hesitate to put to the sword any of the lords of the marches who have supported him: it's right that the king's enemies be fed to the crocodiles. And there are others, the seed of Ahriman, who oppose my rule in their hearts, who ignore the righteous things I have done, and whom Nushzad's rebellion has brought to light. But even if he has turned to evil ways, he is still my son, and my heart reminds me of this. Publicly brand the tongues of those who led Nushzad astray with their evil councils; my curses on their mouths and tongues! They are men who looked for me to weaken, who followed Ahriman and went by devious paths; they do not deserve to live in my kingdom, whose glory and crown belong to me."

Ram-Borzin Prepares for Battle against Nushzad; Piruz's Words to Nushzad

The king's seal was set on the letter and a messenger quickly set off with it. He told Ram-Borzin all he had heard from King Kesra and handed over the letter with its orders to prepare for war. At cockcrow, the morning after the old man had read the letter and heard what the messenger had to say, the din of drums was heard before his palace and Ram-Borzin led the army out from Ctesiphon.

The news reached Nushzad, who mustered his troops and gave them pay and provisions. The Roman priests and patriarchs, with Shemas at their head, took their places in his army, whose hands were soaked in blood. A cry sounded from the gateway of Nushzad's palace, and his men surged forward, like a wave of the sea before the wind. They marched out of the city to the plain, their heads filled with warfare, their hearts with poisonous hatred. When they caught sight of the dust raised by Borzin's forces, they drew up their ranks in battle formation, and the brass trumpets were blown. The dust sent up by the cavalry obscured the sun, and the blows of heavy maces split the granite rocks. Nushzad, a Roman helmet on his head, was in the center of his forces, surrounded by so many Roman priests that their horses' hooves hid the ground. The earth seemed to seethe, and the air above their heads to groan in anguish.

A brave warrior, whose name was Piruz-Shir, came forward and cried out, "Nushzad, who turned your head away from justice? You have deserted the faith of Kayumars, Hushang, and Tahmures, and Christ the Deceiver himself was killed when he abandoned God's faith! Don't follow the faith of someone who didn't know what he was doing. If God's *farr* was with him, how were the Jews able to overcome him? Have you heard what your noble father did to the Romans and their emperor? And now you're fighting against him and lifting your head up to the skies! For all your handsome face and *farr* and strength, for all your massive shoulders and great mace, I see no wisdom in you: your soul is dark and bewildered. I pity that head and crown of yours, and your fame and lineage, which you are flinging to the winds. You are no mammoth or ravening lion, and you cannot withstand the might of Kesra's forces. O prince, I have never seen a picture in a king's palace that portrayed a horseman like you, with your reins and stirrups, your mighty arm and thigh, your ardor, and strength, and mace. No Chinese painter ever saw such a painting, and the earth has never seen a prince like you. Young man, don't burn Kesra's heart like this, don't muddy the splendor that illuminates the world. Dismount from your horse, ask for quarter, throw your mace and Roman helmet to the ground! If far away from here a cold wind blew black dust in your face, the king's heart would ache for you, the sun would weep for you. Don't sow the seeds of rebellion in this world, such quarrels don't become a king; but if you ignore my advice and choose the way of pride and confrontation, I hope my words come back to you often enough, and that your evil advisors' talk turns to wind."

Nushzad answered him, "Feeble old man, your head's filled with wind, you can expect no surrender from my army of heroes, nor from me, a king's son. I reject Kesra's faith and cleave to my mother's way. Her faith is that of Christ, and I shall not swerve aside from his glorious path. If Christ who brought our faith was killed, this does not mean that God's glory had abandoned him; his pure soul went to God because he saw no nobility in this dark world. If I am to be killed, I am not afraid, since death is a poison against which there is no antidote."

This was Nushzad's answer to the old warrior Piruz, and the air became thick with arrows. The drums and trumpets sounded and the two armies closed with one another. Nushzad urged his horse forward like fire and pushed back the left flank of the king's army; he killed many of their warriors and no one dared to oppose him. Ram-Borzin was roused to action and gave orders for arrows to rain down like springtime hail. Nushzad was wounded in the attack and recalled the words of Piruz; he retreated to the center of his army, his body pierced by arrows and his face sallow with pain. He said to his Roman warriors, "It is a sad and shameful thing to fight against one's father." He groaned and wept, and asked for a bishop, to whom he told everything that was in his heart.

> "It's I who brought this sorrow on my head:
> Send tidings to my mother when I'm dead,
> And say that Nushzad's earthly course is run,
> The good and evil of his life are done.
> Tell her she should not grieve for me, and say
> That in this world all things must pass away.
> This was my lot, and how could I have known
> Delight here, or the glory of a throne?
> All life is born to die, and when you see
> The truth of death you will not mourn for me.
> It's not my death I grieve for now, but rather
> That I've provoked the anger of my father.
> Build no great tomb for me, and do not bring
> The musk and camphor that preserve a king:
> Grant me a Christian grave." He spoke and sighed,
> And so the lionhearted Nushzad died.

The Story of Bozorjmehr

It's unwise to think of dreams as meaningless. You should consider them as a kind of revelation of hidden things, and this is especially so when the king of the world sees them. The stars, the moon, and the heavens gather their scattered languages together into one path, so that bright souls can see in dreams all that exists, like fire reflected in water. One night, as King Nushin-Ravan slept, he saw a majestic tree growing before the throne, and his heart was so delighted by it that he called for wine and music. All was peace and pleasure, but then a boar with sharp tusks sat down beside him and wanted to drink from Nushin-Ravan's goblet.

When the sun rose in Taurus, and the lark's song was heard on every side, Kesra sat on his throne, and his heart was filled with melancholy because of his dream. A dream interpreter was summoned, and the high priests took their places in the court. The king explained to them what he had seen in his dream, but the dream interpreter gave no answer, because he had no knowledge of such a dream. A person who confesses his ignorance avoids having to make a judgment. When the king received no answer from this expert, his heavy heart looked for another solution. He sent distinguished men to every quarter, each with a chest of gold containing ten thousand coins to help them search throughout the world for a knowledgeable dream interpreter who could say what the king's dream meant, and he eagerly awaited their return.

One of these envoys was Azad-Sarv, and he traveled from Kesra's palace to Marv. He scoured the city and came across a priest with the Zend-Avesta before him; he was teaching little children the scriptures, and shouting at them in his anger and irritation. One older boy, whose name was Bozorjmehr, was studying the Zend-Avesta, poring over it with love. The envoy drew rein, and asked the teacher about the king's dream. The man replied, "This is not my business; the Zend-Avesta's the only branch of knowledge I care about." But when Bozorjmehr heard the envoy's question, he pricked up his ears and smiled. He said to his teacher, "This is sport for me: interpreting dreams is what I'm good at." The teacher yelled at him, "Have you done your exercise properly?" But the envoy said, "Perhaps he knows something; don't discourage him." The teacher was irritated with Bozorjmehr and said, "Say what you know then." But the boy answered, "I won't say anything except in front of the king, in his court."

The envoy gave him a horse and money and everything he needed for the journey. The two traveled together from Marv, as splendidly as pheasants strutting beneath the flowers. And so they went forward, chatting about the king, his commands, his *farr*, the crown and court, until they reached a place where there was water. They dismounted under the trees, and ate and rested. Bozorjmehr slept in the trees' shade, with a sheet pulled over his face. The envoy was still awake, and as he watched his companion, he saw a snake slither beneath the sheet and seem to sniff eagerly at the sleeping youth, from head to foot: then it gently glided away toward the trees. As the black snake eased its way to the top of a tree trunk, the boy lifted his head from sleep, and when the snake heard him moving it disappeared among the branches. The envoy was astonished and repeatedly murmured the name of God over the boy. To himself he said, "This clever child will reach an exalted position in the world." Then they galloped on, until they reached the king's court.

Bozorjmehr Interprets the King's Dream

The envoy preceded the youth to Kesra's throne and said, "I traveled from the king's court to Marv, searching like a pheasant through a rose garden, and I found a child at school, whom I have brought here as quickly as I could." Then he told the king what the youth had said, and he also described the strange incident involving the snake. Kesra called the boy forward and talked to him about his dream. The boy's head seemed so filled with words that they tumbled from his mouth: "In your palace, among the women of your harem, there is a young man who has dressed himself as a woman. Clear the court so that no one will realize what we're going to do. Then have your women walk before you, and as they set one foot before another we'll ask that foolhardy intruder how it is that he's found his way to the lion's couch."

The court was cleared of strangers, and the palace door locked. The king's women, in all their tints and scents, smelling of jasmine, filled with grace and modesty, walked slowly before Kesra. But no man was seen among them, and Kesra was as enraged as a lion. Bozorjmehr said, "This is not right; there is a young man somewhere among these women. Have them walk before you again, but with their faces unveiled." Once more the women paraded before the king, and this time a young man was discovered among them, tall as a cypress and with a face like a Kayanid. His body trembled like a willow, since his heart had despaired of life's sweetness.

There were seventy women in the harem, each as elegant as a cypress tree. One, who was cypress-tall and whose body was like ivory, was the daughter of the lord of Chaj. When she was living in her father's house, a young man, whose face was like jasmine and who was as enticing as musk, had fallen in love with her. He had paid court to her like a slave, following her wherever she went. The king asked her, "Who is this young man foolhardy enough to live in Nushin-Ravan's harem? And who has been looking after him?" She replied, "He is my younger brother, and we're both from the same mother. He dressed like this because he was ashamed before the king; he didn't dare look you in the face. If my brother veiled his face from you, it was out of respect for you, and you shouldn't think it was for any other reason." Nushin-Ravan was astonished at her explanation and at their behavior. He turned angrily to his executioner and said, "These two deserve to be in their graves." The man hurried them away and they were hanged in the king's harem, with their bodies upside down and covered in blood.

The dream interpreter was given a purse of coins, horses, and clothes; the king was amazed at his knowledge, turning his words over in his mind. They wrote his name down as one of the king's advisors, among the priests who give counsel; the heavens looked kindly on Bozorjmehr. Day by day his good fortune increased, and the king delighted in his presence.

Kesra's heart was just, and his heart and mind were ennobled by knowledge; he kept priests at his court, and experts in all branches of knowledge. There were always seventy savants who slept and ate in his palace, and whenever he rested from the labors of administering justice and from his banquets, he asked for some new discourse from one of them, and in this way his heart gained in knowledge. At this time Bozorjmehr was still a young man, eloquent, ingenious, and handsome. He learned from these priests, astrologers and wise men, and soon he surpassed them all.

*B*ozorjmehr *became Kesra Nushin-Ravan's vizier, and much of Ferdowsi's account of Kesra's reign consists of Bozorjmehr's advice on how to rule. This advice, combined with Kesra's own naturally just and careful character, ensured Persian prosperity during his reign. The emperor of China went to war with Iran's neighbors in Soghdia, and he and Kesra, although mutually suspicious of one another, concluded a treaty of friendship. The emperor sent an envoy to Kesra, with a letter suggesting that the Persian king marry his daughter.*

Nushin-Ravan Sends Mehran-Setad to See the Emperor of China's Daughter

King Kesra Nushin-Ravan summoned a scribe, talked at length about the emperor of China, and then dictated an answer to the emperor's letter. He began with praise of God, who is victorious and who maintains the world, who is our guide to good and evil, who raises whomever he wishes from misery to the high heavens, while another man lives in wretchedness because God does not desire his prosperity. The letter continued: "I am grateful to him for all benefits, and if I do evil, it is his wrath that I fear: may my soul be divided from my body if my hope and fear turn away from him. The envoy bearing the emperor of China's kind message arrived here, and I heard all he had to say concerning a marriage and the emperor's daughters who live secluded in his palace. I will be happy to become allied to you, especially if it is by marrying your veiled daughter. To this end I am sending you a wise ambassador, and when he arrives he can tell you of my secret thoughts about this alliance. May your soul and body always be filled with sobriety, may your heart be happy, and your friendship toward us continue." When the scribe's pen ceased to move and the ink was dried, he folded the letter and sealed it with musk. Kesra gave the emperor's envoy a robe of honor, and his escort was astonished by its quality.

Then he chose a wise high priest whose name was Mehran-Setad, and as his companions a hundred eloquent and noble Persian horsemen. To Mehran-

Setad he said, "Travel with joy and victory, kindness and justice; your thoughts and speech must be astute and eloquent, with wisdom to guide you. First examine his harem, and see that you can accurately distinguish the women there. Don't let a well made-up face or splendid clothes, or fine jewelry deceive you; there are many young women in his private apartments, all of them tall and splendid and crowned. Someone born from a serving girl is no good to me, even if her father is the king. Look to see which of them is modest and acts appropriately, someone whose mother is from the emperor's family, who is of true royal lineage. If she is as lovely in her body as in her descent, she will make the world happy and be happy herself."

Mehran-Setad listened to the king and called down blessings on the throne and crown. He set out on an auspicious day in the month of Khordad, and when he arrived at the Chinese court he kissed the ground and paid homage to the emperor, who welcomed him and assigned him splendid living quarters. But the emperor was troubled, and he went to the apartments of his wife, the empress. He told her of what Nushin-Ravan had said and talked to her at length about his wealth and army. He said, "This King Nushin-Ravan is young and intelligent, and fortune smiles on him. It would be a good idea to give him a daughter as a bride; it would increase my standing with him. You and I have a daughter in purdah here who is the crown of all princesses, but I love to see her face and could not bear to be parted from her. I've four other daughters born from servant girls. I'll give him one of them, and that'll save me both from war with him and from gossip." The empress said, "No one in the world's as cunning as you are!"

Having made this decision, the emperor slept until the sun rose above the mountains. Then Mehran-Setad appeared before his throne and handed over Kesra's letter. When the emperor read the letter he laughed with pleasure, both because of the alliance, and because a bride was to be chosen. He gave the Persian envoy the key to his harem and said, "Go and see who is hidden there." Four servants who were in the emperor's confidence accompanied him. The envoy took the key and entered the private apartments, while the servants told him tales of what to expect. They said, "Neither the sun nor the moon nor any wind have ever set eyes on those you will see." The apartments were arranged like a paradise, one that contained the sun and the moon and was filled with luxury. Five young women sat there with crowns on their heads and treasure at their feet,

> All but the great queen's child, whose elegance
> Did not require such gaudy ornaments:
> Her dress was old and plain, her head was bare,
> Crowned only with her coiled and musky hair,
> While her unpowdered and bewitching face
> Shone with a lovely God-created grace:

She seemed a cypress with the moon above,
Filling the women's rooms with light and love.

Mehran-Setad knew he had never seen anyone as lovely as she was, and his quick mind saw that the emperor and empress were being far from honest. The young woman covered her eyes with her hands and veil, and this increased Mehran-Setad's anger at their duplicity. He said to the servants, "The king has plenty of crowns, thrones, and bracelets; I choose this one, who has no crown or fine adornments, since she is worthy to be elevated in such a fashion. I undertook the pains of this journey to make a good choice; I didn't come here for Chinese brocade."

The empress said to him, "Old man, you have not said one pleasing word. There are women here who have splendor, beauty, and good sense, who delight the heart and are of marriageable age, tall like cypresses, with faces as lovely as springtime and who know how to serve a king, and you have chosen an immature child—this is not sensible of you!" Mehran-Setad replied, "If the emperor had deceived me, then my king would also say I wasn't sensible. I choose this young woman, who has no ivory throne, no crown or torque or jewelry. If your majesties do not approve, I shall return home as soon as I am permitted to do so."

The emperor considered his words, astonished by his understanding and by his decision. He saw that this old man's mind was clear, and that he was a great personage who was fit to carry out such delicate tasks. The wise ruler sat with his advisors and emptied the court of strangers. He ordered astrologers with Western charts in their hands, together with the great men of the country and all who felt benevolent toward the throne, to search for the will of the heavens. A priest studied the stars as they affected the emperor's alliance with the king and said at last, "Do not trouble your heart about this matter, it can only end auspiciously and will not deliver the world into your enemies' hands. This is the secret of the high heavens and of the favorable stars that turn there; a king who will be an ornament to the throne will be born from this daughter of the emperor and from the king's loins. Princes will pay homage to him, as will the noblemen of China."

The Emperor Sends His Daughter with Mehran-Setad to Nushin-Ravan

When they heard this, the emperor's heart rejoiced and the splendid empress smiled with pleasure. Once their hearts were set at rest, they sat the envoy down before them and told him whatever he needed to know about the empress's daughter. Mehran-Setad accepted her from her father, in the king's name. Servants came joyfully before the king bringing her splendid dowry, which included gold coins, jewels, torques, crowns, turquoise seals, an ivory throne, another throne of Indian aloes wood encrusted with gold and gems, a hundred finely saddled horses, a hundred camels laden with Chinese brocade, forty pieces of golden brocade woven with emeralds, a hundred camels laden with carpets, and three hundred serving girls. The emperor waited until the company had mounted in the Chinese fashion, with banners in their hands, and then he ordered that a throne covered in gold and silver cloth encrusted with gems be placed on an elephant's back. A hundred men lifted it into place, and beside it there was a banner of Chinese brocade so huge that it hid the ground. A golden litter was draped in brocade, and within it was the uncut jewel, the emperor's daughter, while the three hundred beautiful serving girls accompanied her with happiness in their hearts. Fifty servants and forty eunuchs formed an escort, and this was the manner in which the emperor sent his daughter to the Persian king.

When this had been accomplished, a scribe came forward bearing musk, rosewater, and silk, and the emperor dictated a letter of great splendor. He began with praise of the Creator, who maintains the world, who is vigilant and all-seeing, and whose creatures fulfill the destinies he appoints for them. He continued, "The Persian king is like a crown to me, and my alliance with him is not simply for my daughter's sake. I have always heard from those who are wise and noble, and from priests who have insight into such matters, about his glory and greatness, and this is why I have sought to be allied with him. No ruler in all the world is as just as he is; none has his magnanimity, or is as victorious and powerful as he is, none has his glory and might, and his faith in God nourishes his knowledge and understanding. I have sent my child to King Kesra, according to our custom, and have told her to act as his slave, as is fitting when she is in his women's quarters, to imbibe wisdom from his glory, and to learn his court's ceremonies and manners. May good fortune and wisdom guide you, and may greatness and knowledge be your support."

They set a seal of Chinese musk on the letter, which the emperor gave to the envoy and called down blessings on him. Then he gave Mehran-Setad a robe of honor more splendid than any given before by a king to a messenger. He also

delighted Mehran-Setad's companions with presents of gold coins and musk. He traveled with his daughter and her wealth, the cavalry and richly caparisoned elephants, as far as the shore of the River Oxus, and there heartfelt tears fell from his eyes. He waited until they had crossed over the river and gained the further shore. Then, with his heart filled with sorrow at being parted from his daughter, he turned back from the Oxus.

When the good news came from Mehran-Setad, people happily gathered at the court with presents, calling down blessings on the king of Persia and the emperor of China. They decorated the towns and roads of the route, and the road to Amui and Marv was as resplendent as a pheasant's feathers. By the time the travelers reached Gorgan and Bestam, the ground had become invisible beneath the finery and press of people; all the men, women and children of Persia crowded the road where the Chinese idol was to pass. They rained down jewels on her from the houses' upper storeys, and silver coins and saffron were scattered in her way. Bowls of sweet-smelling scents were set out, and the world re-echoed with the sound of drums and trumpets. The horses' manes were soaked in musk and wine, they trod on sugar and silver, and such was the din of flutes and harps and lutes that there was no place where a man could be quiet and sleep.

The princess was brought into the women's apartments, and Kesra looked into the litter. He saw a cypress tree with the full moon above it, crowned by her sweet-smelling hair that fell in cunningly woven braids; its musky ringlets framed the roses of her face, which shone as brightly as the planet Jupiter. King Kesra stared at her and repeatedly said the name of God in his wonder at her beauty. He selected apartments that were worthy of her, and a throne was prepared in her honor.

An Indian Rajah Sends the Game of
Chess to Nushin-Ravan

One day, when the king's audience hall was hung with Byzantine brocade, the royal crown suspended above his throne, and the room was thronged with priests and lords of the marches from Balkh, Bamyan, and Karzeban crowned and seated on ivory thrones, the court learned that an envoy from an Indian king was approaching with a caravan of horsemen from Sind, elephants shaded by parasols, and a thousand laden camels. As soon as the king heard this, he sent an escort to welcome the caravan. The envoy entered the court and made his obeisance and called down God's blessings, as is the custom of noble men, and spread many jewels before the king as an offering, as well as ten elephants, earrings, and a parasol decorated in gold, with gems woven into its fabric. Then he unpacked the goods in his train and brought them all before the king. There were great quantities of gold and silver, musk, ambergris, fresh-cut aloes wood, rubies, diamonds, and glittering Indian swords; everything that Qanuj produced was there, and the servants hurried to lay his wealth before the throne. Kesra examined the presents that the Indian rajah had labored to collect, and had them taken to his treasury.

Then the envoy presented a letter written on silk to Nushin-Ravan, from the Indian king, together with a chessboard and its pieces, made with such skill that they were worth a treasury in themselves. The rajah had written: "May you reign for as long as the heavens turn. Set this chessboard and its pieces before your most learned men, to see if they can understand this subtle game, the names of its pieces, and where each one's home is on the board. See whether they can comprehend what the pawns and elephants do, and what the moves of the rook, the knight, the king, and his advisor are. If their intellects can fathom this subtle game, we shall gladly send the tribute and taxes that the king has demanded. But if the famous sages of Iran are all deficient in such knowledge, if their knowledge is not equal to ours, then Iran should no longer demand tribute from us. It is we who should accept tribute from you, since knowledge is the best of all things that confer glory."

Kesra listened carefully to what was said; then they set the board before him, and he looked at the pieces. On one side they were of painted ivory, and on the other of teak. The great king asked about the game, the pieces, and the board. The envoy answered, "Your majesty, the rules are those of war: see if you can work out the moves of the rook and the elephant, and how the pieces are drawn up for battle." The king said, "Give us a week, and on the eighth day we'll be happy to play this game with you." Fine apartments were set aside for the envoy, and all his needs were taken care of.

Priests and learned men came and they pored over the chessboard and its pieces. They tried various solutions and discussed the possibilities with

one another, but none of them could work out the game's rules, and, frowning, they gave up the attempt. Bozorjmehr came to the king and saw that he was very disappointed by their remarks. But the vizier knew how to resolve the matter, and he said to Kesra, "Your majesty, I shall take wisdom as my guide and solve the riddle of this subtle game." The king said, "You are the man for this problem: may your soul see its way to a solution. Otherwise the rajah of Qanuj is going to say, 'The king has no one who can fathom such secrets,' and this will be a defeat for our priests, our wise men, and the court."

Bozorjmehr took the chessboard and pieces, and for a day and a night he studied them carefully, moving the pieces to left and right and taking note of their positions. Then he hurried from his apartments to the king and said, "Victorious king, I have studied this board and its pieces, and by the good fortune of your majesty, I now understand the game. Summon the rajah's messenger, and whoever else wishes to see this; but first you must witness it, because the game is exactly like a battle."

Overjoyed by his words, the king said that Bozorjmehr was a man able to solve all difficulties and favored by fortune. He summoned the rajah's envoy and seated him appropriately. Bozorjmehr addressed him, "You are the envoy of a rajah whose face is as splendid as the sun, and may wisdom be your soul's companion. What did your master say about these chess pieces to you?" The envoy replied, "When I left, the rajah said to me, 'Take these pieces of ivory and teak before the throne of the crowned king and tell him to have his priests and wise men examine them; if they can understand this subtle game, and play it correctly and elegantly, then, as far as we're able to, we shall send the purses of gold, the slaves, and the tribute they demand. But if the king and his advisors cannot understand the game, if their souls are not equal to it, then the king has no right to demand tribute from us. If he despairs of understanding the game, he will realize how fine our hearts and souls are, and he will send us his surplus wealth.'"

Bozorjmehr brought out the chessboard and said to the assembled priests and advisors, "You are wise, and your hearts are pure; take note of what he has said and of his master's views." Then the knowledgeable vizier set out a battlefield: the king's place was in the heart of his forces, his horsemen were to his right and left, and his infantry, armed with lances, stood before him. The clever vizier was next to the king, to show the way when battle was joined. As the horsemen attacked from both sides, the warlike elephants were there on the left; infantry went ahead of the horsemen, to watch for ways forward. When Bozorjmehr set out the army's ranks, the whole assembly was astonished. The Indian envoy was dumbfounded and dispirited. This man of magic was bewildered, and he brooded in his heart on what he had seen:

"This man has never been in India, nor
Has he so much as seen the game before—
How did he understand its rules? The earth
Can't show another man of equal worth."

Kesra was so pleased with Bozorjmehr that it was as if the heavens themselves were smiling on him. He praised his vizier at length and ordered that
he be given a goblet filled with splendid jewels, a saddled horse, and a
purse of gold coins.

Bozorjmehr Invents the Game of Nard, Which Nushin-Ravan Sends to India

Bozorjmehr went to his own home, where he shut himself away with a board
and a pair of compasses. Carefully considering the game of chess, which the
Indians had sent, he cudgeled his brains until he conceived of the game of
nard. He had two dice made of ivory, with designs on them the color of teak.
He made a board similar to a chessboard and set the combatants out on either
side. The two armies were distributed in eight stations, where the pieces were
drawn up ready to take the opposing city. The battlefield was divided into four
sections, and there were two noble and magnanimous kings, equal in their
forces and obliged not to harm one another. At their command the armies set
off from each side, ready for war. If two pieces came on a solitary piece, that
piece would be lost and its side would suffer a setback. The two kings were in
the thick of the fighting, each overtaking the other in turn, and sometimes the
battle was in the mountains, sometimes in the plains, and so the two kings
and armies advanced until one was defeated. When he took his game to the
king and explained it to him in detail, Kesra was astonished. He thought long
and hard about the game and then said, "Your soul is clear and bright; may
your good fortune remain young and vigorous!"

He ordered that two thousand camel drivers bring their animals to the
court gates, and there they were loaded with goods from Byzantium, China,
Central Asia, Makran, and Persia. When they were ready to set off, the king
summoned the rajah's envoy, and talked with him at length about the nature

of knowledge. He wrote a letter filled with wisdom and splendor, which began with praise of God, his refuge from evil. It went on, "To the king of India, from the Lake of Qanuj to Sind: your wise envoy, with his elephants and parasols, arrived at our court and delivered your message and the game of chess to us. We asked for time, and one of our learned men considered the matter deeply, until he discovered the game's rules. This wise man has now

come to Qanuj, and to your majesty, bringing with him two thousand camels laden with royal gifts. We send the game of nard as an exchange for chess, and now we shall see which is the finer game. You have many pure-souled Brahmins with you; let us see if they can understand this game. Send the goods that my messenger has taken such pains to bring to you to your treasury. If the rajah of Qanuj and his advisors cannot fathom our game, he must send us an equivalent number of camel-loads of goods: this is the agreement between us."

The shining sun rose in the sky, and Bozorjmehr set off from the court. As he approached the rajah's kingdom with his gifts, the letter, and the game of nard, Brahmins gladly came to guide him. His head was filled with thoughts of the coming contest. When he was admitted into the rajah's presence, and saw his crown and the splendor of his court, he praised him at length in Pahlavi, then handed over the king's letter. He talked in detail about his journey, the game of chess, and the trouble he had taken to understand it; then he conveyed the greetings of the King of Kings, and the rajah's face opened like a blossoming flower. Next he produced the game of nard, pointing out the dice and its pieces, and put forward his king's proposal; lastly he said that when the king's letter had been read, he was sure that the rajah would not act unjustly. The rajah's face turned pale at this talk of chess and nard.

The Indian Sages Are Unable to Understand the Game of Nard

A nobleman conducted Bozorjmehr to suitable quarters, a hall was prepared for feasting, and wine and musicians were called for. The rajah asked for seven days' grace, and the country's sages gathered together to examine the game of nard. For a week the most intelligent of their men, young and old, competed against one another in trying to work out how the game of nard was played. On the eighth day their chief priest said to the rajah, "No one can make head or tail of this game; wisdom will have to help our souls if we're to construct a game from these pieces."

On the ninth day Bozorjmehr came forward with a frown on his face and hope in his heart. He said, "Kesra did not tell me to stay here for a long time; I must not disappoint my king." The Indian priests were discouraged by this; frowning in sorrow, they confessed their inability to fathom the game. Bozorjmehr sat himself down and the sages watched him intently as he set out the game and taught them how the pieces moved, which was the commander, how the war was fought, how the troops were drawn up, and how the king gave his orders. The rajah and his country's sages were astounded. All of them acclaimed Bozorjmehr, and called him a priest of the pure faith. The rajah questioned him about every branch of knowledge, and he answered each question appropriately. The raja's sages and advisors cried out, "This is truly an eloquent and wise man, quite apart from the business of chess and nard!"

They brought two thousand camels and loaded them with Qanuj's treasures; there were aloes wood and ambergris, camphor and gold, robes and cloth woven with jewels. All this was sent, together with a year's tribute, from the rajah's court to the Persian king's. Then the rajah asked for a crown to be brought from his treasury, together with a robe made of cloth of gold from head to foot, and these he presented to Bozorjmehr, praising him as he did so. He also gave many gifts to Bozorjmehr's companions. The two thousand camels laden with tribute and presents made a caravan the like of which no man had ever led before, and as Bozorjmehr traveled home from Qanuj he lifted his head up to the heavens with pride. He was happy to be carrying the rajah's letter, written on silk in Devanagari script, which said, "The rajah and his nobles bear witness—and not out of fear, but as their true opinion—that no one has ever seen a king like Nushin-Ravan, or heard from learned priests of one like him; and there is no one more knowledgeable than his vizier, whose wisdom is guarded by the heavens. We have sent a year's tribute in advance, and if more is required we shall send that too; we have sent all that was agreed according to our wager."

When the king learned that his wise advisor had been successful and was on his way home, he was overjoyed and gave orders that the noblemen in the city and army be informed, so that they could go together to welcome him. Bozorjmehr made a triumphal entry into the city, like a victorious prince, and when he approached the throne, the king heartily congratulated him, embracing him and questioning him about the rajah and the difficulties he'd encountered along the way. Bozorjmehr told the king about his journey and his good fortune, and then laid the rajah's letter before the throne. The scribe Yazdegerd was summoned, and when he read the rajah's letter the whole company was astonished at Bozorjmehr's knowledge and good fortune. Kesra said, "Thanks be to God for my wisdom, and for my knowledge of what is good; kings bow as slaves before my crown and throne, and their hearts and souls are filled with love for me."

Borzui Brings the Book of Kalileh and Demneh from India

The King of Kings, Nushin-Ravan—may his name live forever—always kept learned men and priests at his court, and they were an adornment to his reign. There were eloquent doctors, scholars, nobles, and men skilled in various professions. One such was the doctor Borzui, who was advanced in his skill and an eloquent speaker. He had some expertise in every branch of knowledge and was famous throughout the world for this. One day, during a royal audience, he came before the king and said, "Your majesty, you love knowledge, and your inquiring mind delights in learning things. Today my spirit was alert and at ease, and I read in an Indian book that a plant grows in the mountains there that looks like silk from Byzantium. If someone gathers this plant and prepares it in the correct way and then sprinkles it on the dead, they will begin to talk. Now with the king's permission, I shall make this difficult journey; I shall employ all my knowledge to see if I can find this wonder. If a corpse can live again, this is only to be expected now that Nushin-Ravan rules the world."

The king responded, "This is not possible, but we should inquire into it nevertheless. Take a letter from me to the ruler of India, and study the nature of these Indian idol-worshippers. Find a companion for this search, and ask good fortune to help you too; these mysterious words you've read perhaps point to some new wonder in the world. Take all your requests to the Indian king; you will certainly need him to provide you with a guide." Then Nushin-Ravan threw open the gates to his treasury and provided Borzui with three hundred camels laden with royal goods—gold coins, bro cades, silks, seals, crowns, musk, and ambergris. Borzui set off and arrived at the Indian court, where he handed over his king's letter and spread the goods he had brought before the rajah. After reading the king's letter, the rajah said, "Kesra has no need to send me presents in this way; my people and my realm are themselves presents he has bestowed on me. Given his just rule and *farr*, his glory and good fortune, it would be no surprise if the world-ruler could resurrect the dead. The Brahmins who live in the mountains will help you carry out your plan. My vizier, my wealth, my treasurer, and all that's good and evil in India, are at your disposal; I measure my greatness by how I am able to aid you."

They provided him with suitable apartments close to the rajah, as well as with a cook, food, fine clothes, and carpets. He spent that night with the wise men of Qanuj, discussing his plans. When day broke over the mountains and the world-illuminating torch appeared, the rajah summoned his learned doctors, and those who could offer advice. Borzui set off for the mountains on foot, with a knowledgeable guide, and the doctors accompanied him. He gathered plants that were dry, fresh, withered, or flourishing, and he made various concoctions from them; but when he sprinkled these on the dead not a single corpse came to life, and it was clear that the mixtures were power-less. Though he walked over the whole mountain, his efforts were fruitless, and he knew that the dead could be revived only by that king who is eternal and rules all things. He was tormented by the pains of his journey, by the shame he would feel before his king and the courtiers, by thoughts of the wealth that had been given to the rajah, and by the foolish things he had said. He was sick at heart when he remembered the book he had read and said to himself, "Why did that foolish, senseless man write such ridiculous things, which could only lead to trouble and reproaches?"

He turned to the learned men who had accompanied him and said, "You are experienced, well-regarded men: do you know of anyone more knowl-edgeable than yourselves, who might outdo you in wisdom?" They all agreed on their answer: "There is an old sage, who surpasses us in both years and wisdom, and who is more knowledgeable than every master." Borzui replied, "You are noble and magnanimous men, and I ask you to take yet more trouble and to guide me to this sage. It may be that this eloquent and wise old man can help me in my search."

As they led him to this man Borzui's heart was preoccupied with wor-ries, his mind with what he would say. When he met him, he eloquently described his troubles that had begun with the book he had read and with the words he had heard from various savants. The old man spoke to him about the different kinds of knowledge, and then said,

> "When I was young I also read the book
> You mention, and like you began to look
> For this same plant; my time was vainly spent,
> Until I saw that something else was meant.
> Let me explain: the plant that you have tried
> So hard to find is speech, the mountainside
> Is knowledge, and the corpse is any man
> Who's ignorant, since only knowledge can
> Give life to us; if there's no knowledge there
> You won't find life within us anywhere.
> The plant you seek's a book called Kalileh,
> Its language is the guide to wisdom's way—
> You'll find this book, if you search carefully,
> Locked away in the rajah's treasury."

Borzui was overjoyed when he heard these words, and it seemed to him that all his troubles disappeared like the wind that blows and is gone. He called down blessings on the sage and hurried to the court, traveling as fast as fire. When he reached the rajah he bowed down before him and said, "May you live for as long as the world remains. Great king, there is a book called in the Indian tongue *Kalileh*; it's kept under seal, in your treasury, in the archives there, and it is a guide to wisdom. If it will cause you no distress, I ask that you order your treasurer to give this book to me."

The king's soul was upset at this request, and for a while he pondered what to do. Then he said to Borzui, "No one has ever asked me for this, but if King Nushin-Ravan wanted my body or my soul, or one of my nobles or subjects, I could not withhold any of them from him. But read the book here, from beginning to end, so that those who hate me cannot say that I allowed it to be copied." Borzui replied, "I want no more than you wish to grant me, your majesty." The king's treasurer brought the book of *Kalileh and Demneh*, and guided Borzui through it. Throughout the day he committed to memory whatever he read, and went over it again at night until the dawn broke. He was delighted by the book, and he washed his soul in its wisdom. He secretly wrote the book out in Persian, and this is how it was sent to Nushin-Ravan. As soon as Nushin-Ravan's reply came saying, "The ocean of knowledge has reached us," Borzui went to the rajah and asked for permission to return home.

The rajah made much of him and gave him an Indian robe of honor, two costly bracelets and two sets of earrings, a torque set with royal gems, an Indian turban, and an Indian sword made of iron that glittered like silk. Borzui left Qanuj having learned a great deal and in high spirits; when he arrived home he made his obeisance before the king, told him what he had seen and heard at the rajah's court, and explained that the plant he had sought had been knowledge. The king said to him, "You have done well, and the book called *Kalileh* has given my soul new life. Take the keys from my treasurer, and choose whatever you wish." Wise Borzui went to the treasury, but he gave the treasurer little enough to do. There were gold and jewels to right and left, but he wanted no more than a suit of royal clothes. He clothed himself in fine fabrics and quickly made his way back to Kesra's court. As he bowed before the throne the king said to him, "You have been through so much, so why did you leave my treasury without taking either money or jewels? A man who has endured a great deal deserves a great deal." Borzui replied, "A man who wears his king's clothes has found the way to good fortune and the throne of greatness. And then unworthy men will see these clothes, and their evil hearts will be darkened, while our friends' faces will rejoice in our good fortune. I have one request of the king, and this is so that I shall be remembered in the world: when Bozorjmehr writes out this book, may he recall the trouble that Borzui took to obtain it. If the victorious king so commands, may he start the book with a mention of me, so that after I die learned men will not forget the difficulties I went through." The king said,

"This is a noble desire, one that is fitting for a man with a free spirit. Your words exceed your station, but they are justified by the pains you have taken." Then he said to Bozorjmehr, "This request should not be denied," and when the scribe had cut his pen and was ready to write, he began his account with mention of Borzui.

This copy was a royal one, and the book existed only in Pahlavi script at that time. It was kept with care in the king's treasury, so that no one unworthy could look at it. It was read in Pahlavi until men spoke Arabic, then the caliph Mamun renewed the book, so that its sun could shine on other men. He had the heart of a learned priest and the mind of the Kayanid kings, and he was skilled in all kinds of knowledge. *Kalileh* was translated into Arabic, in the form in which you now hear it recited. It remained in Arabic until the time of King Nasr; his vizier and librarian was Abul Fazl, and he gave orders that the book be translated into Persian and Dari, and so the matter was settled. Then Nasr was guided by wisdom and desired that there might remain some memorial to himself in the world. He had a man recite the whole book to Rudaki, who strung its rich pearls, turning prose into verse. For a man who is literate, this is an added adornment to the tales, and for the ignorant it is a blessing: verse satisfies both the soul and the mind.

Nushin-Ravan Is Angry with Bozorjmehr and Has Him Imprisoned

Now hear what happened to Bozorjmehr, who was raised from the earth to the heavens, and brought down to base earth again by the same man who had raised him up.

One day Kesra rode out from Ctesiphon to hunt horned sheep and deer on the plain. The flock of sheep dispersed, leaving Kesra behind, and he came on a grassy spot shaded by trees. Bozorjmehr was with him, keeping him company out of affection and in order to serve him. The king dismounted, intending to rest; none of his servants were nearby, but the one kind face that was there was enough. He stretched out and turned from side to side on the grass; then he laid his head down, with Bozorjmehr watching from a little way off. The king always wore an armband encrusted with jewels, and as he lay sleeping his arm was uncovered. A black bird swooped down from the clouds, perched beside the sleeping king, and saw the jewels on his naked arm. The bird saw no one else there; the men in the king's entourage were off hunting by themselves, and the sleeping king seemed to be alone with no one nearby to advise him. Seeing the armband, the bird pecked open the jewels' settings, and as the precious pearls and topazes fell out, he ate them one by one. Then he flew up and disappeared from sight.

Bozorjmehr's heart was filled with foreboding at what the heavens had brought. He knew that fate brings prosperity and hardship, and that now a time of hardship had come. When the king woke and saw Bozorjmehr biting his lip, he thought that this man whom he had treated so well had acted disrespectfully toward him, and said, "You dog, who told you a man's nature could be hidden? I'm not some celestial being like Hormozd or Bahman; my body is made of earth, air, and fire." But although the king tired out his tongue reproaching Bozorjmehr, he received no answer from him but sighs. Bozorjmehr seemed to shrivel away before his king and the turning heavens, because he had seen the signs of his downfall, and in his fear the wise counselor remained silent. The soldiers in the king's entourage were now all around the meadow where their master had rested. The king mounted his horse and looked at no one on the way back to his palace; he bit his lip as he rode, and when he dismounted he muttered to himself in anger. He ordered his men to harden their hearts against the vizier and to confine him to his palace.

Bozorjmehr sat in his palace, deprived of the king's favor. One of his relatives, a young, energetic man who waited on King Nushin-Ravan, lived there with him. This man followed Nushin-Ravan about his palace, and was quite forward in his conversations with the king. One day Bozorjmehr asked him how he served the king, and told him he should look for ways to improve his skills. The servant replied, "You are our chief priest, so let me tell you what happened today. After he finished eating I went forward and poured water on his hands, and he found the floor was wet from my ewer. He looked at me with such fury that I said to myself, 'I'll never eat or sleep again!' When the king of the world became angry with me like that, my hand holding the ewer went weak and I dropped it." Bozorjmehr said to him, "Go and get some water, and pour it as you did over the king's hands." The young man brought warm water and bit by bit poured it over the hands of the vizier, who said, "Next time, when you pour the water for him to wash his hands, try to do it smoothly, with no violent movements, and when the king raises his hands to touch his lips with perfume, stop pouring."

The next day, when King Nushin-Ravan was eating, the young man stood there filled with apprehension until he once again had to bring the ewer and basin for the king to wash his hands. He performed his task just as the knowledgeable vizier had told him, pouring the water not too slowly and not too quickly. The king said to him, "Your service has improved: who taught you how to do this?" He answered, "Bozorjmehr taught me how to do this properly, in the way the king has just seen." The king said, "Go to that clever man and ask him, 'What evil nature was it, what despicable ambition, made you choose to sink down from the splendid and honorable rank you held?'" Hearing the king's words, the young steward ran to his uncle with grief in his heart. He told him what the king had said, and Bozorjmehr quietly answered him: "In ways that can be seen, and in ways that cannot be seen, my state is finer than the king's." The servant went back to the king and told him what Bozorjmehr had said. Nushin-Ravan started up in fury and ordered that Bozorjmehr be kept chained in a dark pit, and then told the servant to ask this foolish man how his days passed when he was imprisoned in this way. With his face covered in tears the young man asked Bozorjmehr the king's question, and the good man's answer was, "My days pass by more easily than the king's do." The messenger ran to the king like the wind and told him what Bozorjmehr's answer was. The king raged like a leopard. He drove all love for Bozorjmehr from his heart and ordered that he be imprisoned in a metal chest with spikes on the inside and with his head held by iron bands. He could not rest by day or stretch out to sleep at night; his body was in constant pain and his heart was in torment.

After four days the king of the world said to his servant, "Go to that wise man once more; be quick taking my message and bringing his answer. Ask him how he finds his body, now that its shirt is made of sharp spikes." But when the servant gave him the obstinate king's message, Bozorjmehr said to the young man, "My days are better than Nushin-Ravan's days." Nushin-Ravans' face turned pale when he heard this reply; he chose a man in the palace who was honest and would understand what Bozorjmehr meant by his words. With him he sent an executioner, and said, "Go, and say to this malignant man that either he returns me a proper answer, not some foolishness about the spike-lined chest where he's chained being better than the king's throne, or this executioner will use his sword to show him how the Day of Judgment will arrive."

The man came to Bozorjmehr, and his heart was moved to pity by the sage's plight; he repeated the king's words for Bozorjmehr who said,

> "Whether our lot is vile or glorious
> Fortune has never shown her face to us.
> But, king or commoner, we know that we
> Must leave this earth soon for eternity.
> No man has an abiding foothold here
> And, good or bad, our lives will disappear:
> Then kings know fear, and cling to life, and grieve—
> But wretchedness is never hard to leave."

The messenger and the executioner returned to their proud sovereign and told him what they had heard. The king's heart was troubled by this answer, and he gave orders that Bozorjmehr be taken from his prison to his palace again.

And so the heavens turned for a while; Bozorjmehr's face became wrinkled, his wealth could not assuage his grief, and he wasted away in sorrow.

The Emperor of Byzantium Sends a Sealed Casket, and When Bozorjmehr Guesses What Is Inside It He Is Released

At this time, the emperor of Byzantium sent an envoy to the king, with a letter and gifts and a locked strongbox. The envoy said, "The message from my master is as follows: 'The king has many wise priests at his court; if, without opening it, they can say what is inside this locked box, we shall send tribute and presents beside, according to our custom. But if your clever priests cannot penetrate this mystery, the king should not demand any more tribute from us, and neither should he send armies into our realm. Answer as seems fitting to you.'"

The world's king said to the envoy, "Even this is not hidden from God; with his grace I shall solve the problem, and I have clear-thinking advisors to help me. Spend a week as our guest, and give yourself freely to wine and pleasure." The king was bewildered as to what to do. He summoned his courtiers and wise men, and each of them looked at the keyless casket from every angle, but all of them had to confess their ignorance of what was inside it. The king became worried when none of the group had had any success. He thought, "This secret of the heavens is a problem for Bozorjmehr." But, embarrassed by the suffering his wise counselor had been through, he frowned and his face turned pale. His painful thoughts prompted him to have a suit of clothes brought from the treasury, and a fine horse with a royal saddle. He sent these to Bozorjmehr with a message: "I cannot deny the suffering you have endured; it was the high heavens that had me hurt you in this way. Your talk infuriated me, and you put your own body at risk. Now something has happened that is troubling my heart. The emperor of Byzantium has sent me one of their priests, a famous man in his own land, who has a golden casket with him that's completely closed, with a lock, and a seal of musk. The emperor says that our counselors should explain what is hidden inside the casket. I thought that this secret is something the soul of Bozorjmehr could understand."

When Bozorjmehr heard these words, his heart was filled with his old sufferings. He left the place where he had been confined, washed his head and body, and prayed before God who rules the world. He was an innocent man and his king was quick to anger, and Bozorjmehr was afraid that he would be harmed by the king again. It was still dark night when the king's message reached him and day had not yet dawned. As the sun showed his crown and night veiled her face, Bozorjmehr peered up toward the stars, and when the shining sun rose in the sky he washed the eyes of his heart with the water of wisdom. He sought out a wise man on whom he could rely and said to him, "My affairs are in a wretched state because the sufferings I have been through have darkened my eyes. Watch for who meets us on the road, and ask them about their lives, but don't inquire as to their names."

Bozorjmehr set out from his house, and there was a beautiful woman hurrying toward him. His companion described everything he couldn't see, and Bozorjmehr said, "Find out if this lovely woman has a husband." When she was asked, the woman answered, "I have a husband, and a child too, at home," and Bozorjmehr smiled at her words as he rode forward on his high-stepping horse. Then another woman appeared, and Bozorjmehr's guide asked her, "Do you have a husband and child, or do your arms embrace nothing but the wind?" She said, "I have a husband, but no child; and now that you have heard my answer, get out of my way." And at that moment a third woman appeared and she too was questioned: "You have a lovely face, and a proud, provocative walk; who keeps you company?" "I've never," she replied, "had a husband, and I don't want to show my face to anyone." Now when Bozorjmehr heard these answers, he turned them over in his mind.

His face was melancholy as he hurried forward. When he arrived, he was taken to the king, who commanded him to approach the throne. And then the king's heart was filled with sorrow, and he sighed deeply, because he realized that his wise advisor could no longer see. The king apologized at length for his anger against this innocent man, and then talked about Byzantium and its emperor and the locked casket. Bozorjmehr said to the world's king, "May you shine for as long as the heavenly bodies shine. We should call an assembly of wise men and priests, as well as the envoy from Byzantium and have the casket placed before the king and his courtiers. Then by the power of God who gave us thought and has made my soul delight in truth, I shall say what is inside the casket, without touching either the box itself or its lock. Even if my eyes are now dark, my heart is bright, and my soul is armored with knowledge."

The king was happy to hear his words, and his heart revived like a flower in the springtime. He drew himself up as his worries fell away, and he had the envoy and his casket summoned, together with his priests, advisors, and sages, whom he seated before Bozorjmehr. The he addressed the envoy: "Give us your message, and make your demands." The envoy repeated what his emperor had said: "A victorious king should have wisdom, knowledge, and a good reputation. You have the *farr* and strength of a world-conqueror, greatness, knowledge, and might, priests who seek out the truth, and heroes who support you here at your court or take your part in the world at large. Let your clever courtiers see this locked and sealed casket, and let them in their wisdom say clearly what is hidden there. Then we shall send you tribute and taxes, since my country is wealthy enough to do this; but if they cannot do this, then they should no longer ask us for tribute."

Bozorjmehr then invoked God's blessing and said, "May the world's king always be happy, understanding, fortunate, and generous! I thank the Lord of the Sun and Moon, who shows our souls the way to wisdom, who alone knows what is open and what is secret. He has no need of knowledge, but knowledge is my desire. There are three shining pearls inside the casket, within a number of coverings; one is pierced, one is half pierced, and iron has never touched the third." When the envoy heard this he brought the key, while Nushin-Ravan watched. There was a box inside the casket, and inside this there were layers of silk, in which three pearls were hidden, just as the Persian sage had said. The first of them was pierced, the second half pierced, and the last untouched. All the priests who were present cried their congratulations, and showered Bozorjmehr with jewels. The king's face cleared, and as a reward he filled Bozorjmehr's mouth with splendid pearls. His heart was tormented by the thought of what he had done before; he writhed within and frowned to think how he had treated this man who had shown him such love and loyalty.

When Bozorjmehr saw that the king's soul was suffering, he spoke of those things from the past that he had kept hidden—the armband and the black bird, his anxiety for the jewels, and the king's sleep. Then he said to the king, "This was fated to happen, and there is no point in suffering regret because of it; the heavens bring us good and evil, whether to the king, or to his priests, or to Bozorjmehr. The signs of the seeds that God has sowed in the stars are written on our foreheads. May Nushin-Ravan's soul rejoice and always be free from pain and sorrow. However glorious a king might be, it is his vizier's job to be an ornament to his court. The king's business is hunting and warfare, wine and rejoicing, generosity, justice, and feasting; he knows how his predecessors reigned and follows their example. It is the vizier who must accumulate wealth, maintain the army, combat gossip, and hear suppliants for justice; it is his heart and soul that are troubled by worries about the administration and treasury."

*A*s Kesra Nushin-Ravan's life drew to a close he nominated his son Hormozd as his successor and wrote a document to him setting out his advice and final wishes.

He began by invoking God and continued, "This is the advice of the son of Qobad. Understand, my son, that this world is faithless and filled with sorrow, hardship, pain, and adversity. And whenever you are happy here and your heart is free of sorrow, and you rejoice in your life, remember that you must leave this fleeting world. When thoughts of my departure came to me in the bright days and the long nights, I searched to see who would be worthy of the crown. I have six wise sons, all of them are generous and just, and they delight my heart. I chose you because you are the oldest, and you have wisdom and will be an adornment to the crown. Qobad was eighty when he made me his successor; I am now seventy-four, and I name you as the world's king. In doing this I seek only rest and the public good, in the hope that my soul will be blessed. I hope too that God grants you nothing but happiness and prosperity. If you make men secure by your justice, you will also ensure your own security, and heaven will be your reward: great is the man who sows the seeds of righteousness.

"See that you are always patient, since it is not becoming for a king to rush into decisions. A king who is alert and seeks for instruction keeps his good reputation forever. Have no dealings with lies, because if you do, your luck will wither away, and keep your heart and mind far from haste because haste sends wisdom to sleep. Do good and strive for the good, and in all things, good and evil, attend to the words of the wise. Do not let evil come near you, for it will certainly have its effect on you; dress appropriately, eat appropriately, and pay attention to your father's advice. You come from God; see that you turn to him if you would have him as your guide. If your justice makes the world prosper, your throne will be secure and your subjects will be happy. If men do well, reward them so that they forget the pains they took. Keep the wise happy and close by, and make the world dark for those who are malevolent. Consult with the wise on every subject, and do not complain about the difficulties that kinship imposes on you. If the wise can always reach you, you will be able to keep your crown and throne.

"Do not let your subjects live in wretchedness, and see that the country's nobles benefit from your justice. Do not look kindly on those of low character, and entrust no task to an unjust man. Incline your ears and heart to the poor, and take their sorrows on yourself; in this way you will sow seeds of righteousness in your orchard, and your enemies will become your friends. When a powerful man acts justly and from the heart, the world is happy in his reign, and he too is made happy. Do not withhold your wealth from the deserving, and be generous to the virtuous. If you follow my advice your crown will keep its eminence. May he who bestows all benefits look kindly on you, and may your good deeds be a refuge for you. Do not forget my words, even though you can no longer see me. May your mind remain fresh and strong, your heart happy, your body pure and safe from all malevolence. May wisdom always guard you, and may your mind be filled with good thoughts.

"When I have left this great world, build me a tomb like a palace, in a place where few men go, and so high that the vultures cannot fly over it. Its entrance must be high in the vault, as high as ten lariats would reach, and over it must be written that this is my court, together with an account of my greatness, my wealth, and my armies. See that the chamber is spread with carpets and cushions, preserve my body with camphor, and sprinkle musk on my head for a crown. Bring five unused brocades of cloth of gold from my treasury, and wrap me in them according to the custom of the Kayanids and our ancestors. Construct an ivory couch and place it there, and over it suspend my crown. Then to its right and left set out all my gold dishes, goblets, and jewels: twenty goblets are to be filled with rosewater, wine and saffron, and two hundred with musk, camphor, and ambergris. Do not exceed or fall short of what I order you. The blood must be drawn off from the trunk of my body, so that it dries, and then it must be filled with camphor and musk. Then close the door to the chamber, since no one must see the king. If the tomb is built in this manner, no one will be able to find his way to me.

"Let my children and family, and all those who will grieve for my death, abstain from feasts and festivals for two months, since this is the custom when a king dies. And it would be right if all who are noble and benevolent would weep for the death of their king. See that you do not disobey the commands of Hormozd, or so much as draw breath without his knowledge."

Everyone wept when they heard of this document. Kesra Nushin-Ravan lived for one more year after he had written it, and when he died these words of his were his memorial; see that you preserve his memory. Now I shall tell of the crown of Hormozd, and place him on his throne.

◄§ THE REIGN OF HORMOZD §►

As Hormozd established his power and was finally able to reign as he wished, his evil nature became apparent and he strayed from the paths of righteousness. One by one, he destroyed his father's confidants and advisors, men who had lived peacefully and with no fear of danger. There were three in particular who had been scholars at Nushin-Ravan's court—one old man and two younger men. The first was Izad-Goshasp; the second, the wise Bozorjmehr, a man blessed with the divine *farr*; and the third Mahazar, also wise and of a serene and cheerful character. These three had served Nushin-Ravan's throne as courtiers and viziers, but Hormozd feared that one day they would feel no gratitude toward him, and he was determined to bring each of them down into the dust.

He had Izad-Goshasp thrown into prison for no reason. The chief priest at that time—a man called Zardhesht—was filled with anxiety for Izad-Goshasp's fate. It was as if an arrow had wounded his heart, and this good and noble priest became pale with worry. After a day in which Izad-Goshasp had had neither a servant, food, clothing, or any companion, he sent a message to the chief priest: "You have always been as dear to me as my own marrow and skin; I am now friendless in the king's prison, and no one visits me. I'm hungry and my aching stomach longs for nourishment. Send me some food, some antidote to the pains that gnaw at me." The priest's heart was moved to sympathy for his friend's situation, but he sent a cautious reply, "Despite your chains, be thankful you have not been physically harmed yet." He grieved inwardly and pondered what to do. He sent some food to the prison, but his heart trembled with apprehension at what he was doing, and he said to himself, "If that unchivalrous and luckless ruler finds out that his priest has sent something to the prison, my life won't be worth a copper coin. The king will find some way to harm me, and his face will turn pale with anger against me." But his heart was wrung for Izad-Goshasp's sufferings, and his face was sallow with grief. He ordered his cook to take food to the prison, and then he mounted his Arab horse and rode there himself. The two men embraced, and their eyelashes were as

wet as the clouds in spring; they talked at length about the king's evil disposition. A table was set before Izad-Goshasp, who took the sacred barsom in
his hand and murmured his prayers while Zardhesht listened. He talked of
his wealth and his palace, and then said,

> *"Now go directly to Hormozd and say*
> *On my behalf, 'Don't turn your head away*
> *But think of all that I have undergone,*
> *Protecting you as if you were my son:*
> *Is my reward to be imprisoned here,*
> *To live in chains, consumed with grief and fear?*
> *My heart is innocent and will display*
> *The wrongs it has endured on Judgment Day.'"*

As the priest was returning home, one of the king's spies ran and told Hormozd all he had heard, and the king decided on an evil course. He hardened
his heart against Izad-Goshasp, and sent someone to the prison and had
him killed. He continued to act toward Zardhesht as if nothing had happened, but he had the priest's words repeated to him at length and began to
consider how to kill him.

He ordered his cook to prepare a dish that had been secretly poisoned. When the priest came to court for the royal audience, the king said to him, "Don't leave us today; I have found a new cook." The priest sat, and a table was set before him, and his face turned pale. He knew that the table signified his end, and he was not mistaken in this. The cooks brought in the dishes and the king ate some of everything. Then the poisoned dish was brought in, and the priest looked at it and knew in his heart that what was being offered to him as nourishment was poison. Hormozd watched and said nothing: he stretched out his hand to the poisoned dish, in the way kings do when they want to bestow a favor on one of their subjects. He took some brains from the dish and said to the priest, "What a fine brain you have. I've reserved this tender morsel just for you. Open your mouth and eat it; it will nourish you well." The priest replied, "By your soul and mind—and may you reign forever—do not order me to eat this morsel. I am full; don't urge me to eat more." Hormozd said, "By the sun and the moon, by your king's pure soul, take this food from my fingers; do not break my heart by denying me." The priest replied, "The king orders me and I have no choice."

He ate the morsel and, tormented by pain, rode quickly to his own house. He told no one of the poison he had eaten, but lay down on a mattress, groaning in agony. He ordered that antidotes for poison be brought, from his own treasury or from the town, but when he ate them they had no effect, and he complained bitterly to God about Hormozd. The king sent one of his confidants to watch the priest and see whether the poison had taken effect or his plan had failed. The priest saw the envoy, and tears coursed down his cheeks as he spoke: "Tell Hormozd that I say this to him: 'Your fortunes will decline, and you and I shall both go before our heavenly judge. From now on you will not be safe from harm, because God's justice will find you out. You are a malevolent man, and I bid you farewell; evil will come to you from the evil you have done.'" The envoy wept to hear these words and reported them to the king. Hormozd regretted what he had done, and he brooded on the truth of the priest's words. He sighed deeply, but could see no way to avoid the pains the priest had spoken of. Then the priest died, and the wise men of the country wept bitterly for him. This is the way of the world, which is full of pain and sorrow. Why strive for a crown, or glory in wealth? For the moments of pleasure pass, and time counts our every breath.

Hormozd Kills Sima-Borzin and Bahram Azar-Mahan

The sad incident of the chief priest put the whole country into a turmoil of distress. This bloodthirsty king, who was unworthy to sit on the throne, gave no thought to the evils that were to come. He prepared to shed more blood and decided to use Bahram Azar-Mahan for this purpose. At dead of night he summoned him, had him kneel before him, and said, "If you want to be safe and never suffer because of my anger or irritation, when the sun rises tomorrow and makes the mountaintops glisten like armor, come with the nobles of Iran and stand before my throne. I will question you about Sima-Borzin; make your heart pliant to my wishes when you answer. I will say, 'Who is this friend of yours? Is he evil, or is he a God-fearing man?' And you will say, 'He is evil, malevolent, the spawn of Ahriman.' After that you can ask me for whatever you desire—slaves, a throne, a seal of authority, a crown." Bahram replied, "I shall say that he is a hundred times worse than you have said." And in this way Hormozd sought for some excuse to ruin Sima-Borzin, even though he was a nobleman and had been a favorite of Hormozd's illustrious father.

When dawn's ivory veil appeared, and the sun rose in the sign of the Twins, the king sat on his ivory throne, above which was suspended his precious crown. The nobility of Iran presented themselves at court and when the chancellor drew back the curtain they went in together to the king, with Bahram Azar-Mahan and Sima-Borzin among them. One by one they sat according to their rank, and a number of them stood before the king. Hormozd said to Bahram Azar-Mahan, "This Sima-Borzin, who is here at this audience, is he worthy of his wealth or is he an extortionate man? Someone with an evil character does not deserve to be wealthy." Bahram Azar-Mahan knew what the king's question meant, he knew it root and branch. He understood that Sima-Borzin was already a man to be mourned, and that he would receive nothing but a tomb, without so much as a shroud, from the king. He answered, "Your majesty, think nothing of Sima-Borzin. He is the cause of Iran's ruin, and would that his body had neither marrow nor skin to it. His talk is all slander, which he uses to stir up quarrels."

When Sima-Borzin heard these words he said to him, "We are old friends—don't vilify me in this way; don't make common cause with demons like this. What have you seen in me, either in word or deed, since

we've been friends, which is the work of Ahriman?" Bahram Azar-Mahan answered him, "You will be the first to harvest the seeds you have sown in the world, and this fire you lit will give you back nothing but black smoke. When Kesra summoned you and me to sit before his throne with the priest Bozorjmehr and that noble courtier Izad-Goshasp, he asked us who was worthy of the crown, who had the divine *farr*, whether his older or younger son was more worthy of the crown, and to which of them he should give it. We all stood and answered him together, saying, 'This prince who was born of a Turk is not worthy of the throne, and no one wants him as king. He is descended from the emperor of China and has an evil nature, and in his face and stature he looks like his mother.' But you said that Hormozd was worthy to be king; well, this is the reward you've received from that worthy man. This is why I have spoken against you and cursed you."

Hormozd shrank back in shame when he heard this man's true words. In the darkness of the night he had both men sent to his prisons and muttered angrily against them. On the third night, when the moon rose above the mountains, the king got rid of Sima-Borzin: he had him killed in the thieves' prison, but all that he gained by this was sorrow and curses. Learning of this honorable man's death Bahram Azar-Mahan sent a message to the king: "Your crown is higher than the moon's sphere. You know how hard I have tried to keep your secrets, and that before that noble king, your father, I always spoke in your favor. If you summon me to your throne I shall give you some advice that will benefit Iran and keep those who are wise safe from harm." Hormozd sent one of his confidants to fetch Bahram to the court in the darkness of the night, and the king spoke kindly to him, then said, "Tell me what this advice is, which will improve my fortunes."

Bahram answered, "I have seen a simple black chest in the king's treasury: within it there is a casket, and within that there is a document written in Persian on white silk, and it is this on which the Persians' hopes depend. It is written in the hand of your father, the great king, and you should look at it." Hormozd sent someone to the treasurer saying, "Search among my father's treasures for a simple sealed chest: on the seal is the name Nushin-Ravan (may his soul live eternally). Find it quickly and bring it here to me now, in the darkness of the night." The treasurer hurried to find the chest, and ran with it to the king, with its seal still intact. The king broke the seal, repeatedly invoking the name of Nushin-Ravan as he did so. He looked in the chest and hurriedly pulled out a sheet of silk; then he stared at the words that Nushin-Ravan had written there:

> "For twelve long years, unequaled among men
> Hormozd will rule this land as king; but then
> Disturbances will fill the world, his name
> Will be obscured and lose its former fame.

Foes will attack, and one will prove to be
An evil and malignant enemy:
The forces of Hormozd will flee and fail.
His rival will dethrone him and prevail,
His wife will put his eyes out, mourners' cries
Will rise above his body to the skies."

When Hormozd saw this message in his father's handwriting, he was terrified and tore the silk in pieces. His face turned pale and his eyes filled with bitter tears. To Bahram he said, "You live by doing evil! What did you want to do with this document—tear the head from my body?"

Bahram said to him, "You are born of a Turkish woman, and you can never be sated with bloodshed. Your ancestry is from the emperors of China, not from Kay Qobad, even though Kesra bestowed the crown on you!" Hormozd knew that if this man stayed alive he would need no prompting to shed his king's blood; hearing these unwelcome words, he had Bahram taken back to the prison. On the next night, when the moon rose above the mountains, the executioner killed him in the prison. Now there were no wise advisors or priests left at his court.

Saveh Shah Attacks Hormozd

When Hormozd had reigned for ten years, voices rose against him in every country. Saveh Shah advanced from Herat, with elephants, war drums, wealth, and an army. To number his troops, count to a thousand four hundred times: he had one thousand two hundred war elephants, and you would say there was no way left unblocked on the earth. From the plain of Herat to Marvrud the land was filled with his warriors, as dense as warp woven with weft. He marched on Marv, and the land disappeared beneath the dust raised by his troops. He wrote a letter to Hormozd, saying, "Gather your armies and make a way for us; provide us with foraging, and remember our swords. I wish to travel through your kingdom; my troops cover the rivers, the mountains, and the plains." When the king read this letter, he grew pale at the thought of such an immense army.

And from the opposite direction the emperor of Byzantium led his army toward Persia, subduing the land as he did so. The Byzantine army was a hundred thousand strong, and included their renowned, warlike cavalry; they re-conquered the territory called Qeisar-Navan, which Nushin-Ravan had conquered. From every country armies led by famous noblemen were approaching. An army came from Khazar, and the land on their route was blackened by the mass of men. They were led by the experienced warrior Bedal, who marched with his own wealth and men and overran the countryside from Armenia to Ardebil. And an innumerable army came up from Arabia, led by young, proud riders like Abbas and Hamzeh. As they came they plundered the land that had provided Hormozd with regular tax revenues. They reached the Euphrates and left not a blade of grass still growing in the province.

Hormozd's days grew dark as messages came in from his forces, and this once-flourishing king seemed to wither away. He sent out messengers summoning the Persian nobility to his palace, laid the private information he had gathered before them, and said, "No one can remember a time when Iran has been attacked by so many different armies." The nobles were perplexed as to what to do and made various suggestions; then they said, "You are a clever and capable monarch, listen to our opinion in this matter. You are the wise king and we are only your subjects, we don't think of ourselves as learned people. You must consider what is to be done, and who can be our country's savior."

The priest who served Hormozd as vizier said, "Your majesty, you are knowledgeable and you accept knowledgeable advice. If the army from Khazar attacks, we will make short work of them. We can parley with the Byzantine Romans, and we'll utterly destroy the Arabs. My heart has no fear of Arabs. It hurts the eyes just to look at them, they eat snakes and lizards and they have no skill at fighting. It's Saveh Shah you should worry about, he's the real threat to us. Troubles come to us from the road to Khorasan, where our armies and wealth are being destroyed. When the Turks cross the Oxus and attack, we should respond without delay." Hormozd asked the priest how he thought they should deal with Saveh Shah. The priest replied, "Prepare your army, since it's an army that gives a king confidence. Summon the keeper of the muster rolls and have him tell you how many men under arms you have." The keeper brought in the rolls; the army came to a hundred thousand men, and this number included both infantry and cavalry. The priest said, "With an army like this we need not worry about Saveh Shah. If you act chivalrously and righteously, and avoid all evil, you will be able to save your subjects as a king should."

The king said, "The Byzantine emperor will not try to attack us. I'll return him the cities that Nushin-Ravan conquered, and he'll go back to where he came from." He found an envoy who was both a warrior and a scribe, a wise, eloquent, and clever man, and instructed him, "Tell the emperor I no longer require tribute from Byzantium, and that if he wishes to prosper, he should not set foot on Persian soil." As soon as the envoy passed on the king's message, the emperor returned to Byzantium and gave up all thoughts of war. Hormozd also sent an army commanded by the splendid and just warrior Khorad against the forces of Khazar. When they reached Armenia the enemy blocked their way and gave battle. The Persians killed a great number of them and brought back large amounts of plunder from the area. Once Hormozd knew that Khorad and his army were victorious, he concentrated all his thoughts on the one remaining problem—Saveh Shah.

Mehran-Setad Recommends Bahram Chubineh to Hormozd

The king had a wise, contented servant called Nastuh who said to the king, "May you live forever, and may evil always be far from you. You should ask Mehran-Setad what he remembers of former days. He sits in a corner, conning the Zend-Avesta; he's grown old and weak and has no hopes of the world now. I recently spent a day and a night with him and told him about Saveh Shah, his war elephants, and his huge army, but when he answered me he spoke only of former times. I asked him what he remembered, and he said that he would tell what he knew if the king of the world asked him."

The king immediately sent a courtier, who brought the old man in a litter to the king. When the old man entered, his heart filled with wisdom, his head with talk, Hormozd asked him what he remembered about the warlike Turks. "Your majesty, you are eloquent and eager to learn," Mehran-Setad said. "When the emperor of China sent your mother to Persia, I went with a hundred and sixty brave warriors to ask for her hand. Your father was a wise and just king, and he didn't want the daughter of some concubine. He said to me, 'Ask only for the daughter of the empress; a servant's child wouldn't be suitable for our court.' I went to the emperor and greeted him. He had five daughters, all as lovely as the spring, all tints and scents and beauty they were. He sent me to his harem; they had made the girls' faces up and put chaplets of roses in their hair, all except for your mother, who wore nothing on her head, and had none of the bracelets and necklaces and jewels the other girls were wearing. She was the only one who was the empress's daughter, and she was the one who had no make-up or finery on. Her mother really loved her and was tormenting herself with the thought of her daughter going off to some distant land; she didn't want to endure having to say goodbye to her when she left the emperor's palace. I chose her, out of all the emperor's daughters, and I didn't so much as glance at the others. The emperor told me to choose another one, saying all five were good, accomplished girls. But I said that she was the one I had to have, and that it would be my ruin if I chose a different one.

"Then he called for his learned counselors, and when they had knelt before his throne he asked them to cast his daughter's horoscope, to see what the stars held in store for her. One of his astrologers said, 'May you see nothing but good and hear nothing but righteousness. A child like a raging lion will be born from this girl and the Persian king; tall and strong-armed, in bravery like a lion, and in generosity like a rain cloud. He will be black-eyed, quick to anger, and impatient, and when his father dies he will be king. He will use up much of his father's wealth, but few enough of his days will be spent in evil. Then a fierce king will arise, and attack with an army of Turks, intending to overrun Persia and the Yemen. The Persian king will fear him and his victories; but the king will have a subject living far away, a proud, loyal horseman, tall and wiry, his head covered in black curls, talkative, with a large nose, dark-skinned, quick and fierce in his quarrels. This ambitious man will be named Chubineh, and he will be descended from champions. This subject of the king's will bring his army to the court slowly, then suddenly attack the Turks and break their army's power.'

"I've never seen a happier man than the emperor of China was when he had heard the astrologer out. He gave his daughter, who was the crown of all his daughters, to Nushin-Ravan, and, as the king's representative, I accepted her and started on my homeward journey. He gave us so many jewels that we had difficulty transporting them. He came with us as far as the Oxus, and there placed his beloved child in a boat; then he turned back from the shore, his heart filled with sorrow at parting from her. Now I have told the king all that I saw. Search your country for this man, and tell your envoy to hurry because the king's victories are in his hands. Don't entrust this matter to anyone else, friend or foe." When he had said this, his spirit left his body, and the whole company wept for him.

The king was astonished, and bitter tears rained down from his eyelashes. He said to the Persians there, "Mehran-Setad remembered these true accounts, and when he had told them to me he died, entrusting his soul to God. I am grateful to God that I have learned from this old man such pressing news. Search among our nobility, and the commoners too, until you find the man he spoke of; do your utmost to find him." Among his listeners was a well-known nobleman who was in charge of the king's stables; his name was Rad–Farrokh and he lived only to serve the king. He came to the king and said, "In my opinion the description this praiseworthy sage gave fits Bahram, the son of Bahram, who was Goshasp's son. He is a fine, proud horseman: I have not seen a more able lord of the marches riding in the plains. You gave him Barda' and Ardebil to rule, and he has become a great warrior there, with his war drums and cavalry."

Bahram Chubineh Arrives at Hormozd's Court

Hormozd sent for Bahram and had him told of Mehran-Setad's prediction. The ambitious chieftain hurried from Barda with his warriors, and as soon as he arrived, Hormozd had him admitted into his presence. Bahram looked at Hormozd's face and greeted him respectfully; the king gazed at him for a while, and formed a good opinion of what he saw. He saw the attributes Mehran-Setad had described; he smiled and his face relaxed again. Then he questioned him and made much of him, and had a fine building set aside for him to stay in.

The next morning, when night laid aside its musky cloak and the sun showed her face, the lord of the marches made his way to the court, and the nobles opened a way for him. The king called Bahram forward and sat him on a throne in front of the other courtiers. He questioned him about Saveh Shah and said, "Should I make peace with him, or send an army to confront him?" The warrior answered, "Making peace is not the way to deal with Saveh Shah. If he's determined on war, trying to make peace will only lead to your destruction: a malignant man will become more audacious when he sees you have no stomach to fight. If you stick to feasting when you should be fighting, one of your subjects will take over this realm." Hormozd asked, "Then what should we do? Wait, or march against him?" Bahram replied, "It's a good omen if this malcontent acts unjustly, because justice and injustice can't be together in one place. Attack this evil enemy, bring water to quench his fire; if you don't, the ancient heavens will choose a new ruler here. If we use the strength and skills we have, God will not reproach us and we shall not be ashamed when heroes ask us about our deeds. If there were only ten thousand Persians left alive and we fled from battle, those enemies who love to find fault with you would say that you ran away without fighting. If we can rain down arrows on the enemy and make our bows like the clouds in spring, if a hundred thousand maces and swords are shattered in the lines of battle, and still we are not victorious and must despair of our fortunes, then will be the time to obey the enemy, when we have neither minds nor souls nor bodies left to us."

When the king heard Bahram's words he laughed, and the throne seemed to shine with splendor. The courtiers left the king's presence, and their hearts were filled with anxiety. They said to Bahram, "When the king questions you don't be so foolhardy in your answers. Saveh Shah has such a huge army with him that not an ant or a mosquito can find its way through such a mass of men. After the things you've said in front of the king, who will dare to lead our armies?" But Bahram said to them, "My lords, if the king commands it, I am ready to lead our armies." The king's spies immediately went to Hormozd and told him what Bahram had said, adding ten new words for every one he'd spoken.

Hormozd Makes Bahram Chubineh the Commander of His Army

The Persian king was pleased to hear this, and he no longer feared Saveh Shah's forces. He made Bahram the commander of his army, lifting this warrior's head to the clouds, and all those who looked for renown in the wars hailed Bahram as their chief. Bahram came before his king, armed and ready for combat, and asked permission to review the army's troops, to see who was eager for war and who would hold back when there was glory to be won. The king replied, "You are their commander, responsible for whatever good or evil comes of this."

Bahram went to the plain where the king reviewed his warriors and ordered that the Persian army appear before him. He chose the best of them and registered the names of twelve thousand armed cavalry, whose horses were protected with barding. He enrolled men who were in their forties, and refused to consider those who were older or younger. Bahram had overall charge of the army, and he made his second in command a man called Yalan-Sineh, whose heart longed for war. He was to lead the troops into battle, curveting his horse, reminding the men of their lineage, and filling their hearts with courage. Another of his subordinates was Izad-Goshasp, who would not turn his horse back from a raging fire: his responsibility was to watch the baggage and to see that the two flanks of the army coordinated their attack. The rear of the army was commanded by Hamdan-Goshasp, a man who could seize lions by the tail when he rode. Then Bahram addressed his army:

> "Noble and valiant warriors, see that you
> Act righteously in everything you do—
> If you would have God turn your present night
> To dawn and victory with his glorious might,

See that in darkness when the trumpets sound
You leap into the saddle from the ground,
And ride as if the sun itself arose
At midnight to do battle with our foes.
Don't dream of rest until the battle's done,
Rest is for when our victory is won."

The king rejoiced to hear of Bahram's preparations and his speech, and threw open the doors of his treasury. He made weapons available to Bahram and had his warhorses brought into the town from their pastures, saying that the new commander could choose any of them for himself. Then he said, "You've heard what quantities of troops and arms and treasure Saveh Shah commands, and that the earth trembles when he takes the field, and yet you have chosen only twelve thousand armed men, together with their horses protected by barding, and I don't know if they will be sufficient on the day of battle. And instead of young swordsmen you've asked for men in their forties."

Bahram replied, "Your majesty, you speak truly and are favored by fortune. You have heard tales of the great men who ruled the world before us, and how, when fortune promised victory to them, a few troops were sufficient. If the king will permit me, I shall give you some examples. When Kay Kavus was imprisoned in Hamaveran with a huge army, Rostam chose twelve thousand of the finest cavalry he could find; he freed Kavus from confinement, and the force he had chosen was undefeated. In the same way Gudarz, the chieftain of the Keshvad clan, took twelve thousand armed cavalry with him in his war of vengeance for the death of Seyavash. And the great Esfandyar took twelve thousand warriors against Arjasp; he was able to raze the enemy's fortress and accomplish all his aims with them. If an army has more men in it than this it becomes uncontrollable and the commander is distracted on the battlefield. As for your saying that forty-year-olds can't fight better than younger men, a man of forty has experience, and his courage is the greater for it. He knows what loyalty is and remembers the bread and salt he's received; the heavens have turned many times above his head. He fears shame and the mockery of his detractors, and because of them he won't avoid fighting; a grown man's soul is steeled by thoughts of his wife and children and family. A young man is easily tricked, and when he must wait, he has no patience; he has no wife or children or fields to think of, and he confuses what's important with what doesn't matter. Because an inexperienced man has no wisdom, he can't see things as they really are. If he's victorious on the day of battle, he's happy and laughs and wastes his time, and if victory isn't his, the enemy will see nothing of him except his back."

At these words, the king felt as refreshed as a rose in the spring. "Go, put on your armor," he ordered Bahram, "and make your way to the reviewing ground." The commander left the king and asked for his belt, cuirass, and helmet. He strapped barding onto his horse and tied a lariat to the stirrups. The king came to the reviewing ground with his vizier, bringing arrows, polo mallets, and balls. His commander appeared and prostrated himself in the dust before his king, who gave him his blessing, and in response the commander kissed the ground. Then the king held up a banner, on which was depicted a purple dragon; this was the banner that had gone before Rostam in his wars, and the king lifted it lightly and kissed it, laughing as he did so, and handed it to Bahram. He called down many blessings on the banner and said to Bahram, "This banner belonged to the man my ancestors always called the first of champions, whose name was Rostam, who conquered the world, and was victorious and pure of soul. It is his banner you hold in your hand, and may you be victorious and loyal to your king! I believe you are another Rostam, in your courage, heroism, and loyalty." Bahram called down blessings on the king and said, "May you be victorious, and your soul remained untroubled!" Then he left the reviewing ground for his lodging, grasping Rostam's banner in his fist; the army's warriors dispersed, and their commander was content.

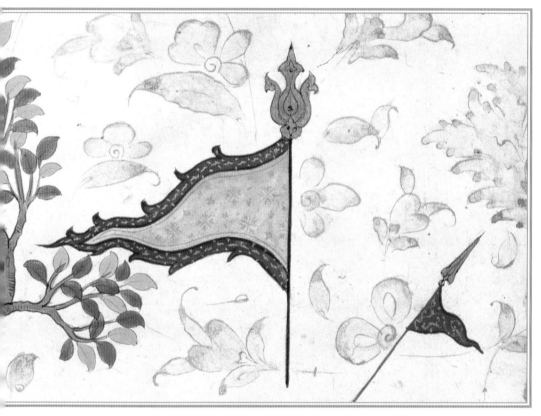

Bahram Chubineh Marches against Saveh Shah

When the first light of dawn appeared above the mountains and the sun's glittering yellow shield shone there, the army's commander came before his king, his arms folded over his chest in submission, to say, "I have all I could wish, and by your *farr* I am the crown of the age, but I have one request to make of your majesty. It is that you send someone trustworthy with me, a scribe who can report back the name of anyone who distinguishes himself in battle and brings the enemies' heads down into the dust, so that his fame may live in the world." Hormozd replied, "The scribe Mehran is young, eloquent, and intelligent," and he gave orders that Mehran accompany the army. Then the commander, alert as a male lion, at the head of his experienced, courageous troops, immediately set off from Ctesiphon.

Hormozd said to his vizier, "He is a brave man and will triumph on the battlefield. But what do you think will happen then? We should discuss this at length." The vizier replied, "May you live forever, since this is what you deserve. This champion, with his great strength and stature, with his quick tongue and confident spirit, will surely be victorious and overthrow the king's enemies. But I fear that in the end he will turn against the king who has favored him. He's very forward in his speech, and he acts like a lion when he talks with your majesty." Hormozd said, "You're the most suspicious man alive! Don't confuse poison with its antidote. If he defeats Saveh Shah, he deserves a crown and a throne. This is my hope, that he reign as a prince, praised and successful." The vizier was abashed, and held his tongue. But in his heart the king pondered what he had said, and before long he chose a spy from among his courtiers, someone who could follow up on this suspicion. He said to him, "Hurry after the army commander, and report back to me on what you see." The man sped after Bahram, and no one knew of his mission. He was both a guide to what was happening and an interpreter of omens, someone who told the king what the outcome of everything would be.

As Bahram rode from Ctesiphon at the head of his army, with his lance in his hand, he saw a seller of sheep's heads in the distance. The man had a tray on which were a number of dressed heads. Bahram urged his horse forward and spitted one of the heads on his lance, lifting up the lance as he rode and then flinging the head down at will. He took this as a sign and said, "This is how I shall deal with Saveh Shah's head; I'll throw it down in the road before his troops, and then I'll destroy his whole army." The man the king had sent saw this and interpreted it appropriately, thinking, "This man has fortune on his side, and his efforts will gain him a throne: but then when he has what he wants in his grasp he'll stubbornly defy his king." He returned, and reported this to the king who grew anxious and worried. The man's words seemed worse than death to him; he became dejected, like a green leaf that shrivels and turns black.

He called for a young messenger to hurry after Bahram, instructing him, "Go and tell the army's commander to halt where he is tonight. At dawn he is to return here to me, where I'll clear the court and give him some advice. I've remembered a number of useful things I have to tell him." The young messenger caught up with Bahram and told him what he had heard from the king, but Bahram answered, "Tell him, 'You're a wise king, and people don't summon armies back when they are on the march. To return as you suggest would be a bad omen, and our enemies would be strengthened to hear of it. I'll come to your court once I'm victorious and I've made your army and country glow with splendor.'" The messenger returned and told the king what warlike Bahram had said. The king was pleased at this answer, and the messenger's efforts had no result.

At dawn Bahram called down blessings on the army and marched them as far as Khuzestan; no one along their route came to any harm. When they pitched camp a woman with a sack full of straw ran between the ranks; a horseman came and bought the sack from her, but he refused to pay and tugged at his reins and rode off. The woman went wailing to Bahram and said, "I had a little straw and I thought I could sell it, so I brought it to your army; but now a horseman has stolen it from me. He has an iron helmet on his head." They immediately searched for the man and dragged him before

Bahram, who said to the thief, "You will lose your head for this sin you've committed." He was dragged stumbling in front of the tents, and his head, arms, and legs were smashed to pieces. Bahram split him in two with a sword, to terrify anyone else there who was inclined to act unjustly. A proclamation was made in front of Bahram's pavilion: "Whoever steals one stalk of straw will find no mercy; I shall split his body open with my sword. Buy whatever you need with silver coins."

Hormozd Sends Khorad-Borzin to Saveh Shah with a Deceitful Message

But Hormozd was constantly troubled by his thoughts, thinking now of Saveh Shah and his wealth and war elephants, then of the anxieties and fear he felt because of Bahram. His soul was full of sorrow, his fearful heart was split in two with worry. In night's darkness, after the moon set, the king said to Khorad-Borzin, "Contrive to reach our enemy: go as quickly as you can and don't rest on the way. Observe his army, who and how many they are, and who their leaders and warriors are." Then he had a letter written,

filled with advice for his dangerous adversary, and it was accompanied by innumerable royal presents. He said to his envoy, "Travel toward Herat; on your way you will meet with Bahram's army. Turn aside from your destination and tell Bahram that I'm sending flattering messages to Saveh Shah in order to lure him into a trap, and that Saveh Shah is not to learn of his identity or intentions."

Khorad-Borzin set out and talked with Bahram as his king had ordered, and from there he traveled on to where Saveh Shah was camped with his elephants and wealth and army. He praised and flattered him, and passed on Hormozd's secret message, amplifying it in every way, so that Saveh Shah would march on Herat. This he did, pitching camp by the river there. A scout then saw Bahram's troops and ran to Saveh Shah saying that a mighty army was approaching. Saveh Shah was alarmed by this news; he summoned Hormozd's envoy from his tent and spoke to him angrily, "You deceitful devil, haven't you seen how far you could fall, up there on the heights? You've come from that wretched king of yours to tempt me into an ambush. You're bringing up a Persian army to attack me; they've pitched camp on the plains of Herat!" Khorad-Borzin answered, "Don't misconstrue things when you see a few troops in front of you. This is some lord of the marches who's going somewhere, or it's someone who's fled from his own country and is seeking asylum with you, or it's a merchant who's traveling with an escort to be safe on the road. Who would be foolish enough to oppose you, unless the mountains and oceans are going to fight?" Saveh Shah was satisfied by this answer and replied, "Let us hope things are as you say."

Night came quickly from the mountains as Khorad-Borzin returned to his tent. He made preparations for flight, to avoid the destruction that was certain to descend on him otherwise. As the darkness deepened, Saveh Shah sent his wise young son with an escort to his enemy's leader. As he drew near the Persian force, the young prince dispatched a horseman to inquire as to who these troops were, and why they were advancing on this territory. A Turk rode forward like the wind and called out, "Mighty warriors, who is your commander, who leads this army, who is the finest fighter among you? Because our crown prince, whom Saveh Shah loves more than his own eyes and heart, wants to see him, without an escort." A warrior came to Bahram and told him what he had heard, and the commander came out of his tent and stood there beneath his glittering banner. When the prince saw him he urged his horse forward, so that it was covered in sweat. He asked, "Where have you ridden from, and why have you pitched camp here? I've heard that you've fled from Persia, that you're a fugitive who has blood on his hands." Bahram replied, "God forbid that I think of opposing Persia's king. I have come here with my army from Baghdad, at the king's orders, to fight. When news of Saveh Shah's army reached the royal court, he told me to march out and block their way with maces, lances, swords, and arrows."

The prince immediately returned to his father and told him what had happened. Saveh Shah grew suspicious at his words and sent for the Persian envoy. But he was told, "Khorad-Borzin has fled, weeping bitter tears of regret that he had come here." Saveh Shah asked his son, "How did that wretch find a route to go by? The night was dark, there is a huge army here; how could our sentinels be so negligent?"

Saveh Shah Sends a Message to Bahram Chubineh

Then Saveh Shah sent an old man, a fine orator, to Bahram, with orders to say, "Don't be such a fool as to lose your reputation here. You should at least realize one thing, that this king of yours is trying to get you killed. He's sent you to fight with someone who has no equal in all the world. He's said to you, 'Go and block his advance,' but haven't you heard the unsettling news that if a mountain is in my way, I can flatten it with my army and elephants?" When Bahram heard these words, he laughed at the man's blustering tactics. He answered,

> "If secretly the world's king wants to kill
> His slave, I cannot contradict his will;
> If it would please him, then it's right that I
> Find my grave here: I am prepared to die."

The messenger returned to Saveh Shah and gave him the warrior's answer. Saveh Shah said, "Go and question the Persian again. Say, 'Why do you need to talk so much? Why have you come here? Ask from me whatever you wish.'" The messenger went to Bahram and said, "Tell us whatever it is you're hiding. My king's star is in the ascendant, and he is looking for subjects like you."

Bahram replied, "Tell him this: 'If you want war, stop all this pretense. But if you want to make peace with the world's king, then I shall entertain you in the borderlands here, and I shall obey your commands. I shall give your troops gold and silver, and crowns and belts of office to those who are worthy of them. I shall send a horseman to the king and he will come halfway to meet you. He will provide you with foraging, as one ally to another. If you want friendship, the king will treat you well. But if you've come here to fight, then you should realize you've entered the sea and it's a sea monster you'll be fighting with; you'll retreat from the plains of Herat in such a wretched state that our nobility will weep for you. I wish you pits before you, winds at your back, rain to accompany you! It's your bad luck that has brought you here, intending to bring down evil on your head.'"

The messenger hurried back like the wind and recounted every detail of what Bahram had said. Saveh Shah was enraged to hear this reply; the cold words ate at his heart, and his face turned pale. He said to his envoy, "Go back again, and take that demon my answer. Say, 'There's no fame to be had from fighting with you, and it'll give me no satisfaction to kill you. I've courtiers crowded at my door like your king; the least of my servants are your superiors. But if you appeal to me for my protection, I'll lift your head above them all; you'll find immense wealth, and all your army will be well equipped. An ambitious man like you doesn't try to prove his courage by pointless, idle talk.'" Once more the messenger returned to Bahram and passed on his master's urgent, heartfelt message. And again Bahram replied, "I cannot hide my answer from your lord. Say this to him, 'If indeed I'm as lowly as you say, I feel no shame because of it. The King of Kings is ashamed to fight with someone as insignificant as you; it's my unimportance that has made me the leader of this army, which I've brought here in order to destroy Saveh Shah's forces. I'll cut your head off and take it to my king, and it's not even worth spitting on my lance to display as I ride there. It would shame you if I asked for your protection, and so in my insignificance I've come to attack you. You won't see me except on the battlefield, with my purple banner fluttering behind me; and when you see the dragon embroidered there, that will be the sign of your death; I shall sheathe my lance in your head and helmet.'"

After hearing such hostile talk, Saveh Shah's envoy turned his back on Bahram. He told Saveh Shah all he had heard and seen, and the Turkish king's head seethed with longing for vengeance. He ordered that his war drums be readied, and his towering elephants be led onto the plain; all the land became black with dust from his army's hooves, and the squeal of trumpets rang out. When Bahram heard that the enemy's troops were approaching, and that the plain had turned red, yellow, and black with their banners, he ordered his men to mount, and he came forward armed, with his mace in his hand. Behind him was the city of Herat, ahead an army with drawn swords. He coordinated the right and left flanks of his forces, all of whom were eager for battle. It seemed that all the world was made of iron, and that the stars were glittering lances.

Saveh Shah looked at the troops ranged against him: Herat was to the rear of Bahram's men, and Saveh Shah's own situation was hemmed in and unfavorable. He said to his horsemen, men of long experience who sympathized with his cause, "That Persian commander has tricked me: he delayed until his army had occupied the city and he's left the reed beds to us." He drew up his army's ranks in the narrow space left to them; the sky was darkened and the earth disappeared. He had forty thousand men on his right flank, but they were so hemmed in that they could hardly wield their swords, and there were another forty thousand in the rear. Because of the limited space many of his troops could do nothing. In the van of his army were his elephants, blocking the way like a wall. Saveh Shah was distraught that his army was unable to maneuver: it seemed that fortune had turned against him, and that his throne would soon be vacant.

Saveh Shah Sends Another Message to Bahram Chubineh

Once again Saveh Shah sent a messenger—a glib, deceitful warrior from the plains of Herat—to Bahram, saying, "The heavens have no love for you; be wise, open your heart's eyes, and listen to my advice. There are two peerless nobles in the world, shining like the sun in the heavens, armed all year round and ready to fight: I, the rightful ruler of the world, am one, and the other is my son. My troops outnumber the leaves on the trees, supposing they could be counted; if I could count my elephants and warriors, they would make the number of raindrops that fall in the spring seem laughable to you. I own more armor and tents and pavilions than you can imagine; the mass of my horses and warriors would terrify the very mountains and deserts. Kings are my servants, or worthy to be counted as such; if the seas could flow here and the mountains run, they would not be sufficient to move the treasures and troops I've accumulated. All the nobles of the world, except that Persian lord of yours, call me king.

"My soul can see clearly enough that your fate is in my hands. If I advance my armies, there will not be space for an ant or a mosquito to pass. I've a thousand armored elephants, and horses flee at the scent of them; who in all Iran can stand before me and block my way? My men occupy the land from here to Ctesiphon, and the number there will grow. Who has deceived you, what fool has tricked you? You've no mercy on yourself, or if you have, it's hidden away because it can't tell good from evil. When did a wise man ever talk so foolishly? Forget this war and come over to me. I won't keep you waiting long for my response: I'll make you a lord, I'll give you my daughter, you'll be an honored man here. You'll be a nobleman, free of all the miseries a subject must endure. When the Persian king is killed in battle, his crown and throne will be yours; I'll go on toward Byzantium, and leave all this land and its wealth and armies in your possession. I say this because I like you, your deeds show you possess the divine *farr*, and you know how to lead an army in war because your father and grandfather were both army commanders. This message is not a trick; I want to help you. Today you're opposing me with your contemptible little army, but even if you don't fall in with my wishes, this is the only message you'll ever hear from me."

Bahram Chubineh's Answer to Saveh Shah

The envoy spoke and Bahram listened, and when he answered his words were somber. He said, "Among those who have pride and nobility you're a byword for evil; an idle king who talks too much has no one's respect. Your previous messages, and this one, show me you're a great talker, certainly; someone whose luck is running out will try to save himself with speeches. In your pointless prattle I can hear that your heart is fearful, that you're terrified of being defeated. When you say you'll kill our king and give me his throne and army, you remind me of how, when a poor man is driven from a village, he will always claim that he was the village headman, that everyone else was his inferior and he was in charge. But the sun will not shine on our deeds for two more days before I send your bloody head spitted on a lance to my king.

"As for your talk about my being grateful to you and hailing you as an honorable king because you'll give me your child in marriage and the throne of Iran, where I'll be your ally, my answer is that my lance is now next to your ear and that I shall cut your head off with my sword. And when you're gone your head and crown and treasure, as well as your daughter and all you've taken such pains to accumulate, will be mine. And your boasts of having more crowns and thrones and elephants and cavalry than anyone can count remind me of the nobleman who, when he was in the thick of battle, said that a thirsty dog barks louder the further away from water he is. Devils must have captured your heart to make you come to fight against my king, but you'll writhe in pain when God punishes you and you remember the evil deeds you've committed. And then you claim that crowned kings are your servants, that all the cities of the world are yours and bear witness to your greatness; well, the way's open to those cities, and servants and kings alike can take it. But if you knock at their gates the only sovereignty they'll grant you is over waste reed beds. You talk about pardoning me, but you've forgotten my courage; you can pardon me when you see my lance, then you won't be calling me your subject. When my army's drawn up for battle I don't care a copper coin for your troops and ambition and elephants and throne. If you're a king, why do you lie so much? That's no way to win glory in the world. I've told my king that in three days' time, when the sun lights up the sky in splendor, he will see your head spitted on a lance before his throne."

The envoy's cheeks turned sallow, as if his once-flourishing fortune were now old and decrepit. He took the message to Saveh Shah, whose face darkened when he heard it; but his son said, "What do such boasts matter? We should weep with pity for their contemptible army." The son went to his pavilion and gave orders for cymbals and Indian bells, elephants and war drums, and directed that the heavens be filled with their din. While his son was preparing for battle in this way, Saveh Shah was filled with anxiety. He said to his son, "All our army loves you, but don't attack until dawn." The two armies retreated to their tents, and sentries were posted before the pavilions. On each side camp fires flickered, and the world was filled with the noise of the two armies.

Bahram's Dream: He Draws Up His Army for Battle

Bahram was alone in his tent when he summoned the Persian commanders, and they discussed the coming battle until nightfall. Then the Turks and Persians alike slept, and ambitious men who were eager to conquer the world forgot its claims. As Bahram slept within his tent, his heart was preoccupied all night with the coming battle.

> And in the lion-warrior's mind it seemed
> As though the Turks had won; great Bahram dreamed
> His army was destroyed, and when he tried
> To flee, the paths were blocked on every side:
> On foot now and alone, he scoured the plain
> For warriors who could help him, but in vain.

He was uneasy when he woke, and his mind, which was usually so resourceful, was filled with foreboding. The night was dark, and sorrow was his companion: he hid his dream and mentioned it to no one.

At that moment Khorad-Borzin arrived after fleeing from Saveh Shah. "Your one hope is to retreat and quickly," he said. "No one in all the world has ever seen an army as massive as Saveh Shah's. What makes you so confident? Look at the devil's trap you're falling into. Don't throw Persian souls to the winds, think of our brave warriors' lives. Find it in your heart to have pity on your own life, because you have never faced anything like this before!" Bahram replied, "All men from your town can do is sell fish, from summer to winter. Your calling is to handle nets by a lakeshore, you're not a man for maces and swords and arrows. But when the sun raises its head above the mountains, I'll show you how I fight with Saveh Shah."

When the sun rose in the sign of Leo and the world turned as white as a Roman's face, trumpets were sounded and the earth trembled with the pounding of horses' hooves. Bahram drew up his army and mounted his horse, flourishing his well-tried mace in his hand. There were three thousand armored and experienced cavalry on the right flank of his forces, and he sent as many warlike horsemen to the left flank. One side was commanded by Azar-Goshasp, and the other by Goshasp; in the rear was Yalan-Sineh, whose men were armed with maces and were to attack last. The van was commanded by Hamdan-Goshasp, whose horse's hooves spread fire in the reed beds. Each of them commanded three thousand cavalry, eager for war.

A herald announced Bahram's message to his troops: "Great warriors with your golden helmets, if anyone flees from this battle, even if he's faced by a lion or a leopard, I swear by God I shall cut his head from his body and give his corpse to the flames." There were two paths from the camp, by which one could easily retreat, and Bahram had both blocked with a high wall of earth, while he himself took up his position in the center of the army. When the king's scribe saw this, he came to Bahram and said, "This is beyond all reason; your foolish boasting has gone on long enough! Look at the armies drawn up here—we're like a white hair lost on a black ox's hide. Things will go badly for Iran in this battle, our land will be destroyed, we'll be overrun by Turks, and not a field or a river or a mountain will remain to us!" Bahram yelled at him,

> *"Stick to your ink and paper, who told you*
> *To count our troops? Do what you're hired to do!"*

The scribe went to Khorad-Borzin and said, "Bahram's been bewitched by some devil!" The two scribes looked for a way to flee, fearing the catastrophe they felt sure would come. They went to a hill overlooking the battlefield and fixed their eyes on Bahram's helmet, to see how he fared when the fighting began in earnest.

When Bahram had drawn up his troops ready for battle, he turned aside, groaning in anguish, from the battlefield. He prostrated himself in the dust before God and cried out,

> "O Lord of truth and justice, if you see
> My cause as wrong, protect my enemy,
> But if it is your cause for which I fight
> Make my heart calm, strengthen my army's might,
> Give us a joyful victory, and bless
> The world with riches, peace, and happiness."

Still weeping, he mounted his horse, his ox-headed mace in his fist.

Bahram Chubineh Fights against Saveh Shah

Now Saveh Shah addressed his troops: "Begin your magic, so that the hearts and eyes of the Persians will tremble, and no harm will come to you." All his magicians set about their business, and fire darted through the air: a wind rose up and a black cloud poured down arrows. Bahram cried out, "Noble lords and Persian warriors, take no notice of this magic; go forward to war with rage in your hearts. If the only hope they have is sorcery and magic, we should weep for the poor wretches!" A cry went up from the Persian side, and they readied themselves for combat. Saveh Shah saw that the magic had done him no good and he attacked on the left, like a wolf falling on a lamb. When he had broken their ranks he turned toward the center, where Bahram was. Bahram saw his men flee; he charged forward and with his lance unseated three horsemen. He shouted, "This is how to fight, this is our custom and how we carry it out. Have you no shame before God, or before our noble warriors?" Then like a hungry lion he made his way over to the left flank and shattered the enemy's ranks so thoroughly that their leader's banner disappeared. From there he turned back toward the center and said to his commander, "This is a desperate business; if the battle goes on for much longer, our army will be scattered; look for some way to retreat." They went and searched, but there was no way back; the road was blocked by a wall of earth. Bahram said to his commanders, "We have an iron wall ahead of us: any man who can get through it will reach safety and take his soul back to Iran and our king. Prepare your hearts to shed blood now: lift your shields above your heads and draw your swords. No one should despair of God's help, even if the bright day turns dark before us."

For his part Saveh Shah addressed his officers, "Bring the elephants forward, into the thick of the fighting, make the Persians' world dark and desperate." Seeing the elephants in the far distance, Bahram grew anxious and drew his sword. He said to his warriors, "Place your helmets on your heads and have your bows from Chach ready. By the head and soul of the world's king, beloved of our chieftains, crown of our nobility, I order whoever has a bow to make it ready immediately. Shoot three of your poplar arrows tipped with heads that draw blood into the elephants' trunks, then flourish your maces and go forward to kill the enemy." Bahram placed his steel helmet on his head and drew back his bow: a hail of arrows rained down and his army charged forward. The elephants' trunks were wounded by the arrows, and the plain grew sodden with their blood. Maddened by their wounds, the elephants turned back and trampled their own troops. Fortune had turned against them; Saveh Shah's army was in turmoil and many died. Bahram's troops pursued the elephants, and the earth was like a Nile of blood.

There was a pleasant hill near the battlefield, to the rear of the struggling army, and Saveh Shah had gone there to sit on a golden throne and observe the battle. He saw his army like a moving mountain of iron, the soldiers' heads covered in dust, their souls downcast, and behind them came the maddened elephants, trampling the troops as they stampeded. With tears in his eyes, Saveh Shah tried to comprehend how his army had been routed. He mounted a dun Arab horse and fled, fearing for his life. Bahram came after him like a raging elephant, his lariat on his shoulder, his bow in his hand. He called to his troops, "Fortune has turned against them; this is no time for reminiscing and talking. Pursue them with your swords, rain arrows down on them, show your mettle as cavalry." He made his way to the hill where Saveh Shah had sat crowned on his golden throne, and saw him fleeing in the distance. He sped after him, moving like a cloud across the sky, and selected an arrow with a glittering head, flighted with four eagle feathers. Placing the thumbstall against the deerskin string, he leveled the bow with his left hand and drew back the string with his right. The Chachi bow groaned as it bent, and as he pulled the deerskin string back to his ear, that too cried out. The arrow sped from his hand and pierced Saveh Shah's spine. Saveh Shah's head descended into the dust, and the earth beneath him ran

with his blood. And so this famous king, with his armies and golden throne
and golden crown, was vanquished. This is the way of the turning heavens,
which show neither love nor kindness: don't pride yourself on your high
throne, and take care to stay far from all harm.

When Bahram reached him, he dragged him facedown through the dust
and cut off his head; none of Saveh Shah's men came near him as he did so.
Later, seeing his headless body lying in the road, they lamented their loss;
the land was filled with wailing, the sky with their distress. Saveh Shah's
son said, "This was the work of God; Bahram's good fortune was with him.
Our army had no room to maneuver, and that was what killed so many of
us. The elephants trampled many of our warriors, and not one man in ten
survived. Men either perished beneath the elephants' feet, or had their
heads cut off on the battlefield."

Bahram Chubineh Kills a Magician

When this evil day had passed, not one of the enemy could be seen alive, except for those who had been taken prisoner; their bodies were wounded by arrows, their souls by sorrow. The way was filled with barding and helmets, heads that the helmets had betrayed to death, Indian swords, arrows, and bows. The ground was like a sea of blood from the dead, and everywhere saddled horses stood ownerless. Bahram searched diligently for the Persian dead, asking Khorad-Borzin for help: "Share my troubles for a day: look to see who among the Persians has been killed, whom we have to mourn for." Khorad-Borzin went over the whole site, peering in every tent and pavilion. For some time a fine cavalry commander named Bahram was missing; he was a nobleman and descended from Seyavash. Khorad-Borzin desperately searched high and low but could find no trace of him; he turned over the wounded and dead, but found nothing. Bahram Chubineh was very distressed, but eventually the man appeared, like a key to open a locked door, and leading a weeping red-haired Turk whose heart was eaten up with sorrow. When Bahram saw Bahram, he said, "May you never lie beneath the dust!" Then he turned to the ugly Turk and said, "You, with the hellish face so far from heaven, what kind of a man are you? What's your name and tribe? Your mother should weep for you now."

The man replied, "I'm a magician: I'm the opposite of a straightforward, honorable man. When my lord goes to war against someone and gets into difficulties, I set to work. At night I show people things in their sleep, and this disturbs even those who are calm and careful by nature. It was I who sent you the nightmare that bothered you so much. But I should try for something stronger, because my spells didn't work. Our stars let us down, and all my efforts dispersed like so much wind. If you'll spare me, you've found a very skillful assistant." Bahram carefully considered the man's words, but his heart was troubled, and his face turned sallow. At first he thought, "This man would be useful on the day of battle, if I got into difficulties." But then he thought, "But what use was magic to Saveh Shah? All benefits come from God," and he ordered that the man's head be cut off. When the man had been killed, Bahram stood up and said, "O Lord of justice and righteousness: all greatness, victory, and the divine *farr*, might and imperial power, misery and joy, come from you. Blessings on the warrior who follows your way."

Then the chief scribe came forward and spoke: "O terrifying champion, neither Feraydun nor Kesra Nushin-Ravan ever saw a warrior like you. All the cities of Iran flourish because of you, all our champions are your slaves. Through you the throne has found good fortune, through you its subjects are exalted. You are a commander born of commanders: happy the mother who bore such a son! Your lineage is splendid and your mind is splendid; you are the pillar that supports all our country." Then all the nobles and the champions of the army left the battlefield.

Bahram Chubineh Sends Saveh Shah's Head to Hormozd

Darkness braided its hair, and the braids covered men's eyes in sleep; night's ebony curtain appeared, and the world rested from the din of drums. Swiftly the heavens turned, as if they thought the night tarried too long, until a golden ship arose from the water, bringing back sorrow and driving away sleep.

Bahram ordered his men to sever the heads of all the slain Turkish nobles and chieftains and to place a banner behind each head. The prisoners and heads were gathered together and taken from the battlefield. Then Bahram summoned his scribe and dictated a letter to the king describing the enemy's innumerable army; the changing fortunes of battle; the stratagems, fighting, and maneuvering against the enemy's forces; the Persians' struggles and prowess; and the cavalry who fought all day without respite. He selected an eloquent envoy from among his soldiers to take the letter and trophies. First he spitted Saveh Shah's head on a lance and put it with

the banner Saveh had carried in battle; likewise, he spitted the heads of the Turanian nobles on lances and sent them with banners of the Chinese cavalry. He ordered that all these be taken directly to the Persian king. The prisoners and plunder he deposited untouched in Herat, awaiting the king's orders as to what was to be done with them. With the heads he also sent a number of horsemen to learn whether the king wished him to attack Parmoudeh, Saveh Shah's son.

For their part, the Turks and Chinese warriors made their way to Turan, naked and bereft of their weapons, horses, and baggage. When news of this reached Parmoudeh, he flung the crown from his head. The Turks bitterly lamented their dead nobles, smearing their heads with dust; they wept, and no one ate or rested or slept. Parmoudeh summoned the warriors and, weeping bitter tears, asked them how their innumerable army had been defeated in battle. Their spokesman replied, "We thought their army of no account, but no one has ever seen a horseman like Bahram when he fights. In battle he's greater than Rostam, and no warrior will stay to oppose him. Their army was not a hundredth of ours, but the best of our warriors was a child compared to them. God guided him, and if I say more you will not want to hear it." Parmoudeh brooded in his heart on Bahram's deed. Then, seething with rage, he decided to attack. He still had a hundred thousand warriors under arms, so he led his army out on to the plains and marched toward the Oxus.

The champion's letter reached Hormozd as he was sitting with his advisors and saying, "My wise counselors, it is now two weeks since we have heard anything from Bahram. What do you think of this? What should we do? We must discuss the matter." And at that moment the chamberlain entered and gave Hormozd the good news: "May the king reign prosperously forever. Bahram has defeated Saveh Shah and made the world splendid by his victory." Bahram's envoy was summoned, and seated in a higher place than the king's advisors. He said, "Great king, the battle turned out as you would wish. May you live peacefully and happily, because your enemies' fortune has grown old. The heads of Saveh Shah and his younger son, whom his father called his crown prince, are spitted on lances at your door, and all the city stares at them."

The king heard this and stood up, but immediately he bowed before God, and said, "O Judge and Guide, it is you who have destroyed our enemies. I was in such despair, and had no hope that my enemy would be overcome. It was not my commander who did this, or his army, it was God who accomplished this victory." Then he brought out a hundred and thirty thousand coins that he had inherited from his father and distributed a third of the sum to the poor, mostly to his own courtiers and servants. Another third he gave to the fire-temples, for the priests who conduct the rites to celebrate the festivals of No-Ruz and Sadeh, and the last third was given to individuals who would undertake to rebuild ruined caravanserais in the desert, so that men could travel there safely and without fear. Then he remitted four years of taxes on both the poor and the nobles who sat on ivory thrones.

Next, he sent a letter to the ruler of every province, saying that Bahram had been victorious and had cut off Saveh Shah's head. Hormozd worshiped God for seven days, and on the eighth he summoned Bahram's messenger and again sat him higher than the other courtiers. He planted a sapling in the garden of greatness by writing a fine answer to Bahram's letter. He sent him a silver throne and a pair of golden shoes, as well as other goods, and wrote a charter making him lord of Khatlan and Badakhshan, as far as the River Barak. He ordered him to give the plunder from the battlefield to his soldiers, except for Saveh Shah's personal treasure, which was to be sent to the royal court; and he directed Bahram to attack Parmoudeh immediately, before he became a formidable enemy.

Before he left the envoy was given a robe of honor. When he reached Bahram, the commander welcomed him warmly and did what the king had ordered, distributing the spoils of war to his soldiers, except for the evil Saveh Shah's treasure, which he sent to the king's court under the care of trustworthy men. Then the commander and his army marched out to war.

Bahram Chubineh's Battle with Parmoudeh, the Son of Saveh Shah; Parmoudeh Flees to His Castle

When Parmoudeh learned that Bahram was ambitious for the imperial throne, he deposited all his gold and silver coins and his jewels in a castle that he felt was safe and secure. Then he crossed the Oxus with his army and went forward confidently to battle. The two armies were soon face to face, and each of them pitched camp in the environs of Balkh. There were two parasangs distance between the two, a space appropriate for a battlefield.

The next day Bahram, who was eager for battle, hurried out to observe Parmoudeh's forces. Parmoudeh was also watching, and saw him as Bahram chose a high hill and ranged his army in front of it, covering the plain. Parmoudeh was taken aback at this show of force and the sight of Bahram before his troops, his warlike head lifted up to the sky. Filled with anxiety, he said to his men, "This leader is like a lion in his pride and ferocity, and the black earth where he stands will run with blood. His troops can't be numbered, and anyone would be reluctant to confront them. When night falls we'll attack, and thereby drive fear and anxiety from our hearts."

When Bahram marched from Persia against the Turks, an astrologer had said to him, "Start no enterprise on a Wednesday; if you ignore this advice, you will be harmed, and nothing you do will bring any profit to you."

Between the two armies, to one side of the battle plain, there was a garden; on Wednesday Bahram went there, saying, "Today will be a day of pleasure." His men brought fine carpets, wine, musicians, and food. Bahram sat there drinking until one watch of the night had passed. A scout went to Parmoudeh and said, "Bahram is in that garden, drinking." Parmoudeh chose six thousand of his horsemen and sent them to encircle the garden without showing any light. But Bahram realized what was being planned and he said to Yalan-Sineh, "Make an opening in the garden wall." Then he and Izad-Goshasp and the other warriors who were with him mounted their horses and rode though the breech in the wall: who knows how they managed it? Trumpets sounded at the garden door, the commander urged his horse forward as a second breech was quickly made in the wall, and the enemy forces were thrown into a turmoil. Bahram fought with a javelin in his hand, like a man who was half-drunk; he was so eager for blood that no one he encountered escaped him. The commanders' cries and the sounds of iron against steel rang out, and from the garden to Parmoudeh's camp the way was littered with headless corpses.

When Bahram reached his encampment again, he too decided on a night attack, and with half the night gone he led his men out onto the plain. They reached the Turkish lines without being seen by the sentries and announced their approach with the squeal of trumpets and the din of drums. The Turkish

warriors leaped up, and the tumultuous noise would have deafened a savage lion. Right and left in the darkness close combats began; in the night and with long lances everywhere men did not know friend from foe; sparks glittered from swords and seemed to burn the earth and air. Few Turks remained alive, and their blood made the stones there resemble nothing so much as coral. Their leader fled like wind-blown dust, his mouth dry and his lips turned blue, and kept going until dawn broke and night drew back her skirts. But Bahram pursued him, and when he reached him he roared like a lion:

> *"Don't mix with warriors if all you can do*
> *Is run away when danger threatens you.*
> *You're just a little boy; you should have stayed*
> *Sucking your mother's milk if you're afraid."*

And Parmoudeh replied, "How much blood must you shed before you'll be satisfied? When they fight, leopards on land and crocodiles in the rivers eventually become sated with blood: but you've never had enough, you're like an insatiable lion. You cut off the head of Saveh Shah, whom the turning heavens loved while he lived, and you destroyed his armies in such a way that the sun and moon felt pity for them. I am that warrior king's son, and you should know that you killed me too when you killed him. But we are all born from our mothers for death, whether we are Turks or Persians. You can pursue me as I flee, but you won't catch me until the end of time. If I return armed either of us might be killed in combat. Don't be so headstrong and fiery; this is not how an army commander should act. I shall return to my castle and try a new tack: I'll write to your king, in the hopes that he will

grant me his protection. If he accepts my petition and helps me, I shall be the slave of his court and give up all hopes of sovereignty. I'll rid my mind of all thoughts of war and vengeance and make a pact of peace with him."

When Bahram heard him speak in this way, he turned back. After his army had rested from battle for a while he went to King Parmoudeh's abandoned camp and toured the area, cutting the heads from the bodies of the dead Turkish noblemen. These he heaped up together and the pile was like a mountain in height and breadth. Everyone still calls this place "Bahram's Hill." Then he dragged all the Turks' armor and equipment to this hill, and finally wrote a letter to Hormozd concerning Parmoudeh and his enormous army. He wrote about the Turks and their warlike king, who out of fear of Bahram's sword had resorted to a trick, and how the king had had to flee ignominiously from the battle. For his part, Parmoudeh closed the doors to his castle and sat conferring anxiously with a crowd of advisors. Many men gathered outside his castle gates, but no one knew what his plans for war were.

Parmoudeh Asks Bahram Chubineh for Asylum

Bahram said, "We should press ahead with this war." He told Yalan-Sineh to select three thousand horsemen, and directed Azar-Goshasp to take four thousand. The two of them were to attack whomever they could find, in the hope that when he saw the plains flowing with blood, Parmoudeh would be lured out of his castle. For three days they scoured the land in front of his castle in this way, and on the fourth, as the sun rose, Bahram sent a message to Parmoudeh, saying, "Lord and king of the Chinese Turks, why have you chosen this castle of all places in the world? Where now is Saveh Shah's ambition to rule the earth? Where are his treasures and power, his elephants with their barding, his clear-minded nobles? Where are his sorcerers' tricks and stratagems, that you've now hidden yourself away like this? The land of the Turks wasn't enough for you. The world had never seen anyone as fine as your father, but now you're holed up in this castle like a woman, beating your hands against your head in desperation, and with bitterness in your heart. Open your castle gates and ask for mercy, ask to be allied with my country's king, and send out whatever wealth you have. I will speak for you at the king's court, and if you have some secret that's lighting up your dark soul, reveal it to me; don't hold yourself aloof now that your situation's so desperate. If you want war, no army's going to help you when you've no money, but if you've allies enough and treasure and cash enough then beat your war drums and come out and fight!"

When the envoy had delivered this message, Parmoudeh replied, "Say to him, 'Don't struggle to know the world's secrets. Because your first trial turned out well, you have become overconfident of the world's ways. Don't be so vain of victory; you may be young, but the world is old. No one knows the secrets of the turning heavens because they never show us their true face. Ridicule does not become a nobleman, and remember that I too once possessed an army, elephants, and war drums. The high heavens weave lies, and you should not give your heart over to presumptuous pride. My father was a brave, experienced warrior, and you saw him on the day of battle; the earth was the slave of his horse's hooves, and the heavens turned as he willed. But he sought what he should not have sought, and his evil designs brought him torment. Merit is obscured by ridicule, and our enemies laugh at us. You say that you have more cavalry and elephants than grain in the hopper of a mill, but this was true of him too; his good luck deserted him, and you will not always be prosperous and hailed as the light of the world. You should fear your fate, for it can turn an antidote into poison. Any man who makes bloodshed his profession will have enemies plot against him, and they will spill his blood as he has spilled the blood of other warriors. If you raise destruction's smoke over the land of the Turks, they will want vengeance sooner or later. I shall not present myself before you because I fear for my life. You are a slave and I am a king; how can I grovel before a slave? And I shall not fight you without an army, because my friends would say I was crazy to do so. If the straits I'm in force me to ask for quarter from your king, there is no shame in that; and then the doors to my treasury and my castle will be yours and you can do as you wish with this noble land.'" The envoy delivered his message, and Bahram was satisfied when he heard it.

Bahram Chubineh Writes to Hormozd, Asking that Parmoudeh Be Granted Safe Conduct

Bahram wrote a favorable letter to his victorious king, saying, "The Chinese emperor is besieged and asks for your favor: he requires a sealed letter of safe conduct, and when he receives it he will come to establish peace between you. He has fallen from greatness into misery and desires our protection."

When this letter arrived, the king's joy seemed limitless. He summoned his courtiers and sat the envoy on a royal throne; as the man read the letter out jewels were poured over him. Hormozd said to his courtiers, "Thanks be to God: I shall pray for three watches of the night, because the emperor of China will be my subject and the high heavens will be my crown. The leader of the Chinese Turks lifted his head up to the heavens and thought of himself as the king of the world, but now he pays homage to me. I give thanks to the Lord of the Sun and Moon, who has granted me this authority. I shall bestow hoarded wealth on the poor, so that goodness will come of this, and you too should praise God, and act with righteousness." He called over Bahram's envoy and spoke to him kindly and at length. He asked for a jewel-studded belt, clothes made of gold cloth, a horse with a bridle worked with gold and jewels; these he handed to the envoy, and added a purse of gold coins and many other presents. Then he declared that Bahram was the chief of all champions, and had a scribe write a proclamation on silk: "Parmoudeh the emperor is my ally; he is under the protection of Hormozd. May God, whose slaves we are, witness this seal and proclamation."

Then he wrote a letter as affectionate as heaven's grace to his ambitious commander: "Allow Parmoudeh and his army to come to my court, and send here whatever is valuable among the spoils you have taken from his army: may God be your guide in this matter. Search out where the enemy might still be hiding, and may your good fortune enable you to capture them and burn their houses. If you think more efforts are required and you need more troops, ask for them and I shall send you as many as necessary. Give me the names of those Persians who have acted well and valiantly in this war, so that they may be rewarded. I shall give your men the border areas, and you will receive a crown of authority over them."

Bahram Chubineh's Anger against Parmoudeh

When this letter reached Bahram, his heart was rejuvenated. He was astonished, and summoned the Persian troops to see the gifts he had been sent; everyone who saw them congratulated him. Then he read them the letter, and such a cry of congratulation went up that the ground seemed to shake. He sent the warrant of safe conduct to Parmoudeh in his castle and brightened the darkness of his soul. That nobleman descended from his castle, blessing Hormozd's name as he did so. Everything of value in the castle was recorded. The proud commander of the castle immediately mounted his warhorse and marched with his men out of the castle, ignoring Bahram. When Bahram saw that, despite having captured this king, he was being treated with contempt, he sent men to bring Parmoudeh before the army on foot. Parmoudeh said to him, "I was the lord of any assembly and now I am a suppliant with no power; I have descended from my ivory throne to a wretched state. You are a malevolent man, and today you have not acted well toward me in having me brought before your troops like this. I have a warrant of safe conduct and I intend to travel to the king, in hopes that he will treat me as a brother and lighten the burden of my sorrows. What business have you with me, now that I have handed over to you my royal throne and wealth?"

Parmoudeh's words enraged Bahram and he lost all sense of proportion; he struck at Parmoudeh violently with his whip, as a man might strike an inferior; he had his legs bound in iron fetters and confined him in a tent. When Khorad-Borzin saw this, he said to himself, "Good sense is no friend to this commander." He went to the chief scribe and said, "This terrifying champion has less sense than the wing of a mosquito, and that's why he has no respect for anyone else. Someone should tell him that this is not the way to act, and that there's no greater danger to a man than his own anger." The two of them went to Bahram, their faces dark with foreboding, their lips filled with advice. They said, "You have thrown away the fruits of your labors; God forbid that a nobleman's head be filled with fire like this!" Bahram knew that he had acted in an ugly fashion, that he had done something as foolish as throwing sun-baked bricks into water. He regretted his actions, held his head in his hands in shame, and had Parmoudeh released from his fetters. He sent Parmoudeh a horse with a gold-worked bridle and an Indian sword in a golden scabbard, and went to him to alleviate his distress. He stayed with him while he prepared to leave, watched him mount his swift horse, and accompanied him along part of his route. But he saw that the king's face did not relax or grow cheerful. When the time came for them to separate, he said, "I think you're angry with me in your heart. If this is so, say nothing about it to Persia's king; it will not do your reputation with him any good."

The emperor replied, "My complaints are against fortune, and I have addressed them to God. Don't think of me as someone who will gossip about everyone, but if your king learns nothing of this, he does not deserve to be king. The turning heavens put me in fetters: I shall not say that some slave injured me." Bahram turned pale at these words; he writhed inwardly but managed to swallow his anger. He said,

> "As far as you are able to, don't sow
> Destruction's seeds—you'll reap them when they grow.

I tried to make your situation better;
I wrote on your behalf, and in my letter
I did not tell the king of all you'd done
In trying to renew the war he'd won."

The emperor replied, "That evil has gone by, and the past is as wind. When a man is defeated in war he has to be patient and make peace. But peace and anger seem to be the same to you, and it's clear you have little enough good sense. If a man follows his lord, he doesn't stumble at every turning. It's God's way we should follow, and cleanse our hearts of darkness. The evil you've done has gone, like the wind: it would be better if you said no more about it."

Bahram said, "I'd hoped this matter would remain secret. But if the sin I've committed is going to produce trouble, I won't try to hide it under a silk veil. When you get there say whatever you want to; my reputation won't be harmed by it." The emperor replied, "I consider any king a fool who takes no account of good and evil, and who is silent when his subjects act in ways that are wrong. Seeing such things from a distance, anyone—enemy, well-wisher, or ally—would say that you are an impulsive and contemptible lout, and that the Persian king is feeble-minded." Bahram was enraged, and his face turned pale. Khorad-Borzin saw this and was afraid that his bloodthirsty master would kill Parmoudeh in his fury. He said to Bahram, "My lord, swallow your anger, and turn back. What the emperor has said is true; you should listen to him and drive evil thoughts from your mind. If you had not spoken so coldly toward him, you heart would not now be so troubled." Bahram replied, "This vicious, talentless son can't wait to rejoin his father." The emperor spoke again: "Don't do this evil to yourself; greatness grows old with anger. People like you, with heads full of dust and hearts full of smoke, think ill of everyone and get on with no one, and their pride is perversity and foolishness. You try to frighten me with talk of the King of Kings, but it is right that my pain and peace should come from him. He is my equal, a nobleman as I am; he's not some malevolent slave. He is wise, dignified, of good lineage, and he remembers those who are wellborn. I command you, by the head and army of the Persian king, to turn back now, and to say nothing further to worsen your situation."

When he heard this, Bahram turned back to his army's encampment. Khorad-Borzin, the chief scribe, and other learned men wrote a letter to the king, recounting everything that had happened, publicly and privately. In the anger of the moment Bahram said to his chief priest, "Go immediately into the castle, hurry like the wind, and see what kind of treasure is there." The scribes went with trepidation in their hearts, and worked from sunrise until three watches of the night had passed: many pages were blackened

with ink, but still the work was not finished. There was hardly room to move in the castle, so many undisturbed ancient treasures were there. From the times of Afrasyab and Arjasp there were gold coins, pearls from the sea, and gems from mines whose excavation was heaven's work. Famous treasures were there, like the belt of Seyavash, which had three bands of jewels on each boss, and also his earrings, the like of which no commoner or nobleman in all the world has ever owned. Kay Khosrow had given them to Lohrasp, who had in turn given them to Goshtasp, and Arjasp had placed them in the castle at a time that no one now remembers. No astrologer or learned man could compute the wealth gathered there: one by one each item was recorded, and Bahram sent an eloquent, honest, and alert scribe to gather everything of value that was in the castle and bring it to one place on the plain.

Among the valuable objects were a pair of earrings and a pair of boots with gold thread braided on them and jewels at the end of each braid. There were also two bolts of Yemeni cloth of gold weighing seven *man* each. In his perversity and arrogance Bahram ignored his duty and set these things aside. Then he ordered Payda-Goshasp to take the treasures to the king, with an escort of a thousand troops. He demanded ten caravans of camels from the emperor and counted off the goods as they were loaded. With the emperor at the head and the baggage train following on behind, the caravans made their way to court.

The Emperor Arrives at Hormozd's Court

While the king of the world sat in state, with a crown on his head and a mace in his fist, news came that the emperor and his train of ancient treasures were approaching. The king went on horseback to the courtyard of his palace to see the emperor's face, and also to see whether, when the emperor caught sight of him, he and his escort would dismount. He waited anxiously for the outcome, as the emperor and Payda-Goshasp came into view. The emperor dismounted and ran toward the king. There was a pause, and then Parmoudeh remounted his black Arab horse. The King of Kings urged his own horse forward and the two conferred together for a moment in the courtyard, but as Parmoudeh tried to follow the king into the palace the chamberlain caught at his horse's bridle. Parmoudeh quickly dismounted, and showed his duplicity by this act of homage. The king too dismounted, took him by the hand, and led him forward to the throne. He showed him great kindness and questioned him; the two talked for a long time together. Apartments worthy of his rank were set aside for him and decorated, and Parmoudeh was provided with everything he could need. His men were given quarters near him, and a scribe was placed at his disposal. The king sent servants to take care of the treasures that had accompanied Parmoudeh.

Hormozd Learns of Bahram's Behavior and Allies Himself with Parmoudeh

A mounted messenger arrived with a letter from the chief scribe, which read: "May the king reign in prosperity forever, and all his actions be generous and just. Know then that the army's champion has taken two bolts of Yemeni cloth, a pair of boots encrusted with uncut jewels, and the earrings of the noble Seyavash that have come down to us as a reminder of his greatness. Since the champion underwent great hardships, this should not be a cause for surprise." The king turned to Parmoudeh and asked him to recount what he had seen, and Parmoudeh confirmed what the scribe had written. Hormozd burst out in fury,

> "This overbearing man has lost his way,
> Forgetting it's his business to obey.
> He dares to strike the Chinese emperor
> As though he were some base inferior,
> And then he takes these earrings—as if he
> Were heir to some imperial family.
> His good deeds have dispersed like wind-blown dust,
> His justice is now shown to be unjust."

He summoned Parmoudeh to the place of honor at his side, and the two sat feasting until night came and spread its dusky curls over the assembly. Hormozd turned to Parmoudeh and said, "You have suffered a great deal from my country." Taking Parmoudeh's hand in his, he said, to the emperor's astonishment, "Renew our treaty, and let us set our agreement on a new basis." Then they swore a solemn oath, by God and their souls, that Hormozd would not turn his heart aside from the emperor, and that he would not change his mind in this for anything that Parmoudeh did. They swore by the throne and crown, by the sun and moon, by the sacred fires of Azar-Goshasp and Azar-Panah, by God who is above all and who maintains Venus and Jupiter in their courses, that when Parmoudeh returned to his people he would not turn aside from Hormozd or from his courtiers. When they had sworn this oath, they rose and retired to their sleeping quarters.

As the yellow sun rose above the mountains the two kings awoke. Hormozd had prepared a robe of honor, woven from gold and silver, together with a horse and crown. He sent these to the emperor and then accompanied him for two stages of his return journey. At the start of the long third stage he said his farewells to Parmoudeh and turned back.

When Bahram learned of the gifts Parmoudeh had received from the king, and that he was returning in triumph, he went out to meet him accompanied by his Persian noblemen. He had a stock of fodder made ready for Parmoudeh at every stage of the route he would take, in the towns and villages, as well as on the plains and mountains. Bahram came before him prepared to apologize humbly for his former behavior. He greeted him respectfully, but the emperor of China turned his head away and refused to accept any of Bahram's gifts, including the fodder he had provided for him and the slaves and purses of gold he had brought. Bahram rode with him, but the emperor would not cast a glance at him, and so they went forward for three days during which time Parmoudeh did not address a word to him. On the fourth day the emperor sent Bahram a message, "Go back, you have tired yourself out enough." Bahram angrily turned back toward Balkh, and there he stayed for a while, regretting his former actions, his heart filled with sorrow.

Hormozd Sends Bahram Chubineh a Spindle and Woman's Clothes

King Hormozd was dissatisfied with Bahram, and his impetuous behavior filled the king's soul with foreboding; first, because Bahram had intentionally mistreated the emperor, and second, because of his presumptuousness in taking spoils to which he was not entitled. He therefore wrote him a letter: "Base devil that you are, you no longer know yourself. You think you have no need of your superiors and do not understand that our abilities come from God. You see yourself seated on the sphere of heaven; you have disobeyed my orders and followed your own inclinations. You have forgotten the troubles I have endured, as well as the army and wealth I command. You do not act as a commander should, but raise your head up proudly to the skies. Now a royal gift has come that is worthy of you, something that is appropriate for the way you are acting." When Hormozd had sealed the letter he gave orders that a black spindle case containing a spindle, raw cotton, and various other unworthy objects be prepared. Then he asked that a purple blouse woven from hair be brought, together with a woman's red coif, and a pair of woman's yellow pants. He chose a messenger who was suitable to take such a present and said to him, "Take these to Bahram, and tell him, 'You are a worthless, useless wretch. You put the emperor of China in chains and you enjoy humiliating your superiors, but I shall bring you down from that throne you've placed yourself on, and I shall not consider you as a man from now on!'"

The messenger memorized the speech and traveled as fast as the wind. When Bahram saw the letter and gifts, he chose silence and patience. He said, "So this is my reward, and this is how my king treats me. But this cannot be the king's idea; it must be because of gossip by those who hate me. The king rules over his subjects, and if he despises me that is his right, but I did not think my enemies would gain access to him so quickly. Everyone has seen what I have done since I set off with all speed from the king's court, with only a small army at my command; everyone knows the difficulties and trials I have undergone. If contempt is my reward for enduring such hardships, and if fortune can only treat me with scorn, I shall complain to God that the heavens have utterly withdrawn their favor from me."

Then he prayed to the Lord of Justice from whom all benefits come, and put on the red and yellow clothes. He set out the black spindle case and the other objects the king had sent, and ordered the king's nobles who were in his army to present themselves before him. His dark soul was filled with conflicting thoughts as they entered, young and old, and saw the manner in which he was dressed. They were all bewildered, and each man's heart was filled with anxiety. Bahram said to his men, "This is the gift the king has sent me. He is our ruler and we are his slaves, and our hearts and souls are filled with love for him. What do you think is the significance of this, and how should I answer our country's king?"

They all began to speak at once, saying, "You are a great champion, and if this is what the king thinks of you, then his courtiers are dogs. Remember what that wise old man said when he was grieved by Ardeshir's negligence: 'I despair of our king's throne and crown, since he pays no attention to whatever I do, for good or ill.'" Bahram replied, "Do not say such things. It is the king who confers honor on his army; we are his slaves, he is the provider, and we are his suppliants." But the Persians answered, "We shall serve no more. None of us will call him the king of Iran, or Bahram his army's commander." They went out on to the plain, and for some time Bahram spoke with them, and his lips were always filled with conciliatory words.

Bahram Sees His Fortune

After two weeks Bahram went out of his castle and onto the plain. He saw a thicket of trees ahead of him that seemed a fine place to pause and drink wine. A wild ass was there, and no one has ever seen a more splendid animal. Bahram rode after the wild ass, but without tiring his horse. After riding across open country for a while, they reached a narrow defile, and when Bahram followed the ass through it a wide desert appeared on the other side. The ass sped ahead and Bahram rode after him across the burning plain, until a magnificent castle appeared in the distance. Bahram rode toward it, with the ass still leading the way. Izad-Goshasp was riding after him, and when they reached the castle, Bahram gave him his horse's reins and said, "May wisdom always be your companion." Then he entered the castle on foot, and went forward without a guide.

Izad-Goshasp waited for a while at the palace gateway, and then Yalan-Sineh, who had been following them on his swift-paced horse, arrived. Izad-Goshasp said to him, "Go into the castle and see where our commander has got to." Anxious to find his master, his heart filled with trepidation, Yalan-Sineh entered the castle. He saw an arch and a hall more splendid than any he had ever seen or heard of in Iran. In the hall there was a golden throne, its feet encrusted with jewels, and on it was laid a tapestry of Byzantine brocade embroidered with figures picked out in jewels on a golden ground. A woman with a crown on her head was sitting on the throne; in stature she was like a cypress tree, and her face was as lovely as the spring. The army's commander was seated on another golden throne, and around him were numerous serving girls as beautiful as idols, with fairy-like faces. As soon as the woman saw Yalan-Sineh she said to one of the serving girls, "Go quickly, dear friend, and tell that lionhearted warrior he is not permitted to be here. He should stay with his companions, and Bahram will come to him soon enough." And immediately she sent the serving girls to Bahram's escort, to take their horses to the stables, where they and their saddles would be taken care of.

At the command of this beautiful hostess, a gardener opened the door to the gardens, and a Zoroastrian priest came forward, praying quietly, the sacred barsom in his hand. Tables laid with many kinds of food were set about the garden. Once the men had eaten, their horses were brought at the gallop, and as he was leaving, Bahram addressed the woman who had entertained them, "May Jupiter protect your crown." She answered him, "Be victorious, always patient-hearted, careful in your councils."

As Bahram left the garden, his eyes rained down bitter tears. His nature had changed, his answers had changed, and his head seemed to lift itself up to the Pleiades. Again he followed the wild ass until it led them out of the thicket. When he reached the town again, he said nothing to his soldiers of what had happened. Khorad-Borzin watched him and said, "My lord, tell me truly, what was this marvel that you saw in the hunting grounds, this thing that no one has ever seen or heard of?" But Bahram gave him no answer: deep in thought, he made his way to his palace.

Bahram Adopts the Customs of a King

On the next day, when the foothills of the mountains turned to silver and the golden lamp of heaven appeared, a carpet of Chinese brocade was spread out, so that the ground looked like the heavens. Golden seats, with cushions made of gold-worked brocade, were set about the palace, and the commander of the army took his place there on a golden throne. He sat enthroned in state, like a King of Kings, with a royal crown on his head. The chief scribe saw all this and realized that it was an act of defiance. He went to Khorad-Borzin and told him what he knew, what he had seen, and what he had heard. Khorad-Borzin now knew that matters had reached a crisis and said to the scribe, "Don't take this lightly. We should say nothing, but in the darkness of the night we should go to the king." Once they had made their decision, they fled from Balkh under cover of darkness.

When Bahram heard of what they had done, he said to Yalan-Sineh, "Take a hundred horsemen and go after those two fools." Yalan-Sineh rode as quickly as wind-blown dust. He soon caught up with the chief scribe and closed in on him like a wolf. He stripped this innocent man of all he had and brought him back in heavy chains, so that Bahram could kill him. Bahram said to him, "Devil's spawn, why did you leave me without permission?" He answered, "My lord, Khorad-Borzin frightened me. He said that if I stayed, only my enemies would be happy; that he and I were in danger of being killed unless we fled." Because Bahram's honor seemed to be impugned before his men, he replied, "We must discuss the good and bad of this." He compensated the scribe for his injuries, returned his wealth to him, and said, "From now on consider more carefully what it is you're doing, and don't try to flee again."

Khorad-Borzin Informs Hormozd of Bahram's Actions

But Khorad-Borzin rode on undetected to the king's court, and there

> He told him all he'd witnessed, every word
> Of all the secret gossip that he'd heard—
> He told him of the thicket, the wild ass
> That guided Bahram, and the narrow pass,
> The jeweled castle and its lovely queen,
> The serving girls, the wonders that he'd seen.
> He detailed all of this, and when he'd done,
> Answered his monarch's questions one by one.

Hormozd was astonished by his words, and everything he heard went straight to his heart. Then he remembered the priest who had foretold that someone would arise who would disobey him, and a cold sigh came from his heart. Immediately he summoned the chief priest and sat him down with Khorad-Borzin, to whom he said, "Tell this man what you saw on that road." Khorad-Borzin did as his king commanded him and went over everything once again. The king said to the chief priest, "What can this mean? We must consider all the parts of it: there was an ass in a thicket and it went ahead as a guide; a castle in the middle of an arid desert, a crowned woman on a golden throne with serving girls standing before her as if she were a queen. All this is like a dream that someone tells in an ancient tale."

The priest answered the king of the world, "That wild ass was a demon in disguise, and when it summoned Bahram away from righteousness, falsehood appeared in his heart. Understand that the castle was made by magic, that the woman on the throne was an evil sorceress who showed Bahram the way of rebellion and promised him the crown and throne of sovereignty. When he returned from seeing her, he became drunk with ambition, and you should accept that he will never submit to you again. Your best course is to find some way to recall the army from Balkh to your court."

Now the king regretted the spindle case, the raw cotton, and the unworthy clothes. Not many days passed before a messenger arrived from Bahram, bringing a basket filled with daggers whose points were bent back. This he placed in front of the king, who stared at the iron weapons. He ordered that the daggers' blades be broken and flung in the basket; then he sent them back as a sign of conflict and warfare. When Bahram, whose judgment was clouded now, saw the daggers broken in half, he called the envoy and his Iranian advisors to him and had them gather round the basket. He said, "Look at this gift from the king, and don't think of it as something of no importance." His men brooded on what the king had done, and on their commander's words. They said, "The king's first present to us was a spindle and brightly colored clothes, and his next was broken daggers—this is worse than wounds and curses. Such a king should never rule, and may his memory be forgotten. If Bahram should once again ride his horse back to that court, curses on him and curses on the father who sired him."

Hearing their words Bahram realized that the soldiers' hearts were weary of the king, and he said to them, "Be careful and clear-headed, because Khorad-Borzin has told the king everything that had been kept hidden. Now each one of you must look to save his soul by swearing fealty to me. I must send lookouts onto the roads, or my luck will be at an end and one by one every man in this army will be killed." He said this, but his plans were quite otherwise: pay attention, and you will be astonished. He sent horsemen throughout the countryside to intercept any letters from the king that might encourage the Persians to fight against him. For some time no one received a letter from the king.

Bahram Takes Counsel with His Advisors; His Sister Gordyeh's Intervention

Then Bahram summoned the nobles of the army and put before them much that he had kept private. Hamdan-Goshasp, the chief scribe, warlike Yalan-Sineh, Bahram who was descended from Seyavash, and the wise counselor Payda-Goshasp were all present. He addressed this band who were eager for battle and had lost their way: "Anyone would be pleased to have you as advisors. Our superior is needlessly angry with us, and has deserted all precedent and good custom. We cannot simply weep over our troubles, like a man who hides his wounds from his doctors; what remedy do you suggest? If we hide our problems from the wise, simple matters become difficult; we are suffering, and it is time to put our troubles before knowledgeable men. We left Iran with a tiny army, eager for battle, and no one in the world will ever see a more numerous army than that of our enemies. Saveh Shah and Parmoudeh marched on Persia, but they considered us of no more importance than a wax bauble, as their real goal was Rome. But Parmoudeh and Saveh Shah were overtaken by events the like of which the world has never known. Even though we underwent all manner of hardships and left them neither their wealth nor their elephants, the king has restored their power and is now threatening war with us. What can we do now to escape his trap, to slip free of his chains? Think of your own lives, and of what balm you can bring to these wounds. I have unburdened my soul to you and told you the secrets of my heart."

In Bahram's private quarters his virtuous sister Gordyeh lived; this wise woman was her brother's confidante and comfort. Listening from behind the curtain separating her from the company, she heard her brother's words and sprang up, her heart quivering with anger. She stepped into the assembly, her head filled with all she wished to say, her tongue with ancient precepts. When he heard his sister's voice, Bahram fell silent, and out of fear the Persians gathered there also stopped speaking. Gordyeh addressed them: "You are noble and ambitious men, why do you remain silent at his words, although you bleed inwardly? You are Persia's leaders, her wise men, her magicians; what's your opinion of all this, what game do you intend to play on this blood-soaked plain?"

The horseman Izad-Goshasp spoke: "You remind us of the ancient heroes, and even if our tongues are sharpened in anger they are silent before the flood of your opinions. All your deeds are from God; they are brave, knowledgeable, and filled with wisdom. We don't have to be like leopards eager for war with anyone. Let no one ask for more from me, this is the extent of my answer. But if you make war, I will be with you, I'll ride at the head of your cavalry. If my commander approves of me, this will keep me young forever."

Bahram saw that Izad-Goshasp was trying to position himself between the two factions. Then he turned to Yalan-Sineh and said, "What thoughts are you keeping hidden?" He replied, "Noble commander, whoever follows God's ways will not turn to evil when he gains victory and glory. If he does so, congratulations will turn to curses, and the turning heavens will hate him. God has given you glory and good fortune, an army, wealth, a diadem, and a throne, and, if you strive for more than this, ingratitude will fill your heart with sorrow."

Next he turned to Bahram, the son of Bahram, and said, "You are a wise man and reason is your friend, what do you think of this search for a throne and crown? Will it end well, or in pain and sorrow?"

> Then Bahram smiled at him, and threw his ring
> Into the air. "A slave can be a king,"
> He said, "for just as long as this will stay
> Up in the air. And there's no simple way
> To gain a royal crown: make no mistake,
> This is an arduous task to undertake."

Then Bahram Chubineh said to Payda-Goshasp, "You're a lion in battle, a man who rides his horse hard, what do you say to this business of mine? Am I worthy of the throne?" Payda-Goshasp replied, "You are like the heroes of ancient times. A priest once gave good advice for a situation like this: he said that if a man is knowledgeable and farsighted and becomes king, his soul will ascend to the heavens. It's better to risk all to be the possessor of the world's wealth than to live a long life as a slave."

Next he turned to the chief scribe and said, "You're an old, cunning wolf; open your lips and give me your opinion." But for a while the chief scribe was silent; he sat sunk in a multitude of thoughts. Finally he said to Bahram, "A man who seeks to satisfy his ambition will do so if he is worthy of what he aims at. Fate's reach is long and sure, and our efforts will bear fruit if God approves of them." Then Bahram said to Hamdan-Goshasp, "You have had experience of life's good and bad fortune. Whatever you say here in front of us will disappear like the wind and have no evil consequences for you. Give us your opinion of this business, say whether you think it will turn out badly or well." Hamdan-Goshasp replied,

> "You're valued by great men, and yet you fear
> Evils to come, troubles that are not here.
> What have imperial crowns to do with you?
> Thank God, and do what you were born to do.
> Don't reach up for the dates if you're afraid
> Their thorns will injure you. Stick to your trade!

A country's king can never be at peace,
The fears and trials he faces never cease."

Their remarks distressed Bahram's sister, and her soul was shrouded in darkness. She said nothing to her brother from the time the sun set until half the night had passed. Then Bahram said to her, "You are a chaste, good

woman; what do you think of what has been said here?" But Gordyeh wept and gave him no answer; she was not happy with the words that his advisors had spoken. She turned to the chief scribe and said, "You have an evil nature, like a wolf's. Do you think none of the noble warriors of the world has ever longed for the crown and throne, for mighty armies, for victory and good fortune? Isn't being king easier than being a slave? One should weep for this knowledge of yours! But we should follow the customs of the ancient kings, we should listen to their words." The scribe answered her, "If my opinions are not acceptable then you should say and do whatever seems right to you; let your heart guide you."

Gordyeh turned to Bahram and his conceited knights and said, "There's no goodness in your knowledge or your opinions; your pride is taking you down a mistaken path. How many times the throne has been unoccupied, but no subject ever glanced at it. They maintained the world in chivalry and had no eyes for the throne. Anyone with intelligence knows that proud sovereignty is finer than being a humble subject, but no one attempted to seize the Kayanid throne; men stood before it ready to serve their kings. A stranger to the royal blood would disgrace the crown, and it is lineage that makes a man worthy of greatness. Let us begin with Kavus, who tried to find out the ways of God, to count the stars and hunt down the secrets of the turning heavens. His perverse thoughts left him wretched and sorrowful in Sari, and heroes like Gudarz and Rostam were troubled in their souls by this. And then he went to Hamaveran and his legs were placed in heavy gyves; but no one ever coveted his throne, they felt only sorrow and sympathy for him. When the Persians said to Rostam, 'You are worthy of the Kayanid throne,' he yelled at the man who had spoken, 'May I see you in your narrow grave! How can a champion presume to sit with the ceremonial that attends a king? Should I occupy a golden throne while our king is imprisoned? My curses on such a suggestion!' He chose twelve thousand warlike cavalry and rescued Kavus from his chains, as well as Giv, Gudarz, and Tus.

"No subject ever sought the throne, no matter how fine his family was. And when this Turk Saveh Shah came seeking the royal seal and crown, the world's Creator prevented him from reaching Iran. You're a slave, so what has put it into your head to desire the throne of the King of Kings? This Yalan-Sineh curvets his horse and boasts that he will make Bahram, the son of Goshasp, into a king, and so leave a name for himself in the world. But the wise old king Nushin-Ravan was rejuvenated by the sight of Hormozd, and the great of the world are his allies or his subjects. In Persia there are three hundred thousand horsemen, all famous fighters and all the king's slaves sworn to carry out his commands. The King of Kings chose you as his commander, as was right since your ancestors successfully fought against their enemies, and you return evil for this good fortune. Well, you should realize that it's yourself you're hurting. Don't make ambition king over good sense; no sensible person will call you wise if you do this. I may be a woman, and much younger than my brother, but I give a man's advice. Don't throw away the deeds of your ancestors, and God forbid that you remember my advice when it is too late."

The whole company was dumfounded by her words, and Bahram bit his lip. He knew that she spoke the truth, and that the way she sought was the right one. But Yalan-Sineh said, "My lady, don't talk in this company about kings and their customs. Hormozd will soon be gone, and our commander deserves the throne. Since Hormozd is as we know him to be, you should consider your brother to be the king of Iran. If Hormozd is so proud of the Kayanid crown and their customs, why did he send that spindle as a royal gift? We've had enough talk of Hormozd, anyway. He's of Turkish lineage, and I curse his people; may they disappear from the earth! You talk about Kay Qobad's line, whose crown and throne lasted for a hundred thousand years, but their rule is finished now, and there is no point in invoking their name. As for Hormozd's son, Khosrow Parviz, he is not worth mentioning. The best of his entourage are your brother's slaves and servants, and if Bahram tells them to, they will shackle their master's feet for him."

Gordyeh answered him,

> "You plot the devil's work in all you do
> And devils lie in wait to ambush you!
> Stop trying to destroy us; all I see
> From you is empty talk and vanity.
> My father was the governor of Rey
> But if my brother acts now as you say
> And carries out your treacherous design,
> He will annihilate his tribe and mine.
> All that we have achieved, at so much cost,
> Will be dispersed upon the winds and lost.
> You servile wretch—go! Be my brother's guide,
> Lay waste our lives, spread ruin far and wide!"

When she had said this, she began to weep and went to her own apartments; in her heart she was now a stranger to her brother. Everyone said, "This wise and eloquent woman speaks so well that her words seem to come from a book; her wisdom surpasses Jamasp's." But Bahram was displeased, and his sister's words angered him. His dark heart was filled with foolish thoughts, and he constantly dreamed of the royal throne. He thought, "Ambitious men can only win this fleeting world through hardship." Then he ordered a meal prepared and called for wine and musicians. "Sing a song of heroes," he said to the singer. "We'll have the song of the Seven Trials while we drink our wine, the one that describes Esfandyar's expedition to the Brazen Castle and the tricks he played in those bygone days." His companions drank Bahram's health a number of times, saying, "May the province of Rey flourish, since a commander like you hails from there, and may God create more as you are!" When the drinkers' heads were confused with wine and night came, the meeting broke up.

Bahram Has Coins Struck in the Name of Khosrow Parviz

The sun lifted its lance into the sky, and the dark night quailed before its brilliance. Bahram called for the chief scribe, and together they wrote a splendid letter to the emperor of China. Bahram wrote, "The need to apologize wracks me with pain; my heart is filled with regret and cold sighs. From now on I shall respect your country, and if I become lord of all the world, I shall treat you as my younger brother. Wash all thoughts of vengeance from your soul, and do not keep China and Iran separate from one another." Then he turned to other business.

He opened his treasury and distributed silver, horses, and slaves to his army; his secret aim in this was to further his ambitions. He chose a worthy warrior from among his troops and made him the governor of Khorasan. Sunk in thought, he himself set off from Balkh to Rey on the day of Khordad in the month of Dey. He turned many ideas over in his mind, and then gave orders that coins were to be minted in the name of Hormozd's son, Khosrow Parviz. He selected an eloquent, trustworthy merchant, one who was suitable to carry out a delicate task, and told him to take a purse of these coins to Ctesiphon. There he was to buy fine Byzantine brocades, worked in silk on a gold ground, so that the coins would be taken to the king and he would see them.

Bahram Writes to Hormozd, and Khosrow Parviz Flees from His Father's Court

He wrote a letter to Hormozd, filled with boasting and vanity. He mentioned many matters—Parmoudeh and Saveh Shah's army, the battles he had fought, and the king's present of a black spindle case and a woman's coif. Then he wrote, "In my dreams I never see the splendor of the king's face; when your noble son Khosrow Parviz sits on the throne, I shall level the mountains and make them plains if he orders me to, and turn the deserts to an Oxus of his enemies' blood." In this way he hoped to have the innocent prince killed. He said to the merchant, "When Hormozd sees the coins, he will be alarmed, and when he no longer has Khosrow Parviz to help him, he'll see the fate I have in store for him. Once I have established my authority over the country I shall tear the Sasanians up by the roots. God did not create the earth for them, and it's time they forfeited his favor."

A messenger took his letter to Baghdad, and when Hormozd read it, his face turned as pale as fenugreek. Then news came of the coins minted in his son's name, and sorrow was piled on sorrow. He writhed inwardly and became suspicious of his son. He confided his suspicions to Ayin-Goshasp, saying, "Khosrow has become rebellious and wants to separate himself from me. He's had coins minted in his own name, and what could be more contemptuous of my authority than this?" Ayin-Goshasp said, "May your horse and the battlefield never be without you!" Hormozd said, "I'm going to get rid of the wretch immediately." Secretly they summoned a man and sat him down with the king that night. Hormozd said to him, "Do as I say: banish Khosrow from the face of the earth." The man replied, "I shall do it; I'll use spells to drive all pity from my heart. Have poison brought from the king's treasury, and when he's drunk at night, I'll mix it with his wine. This will be better than shedding his blood." But the chamberlain learned of this, and could not sleep from anxiety. He hurried to Khosrow and told him the secret plan. When Khosrow Parviz heard that the king of the world was secretly plotting to kill him, he fled in the darkness of the night from Ctesiphon and seemed to disappear from the face of the earth. Not wanting to lose his precious head to no purpose, he made all haste to Azerbaijan.

When news reached the country's governors and lords of the marches that Khosrow had fled with a few horsemen from the king's court, they made inquiries as to where he might be. Men like Badan-Piruz and Shir-Zil, both just warriors with the strength of elephants, Shiran and pious Vastui, Khanjast from Oman, Bivard from Kerman, and Sam, who was descended from Esfandyar, from Shiraz—one by one they came with their warriors and sought out Khosrow Parviz.

Khosrow said to them, "I fear the king and his courtiers, but if you will go to the fire-temple and there solemnly swear to protect me, never to break this oath, I shall stay here with confidence and have no fear of Ahriman's designs against me." The warriors went to the fire temple and swore as he had requested, saying that they would hold him as dear as their own eyes. As soon as he felt safe, Khosrow sent out spies to find out what his father said about his flight, and whether he was plotting anything new. When Hormozd learned that Khosrow had fled, he immediately had Gostahm and Banduy, Khosrow's maternal uncles, thrown into prison, as well as all of Khosrow's other relatives, and there was much talk about this.

Hormozd Sends Ayin-Goshasp to Fight Against Bahram; He Is Killed

At this time the king said to Ayin-Goshasp, "We seem to have no recourse, and pain is our companion. Now that Khosrow has gone, what shall we do against that wretched slave Bahram?" Ayin-Goshasp said, "Your majesty, this business of Bahram has gone on for long enough. It's my blood he secretly wants to shed, because I was the first person to humiliate him. Send me to him with my legs in shackles; it may be that this will benefit you." The king replied, "I can't do that; it would be the work of Ahriman. No, I'll dispatch an army, with you at its head, and you can win glory in battle. But first send someone to him to sound out what he is thinking. If he is ambitious for sovereignty, for the crown and throne, good fortune will finally desert him. But if he is prepared to be my subject and prefers peace, I'll give him a portion of the world to rule, and place a hero's crown on his head. Let me know immediately what he is up to; don't delay, be as quick as you can."

Ayin-Goshasp set about putting the wise king's plan into action. There was a man from his town who was a prisoner in the king's jail, and when he heard that Ayin-Goshasp was going to war, he sent someone to him with a message saying, "I'm a fellow townsman of yours imprisoned here. If you beg me from the king, I'll accompany you on this expedition. I'll fight before you, as your protector in battle, if only I can get out of this narrow prison." Ayin-Goshasp sent someone to the king to say on his behalf, "One of my fellow townsmen is languishing in your jail; give him to me, your majesty, so that he can come with me on this expedition." The king said, "That evil good-for-nothing? When is he ever going to fight in front of you in a battle? He's a violent criminal, a lout, and a thief; you must be hoping for a bribe from him! Well, at the moment I don't want to deny you anything, even though there's no worse blackguard than he is." And he handed this bloodthirsty devil over to Ayin-Goshasp.

Ayin-Goshasp led his army out, and they marched as quickly as the wind as far as Hamedan, where they halted. Ayin-Goshasp made inquiries as to whether anyone there understood the stars and could foresee the future. Everyone said, "You'll be pleased with the astrologer who comes to you. There is a rich old woman who lives here who seems to know all the secrets of the stars. Whatever she says comes to pass, and she can tell you in the summer what will happen in the autumn." Ayin-Goshasp sent someone with a horse to fetch her, and when she arrived he questioned her about the king's business, and about his own military expedition. Then he said to her, "Whisper in my ear whether I will die in bed, or by my enemy's dagger." As he was talking privately with this old woman about his own affairs, the man whom he'd begged from the king passed in front of the woman, glanced at his commander, and went on. The old woman said, "Who was that man? We should weep for the harm he'll do to you. Your sweet life is in his hands; my curses on him, skin and bones!"

When Ayin-Goshasp heard this he remembered something he had heard long before, something an astrologer had told him that he had forgotten: "Your life is in the hands of a neighbor, who is a thief, a lout, and a worthless wretch. He will confront you during a long journey; you will cry out for help, and he will shed your blood." He wrote a letter to the king, saying, "That man I begged from you should not have been freed from prison; he is something worse than devil's spawn. You told me this, but I did not have your royal *farr* and so could not see the truth. As soon as he arrives, have his head cut off." He sealed the letter and when the seal was dry, he summoned his fellow townsman. He heaped praises on him, gave him some money, and called down God's blessings on him. Then he said, "Quickly and secretly take this letter to the king. If he gives you an answer, bring it straight to me; don't stay with the king."

The young man took the letter and set off, brooding as he went. He said to himself, "I was chained and imprisoned, I couldn't move, and I'd no food. God got me out of that terrible mess, and now my blood and brains are boiling at the thought of going back to Ctesiphon." He went gloomily along the road for a while, and then he opened the letter to the king. When he read his commander's letter he was bewildered at the ways of the world. He said, "This is my neighbor who begged me from the king, who said it was a noble deed to spare me, and now he wants to shed my blood. Did this idea come to him in a dream? Well, now he's going to find out what bloodshed means, and all his troubles will be over." His head whirling, he turned back and traveled as fast as the wind. As he approached the commander he saw that there was no one about: Ayin-Goshasp was resting in his tent, brooding on the king and what fate had in store, and there was no servant, or companion, or sword, or horse nearby. When his neighbor entered the tent Ayin-Goshasp knew that he had come to shed his blood. The man clapped his hand on his sword, and Ayin-Goshasp tried to soften him with words. He said, "Young man, you're mistaken, wasn't it I who begged you from the king when you'd despaired of life?" The man replied, "You did, but what did I do to make you want to destroy me?" As he said this he struck at Ayin-Goshasp's neck with his sword, and the commander's days of feasting and fighting were at an end.

He brought the severed head out of the tent, while the army was still unaware of what had happened. Knowing he would be condemned for shedding his commander's blood, he made his way as quickly as he could to Bahram Chubineh. He said to him, "Here is the head of your enemy, who was planning to kill you. He'd led an army here against you, not knowing what you intended." Bahram asked, "Whose head is this? Who should weep over it?" The man replied, "This is Ayin-Goshasp, who came from the king's court to fight against you." Bahram said to him, "This noble man had come from the king's court to make peace between me and the king, and you cut his head off while he was sleeping. You will receive such a punishment from me that all who see you will weep for you." He ordered that a gibbet be erected before his door, in view of the army and the countryside, and there the wretch was strung up alive, so that he understood in his heart what he had done.

When it was known that Ayin-Goshasp was dead, some of the horsemen he had brought with him went over to Bahram, and others to Khosrow Parviz, hoping to revive their fortunes in the world. The army was like a shepherdless flock that disperses on a day of wind and snow.

Gostahm and Banduy Blind Hormozd

When Hormozd learned of his commander's fate, he was so downcast that he gave no audiences and no one saw him with a wine glass in his hand. He found no peace, he could neither eat nor sleep, and his eyes were always filled with tears. Repeatedly he gave orders that no one was to be admitted to him. One of the courtiers said that Bahram was preparing for war and was intent on seizing the imperial throne. Another said that Khosrow Parviz was so angry with the king that he was leading an army against Iran. The chieftains were bewildered, and each one had a different opinion of what was happening. When these rumors spread throughout Ctesiphon, the king's rule lost all authority. His servants became anxious and quarrelsome, and those who had blessed him now cursed him. Few of his men remained at their posts at court, and to the king's heart the world had become a narrow place.

Banduy and Gostahm learned that the king's *farr* had darkened. The prisoners freed themselves from their chains and appointed one of their number to find out what was happening and who among the warlike chieftains was still at the court. When they learned how matters stood, they cast aside all pretense of loyalty and broke out of the prison. Such a tumult arose that the whole plain rang with it, and the troops who were in the city stood powerless against them. Now armed, and with followers and weapons, Gostahm and Banduy marched determinedly on the palace; they washed all trace of shame from their eyes. Then a detachment of troops appeared from the bazaar, heading toward the palace. Gostahm addressed them, "If you wish to join us, renounce your loyalty to the king, because Hormozd has turned aside from all good sense and from the true path; from now on you should not call him a king. Punish him, make Persia's glory as bitter as colocynth for him. We shall have you as our vanguard and place a new king on Persia's throne, and if you do not falter in this enterprise we shall put Persia in your hands, while we ourselves will retire to some corner of the world with our companions."

At Gostahm's words, as one man the troops cursed the king and cried, "May there never again be a king who seeks to shed his son's blood!" Roused by his speech, they became shameless, setting fire to the palace gates and swarming into the audience hall where they snatched the crown from the king's head and dragged him down from the throne. Then they put hot irons into his eyes, and the bright lamps of his life turned dark. They left him, still alive, in this state and looted all the wealth that was there.

ᵈᔓ THE REIGN OF KHOSROW PARVIZ ᔔᵉ

By night, Banduy and Gostahm quickly sent a messenger with a change of horses to Khosrow, who was then at the fire-temple called Azar-Goshasp, to tell him what had happened. But when the envoy described the tumult in Baghdad, the young man's face turned as pale as fenugreek. He said, "Any man who ignorantly leaves the ways of wisdom and has no fear of the turning heavens will lead a profitless life. If this evil you describe were to please me, my sleep and food would turn to fire. Even though my father tried to shed my blood and I fled from Iran, I am still his slave and will listen to all he has to say."

Immediately he set off with a large number of troops from Barda', Ardebil, and Armenia, traveling as quickly as fire. When news reached Baghdad that a new claimant to the throne was on his way, the town grew peaceful again, and Khosrow was encouraged by this calm. The city's chieftains came out to welcome him; they seated him on an ivory throne and placed a golden torque about his neck and a splendid crown on his head. Khosrow entered the town in sorrow and went sighing to his father, his face a witness to the grief he felt. When he saw him, he wept and paid him homage; the two were closeted together for a long time. Khosrow said, "You are a scion of Nushin-Ravan, but misfortune has dogged your reign. You know that if I had been here to support you, not even a needle would have been permitted to scratch the tip of your finger. Think of what your orders are for me, now that sorrow has come to you and my heart is filled with grief. If you command me, I shall be a slave guarding you; I have no desire for the crown or the army and will cut my head off before you if you order me to." Hormozd replied,

> "You are a wise man, and you know this day
> Of hardship and despair will pass away.
> I've three requests to make of you, no more;
> Grant me these three and I'll not ask for four.
> First, that as day breaks, in the morning light,
> You'll sing to me, and drive away the night;

Next that you'll send a warrior to me,
A veteran of our warlike cavalry
Who'll talk of wars and hunts; and see he brings
A book that tells the exploits of our kings,
So that in hearing them I'll find relief
From my incessant pain and constant grief.
Thirdly, see that your uncles understand
They're your inferiors here, and that this land
Is yours to rule, not theirs; blind them, and make
Their days a darkness for my sorrow's sake."

Khosrow replied, "May anyone who does not mourn for your blinded eyes perish, and may your enemies be swept from the earth! But consider, Bahram Chubineh has become a formidable warrior, and he has innumerable cavalry and swordsmen with him. If I dispose of Gostahm, I'll have no one to turn to for help against Bahram. As for horsemen who've known battles and banquets to recite the stories of ancient kings for you, I'll send new ones to you constantly. I wish your heart wisdom and relief from the pain you suffer." He left his father's presence in tears, and told no one of his secret thoughts. The son was a kinder man than the king, and as a sage once said,

"A sweetly spoken youth is finer than
A difficult and quarrelsome old man."

But in the end the virtuous and the vicious both lie beneath the dust.

Bahram Chubineh Learns that Hormozd Has Been Blinded and Leads His Army against Khosrow Parviz

Bahram was astonished when he learned that the king's eyes had been put out with hot irons, that the light had died away from the garden's two narcissi, that Hormozd's good fortune was at an end and his son now sat on his throne. For a while he was taken aback and brooded on this turn of events, but then he ordered that the armies' drums be sounded and his great banner be brought out onto the plain. The baggage was loaded, the cavalry mounted, and Bahram prepared to do battle with Khosrow Parviz. Audaciously he led his army, which was like a moving mountain, as far as the bank of the River Nahravan.

Khosrow grew anxious when he learned of Bahram's aggressive advance, and sent out spies. He said to them, "First you must find out how his army feels about his intentions, whether they're with him in his desire for war, or whether they're moving against us reluctantly. Then notice whether Bahram stays mainly in the center of the army or moves about among his troops. Also, learn how he holds audience, and whether he ever thinks of going hunting while they're on the march." The spies set off on their mission without the army being aware of this, and when they returned they went secretly to Khosrow and said, "From the nobles down to the young recruits, his soldiers are with him in everything he does. When his men are on the march, he is always moving among them, sometimes with the right wing, sometimes the left, and then with the baggage train. He has everyone's confidence and has no need of outside help. He holds court like a king, and hunts in the same fashion. All his behavior is that of a king, and he constantly reads the book of *Kalileh and Demneh*."

Khosrow said to his vizier, "We have a long business ahead of us. Bahram terrifies the monsters in the oceans when he rides out against his enemies. He learned how to act like a king from my father, when he was king of the world; he's taken *Kalileh and Demneh* as his vizier, and no one has a human advisor who's better than this." To Gostahm and Banduy he said, "Sorrow and trouble are my partners now." Men like Gerdui, Shapur, Andian, the leader of the Armenians, as well as other nobles, sat with the king in secret council. After their deliberations Khosrow Parviz led his army out from Baghdad, and pitched his pavilion on the plains. The two armies were now close together: on the one side the commander, and on the other the

king. When the world's light declined in the sky and night spread its dark curls, sentries were posted on each side. Then, as night grew dry-lipped and sick at heart and fled from day's dagger, the din of drums began from both camps, and the sun rose to guide them to battle. The king ordered Banduy and Gostahm to put on their iron helmets, and he went forward with his nobles to the riverbank.

When the sentry reported to Bahram that the enemy's forces were within two bowshots, he summoned his advisors. He mounted his white charger, a proud, fine horse with a black tail and brazen hooves. Grasping an Indian sword, whose blow was like lightning from a cloud, Bahram rode forward, glittering in glory; Izad-Goshasp was on his left, and Ayin-Goshasp and Yalan-Sineh, both longing for combat and filled with courage, accompanied him. There were also three Turkish warriors in his retinue, men who had sworn loyalty to Bahram, saying that if they saw the king become separated from his men, they would bring him dead or as a captive to Bahram.

On the one side Khosrow waited, on the other Bahram, and between them flowed the River Nahravan. The soldiers on both sides watched, to see how Bahram would approach the king.

Khosrow Parviz and Bahram Chubineh Address One Another

Bahram and Khosrow met, the face of the one was open and confident, the other's closed and apprehensive. The king, dressed in a Chinese cloak of gold-worked brocade, sat on his ivory-colored horse. Gerdui preceded him as a guide, and he was accompanied by Banduy, Gostahm, and Khorad-Borzin, who wore a golden helmet; they were all covered in iron, gold, and silver, and wore golden belts studded with rubies. When Bahram saw the king, his face turned pale with anger. He said to his warriors, "So this miserable son of a whore has risen up from wretchedness and stupidity to be a man; he's become powerful and is ready for battle. He's learned how to be an emperor, but I shall bring his days in the world to an end soon enough. Look at his army from one end to the other, and see if there's a single warrior there worthy of the name. I can see no horseman there who'd dare to confront me. Now he will see how men fight: headlong horses, swords and maces, weapons' blows and the hail of arrows, warriors' cries and the give and take of battle. No elephant can keep its ground when I lead my army in an attack; the mountains tremble at my war cry, and savage lions flee. We'll put a spell on the waters with our swords and fill the desert from end to end with blood." Then he urged on his piebald horse, and it leaped forward like a winged bird. To his army's astonishment he advanced to the river's edge and stood opposite the young king; a few Persians, all prepared to fight against Khosrow, accompanied him.

Khosrow turned to his companions and said, "Which of you can recognize Bahram Chubineh?" Gerdui said, "Your majesty, look at the man on the piebald horse, the one wearing a white cloak and a black sword belt, who's riding at the center of that group of warriors." Seeing Bahram, Khosrow knew immediately what kind of a person he was and said, "You mean the dark, tall man, on the piebald charger?" Gerdui said, "Yes, that's him, a man who's never had a benevolent thought in his life." Khosrow replied, "If you ask a hunchback a question, you'll get a rough answer. And can't you see that that man, with his boar's snout and half-closed eyes, is obviously evil and an enemy to God? I can see no humility in him, and no one is going to be able to treat him as a subject." But still hoping to turn the time from one of fighting to one of feasting, he addressed Bahram from a distance: "You're a proud warrior, but what are you doing here on the field of battle? You're an ornament to the court, the throne and crown depend on you, you're a pillar of the army in warfare, a shining torch at feasts, an ambitious God-fearing warrior; may God never abandon you! I have considered your position and weighed well the things you have done. I shall treat you and your army as my guests and refresh my soul with the sight of you; then I shall name you the commander of Iran's armies, as is just, and pray to God for your welfare."

Bahram heard him out. He let the reins in his hand drop and saluted Khosrow from his horse, then stood silently before him for a long while. Finally, still mounted on his piebald charger, he said, "I rejoice in the life I lead, and fortune favors me. I don't wish you greatness, because as a king you know neither justice nor injustice, and when the king of the Alans rules it's the most miserable wretches who support him. I've considered your position too, and I have a noose ready and waiting for you. Soon I'll construct a tall gibbet and tie your two hands together with my lariat; then I'll string you up as you deserve, and turn your days to bitterness."

When Khosrow heard Bahram's answer, his face turned as pale as fenugreek. He said, "Ungrateful wretch, no God-fearing man would speak as you do. A guest approaches, and you greet him with curses when you should be welcoming him. This was never the way of kings or noble warriors; neither Arabs nor Persians have ever acted like this, not if you go back for three thousand years. A wise man would be ashamed of such behavior. Think again, don't follow this ungrateful course. When a guest greets you kindly, you must be a devil to answer in such a fashion: I fear that I shall see you fall on evil days, ruined by your own obstinacy. Your well-being is in the hands of that king who lives eternally and rules all things; but you are an ungrateful sinner against God, and you'll bring contempt on your body, terror on your heart. When you say I'm king of the Alans, you only mention a third of my lineage; in what way am I unworthy to rule, how is this crown unsuitable for my head? Nushin-Ravan was my grandfather, Hormozd my father; who can you name who is more entitled to the crown than I am?"

But Bahram answered him, "You're evil, and you talk and act like a fool. You prattle about being a guest, but your nature is wicked and all you can do is repeat old stories. What do you know about what kings say? You're neither wise nor a good warrior. You were king of the Alans and now you're a contemptible wretch, lower than a slave of slaves. You're the most wicked man in the world; you're not a king and you have no right to lord it over other chieftains. The people have proclaimed me king, and I shall not leave you space on the earth to set your foot down. You say that bad fortune's in store for me, and that I'm unworthy of sovereignty, but I say that you're unfit to be a king, and may you never occupy the throne again! The Persians are your enemies, and they'll fight till they tear you up by the roots and flay the skin from your body and fling your bones to the dogs!"

Khosrow said to him, "You villain, what has made you so angry and insolent? Ugly talk is a fault in a man, and your nature has had this trait from the beginning. Fortunate the man who lives by wisdom, but wisdom has deserted your brain, and when a devil's hard-pressed he'll say anything. But I wouldn't want a fine warrior like you to be destroyed by anger: you should drive anger from your heart, control yourself, and put a spell on your rage. Remember the just God who rules all things, and in doing so make wisdom your guide. There's a mountain of troubles ahead of you, and, if you look, you'll see it's higher than Bisitun; the desert thorns will bear fruit before someone like you becomes king. Your heart's filled with thoughts of sovereignty, but we'll see what God wills. I don't know who has taught you this villainy and these councils of Ahriman, but whoever it was wanted to bring about your death with his words." Then Khosrow dismounted from his ivory-colored horse, removed the precious crown from his head, and turned lamenting toward the sun. His heart was filled with hopes of God's grace, and he said, "Bright Lord of Justice, it is you who makes the tree of hope bear fruit. You know this slave who stands before me, and that one should weep for the shame he has brought to the crown." And then he went aside to pray, and opened the secrets of his heart to God:

> "If I'm to give up my authority
> And see my lineage lose its sovereignty,
> I'll be your servant, and my one desire
> Will be to tend your temple's sacred fire.
> I'll take no food but milk, the clothes I wear
> Will be of wool and animals' coarse hair;
> I'll have no gold or silver, and I'll stay
> Within your temple's precincts night and day.
> But if my sovereignty's to stay with me,
> Guide my great army on to victory

And do not hand my crown and throne to one
Who's shown himself a slave in all he's done.
If I achieve my heart's desire, I swear
This horse and crown, the royal jewels I wear,
My clothes of cloth of gold—all these will be
Devoted to your temple's treasury;
Over your temple's lapis dome I'll pour
Ten purses of gold coins, and when I'm sure
That I am once again Iran's sole king,
I'll add ten thousand more gold coins, and bring
The captives from this war, so that they'll be
Your temple's slaves in perpetuity."

This sorely pressed man stood again after he had prayed, and quickly went back to the riverbank. He called out to Bahram Chubineh, "You have no wisdom, no manners, no royal *farr*; you're the hellish slave of some monstrous irascible demon who has blinded you. You've found rage and revenge instead of wisdom, and hell's demons applaud you for it; thorn brakes seem cities to you, hell seems an orchard; wisdom's torch has died before your eyes, and taken all the light from your heart and soul. Some wily magician has raised your ambitions and shown you the abyss, but the leaves of the tree for which you reach are poisonous, and its fruit is bitter. None of your family has ever shown such pride and ambition; God has not granted you the exalted position you crave, and you should not dream of things that can never be. A crab cannot sprout an eagle's wings, and an eagle cannot fly beyond the sun. I swear by God and by the throne and crown that if I find you without your army, I shall do you no harm. I have heard your savage language, but it is God who gives us victory and on him I rely. If I am not worthy to be a king I've no wish to live as anyone's subject."

Bahram replied, "You're foolish and in thrall to Ahriman. Your father was a God-fearing man, but you didn't respect him for what he was, and you pushed him ignominiously from the throne. You want to be a wise and capable king in his place, but you're perverse and an enemy to God, who will send you nothing but evil. It's true that Hormozd was unjust at times, and the land groaned beneath his oppression, but you're unworthy to be his son and to rule Iran and Turan. You don't deserve a throne, or even life; good fortune has so deserted you that a tomb is all you're good for. I shall avenge Hormozd, and I shall be king in Iran. And tell me again the story that everyone agrees on, about how you thrust hot irons into the king's eyes, or that you at least gave the orders for this to be done. From now on you'll see that sovereignty is mine, and I rule the heavens, from the sun to Pisces."

Khosrow said, "God forbid that a man should rejoice at his father's pain. It was written thus; what had to be came to pass, and there is no point in discussing it endlessly. You call yourself a king, but when death comes you won't even have a shroud to your name. You've your horse and barding, and because of these you hope for a sovereignty that will never exist. You've no home, no wealth, no country, no lineage; you're a king who's filled with wind. For all your army and wealth and false titles, you'll never know the splendor of a royal throne. Subjects have never sought to be king because they knew they were not worthy of the throne and crown. God created sovereignty out of justice, ability, and lineage; he bestows it on the most worthy person, the wisest, and the most compassionate. My father made me king of the Alans, and I was troubled enough by you then; now God has conferred imperial sovereignty, greatness, and the royal crown and throne on me. I shall do good in the world, so that my name shall not disappear after my death. When Hormozd ruled justly, the world rejoiced in his reign, and I as his son have inherited his throne, as is right, and with the crown and royal belt I have found good fortune. But you—you are filled with sin and deceit: first you attacked Hormozd, and all the evil in his reign was from you and your tricks and plots and lies. If God wills it, I shall avenge him and turn your sun to darkness. Who is worthy of the crown? If I am not worthy of it, who is?"

Bahram replied, "You're a warrior, and whoever snatches sovereignty from you is worthy of it. The Ashkanians ruled when Babak's daughter gave birth to Ardeshir. And isn't it true that Ardeshir became powerful and seized the throne through killing Ardavan? But five hundred years have passed since then, and the Sasanian crown has grown cold. Now it is time for me to possess the throne and crown, and my victorious fortune will ensure this. I look at your face and your fortune, your army, your crown, and your throne, and I stretch out my hand against the Sasanians as a savage lion leaps on its prey. I shall erase their names from the records and trample the Sasanian throne beneath my feet. If one listens to those who know the truth, it's the Ashkanians who deserve to rule. The truth is that you're a Sasanian and your lineage is a contemptible one, because Sasan was a shepherd, and the son of a shepherd. Didn't Babak employ him as a shepherd for his flocks?"

But Khosrow answered, "You ungrateful criminal, wasn't it the Sasanians who raised you up in the world? Your words are nothing but lies from one end to the other, and no honor will come from such talk." Bahram replied, "It's no secret that Sasan was a shepherd." Khosrow said, "When Dara died, he was unable to bequeath the crown to Sasan; but though fortune turned against him, the race survived, and no justice will come from your unjust chatter. And this is the intelligence and good sense and glory with which you hope to gain the imperial throne?" As he spoke, he laughed and turned away toward his own army. But one of the three savage Turks, who were as wild as wolves, and who had promised Bahram that on the day of battle they'd seek fame by bringing the king before him dead or alive, rode fearlessly forward and flung a lariat of sixty coils, which caught on Khosrow's crown. Gostahm severed the rope with his sword and the king's head was unharmed. Bahram turned on this wretched Turk and said, "You deserve to be in your grave for this! Who told you to attack the king; didn't you see me standing there parleying with him?" Then he returned to his camp, his soul filled with sorrow, his body with disquiet.

Vehemently, Gordyeh tried once again to dissuade her brother from his plans, but to no avail. Bahram attacked the king's army at night, and Khosrow Parviz was forced to flee back to Ctesiphon. There he consulted with his blind father Hormozd, who advised him to ask the emperor of Byzantium for help. As they were talking, news came that Bahram's army was approaching, and Khosrow fled westward into the desert. Khosrow's advisors, Gostahm and Banduy, remained behind and, unbeknownst to Khosrow, strangled Hormozd. Then they set out after Khosrow, who had taken refuge in a monastery. Bahram's army reached the monastery, but through a ruse of Banduy's Khosrow was once again able to flee westward. Banduy fell into Bahram's hands and was imprisoned, but he managed to escape. Bahram crowned himself king. Khosrow meanwhile had reached Byzantium and entered into lengthy negotiations with the emperor there, using Gostahm as his go-between. Eventually, the emperor agreed to help him against Bahram Chubineh.

The Emperor of Byzantium Sends Khosrow Parviz an Army and His Daughter

The emperor selected a hundred thousand of his troops, all fine men ready for battle, and these he assigned to Khosrow Parviz, together with armor, cash, and warhorses. In this way the king's long wait came to an end. The emperor had a daughter named Mariam, who was a wise, dignified, and intelligent young woman. He affianced her to Khosrow, with the rites of his religion, calling down God's blessing on her. Gostahm received her from the emperor, and with all due ceremony he handed her over to Khosrow. The emperor presented them with such a dowry that the splendid horses carrying it were exhausted by the weight. There were gold vessels and imperial jewels, rubies, and clothes embroidered with gold-worked designs, carpets, and Byzantine silk brocades bearing figures woven in gold. There were also bracelets, torques and earrings, and three splendid crowns

encrusted with jewels. Four golden litters were prepared, their facings studded with gems, as well as forty closed couches of ebony, glittering with
gems like a rooster's eyes. Following them came serving girls as lovely as
the moon, and five hundred young male servants mounted on horses with
trappings of gold and silver. Then there were forty handsome, charming
Byzantine eunuchs, together with four wise and famous philosophers; to
these last the king told everything that was necessary. He also spoke with
Mariam in secret, advising her on obedience and her duties, on when she
should be generous, on her food, and on what behavior was appropriate.
When the gifts were reckoned up their value was estimated at more than
three hundred million dinars.

The emperor consulted with astrologers as to when would be the best
time for the journey and set off on an auspicious day. After two stages of
the journey he gave orders that Mariam come to him, and he spoke with her
at length. He said, "Keep yourself secluded, and do not loosen your belt
until you reach the Persian border; Khosrow must not see you naked before
then, since this could lead to unforeseen consequences." He then bade her
an affectionate farewell. To his brother Niatus, who was in charge of the
Byzantine troops sent to Khosrow, he said, "Mariam is of your own blood,
and so I have entrusted her to you. I am giving my daughter, my wealth, and
a well-equipped army into your safekeeping." Niatus accepted the charge,
and when he and the king had spoken together, he wept as they turned
aside from one another.

Niatus, bearing his sword and mace, marched at the head of the army.
Khosrow heard of their approach and set out from the town where he was
waiting. As the dust sent up by the approaching troops became visible, followed by their banners and their splendid armored cavalry bearing down
toward him like the wind, Khosrow laughed from his heart, as a flower
blossoms in the spring. His spirits lifted and he dug his heels into his
horse's flanks. He saw Niatus and embraced him, questioning him at length
about the emperor who had gone to such trouble on his behalf and offered
him so much wealth. Then he went over to the litter, where he saw Mariam
and glimpsed her face beneath her veil; he questioned her too, and kissed
her hand, rejoicing in his heart to see her beauty.

Khosrow brought the army to his royal pavilion, where he had a private
chamber prepared for Mariam. He sat talking with her for three days, and
on the fourth, as the sun lit up the world, he had a splendid tent prepared,
and there he summoned Niatus and his subordinates Sergius and Kut, as
well as the other Byzantine commanders. He asked them, "Who are your
leaders, your finest warriors?" Niatus chose seventy men to lead the attack
on the day of battle, and each of them had a thousand picked cavalry following his banner. When Khosrow saw this fine force of cavalry all eager

for war, he praised God who has created time and the world, and called down his blessings on Niatus and the army, as well as on the emperor and his country. To the commanders he said, "If God is with me in this battle, I shall show my mettle, and make the earth as splendid as the Pleiades. May our thoughts now be only of friendship; the heavens are with us, and the kindness of noble men is as an orchard for us to rest in."

*K**hosrow Parviz traveled to Azerbaijan, where the people welcomed him. Bahram Chubineh's attempts to rally support began to fail, and there were a number of skirmishes between Bahram and Khosrow's allies. For a while, Khosrow became separated from the main body of his army.*

Khosrow Fights against Bahram Chubineh

At that moment a cry went up from the sentries, and Bahram was told that a group of men was approaching. Eager for conquest, with his wits about him, Bahram mounted his horse, he grasped his sword, and fastened his lariat to his saddle. From his horse's height he surveyed the little group of men who were approaching, and then chose a few of his own warriors. He said to Yalan-Sineh, "That wretch wants to prove his worth in battle: I know it can't be anyone but him who would dare to fight against me. He's come to attack me with his handful of men, and he's walking into the mouth of a monster. There can't be more than twenty warriors with him, and I don't recognize any of them. If he confronts me and I don't overcome him, I'm a nobody." To Izad-Goshasp and Yalan-Sineh he said, "Men don't hide their bravery; we don't need more than four of us to defeat them." There was a man there called Janforouz, who preferred night to day; Bahram put him in command of his troops, while he and three companions went out to confront the enemy.

When Khosrow saw Bahram, he said to the Persians, "Their men are coming. Don't let your hearts fail now, because I'm finally face to face with my destiny. I'm here with my mace, and there is that malignant Bahram; fight against these rebels to my rule! There are fourteen of you, three of them; God forbid that they defeat you!" Niatus and his Byzantine companions had no choice but to prepare for combat. Other men made their way into the mountains where they could look down on the two groups, and everyone said, "Why is the king throwing his life away like this? Why should he leave behind all his fine cavalry and go into battle alone?" They raised their hands to the heavens in horror, believing that Khosrow was as good as killed already.

Bahram urged his horse forward and Yalan-Sineh and Izad-Goshasp accompanied him. When Khosrow's companions saw the enemy, most of them were like a flock of sheep scattering before a wolf. The king stood his

ground as they fled, but he too had no choice but to wheel his horse about as Izad-Goshasp bore down on him. Gostahm, Banduy, and Gerdui were still with him: the royal hero called on God's help and said to Gostahm, "What is the point of my fighting if my men flee from me?" Gostahm replied, "Their cavalry are upon us, you can't fight them alone!" Khosrow looked back at their pursuers and saw that Bahram rode ahead of the rest. To save his skin, he cut away the straps of his horse's black barding, so that it could flee more quickly. His companions lagged behind, but his enemies began to close on him. As he rode, he came up against a mountain in which there was a narrow defile. He turned and his three enemies faced him; behind him was the defile, which narrowed to a cul-de-sac. The world's king was alone, cut off from his companions. He dismounted from his horse and began hurriedly to climb the mountain, but there was no way forward and the watching warriors despaired of his life. There was no place to make a stand, and no way to escape, and Bahram came rushing toward him. He called out to Khosrow, "Deceitful fool, now the abyss is opening beneath your glory! Why did you deliver yourself into my hands?"

When the king saw the desperate straits he was in, with his enemy's sword behind him and the rock ahead, he prayed aloud to God, "O world Creator, you are above the turnings of fate! Help me in my distress! It is you I turn to, not Saturn or Mercury."

> *Before the echo of this prayer had died,*
> *Redoubled from the flinty mountainside,*
> *Sorush appeared; Khosrow stared in dismay—*
> *The angel's clothes were green, his horse was gray.*
> *He paused, then lifted Khosrow by the arm,*
> *And set him down where he was safe from harm*
> *(There's no surprise in this; the miracle*
> *Was God's, with him all things are possible).*
> *Now Khosrow wept and asked: "What is your name?"*
> *The angel said, "I am Sorush. I came*
> *In answer to your faith, and soon you'll be*
> *The world's king, glorious in your sovereignty:*
> *You'll reign for thirty-eight long years if you*
> *Act righteously in everything you do."*
> *He vanished, and the world has never known*
> *A vision like the one Khosrow was shown.*

Bahram was astonished at all this and called repeatedly on God, saying, "When I fight with men I hope I'll never lack for bravery, but now I think I am fighting with the spirit world, and I must weep for my bad fortune."

On the other side of the mountain Niatus prayed to God for help, while Mariam scored her face with her nails in her anxiety for her husband. The hearts of the Byzantine troops on the plain and in the foothills were filled with foreboding, and when Niatus lost sight of Khosrow, he drew Mariam's golden litter aside and said to her, "Stay where you are. I fear that the Persian king has been killed." At that moment, Khosrow appeared in the distance on the mountainside; all of the army rejoiced, and Mariam's heart was freed from dread. Khosrow came down from the mountain and told Mariam what he had seen: "My lovely Byzantine princess, it was God who saved me," he said. "I didn't flee out of cowardice or hang back from the fight. I was trapped in a rocky defile and called on the Creator for help, and he revealed to his slave secrets he had kept hidden. I saw things that the great Feraydun, Tur, Salm, and Afrasyab did not dream of, and they are portents of victory and royal power." The king told her what he had experienced, and then he ordered his army to prepare for battle and to remember Khosrow as they fought. For his part, Bahram was filled with consternation and regretted all he had done.

The Battle between Khosrow Parviz and Bahram Chubineh

Khosrow's army came down from the foothills, and the world turned black with the dust sent up by its cavalry, while from the other direction Bahram led his army forward, so that there was no brightness left in the day. Bahram said, "Whoever leads an army needs to be wise, brave, and capable; the warriors who have seen my lance and my heroic spirit have chosen me over Khosrow, and I shall hurl the name of Nushin-Ravan into the dust." Making wildly for the king, he went ahead of the main body of his army, readied his bow, and notched an arrow to the string. Quickly he loosed the arrow toward the king's waist, but the arrow faltered in its flight, and when a slave saw it strike, he was able to pluck it out from the brocade in which the king was clothed. The king rushed forward against Bahram and lunged with his lance. Bahram's body was protected by a cuirass and the lance split with the impact; nevertheless, Bahram was terrified by the blow. The king sprang forward once again, bringing his sword down on Bahram's helmet; his sword, too, broke in pieces, and the blade stayed lodged in the helmet. Everyone who saw this or who heard the clash of metal on metal praised the king's courage. Their warriors followed the two, and battle was joined. Banduy hurried over to the king and cried, "Your crown is more exalted than the moon; this army is like a host of ants or locusts, covering all the desert and wastelands. It is not right that blood should be shed needlessly, or that a king attack his subjects. If anyone asks us for quarter, it would be better to grant it than to kill or wound him in battle." Khosrow replied, "I've no desire to avenge myself against those who repent of their sins; they are all under my protection, they are the jewels in my crown."

Night came down from the dark mountains, and the two armies separated and went back to their camps. The cries of the sentries and the jingling of bells meant that few of the soldiers fell asleep. Ambitious Banduy selected a brave herald with a strong loud voice and ordered him to mount his horse and get ready to wake anyone who slept. The two went out into no-man's land between the two armies and, when they were close to the enemy's camp, the herald cried out: "You slaves who have sinned and whose luck has run out, even if you have sinned more than any other man and distinguished yourself in battle against him, the king swears by God that he will forgive the crimes you have committed in public and in secret." When this cry was heard in the darkness everyone pricked up his ears, and Bahram's famous warriors prepared to steal away.

When the bright sun appeared above the mountaintops, and day made the land shine like silk, the plain was empty of people; they had crept away in the night, unbeknownst to Bahram. No one was to be seen in the tents, except a few of Bahram's closest friends and advisors. As Bahram walked among the empty tents and realized what had happened, he said to his companions, "Fly from this place, don't wait for disaster to strike." He asked the cameleers for three thousand camels, fine mounts that would foam at the mouth and bear heavy burdens. He loaded them with all the portable wealth he had—carpets and provisions, gold and silver, his ivory throne, bracelets, gold torques and crowns—then he mounted his horse and prepared to retreat.

Bahram Chubineh Flees to the Emperor of China

Bahram and his remaining soldiers trusted neither the road nor the loyalty of the countryside they were traveling through. With terror in his heart, Bahram took his gold and silver by trackless ways. Yalan-Sineh and Izad-Goshasp rode to one side of the army, telling stories of ancient kings as they went; Bahram rode ahead, his heart filled with regret and anguish. A humble village, too lowly to supply the wants of a nobleman, came into view in the distance. Because their throats were dry with thirst, Bahram stopped at an old woman's house. Politely they asked for bread and water. The crone heard them out and set an old basket containing barley bread in front of them, together with a tattered water skin. Yalan-Sineh handed the barsom to Bahram, but he was so sunk in sorrow he forgot to observe the ritual silence while eating. They ate the bread, asked for wine, and murmured their prayers. The old woman said, "You want wine, do you? I've wine and an old dried gourd: I split the gourd when it was fresh, and I dried it to use as a cup, and placed it over the wine." Bahram said, "As long as there's wine, we don't need any finer cup than that." The old woman went and brought her cup, which delighted Bahram. He filled it with wine, to please her, and said, "Now, mother, tell us what news you've heard about the world's business." The crone said,

> "My brain's grown tired with all I've heard today:
> So many folks from town have come this way
> And all they'll talk about is Bahram's battle
> Against the king, and such like tittle-tattle.
> He had to run away, so people claim,
> And hasn't got a soldier to his name."

Bahram said, "Tell me then, do you think Bahram was wise to do what he did? Or do you think he's an ambitious fool?" The woman said,

> *"Good sir, what devil's darkened your clear eyes?*
> *Bahram rebelled, and everyone who's wise*
> *Just laughed at him; nobody reckons he*
> *Could win against a royal enemy."*

Bahram said, "If he asks you, tell him to drink wine from a gourd, and keep a basket of barley bread for him till the next barley harvest comes round." This was Bahram's supper, and he stayed there that night, hoping to find some rest for his spirit, though he was unable to.

At this point, Ferdowsi unexpectedly breaks off his narrative for a moment to insert a lament for the death of his son.

Now that I'm more than sixty-five years old,
It would be wrong of me to hope for gold.
Better to heed my own advice, and grieve
That my dear son is dead. Why did he leave?
I should have gone; but no, the young man went
And left his lifeless father to lament.
I long to overtake him; when I do
I'll say, "I should have quit the world, not you,
And in your going, my belovèd boy,
You left your father destitute of joy.
You were my help in all adversity;
Why, now I'm old, have you abandoned me?
Did you perhaps find younger friends, who led
You from my side, to travel on ahead?"
At thirty-seven, his unhappy heart
Despaired and he was ready to depart;
When difficulties came he'd always shown
Me kindness, now he's left me here alone.
He went, while grief and bitter tears remain,
And inward suffering, and heartfelt pain.
He's gone into the light, and he'll prepare
A place to welcome his dear father there:
So many years have passed, and surely he
Is waiting there impatiently for me!
May God illuminate your soul, my son,
And wisdom keep you safe where you have gone.
May God forgive my sins, and may the night
In which I labor be suffused with light.

*N*ow that Bahram had fled, Khosrow Parviz had no more need for his Byzantine allies, who returned home. Bahram reached China, where he ingratiated himself with the emperor by killing a rebellious chieftain who was threatening the court, and then by slaying a lion that had killed one of the emperor's daughters. Bahram's reward was to be married to another of the imperial daughters. Khosrow Parviz sent a letter to the emperor demanding Bahram's extradition; the emperor's response was to put Bahram in charge of an army to invade Iran.

Khosrow Sends Khorad-Borzin to the Emperor

When the king learned that this wolf Bahram had emerged from his thicket once more and was at the head of an army whose dust obscured the sky's brightness, he said to his counselor Khorad-Borzin, "Hurry to the emperor, and speak to him with all the persuasiveness you can muster. In Persia and beyond, you are the most knowledgeable of men, and you have the most eloquence." He opened the doors to his treasury and brought out such jewels, swords, and golden belts that Khorad-Borzin murmured the name of God in wonder. He took these objects as gifts and made his way to the Oxus; from there he continued by a secret route. When at last he reached the palace, he selected a messenger to announce his arrival to the emperor.

As soon as he heard the news, the emperor had the audience hall prepared and gave orders that the envoy be admitted. Khorad-Borzin entered humbly, made his obeisance before the emperor, and said briefly, "Your slave will speak when you order him to." The emperor replied, "Eloquent talk will make an old man's heart young again: tell us the profitable things you have to say. What's said is the marrow of a meeting, things left unsaid are only the skin." These words reminded Khorad-Borzin of the ancient enmity between their countries. He began his speech by invoking the world's Creator, who has made the heaven's sphere and the earth and time, and both the weak and the powerful; then he spoke of the certainty of death, and the history of the Persian kings. He continued: "Now the king of Persia is your relative, and his happiness and sorrow depend on your good and bad fortune. In the time of great kings, his mother's father was the emperor of China. Now in these days, when many things have changed, our alliance is renewed. May God who bestows victory keep you, and may the nobles of the earth be as your slaves." The emperor listened to him, then said, "You are a wise man; if there is another like you in Persia he must be eloquent enough to praise the heavens!" A place was set aside at court for the envoy, and the emperor kept him close by. At his command the gifts were counted out to the court treasurer, and the emperor said to him, "May you never want for wealth in the world. If there is something I can give you in exchange for all you have brought, tell me what it is. But you are more splendid than all gifts; you are the crown of the world's wise men."

Khorad's lodgings were beautifully decorated with all kinds of fabrics, and he was always welcome to join the emperor at table, out hunting, during the court festivities, or to drink wine with him. He waited for a chance to make his case; one day he saw an opportunity and bravely spoke up: "Bahram has an evil nature," he said. "He's more malevolent than Ahriman himself. He sells men of experience and understanding for profit, and for a paltry profit at that. It was Hormozd who promoted him, who lifted him up above the sun's sphere. Before that no one had heard of him, but then he was successful in everything he touched. He might act very well toward you now, but in the end he will betray you, as he betrayed the Persian king; he has no respect for either kings or God. If you send him to the Persian king, you'll lift the king's head above the moon with happiness. All Persia and China will then be yours, and you can have your palace anywhere you wish." The emperor was astonished at these words. His eyes darkened, and he said, "If you would keep my goodwill, don't say such things. I'm not a suspicious man and I don't break my word; a man who breaks his word has the dust as his shroud." When Khorad heard this, he knew that his mission had failed and that Bahram had encouraged the emperor with hopes of conquering Persia: to talk further with him would be a waste of breath.

Having lost hope of winning over the emperor, he decided to approach the empress, and he looked for someone with access to her. He met with a palace chamberlain and beguiled him with stories about Khosrow Parviz. Then he said to him, "I need to meet with the empress; help me be introduced to her as a scribe." The man replied, "There's no hope of that; Bahram Chubineh's her son-in-law, and all the power he has here is derived from her. You're a learned man—seek some other way, and tell no one of your secrets." Khorad-Borzin could see no solution to his difficulties.

There was an old Turk named Qalun, who was held in contempt by the other Turks; he wore sheepskins, and lived off whey and millet. Khorad-Borzin summoned this man to his fine quarters, where he gave him gold and silver coins, clothes, good meals, and entertained him with men of standing and importance. Khorad was cautious and patient, sly, and careful, and while he was cultivating Qalun he also continued to question the chamberlain of the empress's palace. This man, who visited the empress day and night, was tight-lipped and revealed nothing, but one day he said to

Khorad, "You're a scholar, and a learned man, and if you had some knowledge of medicine too, and were famous for it, you would be as welcome as a new crown on the empress's head, because her daughter is ill." Khorad replied, "I have some medical knowledge. If you tell the empress, I will do my best in this business." The chamberlain hurried to the empress and said that a new doctor had arrived. She replied, "May you live in happiness for this news: bring him here, and don't stand scratching your head, get on with it!" He ran to Khorad-Borzin and said, "See that you do this secretly. Go to her and don't tell her your name; just be an amiable doctor."

Khorad went to the empress and saw that her daughter was suffering from a liver complaint. He asked for pomegranate juice and a particular kind of cress that grows on the banks of streams, and with these he tried to bring down the fever in her brain. By God's will, after seven days the girl was well again, and as resplendent as the new moon. The empress brought a purse of gold coins from her treasury and five lengths of gold cloth. She said, "Take these worthless gifts, and ask for anything else you desire." Khorad replied, "Keep these things for now; I shall ask for your help when I need it."

Khorad-Borzin Sends Qalun to Bahram Chubineh

For his part, Bahram had reached Marv, where he had drawn up an army as splendid as a pheasant's feathers. A messenger from the emperor reached him, saying, "Let no one go into Persia, because if Khosrow Parviz learns of our plans, he'll change his disposition toward us; have it announced that if anyone crosses into Iran without a sealed order from me, I'll have him hacked in two, and I swear by God that I won't let him ransom his life with silver."

For three months Khorad watched these secret preparations. Then, sick at heart, he summoned Qalun and made much of him. He said, "Every man in the world has some kind of secret in his heart. You used to beg door to door in China for coarse barley bread and millet, and sheepskins to wear; now your food is fine bread and lamb, and you dress in white silk. Look how you were and how you are, how men's curses have turned to congratulations! Now your life is drawing to an end; you've seen many days and nights, mountains and plains. There is something I want you to do. It's dangerous, and you may gain a throne from it, or you may end up in the black earth. I've obtained a copy of the emperor's seal, and I want you to travel quickly to Bahram and stay in Marv. There you're to put on your black sheepskin, and take a knife with you. Wait for the day of the month that is called Bahram, because he believes that's an inauspicious day for him. I've watched him for years, and on that day he never wants a crowd of people near him; he hides himself away wrapped in Chinese brocade. Say that you're bringing the great lord Bahram Chubineh a message from the emperor's daughter; see that you keep the knife in your sleeve until he calls for you. When you're admitted say, 'Her majesty ordered me to whisper her message in your ear, so that no one else may hear it.' And when he asks, 'What message?' run to him and plunge the knife into his gut, and then look for some way to escape. Whoever hears him cry out will flee from him—to the stables, or to look to the carpets or treasury; no one's going to harm you for this murder. And if you are killed for this, you've already experienced the good and bad that this world has to offer. But it's likely that no one will pay any attention to you, and if you can get away with this, you have bought the world and paid its price; King Khosrow Parviz will give you a city, a portion of the world for your own."

Qalun said, "I'll need a pass to get to him. I've reached the age of a hundred; how much longer am I going to live in want? My body and soul are ready to sacrifice themselves for you, since you've looked after me in the days of my wretchedness." When Khorad heard this he hurried to the empress and said to her, "The time has come, your majesty, for me to ask for your help. Two of my men have been thrown into chains, and I need your assistance to set them free. Get me a copy of the emperor's seal; you'll be giving me my life back if you do this." The empress said, "He's in a drunken sleep; I'll take an impression of his seal from his finger." She asked Khorad for clay, and then she went to her husband's bedside and impressed his seal ring on the clay; this she gave to Khorad, who thanked her and handed it over to the old man, Qalun.

Bahram Chubineh Is Killed by Qalun

Qalun took the impression of the seal and made his way quickly to Marv. There he waited until the day of Bahram, the one Bahram thought of as inauspicious. Bahram was alone in his house with a slave, eating a meal of pomegranates, apples, and quinces. Qalun went there and said to the doorman, "I'm not a warrior or a free man; I've been sent by the emperor's daughter. Her ladyship told me a secret to whisper in the king's ear: by his grace, she is pregnant, and unwell. If you could announce me, I'll give the message to his majesty." The doorman hurried to Bahram and said, "An ugly messenger dressed in a sheepskin is here; he says he has a message for your majesty from the emperor's daughter." Bahram said, "Tell him to show his face in here."

Qalun approached and put his head inside the door. Bahram saw a weak old man standing there and said, "If you've a letter, bring it here." Qalun replied, "It's something she said, that's all. I don't want to say it in front of anyone else." Bahram said, "Be quick, then, come and tell me in my ear; don't stand on ceremony." Qalun went forward with the knife in his sleeve, and then his treachery became apparent: he bent as if to whisper in Bahram's ear and plunged the knife into him, and the house was immediately in an uproar. As Bahram cried out, "Ah, I'm dead," people came running to him. He said, "Grab that man! Ask him who sent him here." Everyone who was in the house descended on the old man; they broke his legs, and the servants slapped and punched him, but no matter how hard they hit him he never opened his lips, though they tormented him from midday to midnight. By then his arms were also broken; they flung him into the courtyard, and with grief in their hearts they returned to Bahram.

Blood flowed from his wound; his cheeks were flushed and sighs escaped his lips. At that moment his sister Gordyeh came to him, tearing out her hair in her anguish. Distracted with grief, she laid her wounded brother's head against her breast and cried out,

"You were a knight whose presence spread such fear
That lions would slink away when you came near;
Who felled this pillar of the world? Who planned
This crime and put the dagger in his hand?
Alas for your ambition and your might,
Your prowess that put savage lions to flight;
You bowed to neither God nor king; whose blow
So cruelly laid your mammoth body low?
Who wrenched the roots up of this mountainside?
Who felled this cypress in its noble pride?
Who stretched his hand out to this princely crown
And flung it so contemptuously down?

Who filled this sea with earth? Who shattered this
Great rocky peak and made it an abyss?
We're strangers here, with no one to protect
Our lives and wealth, or treat us with respect—
My lord, I said to you repeatedly,
'Do not uproot the tree of loyalty,
Because if one Sasanian girl remains
And crowns herself, it will be she who reigns,
And all the provinces in Persia's land
Will willingly submit to her command:
Their hearts will not betray this family.'
But you ignored my words, my lord, and me.
Regret your actions, and the paths you trod,
And take your guilty soul from here to God.
Evil has come to our great house; I weep
That all our foes are wolves, and we are sheep.'

When the wounded man heard her words, and understood the wisdom of her heart, and saw her face scored by her nails, her hair torn from her head, her heart filled with anguish, and her eyes with tears, he spoke sadly and falteringly: "Your advice lacked for nothing, but now my life draws to an end. Your advice had no effect on me; a demon misled me. There never was a king greater than Jamshid—the world lived in awe and hope of him— and yet he was misled by demons and made the earth a dark and fearsome place for himself. There was King Kavus, who ruled the world and was blessed by fortune, and he too was destroyed by a wretched demon; he ascended into the sky to see the turning spheres, the moon, and the sun, and you know the evil that came to him because of this. A demon misled me too, and I strayed from righteousness. I regret the evil I have done, but I trust that God will pardon me. Thus was it written on my forehead; why should I grieve for old sorrows again? The waters rise above my head, and all my joys and sorrows are as so much wind. Thus was it written, and what had to be came to pass, neither more nor less. I remember the words of advice you gave me. They are like jeweled earrings in my ears, but now that justice and injustice come to an end for me, do not repeat those words any more. Turn your face toward God, trust that fortune will smile again for you. The only friend you have against evil is God; speak with no one of either sorrow or joy. This is the portion I have had in the world, this and no more; now it has come to an end, and I must depart."

Then he said to Yalan-Sineh, "I hand the army over to you; pray for good fortune. Look after my virtuous sister; there is no finer advisor in the world than she is. Don't be separated from one another, stay always together. Don't remain in this enemy land; I have traveled here and am sickened by it. Go immediately to Khosrow Parviz; tell him your story and hear what he says. If he forgives you, have only him as the sun and moon of your lives. Build me a tomb in Persia, and destroy the palace I made for myself at Rey. I undertook so much for the emperor of China, and I had no thanks for it; this was not a just reward for my pains, that he should send some devil to kill me. Thus has it always been for the Persians; there has always been some evil demon guiding them."

Bahram had a scribe come and write a letter on silk. He said, "Tell the emperor: 'Bahram has gone; he has gone wretchedly and in sorrow, and with his ambitions thwarted.' Write, 'Look after those I leave behind and save them from their enemies, since I never did you any harm, and sought only right-eousness and wisdom on your behalf.'" Then he spoke at length to his sister, first pressing her beloved head against his chest, then putting his mouth to her ear; in this fashion, his eyes filled with blood and he gave up his soul.

Everyone there wept bitterly for him, and their hearts were filled with anguish. His sister was loud in her laments, going over in her mind all he had said to her, and her heart was split in two with grief. They constructed a narrow coffin of silver and put a muslin undershirt on him, then wrapped his warlike body in brocade. Lastly they sprinkled camphor over the body until his head was hidden beneath it.

Khorad escaped back to Iran, where he was warmly welcomed by Khosrow Parviz. The emperor of China wished to honor Bahram Chubineh's memory by proposing marriage to his sister Gordyeh, and he sent a letter to her to this effect.

Gordyeh Consults with Her Advisors and Flees from Marv

This young, wise woman sat and deliberated with her advisors. She said, "A new proposal has come to me, and it will always be remembered in my heart. The emperor of China has asked for my hand in the most ornate language. He has no faults; he is a great king, a brave man, and the lord of Turan. But whenever the Turks and Persians have tried to ally themselves in this way, the result has been sorrow and trouble. Look at Seyavash and Afrasyab; what did Seyavash gain except exposure to the burning sun? No mother ever bore such a fine young man, and yet he was destroyed. And what did Seyavash's son do but raise the dust of battle over Iran and Turan? We must arrange matters so that we flee in secret from these Turks to Persia. I have been worried about this for some time and have written a letter to Gerdui, asking him to intercede for us with Khosrow Parviz, and to tell him all that we've suffered."

Everyone there said, "You are our mistress, an iron mountain cannot make you quail, we will follow wherever you lead. You are more clever than a wise man, more intelligent than a knowledgeable vizier. We are all your servants and yours to command, and we will support you in your response to the emperor's request." She reviewed her troops, and had money made ready. She watched the army as it passed before her and chose one thousand one hundred and sixty men, champions who would not desert even if each faced ten enemies. She paid them and then returned to her house, where she said to the army commanders, "Once a man has decided on a journey his heart should be steadfast through good and bad fortune. He does not fear the might of the enemy, even if severed heads rain down on him from the clouds. We are strangers in Turan; we have no friends or allies here, we are weak and helpless among these Chinese noblemen. We must travel in darkness when our enemies are bewildered by sleep. Don't be anxious about the journey, even if a Chinese army attacks us, for surely their chieftains will come after us with their heavy maces. And if they come, stand together and give blows as good as those you receive. If any of you are not with me in this, you can stay here."

With one voice they replied, "We are your servants, and we will not turn aside from your commands." Then they prepared for battle against the Chinese forces; Yalan-Sineh, Mehr, and Izad-Goshasp mounted their horses and said, "It is better to die with honor than to live with the Chinese triumphing over us." Meanwhile Gordyeh visited the camel caravans and asked to see camels paraded before her; she chose three thousand of them and loaded them with their baggage. When night fell Gordyeh mounted her horse; she sat like a proud warrior, grasping a mace in her hand. Her horse was covered with splendid barding, and she wore armor and a helmet and a sword at her side. Her army rode forward like the wind, through the dark night and the bright day.

The Emperor Sends Tovorg after Gordyeh: She Kills Him

Many of the Persian soldiers threw themselves on the mercy of the Chinese emperor. His brother Tovorg came to the emperor and said, "You are a warlike lord; though many Persians have appealed to us for quarter, their army is making its way to Iran. If they escape, this will shame you forever, and your soldiers and people will laugh at you." The Chinese emperor's face clouded with fury and he said, "Hurry and get an army together; see how far they've gone. When you catch up with them, don't use force at first, but try to see what persuasive talk will do. They don't know how we go about these things; it may be that you can break their determination by talk. Speak kindly to them, make much of them, treat them respectfully and chivalrously. But if one of them should attack you, then play the man and don't hesitate to fight: make Marv their graveyard and its earth as bright as a pheasant's feathers with their blood."

Tovorg set off with six thousand Turkish cavalry and on the fourth day caught up with the Persians. When their lionhearted leader saw them, she felt no anxiety. She hurried over to the leader of the caravan of camels and had the baggage placed behind the troops, and then inspected the plain where it was likely that a battle would be fought. She donned her brother's armor and mounted a high-stepping charger. The two armies drew up their forces, face to face, and every man there was ready to sacrifice his life. Tovorg, whom the emperor referred to as an old wolf, was at the head of his men, and he called out to the Persians: "Isn't that noble woman somewhere in your ranks?" Because Gordyeh was dressed in heavy armor, Tovorg did not recognize her, and once again he called out, "Where in this company

shall I find the sister of the murdered king? I need to talk with her, both about the days that are gone by and about new matters." Gordyeh replied, "I am the person you're looking for, and I'm ready to ride my horse against a ravening lion."

When Tovorg heard her, and saw her seated on her warhorse, her mien as threatening as a lion's, he was astonished and said, "The emperor has chosen you from all his realm, so that you will be a reminder to him of that great knight Bahram. He said that if you listen to his words he will reward you handsomely. He said to me, 'Hurry to her, and tell her that if she is not pleased with my offer then I can change my mind. Talk to her and come to an agreement with her, and only if she won't accept your advice should you detain her.'"

Gordyeh said, "Let us move aside from the main body of the army. There I'll answer everything you've said." Tovorg came forward from his troops, to where the valiant warrior stood. When she saw that he was alone, this resourceful woman glared at him from beneath her dark helmet. "You saw Bahram; you admired him as a horseman and a warrior," she said. "He was a mother and a father to me, but his days have come to an end. Now I shall test your mettle and fight against you. Then, If you think I'm ready for a husband tell me, and we'll see if there is a husband who pleases me." She urged her horse forward, and Izad-Goshasp rode behind her. She lunged with her lance at Tovorg's waist, and split the fastenings of his armor, piercing his body. Yalan-Sineh led her troops in a general attack, and the Chinese army was thrown into confusion; many were killed, or hurled to the ground, or wounded. The Persians pursued them for two parasangs, and few of them remained mounted; the plain was like a river of blood, with headless bodies and others sprawling in the dust.

After her victory she crossed into Persia, and there wrote a letter to her brother Gerdui, explaining all that had happened to Bahram and herself.

Gostahm Revolts against Khosrow Parviz and Proposes Marriage to Gordyeh

At this time Khosrow Parviz sent a messenger into Khorasan and said to him, "Speak with no one on your journey, but go straight to the lord of the marches, Gostahm, and say that he is to come to me as soon as he reads my letter." When the messenger reached Khorasan he went to Gostahm's court and repeated the king's message. But knowing that Khosrow Parviz was young and bloodthirsty, when Gostahm received this order he gathered his forces together and went to cities ruled by men of authority, visiting Sari, Amol and Gorgan. In a drunken rage the king killed Gostahm's brother, Banduy, and when Gostahm heard about this, he bit his hand, dismounted from his horse, tore at his clothes, and heaped dust on his head. He knew that the king wished to destroy him, in revenge for his part in the death of the king's father, Hormozd. He rode like the wind, lamenting and mourning, to the forest of Narvan, gathering men as he went. Near the mountains at Amol he hid his army in the woods and began a series of raids on the area. Wherever there were men without work, he gave them bread, and they joined with him. Whenever he heard that the king's troops were nearby, he attacked and destroyed them.

Meanwhile Gerdui went to Khosrow Parviz and told him of his sister Gordyeh's exploits, and of how she had defeated the emperor's forces at Marv. Gostahm too heard that Bahram's days had come to an end, and that Gordyeh had left China's savage ruler and defeated his forces in battle. Gostahm led his forces out to welcome her, and when she heard of this, Gordyeh and her chief advisors set off from Amui. When he saw her troops in the distance, Gostahm urged his horse ahead of the main body of his men. He came before Gordyeh lamenting for Bahram, and then told her of his grief for Banduy, wiping his tears away with the sleeve of his robe. He saw Yalan-Sineh and Izad-Goshasp, and as he wept he dismounted from his horse. He told them how the king had killed Banduy, and how evil days had befallen him. He said, "It was as though the king had forgotten that he is the son of Banduy's sister, and that Banduy had shed his own blood for him. He cut off Banduy's hands and feet, just as one would expect from a man of his nature. What hopes can you have of such a man? He will do worse than this to you and your friends, and meat will be cheap in the town when he butchers you. As soon as he sees Yalan-Sineh in the distance he'll be eager for revenge, because you were Bahram's commander, and it was through him you became powerful in the world. Whoever knows Khosrow Parviz avoids him; the best thing for him is a sharp knife at his throat! But join with me, and we'll plan something." Hoping to save themselves from harm, all those who heard him accepted his suggestion. Then he spoke earnestly to Gordyeh about Bahram's exploits, and at his words she softened, and many thoughts filled her mind. All of her men went over to Gostahm, and hope brightened their dark forebodings.

One day Gostahm said to Yalan-Sineh, "What would this woman say to being married?" Yalan-Sineh replied, "I'll prepare her mind for the idea." Seeking out Gordyeh, he said, "I know the world, and I have seen you are a wise woman. It was right that you put off the emperor and chose to come back to Persia. What do you think of Gostahm as a husband? He's the king's uncle, and a powerful commander." Gordyeh answered, "If I take a Persian husband, my family won't die out." Yalan-Sineh gave her to Gostahm, who was a fine warrior, and of noble lineage. Gostahm thought her as sweet as a fresh apple, and in his good fortune he had no suspicion of disaster. His days were renewed in fighting against the armies the king sent, and as they were defeated his confidence increased.

Gostahm Is Killed by Gordyeh

As time passed the king became more alarmed by Gostahm. One day he burst out to Gerdui, "Gostahm has married Gordyeh; her warriors went over to him, and I think they did it on her advice. One of my informants has come from Amol and told me of everything they'd kept hidden." He talked in this way until night fell, and men's eyes grew weary, tired out by his words. As the servants brought candles and wine he cleared the hall of strangers and sat alone with his advisor, Gerdui. The two of them talked over the business of Gordyeh at length, and Khosrow said, "I've sent any number of armies against Amol, and the men have either been killed or returned wounded and complaining about their misfortunes. I can only see one solution to this, because so far my plans have weakened the crown and throne. When Bahram Chubineh forgot his duty, Gordyeh always supported us. I've an idea, but don't spread it abroad. I must write a letter to Gordyeh, one that's as beguiling as a stream of wine in the garden of paradise. I'll say to her, 'I shall be your friend everywhere and in every way. For a long time my tongue has not revealed the secrets of my heart, but now it's time to speak out, and Gerdui is my confidant in this. Find some means to get rid of that wretched miscreant Gostahm; if you can put him beneath a gravestone, my heart and household are yours. When you have done this I'll give provinces to your army and your companions, everyone you wish, and they will rule in those lands. You will have the golden chamber in my women's apartments, and all my desire for vengeance will be at an end. I swear I will do these things; I will add more oaths to this oath, and if I break my word, may all my alliances fail.'"

Gerdui responded, "Long may you flourish, as shining as Venus in the sign of Virgo! You know that, compared with your life, I set no value on my soul and children, or my land and friends, precious though they are to me. I'll send someone with this letter to Gordyeh and make her dark soul bright again. I shall send my own wife, and this will allay any suspicions; this is a woman's work, especially a clever woman's. The more I consider this, the more I see the message must be sent to my sister. This matter will soon be over with, and to your advantage; we must do neither less nor more than you have said."

Khosrow was overjoyed when he heard this, and all his worries disappeared like the wind. He asked that paper and ink made from musk be brought from the treasury, and then he wrote a letter as lovely as a garden, as a rose whose petals are like the beloved's cheeks. It was filled with promises and oaths, adulation and advice, and when the ink on the greeting had dried, the letter was sealed with black musk imprinted with the name of King Khosrow Parviz. Gerdui also wrote a letter filled with advice and other matters; the king's letter was placed inside his, and the two were wrapped in silk. His resourceful wife heard all these words, took the package, and rode to the forest of Narvan as one woman bearing a message to another.

Gordyeh's face lit up like the springtime to see her. They talked about Bahram for a while and tears dropped from their eyes. Then the messenger handed over her husband's letter, with the king's hidden inside it. When this lionhearted woman saw the king's missive it was as if she saw the moon before her. She smiled and said, "If someone has five friends, this will be no trouble." She kept the letter secret from the court, but read it to five of her confidants, who took one another's hands and swore to aid her. She hid the five in her sleeping apartments, and when night came she extinguished the lights and placed her hand over her husband's mouth. The five accomplices rushed to the bedside and struggled with the man, who was drunk, until finally they suppressed his cries and smothered him. The town was soon in an uproar, and fires were lit in the streets. When she heard the noise, this intrepid woman put on her Byzantine armor; she called her Persians to her in the darkness and told them she had killed Gostahm. Then she showed them the king's message and encouraged them to be of good heart. Her men acclaimed her for what she had done and scattered jewels on the letter.

Gordyeh's Letter to Khosrow Parviz

This fearless woman asked for ink and a pen case, and sat with her advisors. She wrote a letter to the king concerning his enemies and allies. She began with praise of those who cleanse their hearts of vengeance and continued, "The deed that the king commanded has been accomplished, and all that his allies would wish has come to pass. Gostahm's forces are in disarray, by the grace of the world's king. What orders have you for me now; what will you demand of your slave?"

When the letter reached Khosrow, his approval of Gordyeh flourished again. He summoned an eloquent messenger, one who knew all the ancient stories, and wrote a letter as beautiful as a painting by the Chinese master Arzhang. In it he summoned her to his court and called her the moon's diadem. The messenger came to Gordyeh like the wind and told her what Khosrow had said, and when that lionhearted woman read the king's letter she was like a rose that blossoms in springtime. She mustered her troops and gave them their provisions, and at daybreak the baggage was loaded.

A great company of men came out to greet her, and when she reached the court she found the king's heart filled with anxiety to please her. She and her chieftains brought before him innumerable gold coins and jewels, brocades woven with gold, crowns and belts, golden thrones and golden crowns, and all these were counted out to the king's treasurer. The king looked at this elegant cypress, whose face was as lovely as the spring, and whose walk was like that of a pheasant, and had her conducted to the harem, where she was a given a rank higher than all his other women. Then he sent for her brother, his vizier, Gerdui, and asked for and obtained her hand in marriage, according to the rites of their religion. He rewarded her companions with robes of honor, as well as gold and silver, and every kind of wealth.

The Destruction of the City of Rey

Many long days passed, and Gordyeh wanted for nothing. One day, when Khosrow Parviz was drinking wine with the wise men of the court, and with his noblemen and warriors, a goblet was discovered with the name of Bahram written on it. The king ordered that it be thrown away, and everyone cursed Bahram, the goblet, and the man who had brought it there. He said, "Let Bahram's town, Rey, be trampled beneath war elephants' feet, its inhabitants driven out, and let it be turned to a wasteland." His vizier said to the king, "You are a living memorial of the Kayanid kings, but consider, Rey is a great town and it would be wrong for it to be trampled beneath elephants' feet. God would not approve of this, and neither would the wise men of the world." The king replied, "Then the place needs an ill-natured governor, an incompetent fool, someone who is ignorant and foul-mouthed." A courtier called Bahman said, "If the king wishes, we will look for such an incompetent, but we need some kind of guide." Khosrow said, "He should have red hair, a crooked nose, and an ugly face; he must be an infamous man, with a sallow complexion, someone who's malevolent, short in stature, his heart filled with anguish, base in his nature, vengeful and with a lying tongue; his eyes should be green and squinting, he should have big teeth, and he should lope along the road like a wolf."

The priests were astonished to hear Khosrow talk in this way, and wondered how they would find such a man. People searched the world, inquiring among both rich and poor, and then one day a man came to the king and said, "I saw someone of this description on the road. If the king commands me, I shall bring him here, and he can be sent to Rey." The king gave orders that the man be brought to the court, and when he entered everyone laughed at his appearance. Khosrow said to him, "Well, fool, tell us about how evil you are." The man replied, "I never stop doing evil things, and there's not an atom of wisdom in me. Tell me to do one thing and I'll do another, and I'll fill men's bodies and souls with anguish. I live off lies and I'm incapable of doing good." The king said to him, "And may your evil star keep you that way."

His name was written down in the court records as the governor of Rey, and this shameless man rose to greatness because he was so ugly. He was given a motley army and went off to his new post, taking his evil reputation with him. When he arrived in Rey he banished all shame from his heart. He gave orders that all the gutters on the roofs be torn down, and he took pleasure in watching this done. Then he had all the cats killed, which annoyed the city leaders. Everywhere he went he had a herald go in front of him shouting, "If I see a gutter in place, or a cat in a house, I'll burn the house down and stone its inhabitants." He searched everywhere and, if he found as much as one silver coin, he made its owner wretched. Mice took over the houses, and people despaired of the city. When it rained there were no gutters to carry away the downpour, and there was no one to care for the city. And that is how this ugly, shameless wretch sent from Khosrow's court caused a flourishing city to fall into ruin. The sun beat down on men's heads, and all the city was filled with pain and anguish, while the world ignored their sufferings.

This went on until spring and the month of Farvardin, when the land is adorned with flowers, the world becomes moist with dew, and the mountains and valleys are filled with tulips. The nobility went to their gardens to enjoy themselves, and the foothills of the mountains were dotted with deer and sheep. When Khosrow opened the gates to his gardens, he saw the fountains were filled with doves; he ordered that trumpets be blown, and bowls filled with sweet scents were set down there. He and his courtiers sat on the grass and called for wine, while they chatted amicably together. Gordyeh brought a little kitten, which she had dressed up just like a child. Sitting on a pony, on a gold saddle ornamented with jewels, the kitten had earrings hanging from its ears, and its nails had been painted as red as tulips. Its face was as sweet as springtime; its black eyes looked sleepy, because it had drunk some wine. A golden bridle hung from the pony, and Gordyeh led the kitten around the garden as if he were a child. The king of Persia burst into laughter at this sight, and all his courtiers copied him. He said to Gordyeh, "My beauty, what do you want from me? Tell me what it is you wish for."

This resourceful woman bowed before the king and said, "Great king, give me Rey: consider wisely, and free its sorrowful inhabitants' hearts from their grief. Recall that shameless wretch from Rey. Know him for what he is, a faithless, evil man. He has driven the cats from their houses and destroyed the town's gutters one by one." Khosrow laughed at his wife's words and said, "You are as lovely as the moon and strong enough to destroy an army. Recall that malevolent wretch, that Ahriman, from Rey." And so her good fortune grew in the shadow of the royal tree.

⇥ THE STORY OF KHOSROW AND SHIRIN ⇤

*K*hosrow Parviz's Byzantine wife, Mariam, bore him a son, Shirui. But the court *astrologers predicted that the country would suffer as a result of this child, and that the army would never acclaim him as their leader.*

When Khosrow Parviz had been a fearless young man, in the period while his father was still alive, he had loved Shirin, and had cherished her more than his own sight. In all the world only Shirin pleased him, and he had eyes for no other beautiful women, or for the daughters of the nobility. But then his time was taken up with traveling about the world, and by his battles with Bahram; he seemed to have forsaken his love, and the beautiful Shirin wept day and night for him.

Khosrow Parviz Goes Hunting, Meets with Shirin, and Takes Her to His Harem

One day Parviz decided to go hunting, and the expedition was arranged as had been customary with former kings. Three hundred horses with golden bridles were led out; there were one thousand six hundred loyal footmen carrying javelins, and one thousand four hundred more who carried staves and swords and wore brocade beneath their armor. Following them came five hundred falconers, with sparrow hawks, merlins, and falcons, and then three hundred horsemen leading cheetahs. There were also leopards and lions, whose mouths had been muzzled with gold chains, and a hundred dogs with golden leashes, for running down deer. After them came two thousand musicians, all mounted on camels and wearing golden crowns; they had prepared songs to celebrate the hunt. There were thrones, tents, and pavilions, loaded on camels, as well as stalls for the animals. There were two hundred slaves with censers that burned aloes wood and ambergris, together with two hundred young servants carrying narcissi and crocuses, and they carried these so that the wind bore their scent to Parviz. In front of them went men who scattered water in which musk had been mixed, so that the wind would not suddenly stir up the dust and disturb the king.

When Shirin heard that this entourage was approaching, with the king at its head, she put on a golden dress scented with musk, and over it a surcoat of red Byzantine brocade with a gold ground worked with jewels. She made her cheeks the color of pomegranates, and on her head she placed a crown of imperial splendor. She went up from her royal chamber onto the roof of her palace, and the days of her youth brought her no pleasure. She waited there, with the tears trickling down her cheeks, until Khosrow Parviz approached. When she saw the king's face she stood so that he could see her, and she spoke gently to him about their former days; her eyes were like narcissi that droop with sorrow, and they bathed her cheeks' rosy color as she wept. Beautiful, and in tears, she reproachfully addressed the king:

> *"My lord, my warrior, my king, who lives*
> *Favored by all that heaven's fortune gives,*
> *Where is your love now? Or your tears that I,*
> *And I alone, could comfort once and dry?*
> *Where are the endless nights we turned to day*
> *With tears, and smiles, and amorous sweet play?*
> *Where are our oaths and promises, and where*
> *Are all the vows we vowed we'd always share?"*

And as she spoke her tears fell onto her imperial clothes. Tears welled too in Khosrow's eyes, and his face turned as yellow as the sun. He sent a horse with a golden bridle for her, and forty reliable Byzantine servants, to accompany her to the golden, bejeweled apartments of his harem.

From there he went to his hunting grounds, taking wine and musicians to entertain him, and when he had had his fill of hunting in the plains and hills, he set off in high spirits for the city. All the roads and buildings were decorated to welcome him, and a confused din of trumpets and songs of welcome resounded through the air. He made a royal, imposing figure as he strode into his high castle; Shirin came forward from the inner apartments and kissed his feet, the ground before him, and his chest. The king turned to his chief priest and said, "I want you to think only well of me: marry me to this beautiful woman, and give the good news to the world." Then he married her according to the ancient rites that were customary in those days.

Khosrow Parviz's Nobles Give Him Counsel

When the nobility and army learned that Shirin had joined Khosrow Parviz's harem and that this old relationship had been renewed, the city was filled

with discontent, foreboding, and curses. No one approached Khosrow for three days, and when the sun rose on the fourth day Khosrow summoned his nobles to an audience with him. He said, "I have not seen you for a few days, and this has worried me. I am troubled that something troubles you, and your sorrows fill me with anxiety." When he had finished speaking everyone present held his tongue; no one gave him an answer. Then, one by one, they looked at the chief priest, who, when he perceived this, stood and addressed Khosrow. "You are just and righteous, my lord," he said. "You became king when you were still a young man; you have seen a great deal of both good and evil fortune, and you have heard much good and evil in the world, concerning the great and their actions. But now the lineage of our nobility has been polluted; our greatness has been sullied by this alliance. If the father is pure and the mother is worthless, you should realize that purity cannot issue from them. No man seeks righteousness from a perverse source, which can only harm righteousness. Our hearts are saddened that this vicious demon has become the great king's consort. Is there no other woman in Persia, apart from this one, who pleases the king? If Shirin were not present in the king's harem, his face would shine with righteousness everywhere. Your ancestors, who were wise and just men, never heard of such a matter." The chief priest spoke at length, but the King of Kings gave him no answer.

At dawn the next day the court prepared to assemble. One said, "The chief priest didn't know what he was talking about." Another said, "What he said was full of wisdom." A third remarked, "Today the king will answer him; let's hope he has a good reply ready." All the counselors made their way into the king's presence, and the nobles took their places there. Then a man came in bearing a bowl that glittered like the sun, and he took it to each of the noblemen in turn. Warm blood had been poured into the bowl, and he offered it gently to each of them, but each man turned his face away. A murmuring spread through the assembly and everyone looked at the king, afraid of what he would do. Finally the king said to the Persians gathered there, "Whose blood is this, and why has it been placed in this bowl?" The chief priest said, "This blood is polluted, and everyone who sees it loathes it." He picked up the bowl and had it passed from hand to hand. Then it was cleansed and made shining again with water, and earth was used to scour it.

When the polluted bowl had been purified and shone again, it was filled with wine, with which musk and rosewater were mixed, and it glowed like the sun. Khosrow Parviz said to the chief priest, "Is the bowl what it was, or has it changed now?" The priest replied, "May your majesty flourish, good has been distinguished from evil. At your command what was hellish has become heavenly, and you have made what was ugly beautiful." Khosrow said, "In this land Shirin was considered to be like that bowl of polluted blood; but the bowl in my harem is now filled with wine; it is my scent that fills her now. Shirin's reputation suffered because of me, and it was because of me that she never sought for a partner among the nobility." All his nobles called down blessings on him, saying, "May the earth never be deprived of your reign. Greatness is increased by your greatness, and those you ennoble are the earth's nobility; you are our king, priest, and guide, and the very shadow of God on earth."

Shirin Kills Mariam; Khosrow Parviz Imprisons Shirui

Then the king's magnificence increased, and if before he had shone like the moon, he was now as splendid as the sun. He spent all his time with Mariam, the daughter of the emperor of Byzantium, and she was his favorite of all the women in his harem. Shirin was tormented by this, and her cheeks were always pale with jealousy. Finally, she poisoned Mariam, and the Byzantine princess died. Shirin did this alone, in secret, and no one was aware of what she had done; and a year after Mariam died, Shirin was given the golden apartments in the harem.

When Mariam's son, Shirui, was sixteen he had the stature of a thirty-year-old: his father brought him teachers, so that he could learn to be an accomplished nobleman, and a priest supervised him day and night, according to the king's orders. One day the priest came from the king to the prince and saw that he sat idly playing. In front of him lay his book, *Kalileh and Demneh*, but in his left hand the loutish youth held the dried paw of a wolf and in his right a buffalo's horn, and he sat there willfully banging the one against the other. The priest's heart was troubled by this pointless game; he took the wolf's claw, the buffalo's horn, and the youth's loutish behavior as a bad omen. He had seen the boy's horoscope, and had heard more details from the vizier and court treasurer, and he feared what fate held in store for the prince. He went to the chief priest and said, "All the prince cares about is trivial games." Immediately the chief priest passed this on to Khosrow, who was troubled by the report; his cheeks turned sallow at the thought of his son, and he brooded on what fate would unfold. He remembered the astrologer's words; his heart was troubled, and his vitals were twisted within him. He said, "We must wait to see what the heavens bring forth."

By the twenty-third year of the king's reign Shirui was strong and fully grown; he had become refractory and uncontrollable, and Khosrow grew anxious about him. The king's smiling soul was clouded with sorrow, and he had the prince confined to his palace, along with his companions and those who sought him out for advice; this group came to more than three thousand in all. The place was provided with clothes, food, and furnishings, the rooms were decorated appropriately, and slaves and servants were there in

attendance. The king sent wine and limitless gold, and forty men were set to watch over the revelers, who passed their time in feasting and pleasure.

The Tale of the Musician, Barbad

As time passed the king's greatness increased, and no one received bad treatment at his court. In the twenty-eighth year of his reign news of this reached the musician Barbad, who was told, "The king favors musicians, and if you compete with his current musician, Sarkesh, he'll give you a higher rank than him." When he heard this, although he wanted for nothing, ambition flared up in him; he traveled from his own country to the king's court and presented himself to the musicians there. When Sarkesh heard him play, he was astonished at the newcomer's skill, and his heart grew dark. He went to the court chamberlain and gave him gold and silver and other gifts. He said, "There's a musician at the door who surpasses me in youth and skill: he mustn't enter Khosrow's presence, because if he does, he'll be looked on as a novelty and I'll be thought old-fashioned." The chamberlain agreed to refuse entry to their naïve visitor. And so when Barbad appeared, he was rudely received. The chamberlain would not admit him to the court, and no one came to help him. Despondently he left the

court gates and, carrying his lute, made his way to the royal garden, where the king would go for two weeks of festivities at the New Year.

The gardener there was named Marduy, and Barbad liked him as soon as he saw him. That very day, the two became firm friends, and Barbad said to him, "It's as if you're the soul and I'm the body of one person. I have a favor to ask, something that will be easy for you to do. When the world's king comes to this garden, hide me somewhere so that I can see him; I want to watch his face for a moment, during the festivities." Marduy said, "I'll do it; set your mind at rest."

As Khosrow approached the garden, the gardener's heart glowed with excitement. He hurried to Barbad and said, "The king is coming here for the celebrations." Barbad dressed himself all in green and took his lute in his hand, ready to sing of glory and battles. He went to where the king was to sit, since a new site was selected each spring. There was a green cypress tree there, with abundant foliage and branches interlaced like warriors in a battle. Barbad climbed this tree and waited for the king to arrive. The king came from his palace to the spot that had been prepared for him. A young serving girl with a bewitching face gave him a goblet, and the red wine within rendered its crystal invisible. At the moment the yellow sun set and purple night came on, Barbad took his lute and sang the heroic song he had prepared. Hidden in the tree, he sang his beautiful lay, the one we now call "Dad-Afarid," and the king was astonished at the sweetness of his voice. The whole company was amazed, and everyone expressed a different opinion as to what was happening. The king ordered the company to search the area thoroughly, and they looked high and low but came back empty-handed. One experienced man came forward and said, "It should be no surprise that the king's good fortune has made even the green plants and flowers his musicians: may his head and crown flourish forever!"

The beautiful serving girl brought another goblet, and as the king took it from her, Barbad suddenly struck up another song, "The Heroes' Battle." The skillful musician sang and Khosrow listened, drinking his wine as the song progressed. Then he ordered that the singer be found, and that the garden be turned upside down if need be. They searched everywhere in the garden, taking flaming torches beneath the trees, but they saw nothing but willows and cypresses and pheasants strutting among the flowers. The king asked for another goblet of wine and leaned his head forward to listen. Again a song began, accompanied by the lute's sound; it was the one that is called "Green on Green" today, and is used for magical incantations. Khosrow Parviz stood to drink to the voice: he asked for a goblet that held a deep draught of wine, and he drained the bright liquor in one motion. He said, "If this were an angel compounded of musk and ambergris, or a demon, he wouldn't sing these songs, or know how to play the lute in this way. Search the garden again, left and right, till you find where he is. I'll fill his mouth and arms with jewels, and make him the chief of my musicians."

When Barbad heard the king's generous words, he came down from the branches of the cypress tree, and went forward confidently, in all his glory. He approached the king and bowed down, rubbing his face in the dust. Khosrow said to him, "What manner of man are you, tell me!" He replied, "Your majesty, I am your slave and live in the world only at your command." Then he told the king all that had happened, and of the man who had befriended him. The king's happiness at seeing Barbad was like that of a spring garden in the moonlight, but he said to Sarkesh, "You've no talent, you're as bitter as colocynth, and Barbad is like sugar. Why did you keep him away from me? Now he's come, you've no place in this assembly."

Then he drank wine to the sound of Barbad's voice, draining his goblet of its ruby contents, until his head became sleepy, and he filled Barbad's mouth with pearls of the first water. And so Barbad became the king's musician, and a respected man among the country's nobility.

> Now Barbad's tale is done: I wish for you
> Good fortune and good friends in all you do.

Khosrow Parviz Becomes Unjust

Despite his splendid throne, the great palace he built at Ctesiphon, and all his imperial glory, the world's king was dissatisfied, and he raised dust clouds of strife over Iran and Turan. This king who had been so just became unjust, and he rejoiced in the injustice of his inferiors.

There was a man called Farrokhzad, the son of Azarmegan, who became Khosrow's chamberlain. He was always frowning, and he acted malevolently toward those under his control, stealing people's wealth and pitting them against one another. He set himself ever new tasks, and all his efforts went to gathering ever more wealth. Men's former blessings turned to curses, and they said that the ruler who had been like a sheep had become a savage wolf. Since the populace had neither water nor bread nor any means of support, they fled from Persia to enemy lands, and the land was filled with curses against all those who had any part in this oppression.

And then there was Goraz, a man devoid of virtue, who fulfilled all Khosrow Parviz's dreams and desires, and guarded the frontier against Byzantium. His mind was a demon's, unjust and shameless, and when the once-just king became unjust, he was the first to betray Persia. The next was Farrokhzad, Khosrow Parviz's favorite and his chamberlain, who would let no one near the king. When the king's days were numbered, Farrokhzad's heart became corrupt: he allied himself with the wily Goraz, and their plot spread from

province to province. Goraz wrote to the emperor of Byzantium and stirred up evil desires in him. He wrote: "Rise now, and take Persia; if you do, I will be the first to come to your aid." As soon as he read this, the emperor mustered an army and set off with it toward the Persian frontier.

The Army Deserts Khosrow Parviz and Frees Shirui

When the king heard of this serious development, he dismissed it as of no importance. He knew it was Goraz's doing, and that he had been in secret communication with the Byzantine emperor. Earlier he had summoned Goraz to the court but Goraz had made excuses and acted as if the king could not enforce his orders, even though he was afraid of him. The king sat in council with the Persian nobles, and they considered various ways to rid themselves of this problem. Then the king had a clever notion: he wrote a letter to Goraz saying, "I'm delighted with what you have done, and have praised you before our nobles. When you receive this letter may it brighten your dark spirits. Wait with your forces where you are until I advance, and with one army on this side and another on that, we shall trap the Byzantine emperor between us. We'll bring him back as a prisoner to Persia, and take all his army into captivity."

Then the king chose a cunning courtier, someone who could act as a spy, and said to him, "See that one of the Byzantine scouts catches sight of you and questions you. Then he'll take you to the emperor, or to their army's commander. When you're asked who you are, refuse to answer, then say, 'I'm just a poor man trying to make a living, and I've traveled a long way to deliver this letter to Goraz.' Tie the letter to your right arm, and if they take it from you, so much the better."

The man tied the letter as instructed and left the court. As he approached the Byzantine marches, a man caught sight of him and took him, with his face covered in dust, his cheeks sallow, and his lips purple, before the emperor. The emperor addressed him, "Where is Khosrow Parviz? You had better tell us the truth!" The poor man mumbled in a bewildered way and hung his head in fear. The emperor said, "Search this malevolent, ill-spoken wretch." They found the letter and opened it, and then looked for someone in the area who could read Pahlavi correctly. When a scribe was found who was able to read it, the emperor's face turned black as pitch. He said to himself, "This was a trap set by Goraz; I was marching straight into an ambush. This king with his army of three hundred thousand men and innumerable war elephants wanted to corner me: may his life end in darkness and sorrow!" And he withdrew his forces, forgetting all thoughts of conquest.

*G*oraz and Farrokhzad then made common cause and encouraged the army to revolt against Khosrow Parviz.

Farrokhzad knew that the king was aware of his treachery, and he did not dare approach the throne. He waited by the door and sounded people out, trying to win allies for when the army would declare itself against the king. He told his ideas to everyone and won many people over, saying that another man should occupy the throne, because Khosrow Parviz had forfeited *farr*, glory, and good fortune.

An experienced old man in Farrokhzad's employ said to his master, "The king blames you for the army's disaffection. You shouldn't proceed any further in this matter until another king is available, otherwise the country will go to rack and ruin. We must consider his sons—which of them has the dignity for this position and will cause the fewest problems? Then we must place him on the throne in triumph and pour gold dinars over his crown as is customary. Since Shirui is his eldest son, he is the obvious choice, even though he's imprisoned at the moment."

Everyone expressed the same opinion, and not many days passed before the dust of Tokhvar's intrepid army rose up. Farrokhzad went out along the road to greet him and his numerous troops, and the two conversed for a long time. Farrokhzad went over the injustices that the king had committed and then said, "The army must act with chivalry and discretion and install a new king." The commander replied, "I'm not a man for talk, but when I fight I make the world a hard place for my enemies. When this king was young, he was loved by champions and lords of the marches alike, but may no man make his days as dark as this king has done. He lost everything when he became unjust and rejoiced in the injustice of his inferiors."

At this Farrokhzad chose Tokhvar, from all the Persians, as his accomplice and said to him, "Now we must go to where those poor wretches are imprisoned and fearlessly free Prince Shirui, who is young, brave, and ambitious. His jailer is an army commander, and he and six thousand cavalry veterans keep him and his companions under surveillance." Tokhvar replied, "I take no account of this commander. If Khosrow Parviz's luck revives, every champion in Persia will find himself on a gibbet or imprisoned in a pit; no one will escape injury." Having said this he urged his horse forward, and it leaped to the fray like lightning. The commander set to guard Shirui came out to oppose him, but he was driven back and killed in the battle. Still in his armor, Tokhvar went straight to the place where Shirui was confined and called out to him. Shirui knew why this proud warrior had come, and when he saw his face glowing after the battle, the young man's heart beat faster with anxiety. Weeping, he said, "Where is

Khosrow Parviz? It's not your business to set me free." Tokhvar said to the prince, "If you're a man don't stay here like a lion clawing at its cage. If you're not with us, then declare yourself and withdraw. If we lose one out of sixteen brothers, that's of no importance; there are still fifteen more of you. All of the others are worthy to rule, and the throne will rejoice in their reign." Shirui wept in bewilderment, uncertain whether to set foot outside of the building or not.

Khosrow Learns of the Army's Defection

Meanwhile Farrokhzad acted as court chamberlain and admitted no one to the king's presence, so that he would not hear of what was going on. When the tent of the sun was tattered, and noblemen went to their sleeping quarters, Farrokhzad summoned the city's sentries and all those who had authority over them. Confidently they came to the king's court, where Farrokhzad said to them, "The cry of the watchmen must be different tonight from last night. As each watch of the night goes by, all the watchmen must cry out in the name of Qobad." They agreed: "We will do this and drive the name of Parviz from our minds."

When night's black tent was pitched, the watchmen's cries went up from the city and bazaar, and all of them called in the name of Qobad. The king was sleeping in the darkness of the night, and Shirin was next to him in his bed. When she heard the cries, she was troubled and her heart beat faster. She said, "Your majesty, what can be happening? Listen! We must talk." The king woke at the sound of her voice and said in his irritation, "Your face is as lovely as the moon, but why are you talking when I'm asleep?" Shirin replied, "Open your ears, listen to what the watchmen are crying!" Khosrow heard their voices and his face grew pale as fenugreek. He said, "Three watches of the night have gone by, and now you will learn the truth of the astrologers' words. When this brat was born I secretly named him Qobad; publicly his name was Shirui, but in private, Qobad. Under cover of the night's darkness we must make for China, or Machin, or Makran; we must flee secretly, and ask for soldiers from the Chinese emperor." But his star was waning, and this talk of flight was empty chatter. Tricks did not help him in the night's darkness; he had underestimated the seriousness of what was afoot. He said to Shirin, "My time has come, and those who hate us have triumphed over our plans." She replied, "May you thrive forever, safe from your enemies' hands. Think of some ruse in your wisdom; God forbid that your enemies prevail. As soon as dawn breaks they are sure to come to the palace."

Then the king asked for armor, two Indian swords, a Byzantine helmet, a quiver full of arrows, and a golden shield from his treasury, as well as a slave who would fight in his defense. In the darkness he made his way to his garden, just at the time when the crow wakes up from sleep. Among the trees there was no space for a couch: he hung his golden shield from a branch, in an area where few men came. He sat among the narcissi and crocuses, with an Indian sword placed firmly beneath his knee. As the sun lifted its glittering lance, the king's malevolent enemies made their way to the palace. They went from room to room but found no sign of the king; they looted his treasures and gave no thought to his suffering.

Khosrow Parviz Becomes His Son's Prisoner

Khosrow stayed in the garden, in the shade of a tall tree, and by midday he had grown hungry. There was an under gardener working there who had never seen the king's face. The sun-like sovereign said to him, "Cut a jeweled link from my belt: there are five gold bosses on each link. Take the link to the bazaar; buy me some meat and some bread with it, and see that you go by an unfrequented road." Now, for a man who knew about such things, the jewels on the link were worth thirty thousand gold coins.

The gardener hurried off to a baker's shop and tried to buy bread with the gold link. The baker said, "I don't know what this is worth, but I'm not letting you go!" The two went together to a jeweler and asked him to put a value on the link. When this knowledgeable man saw the piece, he said, "But who would dare to buy this? This is a piece from Khosrow's treasury; each year a hundred new ones of this kind are made. Who did you steal this from? Did you snatch it from a slave while he was asleep?" The three of them then took the gold and jewels to Farrokhzad, who immediately took this link severed from a golden belt to Prince Shirui and showed it to him. Shirui addressed the gardener: "If you don't tell me where the owner of this is, I'll cut your head off, and the heads of all your family too."

He replied, " Your majesty, he's in the garden, dressed in armor, with a bow in his hand. His stature is like a cypress tree's, and his face is like the spring; he seems a prince in every way. All the garden shines with his splendor, and in his armor he's like a shining sun. His golden shield hangs from a branch, and a slave stands in front of him, bow in hand. He cut this link and gave it to me, and said, 'Run and bring me bread and food from the bazaar.' I ran here from his side just a moment ago." Shirui knew that this was Khosrow, whose appearance was unique. Three thousand horsemen went like the wind from the palace to the stream's bank. When Khosrow saw them in the distance he quailed but drew his sword for combat. The soldiers saw the king's face, and they turned back, weeping. One by one they went before Farrokhzad, and each told the same story saying, "We are slaves and he is Khosrow: misfortune is a new thing in this king's life. No one would oppose him, not so much as by a cold sigh, whether in a garden or on the field of battle." Farrokhzad took a number of guards from the palace and went to the king. He went forward alone and said to Khosrow: "If the king will grant me audience, and forgive me for what has happened, I will come and explain the situation. If not, I shall go back to the palace." Khosrow said, "Say what you have to say; you're neither my comforter nor my enemy."

Farrokhzad said, "Look more wisely on what's happening. You could kill a thousand warriors but finally you'll tire of combat. All the land of Persia is against you; all men are united in their enmity for you. Come, and see what the heavens will show; it may be that their longing for revenge will turn to clemency." Khosrow replied, "You are right, this has always been my fear, that unworthy men should come and lord it over me and make me the butt of their ridicule." Listening to Farrokhzad's words, the king had grown sick at heart, and he remembered that in earlier times an astrologer had said to him "Your death will occur between two mountains, and at the hands of a slave, far from other men. One mountain will be of silver, and another of gold, and you will sit between the two with your heart trembling in fear. The heavens will be gold above you, and the earth will be of iron, and fortune will be against you." "And now," Khosrow thought, "this iron armor is like the earth for me, my shield is the golden heavens; and the treasures that have been piled in these gardens, which so delighted my heart, are the two mountains. My days have come to an end. Where now is my star that lit the world with splendor, and my power and happiness that made my name more exalted than crowns?"

They brought an elephant before him; his soul was darkened by grief as he sat in the saddle and was escorted from the garden. He called out in Pahlavi from the elephant's back, "My treasure, even if you are Khosrow's enemy, do not make common cause with those who are against me. Today I am in the clasp of Ahriman, and you were no help to me in my distress; stay hidden, and show your face to no one." Then Qobad ordered his men to treat him well, to have him taken to Ctesiphon, and installed in his vizier's palace, where Galinush would watch over him with a thousand cavalry. When the turning heavens brought his reign to an end, Khosrow Parviz had ruled for thirty-eight years: this happened in the month of Azar, on the day of Dey, at the time when fires are lit, fowls roasted, and wine drunk.

Then Qobad came forward and placed the crown on his head and sat in peace and prosperity on the throne. From all of Persia the army paid him homage, and he gave them a year's pay from the king's treasury. He reigned for no more than seven months; you can call him a king if you wish, or something worthless. But this is the treacherous world's way, and you should not look on it with trusting eyes.

Barbad's Lament for Khosrow Parviz

When Barbad heard that the king had been unjustly forced to quit the throne and that he was now powerless, he traveled from Jahrom to Ctesiphon, his eyelashes wet with tears, his heart swollen with grief. He came to the palace and saw the former king, whose once ruddy face was now as pale as fenugreek. He stayed with him for a while, and then went weeping to the audience chamber. He mourned in Pahlavi, his cheeks sallow with grief, and his heart filled with pain. When the king and those who were there in the palace, including the guards, heard his lament, they all wept, consumed with the fire of their pity. This is what Barbad sang:

> *O great Khosrow, great in your majesty,*
> *In warlike pride, in magnanimity—*
> *Where is that greatness now, your high renown,*
> *Your glory and your throne and royal crown?*
> *Where is your chivalry, your power, my king*
> *Who sheltered all the world beneath your wing?*
> *Where are your wives now, your musicians, all*
> *The nobles who once thronged your audience hall?*
> *Where now is Kaveh's banner, and the lords*
> *Who flourished in the air their glittering swords?*
> *Where are your valiant warriors and your priests,*
> *Where are your hunting parties and your feasts?*
> *Where is that warlike mien, and where are those*
> *Great armies that destroyed our country's foes?*
> *Where is your armor, wondrous to behold,*
> *Studded with jewels, fashioned from shining gold?*
> *Where is Shabdiz, your fiery stallion who*
> *Galloped with such impatience under you?*
> *Where are your glorious gold-shod cavalry,*
> *Whose swords sought out one sheath—the enemy?*
> *Where is that generous, never-failing store*
> *Of your largess? Your eagerness in war?*
> *Where are the camels, horses, elephants,*
> *Their howdahs, trappings, and magnificence?*
> *Where is that wise nobility of mind,*
> *That eloquence, at once adroit and kind?*
> *Why are you left deprived, in this sad state,*
> *Who read you this page from the Book of Fate?*
> *Once you desired a son—to be your friend,*
> *A prop to your old age—and in the end*

Grief came to you from him: a king's son gives
His father strength and shelter while he lives,
But to the King of Kings this son brought pain
And his success destroyed his father's reign.
Count Persia as a ruin, as the lair
Of lions and leopards. Look now and despair,
You were the best of Sasan's line, no one
Will ever reign again as you have done,
And as your seed degenerates, this land
Degenerates beneath an alien hand.
It is the shepherd's fault when wolves descend
And ravage all the sheep he should defend.
God keep your soul, and may each enemy
Of yours die gibbeted in agony!
I swear by God above, my noble king,
By Mehregan, by New Year and the spring,
That if my hand plays any song again
I should be stricken from the roll of men.
I'll burn my instruments and never face
The enemies who've dealt you this disgrace."

Then he cut off his four fingers and went back to his house with his hand mutilated; there he built a fire and burned all his musical instruments.

The Nobility Demand that Khosrow Parviz Be Killed; His Death at the Hands of Mehr Hormozd

All those who had allied themselves with the prince trembled day and night at what fate would bring, since Shirui was a coward and untried in the world's ways. The throne was like a snare to him, and his astrologers knew that his greatness would not last. Those who had been so eager to bring about this evil went to Qobad and talked of what had happened. They said, "We have said this once, and now we repeat it: your mind is set on other things than sovereignty. If two kings are enthroned in one land, one must take precedence and the other be his inferior, and their subjects will rue the day that father and son rule together. We are opposed to this arrangement; do not mention it to us again." Shirui was a slave in their hands, and he was afraid of what would come of this. He answered, "Only a contemptible fool would put his head deliberately into a trap. You must go to your homes and debate what is to be done. Search out someone in the world who can secretly deliver me from this difficulty." The king's enemies looked for someone who would secretly do away with him, but no one had the courage to attempt such a feat, or to bear the mountain of guilt that would come from killing such a monarch.

They searched everywhere until they found a man traveling by road who had blue eyes and sallow cheeks; his body was covered in hair and his face was flushed purple. This evil man's feet were dusty, his belly was wasted with hunger, and his body was naked. No one in the world, rich or poor, knew his name. This ugly wretch—and may he never see the joys of paradise—made his way to Farrokhzad and said, "I'm the man for this business; fill my belly and he's my prey!" Farrokhzad said, "Go, and do it if you can, and speak not a word of this to anyone. I'll have a purse of gold coins waiting for you, and treat you as one of my own." Then he gave him a sharp, glittering dagger, and the man immediately set off on his errand. He found the king, with his feet shackled, in the audience hall.

Khosrow trembled when he saw his assailant, and tears fell from his eyes. He said, "What ugly name is yours? Even your mother should weep to set eyes on you." The man replied, "They call me Mehr Hormozd; I'm a stranger in this land and have no friends or companions here." Khosrow said, "And so my end has come at the hands of a lowborn criminal. His face is inhuman, and no one in the world could expect kindness from such a man." The king said to a servant boy standing near him, "Go lad, and fetch me a bowl of water mixed with musk and aloes; and bring me a fine set of fresh clothes." The boy heard him but didn't know what this signified; he quickly brought the king a golden bowl, a ewer, and fresh clothes. Khosrow took the sacred barsom in his hands and prayed: this was no time for idle chat or frivolity. He dressed himself in the clean clothes and asked pardon for his sins; then he drew a previously unworn cloak over his head so that he would not see his murderer. Dagger in hand, Mehr Hormozd locked the doors to the king's apartments; quickly he went forward and slashed through the king's clothes, plunging the blade into his vitals.

So turns the world, keeping its secrets hidden, and both the prudent, harmless man and the idle boaster find nothing there but vanity. Whether you own treasures or live in pain and sorrow, you cannot remain in this fleeting world. Choose righteousness and benevolence if you would be remembered with praise.

When news spread in the roads and bazaars that Khosrow had perished in this way, evildoers made their way to where his fifteen sons were kept chained in the palace and murdered these innocents on the same day. Shirui did not dare say anything, but grieved over these events in secret. This then was the end of Khosrow, who had been the lord of such armies and ruled with such splendor. He had no rival as the King of Kings, and no one had ever heard of such a monarch from former times.

The Story of Shirui and Shirin, the Wife of Khosrow Parviz

I have finished the tale of Khosrow Parviz, and now I will begin that of Shirui and Shirin. Fifty-three days after the king was killed, Shirui sent someone to Shirin with this message: "You are an abomination, a magician who knows all spells; there is no one in Iran more culpable than you. It was your sorcery, which could bring the moon down from the heavens, that bewitched the king. Tremble now and come before me. You'll strut so confidently about the palace no longer." Shirin was enraged by his message, and its ugly, threatening language. She said, "May no man flourish who spills his own father's blood! I shall not see that criminal even from a distance, neither on a day of sorrow nor on one of feasting." She summoned a scribe and had a document written in Pahlavi; she dictated her will to this man and listed her wealth there.

She had a little poison in a coffer, the like of which could not be found anywhere in the whole country. From then on she kept it on her person, and this cypress of the meadows proceeded to sew her own shroud. She sent a message back to Shirui: "You wear the crown, haughty in your majesty, but the words you've spoken are like leaves in the wind. May the heart of any malevolent wretch who talks about magic and rejoices in such things be brought low! If the king had cared for such sorceries, he'd have kept a witch in his harem so that he could see her face to face; but he kept me there, to delight his heart when he looked on me as evening fell. He would call me from my apartments, and his soul rejoiced to see me. Shame on you for this talk; such lies don't suit a sovereign. Remember God, who is benevolent, and don't say such things before men again."

They took her message to Shirui, who flared up in anger at this innocent woman, and said, "You've no choice but to come! No one in the world is as impudent in her speech as you are." When she heard this, Shirin was troubled and her cheeks turned sallow. She replied, "I will only come to you in the company of others; you must be surrounded by wise and respectable men." Shirui summoned fifty old men, wise in the world's ways, and then sent a messenger to Shirin who said, "Rise, come now, and leave off your excuses." Shirin heard, and dressed herself in blue and black and came before the king. She went straight to the garden called Shadegan, where there was a place set aside for free men to speak; she sat there veiled, as was customary for nobly born women. Shirui sent someone to her with this message: "It is now two months since Khosrow died; be my wife now, as is worthy of you, and in this way you will not be shamed before your inferiors. I shall treat you as my father did, and even more respectfully and kindly than he did."

Shirin replied, "First act justly toward me, and then my soul will be yours; then I will not bridle at your questions, or resist your orders or the wishes of your splendid heart." Shirui agreed to this, and told her to say what she had in mind. The noble woman spoke from behind her veil: "May you be prosperous and victorious, your majesty. You said that I am an evil woman and a sorceress, and that there is no purity or righteousness in me." Shirui replied, "This is true, but such an outburst is not to be taken seriously." Then Shirin said to the nobility gathered in the garden of Shadegan, "What evil have you seen from me, what darkness of soul, or deceit, or foolishness? For many years I was the queen of Persia, and in this time I always supported her brave warriors. I sought only righteousness, and all trickery and deceit were far from my mind. Through my intercession many men gained land and a fair portion of the world's goods. Let those who have lived protected by my shadow and that of my crown and glory say what they saw and heard, and their words will confirm all I did." The nobles who were there affirmed Shirin's goodness and said that there was no other woman like her in all the world, either in public life or hidden away.

Shirin said, "My noble lords, who have traveled the world and know its ways, there are three things that are honorable in a woman and that adorn the seat of greatness. First, that she possess both modesty and wealth, so that she may make her husband's house a place of beauty and contentment; another is that she bear him fine sons, and so augment his splendor; and the third is that she be beautiful of face and of good stature, and that her hair envelope her like a cloak. When I married Khosrow and felt my life to be renewed in the world, he had come from Rome disheartened and despoiled of his wealth, with hardly a home to call his own in this country. But then his reign became so splendid that no one in the world had ever seen or heard of its like. And I bore him four sons—Nastud, Shahryar, Forud and Mardanshah—who rejoiced his heart. Jamshid and Feraydun did not have such sons, and may my tongue turn mute if I am lying."
Having said this she drew back her veil from her face, which shone like the full moon, and the night behind it was her hair. "The third quality is a face such as you see before you, and if anyone believes that I am lying, let him raise his hand. One of my secret attributes was my hair, which no man in the world has ever seen. And here I display to you all my magic, which is not from sorcery or tricks or malevolence; no one has seen my hair before, and none of the nobles have even heard tell of it." The elders were dumbfounded at the sight of her, and they moistened their lips.

When Shirui saw Shirin's face, his soul seemed to take leave of his body. He said to her, "I must have no one but you; you are the only wife in all Iran whom I desire." The beautiful woman answered him, "There are matters I still require from Persia's king. May your reign be long, but I have some requests, if you will grant them." Shirui replied, "My soul is yours; I will grant whatever you wish." Shirin said, "Give me, piece by piece, before this company of nobles, all the wealth that I have owned in this land, and sign this document witnessing that you lay no claim to it." Immediately Shirui did as she requested, and when her requests were fulfilled Shirin went from the garden of Shadegan, walking before the nobles gathered there, to her own home, where she used her wealth to free her slaves and rejoice their hearts. The rest of her possessions she gave to the poor, bestowing most on people of her own household. She gave a portion to the fire-temples, for the celebration of the new year and summer festivals. There was a convent, which was in ruins and had become the lair of lions, and this she rebuilt, dedicating it to the memory of Khosrow, for the good of his soul.

Then she sat in its garden, unveiled, on the ground, divested of her finery. She called her servants to her and sat each one down with kindness. She said in a loud voice, "All of you who have generous hearts, hear what I have to say, since no one will see my face again. Say only the truth; wise people do not lie. From the time that I joined Khosrow and was introduced into the golden apartments of his harem, from when I became the first of queens and the glory of the king, what sins did I commit? Don't speak merely for form's sake—what do such things matter to a desperate woman?" Everyone

487

stood and said: "Queen among queens, you are eloquent, wise, and enlightened in your soul; we swear by God that no one has ever seen a woman like you before, or heard such a voice from behind the veil. From the time of Hushang until now, no one like you has ever sat on the throne." All her servants and slaves said together, "You are praised in China and the west and in Taraz; who would dare to speak ill of you, and how could you ever commit an evil act?"

Shirin responded to them, "This criminal, whom the turning heavens mock, killed his own father for the sake of a crown and throne, and for this may he never know happiness or good fortune again. Does he think he can evade death, having killed his father in such a wretched fashion? He has sent me a message that has darkened my anguished soul. I have told him that while I remain alive I shall devote myself to God; I have told him my intentions, but his evil desires have filled me with sorrow, and I fear that after I die he will publicly slander me." The company wept, both at her words and for Khosrow Parviz.

The king was told of what this innocent woman had said, and he asked her again what she desired. Shirin sent a messenger to him saying that she had only one more wish, that the entrance to Khosrow's tomb be opened for her, and that she be allowed to look at him once more. Shirui responded that it was fitting for her to look on the king again. The guards opened the tomb and Shirin began a mourning lament. She laid her face against Khosrow's face and spoke to him the words they had spoken to one another in times past; then she drank the mortal poison she carried, which began to cloud her soul. Her clothes scented with camphor, she sat beside the king and leaned her back against the tomb's walls. So she died, and her death was praised by the world.

When Shirui heard of this, he fell sick, and the sight of Shirin's body filled him with grief. He ordered that another tomb be constructed, and there she was laid, her head crowned with musk and camphor. Then Shirui sealed Khosrow's tomb, and not many days passed before he too was given poison: the world had had its fill of kings. He was born shamefully and died shamefully, leaving the throne to his son. So a man may reign for seven months, and in the eighth he finds that his crown is made of the camphor with which the dead are anointed.

Shirui was succeeded on the throne by his son Ardeshir, who ruled for six months and was then murdered. Goraz seized the throne, but he too was murdered after a reign of less than two months. Two royal princesses, Puran-Dokht and Azarm-Dokht, reigned briefly, the first for six months, the second for four months; they were succeeded by Farrokhzad, who was poisoned after a month. A grandson of Khosrow Parviz, Yazdegerd III, then became the last Sasanian king of Iran.

⚜ THE REIGN OF YAZDEGERD ⚜

After the death of Farrokhzad, Yazdegerd became king, in the month of Sepandormoz, on the day of Ard. He sat in splendor on the imperial throne and placed the crown on his head. He said, "By the revolutions of the turning sky, I am the descendant of Nushin-Ravan; from father to son the realm is mine, and the sun and the constellations Virgo and Pisces are favorable to my reign. I shall confer greatness on the lowly, and I shall not harm the mighty. I do not seek for glory and knowledge, or for warfare and valor, since time and good fortune, wealth, the royal crown, and the throne stay with no man. It is a good reputation we must strive for, not our own pleasure; pleasure is to be ignored, and reputation made our goal." And so he ruled for sixteen years, while the moon and sun passed over his head.

Sa'd, the Son of Vaqas, Invades Iran, and Yazdegerd Sends Rostam, the Son of Hormozd, to Fight against Him

Omar, who was then the commander of the Arab armies, sent Sa'd, the son of Vaqas, with an army against the king. Hearing news of this Yazdegerd gathered troops from all quarters and ordered the son of Hormozd to lead them against the invader. This man's name was Rostam; he was an astute, intelligent man and a fine warrior. He was also a very knowledgeable astrologer, who paid attention to the advice of priests. He set out with the nobility under his command, and everyone who was capable of fighting well accompanied him.

For thirty months they skirmished, until the army made a stand at Qadesiya. Rostam was a just, kind man; in his capacity as an astrologer he said to himself, "This battle will turn out unfavorably; these times are unfavorable to kings, their current cannot flow in such channels." He took his astrolabe and observed the stars, and when he saw the day of disaster that loomed he buried his head in his hands. He wrote a letter to his brother, beginning with praise of God, who brings both good and evil fates to pass. Then he continued:

"A wise man will be saddened when he learns
Of how the moving sphere of heaven turns:
Caught in the evil clutch of Ahriman,
I am the time's most sad and sinful man;
This house will lose all trace of sovereignty
Of royal glory, and of victory.
The sun looks down from its exalted sphere
And sees the day of our defeat draw near:
Both Mars and Venus now oppose our cause
And no man can evade the heaven's laws.
Saturn and Mercury divide the sky—
Mercury rules the house of Gemini:
Ahead of us lie war and endless strife,
Such that my failing heart despairs of life.
I see what has to be, and choose the way
Of silence since there is no more to say:
But for the Persians I will weep, and for
The House of Sasan ruined by this war:
Alas for their great crown and throne, for all
The royal splendor destined now to fall,
To be fragmented by the Arabs' might;
The stars decree for us defeat and flight.
Four hundred years will pass in which our name
Will be forgotten and devoid of fame.

"They've sent a messenger who says to me
They'll leave our sovereign all his territory
From Qadesiya to the river; but,
For trade's sake, they require a highway cut
Through our domains, no more than this. They'll pay
Us taxes, offer hostages, obey
Our king as theirs. But these are words, not acts,
And have no correspondence with the facts:
There will be war, and in this conflict I
Know many lion-warriors will die.
And all of my commanders, to a man—
Like Merui from wide Tabaristan,
Like Armani and Kalbui, all those
Who fight with heavy maces to oppose
Our enemies—reject their words and say,
'Who are these upstarts who have dared to stray
Across Mazanderan's and Persia's borders?
For good or bad then, issue us your orders

And let our swords and maces drive them back;
We'll press them hard enough when we attack!'
They cannot know the fate the stars foretell,
These stars which always treated us so well!
As soon as you have read this, don't delay
But make plans quickly and be on your way;
Gather together our nobility,
Their wealth and slaves, horses and property—
Azerbaijan must be your refuge now.
If Persian troops come from Zabol, allow
Them all you can in clothes and charity,
Treat them with friendly hospitality,
But watch the turning heavens—it's from there
That we are granted comfort and despair.
Say to our mother all I've said, but then
Tell her she'll never see my face again.
Give her my greetings, comfort her and see
She does not grieve too desperately for me.
If someone brings sad news of me, don't let
Your sorrow weaken you; we should not set
Our hearts on this world where our wealth is won
By pain and is another's when we're gone.
Devote your heart to God, and as you pray
Ignore this fleeting world which fades away.
The king will not see Rostam any more,
Since fate has driven me to fight this war.
Have all our people pray throughout the night,
Both young and old, until the morning light;
Be generous to the poor, and in your sorrow
Trust in God's help, give no thought to the morrow;
And as for me, my fate's to fight, to lead
Our armies in our country's hour of need:
May Persia flourish! But I know that I
Will not survive this battle, and must die.
When once the king is threatened, give no thought
To wealth or life, to all that you have sought,
Do not be weak or hesitant but strive
With all your strength to keep the king alive,
Since of this noble line the king alone
Still lives; the House of Sasan and its throne
Depend on him, and after him the race
Of Sasan will be gone, and leave no trace.

Alas now for their crown, their court, and for
Their throne that will be shattered in this war.
Farewell now: live for the king, be his shield,
Defend him, sword in hand, and never yield!

"But when the pulpit's equal to the throne
And Abu Bakr's and Omar's names are known,
Our long travails will be as naught, and all
The glory we have known will fade and fall.
The stars are with the Arabs, and you'll see
No crown or throne, no royal sovereignty:
Long days will pass, until a worthless fool
Will lead his followers and presume to rule:
They'll dress in black, their headdress will be made
Of twisted lengths of silk or black brocade.
There'll be no golden boots or banners then,
Our crowns and thrones will not be seen again.
Some will rejoice, while others live in fear,
Justice and charity will disappear,
At night, the time to hide away and sleep,
Men's eyes will glitter to make others weep;
Strangers will rule us then, and with their might
They'll plunder us and turn our days to night.
They will not care for just or righteous men,
Deceit and fraudulence will flourish then.
Warriors will go on foot, while puffed-up pride
And empty boasts will arm themselves and ride;
The peasantry will suffer from neglect,
Lineage and skill will garner no respect,
Men will be mutual thieves and have no shame,
Curses and blessings will be thought the same.
What's hidden will be worse than what is known,
And stony-hearted kings will seize the throne.
No man will trust his son, and equally
No son will trust his father's honesty—
A misbegotten slave will rule the earth,
Greatness and lineage will have no worth,
No one will keep his word, and men will find
The tongue as filled with evil as the mind.
Then Persians, Turks, and Arabs, side by side
Will live together, mingled far and wide—
The three will blur, as if they were the same;
Their languages will be a trivial game.

Men will conceal their wealth, but when they've died,
Their foes will pilfer everything they hide.
Men will pretend they're holy, or they're wise,
To make a livelihood by telling lies.
Sorrow and anguish, bitterness and pain
Will be as happiness was in the reign
Of Bahram Gur—mankind's accustomed fate:
There'll be no feasts, no festivals of state,
No pleasures, no musicians, none of these:
But there'll be lies, and traps, and treacheries.
Sour milk will be our food, coarse cloth our dress,
And greed for money will breed bitterness
Between the generations: men will cheat
Each other while they calmly counterfeit
Religious faith. The winter and the spring
Will pass mankind unmarked, no one will bring
The wine to celebrate such moments then;
Instead they'll spill the blood of fellow men.
These thoughts have dried my mouth, my cheeks turn pale,
I feel my sickened heart within me fail,
For since I was a soldier I've not known
Such dark days to beset the royal throne;
The heavens have betrayed us, and they spurn
Our supplications as they cruelly turn.
My tempered sword, that fought with elephants
And lions, will now I know be no defense
Against these naked Arabs, and all I see
Has only multiplied my misery.
Would that I had no knowledge, did not know
The good and evil that the heavens show.
The noble warriors who are with me here
Despise the Arabs, and they show no fear,
They think they'll turn the plain into a flood,
An Oxus flowing with these Arabs' blood;
None of them knows the heavens' will, or how
Immense a task awaits our armies now.
When fate withdraws its favor, why wage war?
What is the point of fighting any more?

"My brother, may God keep you safe; may you
Comfort the royal heart by all you do.
My grave is Qadesiya's battlefield,
My crown will be my blood, my shroud my shield.

The heavens will this; may my death not cause
Your heart to grieve too much at heaven's laws.
Watch the king always, and prepare to give
Your life in battle so that he may live—
The day comes soon when heaven's sphere will be,
Like Ahriman, our bitterest enemy."

He sealed the letter and summoned a messenger, saying to him, "Take this quickly to my brother, and tell him everything that is appropriate."

Rostam's Letter to Sa'd, the Son of Vaqas

He also sent a messenger, who rode like lightning, to Sa'd. The letter was written on white silk, and the scribe's script glittered like the sun. It was addressed "From the son of Hormozd the king, Rostam, the benevolent and foremost warrior of the world, to Sa'd the son of Vaqas, who seeks war and has made the world a dark and narrow place for himself."

The message began, "May the great God, whom we must fear, who has founded the turning heavens, and whose rule is one of justice and love, bless our prince, who is an adornment to the crown, the throne, and the royal seal, who is lord of the sword and crown, and whose glory binds Ahriman's evils. A contemptible business has been set afoot, involving pointless suffering and warfare. Tell me who your king is, and what kind of man you are, and what your customs and intentions are. You're a naked commander leading a naked army; on whose behalf are you fighting? Bread satisfies you, but you hunger for something more; you've no elephants, no thrones, no baggage train. Simple life in Iran would be enough for you; the crown and royal seal belong to another man, who has elephants, treasures, glory, power, and who is king by right of descent from father to son. When he appears, the moon is absent from the sky, and no king on earth has his stature. When he smiles at a banquet he gives away the ransom of the Arabs' leader, and his treasures remain undiminished by the gift. He has twelve thousand hunting dogs, cheetahs, and hawks, all with golden bells and ears decorated with jewels; in a year the plains where the Arabs live could not provide the food that his dogs and cheetahs run down in the hunt. His dogs and cheetahs eat more than you, and the cost is as nothing to the king.

"Is there no shame in your eyes, have you no wisdom or benevolence? And with your appearance, your lineage, your customs and character, you hope to gain the crown and throne? If you have ambitions in the world, and your words are not mere idle chatter, send me an experienced, eloquent warrior who can explain to me what your intentions are, and who has led you to the Persian throne; then we'll send a knight to the king to make your requests known.

"Don't make war against the king, because the end can only be a sorrowful one for you. He is descended from the world-ruler Nushin-Ravan, and his justice makes old men young again; his ancestors were kings and he is king, and time cannot show his equal. Do not make all the world curse you: a just, wise man who is not of royal lineage will not seek the throne. Look carefully at the advice I give you in this letter, and do not close your eyes and ears to wisdom." The letter was sealed and he handed it to the nobleman Piruz, the son of Shapur, who took it to Sa'd, the son of Vaqas. The Persian nobles waited, untroubled in their spirits, dressed in armor lavishly covered in gold and silver, with their golden shields and golden belts.

Sa'd's Answer to Rostam's Letter

Sa'd went out with his warriors to welcome the noble messenger. They brought him to their camp, and Sa'd questioned him about the king, his advisors, his army, and its commander. They spread a simple cloak for Piruz to sit on, and Sa'd said, "Our business is with swords and spears; men worth the name don't talk about brocade, or gold and silver, or sleeping and eating." The noble Piruz handed over the letter and repeated Rostam's words. Sa'd heard him out and read the letter, which astonished him.

He wrote an answer in Arabic, setting out things that were good and

things that were ugly. He wrote about jinns and human beings, about the words of the Hashemite prophet, about the unity of God and the Qoran, about what was promised and what was threatened, about God's support and the new ways; about the burning pitch and icy cold of hell; about the houris and streams, the camphor and water, the trees and wine and honey of paradise. Then he wrote, "If the king accepts this true faith, he will prosper in both this world and the next. He will keep his crown and royal earrings and live forever in splendor. Mohammad will intercede for his sins, and his body will be like distilled rosewater. Sow seeds that you will reap in paradise; it is wrong to plant hatred in the garden of disaster. I would not exchange the sight of one hair of one houri from heaven for the person of Yazdegerd himself, together with the wide earth and its orchards, castles, palaces, throne rooms, feasts and festivals. In this fleeting world your eyes have been dazzled by crowns and wealth; you trust in the ivory throne, in cheetahs and hawks and royal benevolence, but this world is not worth one gulp of sweet water, so why should it trouble your heart so much? Any man who opposes me in battle will see nothing but a narrow grave, and hell; if you join with me, your place will be in paradise. Consider carefully which you will choose." He set the Arab seal on the paper and invoked the name of Mohammad. He told Sho'beh Moghaireh to take the letter to the warrior Rostam.

The Persian commander was told, "A weak, old man is coming as a messenger; he has neither a horse nor armor, and he can hardly see. He carries a thin sword on his shoulder, and his clothes are tattered." Rostam had a brocade tent prepared and spread with Chinese carpets woven with gold; his troops were drawn up as thickly as ants or locusts. A golden chair was placed there, and Rostam seated himself on it; around him were gathered sixty of his warlike cavalry officers, dressed in purple clothes woven with gold and wearing golden shoes, torques, and earrings. The tent itself was royally adorned.

When Sho'beh reached the tent, he did not set foot on the carpets. He stood humbly in the dust, leaning against his sword as if it were a staff. Then he sat on the earth and paid no attention to anyone; he did not even look at the Persian commander. Rostam greeted him, "May your soul rejoice, your spirit know wisdom, and your body flourish." Sho'beh replied: "Your name is well known; if you accept the true faith, I will be satisfied." Rostam bridled at these words; he frowned and his face turned sallow. He took the letter from him and handed it to a scribe, who read it to him. Rostam answered, "Tell your master, 'You are not a king, and you have no right to seek a crown. Speech is not a trivial matter for wise men, and you don't know what it is you're undertaking.' If Sa'd wore the Sasanian crown it would be an easy matter for me to fight on his behalf; but you should realize that your star is faithless. How can I explain to you that today will be a day of disaster? If Mohammad himself were your leader, I could speak according to the old faith about this new faith. But the hunchbacked sky will deal harshly with me. Return in peace, since there is no place for talk on the day of battle. Tell your master that it is better to die honorably in battle than to live while an enemy triumphs over you."

Rostam's Battle with Sa'd; the Death of Rostam

Rostam ordered that the trumpets be sounded and his army surged forward like the sea. A cloud of dust rose up, and there was such a din of war cries that the sharpest ears were deafened. Like fire glimpsed through a purple curtain, diamond lances glittered in the darkened air, spears struck against helmets, and men's heads were trampled by horses' hooves. The battle continued for three days; then thirst made men's blows grow weaker and their horses too faint to fight. Rostam's lips were dry as dust; his mouth was parched and his tongue swollen and split. Both men and horses were so tormented by thirst that they ate damp clay. A cry like thunder went up, from Rostam on the one side and from Sa'd on the other: the two of them rode out from the body of their men and faced each other alone beneath a tall cypress tree. Rostam gave another thunderous cry and struck a sword blow against Sa'd's horse: the horse collapsed beneath him, and as Sa'd disentangled himself, Rostam lunged at him with his sharp sword, to prevent him from rising. He intended to sever Sa'd's head from his body, but the dust of the battlefield hid Sa'd from his sight. He jumped down from his leopard-skin saddle and tied his horse's bridle to his belt, but while he was blinded by dust, Sa'd attacked and struck Rostam's helmet a mighty blow with his sword. Blood poured from Rostam's head, filling his eyes, and the ambitious Arab triumphed over him. Sa'd thrust his sword into Rostam's chest and neck and hurled his warlike body into the dust.

The two armies were unaware of what was happening to their leaders, and began to search for them. When they saw Rostam lying bloody in the dust and his pavilion slashed into pieces, the Persians fled, and many of their noblemen were slaughtered. Many died of thirst while still in the saddle, and in this way the lives of many local kings came to an end. The remnant of the army sought their king, riding hard by day and night. At this time Yazdegerd was in Baghdad, and his soldiers flocked to him there.

Yazdegerd Consults with the Persians and Goes to Khorasan

Hormozd's other son, Farrokhzad, rode furiously to the Tigris, his eyes awash with tears. He reached Kerkh and attacked the enemy with such force that not an Arab warrior remained alive there. At the same time, troops poured out of Baghdad onto the plain and joined battle, but when the dust of combat rose into the sky the Persians were driven back. Farrokhzad retreated and made his way to the king, his armor and weapons smeared with the grime of battle. He dismounted from his horse and made his obeisance before the king, his eyes filled with bitter tears, his heart with anguish. He said, "What are you waiting for? You are putting the Persian throne at risk: of all the royal lineage, no one remains alive but you, there's no one else who's worthy to assume the crown and throne. You are one man and your enemies are a hundred thousand: how in all the world can you go on with this war? Go to the forests of Narvan; there men will join you until you have an army, and then like young Feraydun you will be able to make new plans for the future." The king listened to Farrokhzad's words, and turned over the alternatives in his mind.

The next day the king sat on his throne and placed the Kayanid crown on his head. He summoned an assembly of the wise, the nobility, and learned priests. He said to them, "What do you think of this proposal? What would you say that ancient precedents advise? Farrokhzad tells me to flee with an escort to the forests of Narvan, saying I have followers and supporters in Amol and Sari. When our armies have grown in size, that will be the time to return and give battle. Do you agree with this suggestion?" With one voice they answered, "This is not advisable!"

The King of Kings replied, "I agree with you; my heart cannot go along with this idea. Am I to save my own head and abandon Persia's nobility and its mighty armies, the land itself, and its throne and crown? This is neither noble nor chivalrous nor sensible. It's better that I fight with the enemy than endure such shame; a leopard-like warrior of ancient times once said, 'Never turn your back carelessly on an enemy, because this can only lead to evil days.' In the same way that the king's subjects owe him allegiance in good times and in bad, so the world's king must not abandon them to their sufferings while he flees to safety and luxury." The nobles called down blessings upon him, and said, "This is the way of true kings! Now consider your orders, and tell us what you wish of us."

The king answered, "My heart is destroyed by anxieties. We will travel to Khorasan, and there restore our strength after our enemies' attacks. We have many men there, many champions ready to fight for us. There are noblemen and Turks in the Chinese emperor's service; they will side with our cause, and I will marry a daughter of the emperor to make our alliance stronger. With their help I will have a mighty army of both our nobility and warlike Turks. Mahuy is lord of the marches there, and he has many men, war elephants, and wealth. He was a lowly shepherd, a laborer in the fields, and I promoted him because he spoke well and had a warlike nature. He had no status and I made him a lord of the marches with war elephants and an army and his own territory. He's a nobody, but he owes his good fortune to my court, and learned men have said it's an ancient precept that one should be wary of those to whom one has done evil, and trust in those whom one's generosity has lifted up to the heavens from nothingness."

Farrokhzad clapped his hands together and said, "My God-fearing king, don't trust men who have a lowly nature. There's a new proverb that says however much you try to mold a man's character, you don't have the key to change what God has made, and you won't alter what he is. May you know nothing but sovereignty and greatness!" The king replied, "You're a lion in combat, but no harm can come from this attempt of mine."

Night passed, and at dawn the court set out from Baghdad toward Khorasan, their hearts prepared for hardship. The Persian nobles who accompanied the king were grief-stricken. They invoked blessings on him, praying that the land never lose him, and a cry of sorrow went up from the army when they saw the king was leaving. Persians and subjects of the Chinese emperor alike came forward weeping to the king, their eyes flowing with tears, and said, "How can our hearts rejoice in our land without sight of the king? We shall abandon our homes and sons and wealth and share your hardships with you. We have no desire to live without your throne, and may good fortune never turn against you." Eloquent representatives of the Chinese emperor's men bowed their faces to the black earth and said, "We left our land and sought refuge with you; now we shall go with burning hearts to the emperor, fleeing before the Arabs to the Persian marches." The king's eyes became wet with tears and he sorrowfully addressed his noblemen: "All of you, pray to God, praise him endlessly, that I may see you all once again, and that this Arab attack be short-lived. You are my strength, inherited from my father, and I would not have you harmed, or share with me in an evil fate. We shall see if the heavens can turn toward benevolence again, but make your peace with them since there is no escaping what they will." Then he spoke to the Chinese merchants and said, "Do not stay in Persia long, because the Arabs will bring harm to you and your affairs." Everyone turned away, filled with grief and anguish, weeping and lamenting.

Farrokhzad, Hormozd's son, took command of the army and summoned experienced Persian warriors to serve. The king traveled, weeping and in sorrow, preceded by his commander and the troops. They went stage by stage to Rey, and there rested for a while, consoling themselves with wine and music. From Rey, partly hopeful and partly despairing, they pushed on like the wind to Gorgan; from there they took the road to Bost, their faces filled with frowns, their hearts with anxieties.

Yazdegerd's Letter to Mahuy and the Lords of the Marches of Khorasan

The king summoned an experienced scribe and vented the emotions of his heart. As he traveled toward Marv, he wrote a letter to Mahuy, the son of Suri, who was the governor there. It was a message filled with pain and bitterness, with his heart's desires and his eyes' tears. He opened the letter in the name of the Creator, the lord of knowledge from whom all benefits derive, who makes Mars and the sun turn in the heavens, who rules over both elephants and ants, who raises the lowly as he wishes and needs no precedent for his actions. He continued: "What evil days have befallen us! Our kingdom has lost its glory: Rostam was killed on the day of battle, at the hands of Sa'd, the son of Vaqas, a man who has no country, no lineage, no knowledge, and no wealth, and grief hems us in. Now that their armies are gathered like magpies before Baghdad, summon your troops to service and prepare them for war. I shall follow this letter like the wind and come to you trusting in your probity and generosity." He chose an intelligent man, capable of giving good advice, as his messenger.

The king had the army's drums sounded, and they pushed on from Bost and Nayshapur to Tus. When Mahuy learned of their approach, he went forward to meet the king with a mighty army, all of whom were armored and bore lances. When he saw the splendor of the king's entourage, with the royal banner and so many soldiers clustered about him, Mahuy quickly dismounted, and acted more like a slave than a subject, going meekly forward over the hot earth, his eyes flowing with tears of humility. He kissed the earth and made his obeisance, then waited humbly before the king for a long time. Farrokhzad's heart was filled with happiness when he saw Mahuy's face and his army's ranks, and he spoke with him at length. "I hand this king, descended from the Kayanid royal line, over to your protection," he said. "See that not a breath of wind is allowed to harm him. I must go to Rey, and I don't know when I shall see the royal crown again, since many others like me have been killed on the battlefield by the Arabs. There was no knight in all the world like Rostam, no wise man had ever heard of his equal, and yet he was killed by one of these crows with their black turbans, and the day of his death was a disaster for me. May God give him a place among the blessed, and that black crow a place where he'll be tormented by the lances of hell." Mahuy replied, "You are a great warrior; the king is as my own eyes and soul to me, and I accept your request that I protect him."

At the king's command, Farrokhzad set off for Rey, and soon the malevolent Mahuy forgot all thoughts of kindness. He spent his nights dreaming of the throne, and his manner and bearing changed. He pretended to be ill and neglected to serve the king as he should.

Mahuy Encourages Bizhan to Attack the King; the King Flees to a Mill

There was a successful warrior named Bizhan, whose family was from Tarkhan. His seat was in Samarqand, and he had many allies in the area. When the evil Mahuy was seized by ambition, he wrote a letter to Bizhan: "You are descended from a warrior race, and here is an opportunity for you to profit from battle. The king of the world, with his crown and throne and army, is here. If you attack, his head and crown and throne will be yours, together with his treasures and the black parasol held over the royal head." Bizhan considered the letter, and saw that the world was ambitious Mahuy's to take. He said to his vizier, "As the most honest of my men, what's your advice on this matter? If I lead my army out to help Mahuy, my situation here will be ruined: the Chinese king will have contempt for me and think of me as an opportunist and a time server. And if I don't do this, people will say I am a coward and afraid to fight." His vizier answered, "You are a lionhearted man, and it will be shameful for you to have offered friendship to Mahuy and then to back out of it. Send your ally Barsam to fight this battle; if you fight just because Mahuy encourages you to, serious men will call you frivolous." Bizhan said, "You're right, it's best for me to stay where I am. Send Barsam with ten thousand cavalry to Marv, and we'll see whether he can seize Persia's treasures in his fist."

Glittering like a pheasant's feathers, the army set off from Bokhara and arrived at the city of Marv in a week. Yazdegerd had no notion of Mahuy's treachery: when it was still dark, at the time the roosters crow, the sound of war drums rang out, and as day broke a horseman came galloping to the king, saying, "Mahuy says an army of Turks is attacking, led by the Chinese khan, and they are so numerous it seems the earth could not bear their weight. What are the king's orders?" The king leaped up and strapped on his armor, and the two armies came face to face. When Yazdegerd saw the Turks' forces, he clapped his hands together and drew his sword; he appeared before the army, massive as an elephant, and the ground was awash with blood like the Nile. But when the king attacked the Turks, none of his warriors followed him; they all turned their backs on their monarch and abandoned him to the enemy cavalry. And as Mahuy too drew back from the fight, leaving him in the midst of the enemy forces, Yazdegerd realized his treachery. The king fought furiously, striking out with his sword, urging his horse on with his stirrups, and killing many of the enemy's renowned warriors; but when he became more hard-pressed, he turned his back on the battle and fled. With many Turks in pursuit, a Kaboli sword in his grasp, he rode like lightning flashing from a cloud.

There was a mill by the River Zarq, and there the world's king dismounted and concealed himself from his enemies. Their cavalry were searching everywhere, and all the area was filled with talk of him. The king had abandoned his horse with its golden saddle, his mace, and his sword in its golden sheath, and when the Turks came on these they cried out in their excitement, while the king hid himself away, sitting on dry straw, in the mill. This is the way of the deceitful world, raising a man up and casting him down. When fortune was with him, his throne was in the heavens, and now a mill was his lot; the world's favors are many, but they are exceeded by its poison. Why should you bind your heart to this world, where the drums that signal your departure are heard continuously, together with the caravan leader's cry of "Prepare to leave"? The only rest you will find is that of the grave. So the king sat, without food, his eyes filled with tears, until the sun rose.

The miller opened the mill door, carrying a load of straw on his back. He was a humble man, called Khosrow, who possessed neither a throne, nor wealth, nor a crown, nor any power. He made his living from the mill and had no other occupation. He saw a warrior like a tall cypress tree, seated on the stony ground as a man sits in despair; a royal crown was on his head, and his clothes were made of glittering Chinese brocade. Khosrow stared at him in astonishment and murmured the name of God. He said, "Your majesty, your face shines like the sun; tell me, how did you come to be in this mill? How can a mill full of wheat and dust and straw be a place for you to sit? What kind of a man are you, with this stature and face of yours, and radiating such glory, because the heavens have never seen your like?"

The king replied, "I'm one of the Persians who fled from the army of Turan." The miller said in his confusion, "I've never known anything but poverty, but if you could eat some barley bread, and some of the common herbs that grow on the riverbank, I'll bring them to you, and anything else I can find. A poor man is always aware of how little he has." In the three days that had passed since the battle the king had had no food. He said, "Bring whatever you have, and a sacred barsom." The man quickly brought a basket

of barley bread and herbs and then hurried off to find a barsom at the river toll house. There he met up with the headman of Zarq and asked him for a barsom. Mahuy had sent people everywhere searching for the king, and the headman said, "Now, my man, who is it who wants a barsom?" Khosrow answered him, "There's a warrior sitting on the straw in my mill; he's as tall as a cypress tree, and his face is as glorious as the sun. His eyebrows are like a bow, his sad eyes like narcissi; his mouth is filled with sighs, his forehead with frowns. It's he who wants the barsom, to pray; if you saw him, you'd be astonished. I put an old basket with barley bread in it in front of him."

The headman said, "Run from here and tell Mahuy what you've said. But God forbid that evil-minded man should show his foul nature once he's heard this." And he immediately handed him over to a man who took him to Mahuy. Mahuy questioned him and said, "Who wanted a barsom? Tell the truth now!" Fearfully, the miller said, "I was carrying some materials I needed on my back, and I opened the mill door in a hurry, and it was as if I saw the sun shining in front of me. He had eyes like a deer's when it's afraid—they were as dark as the third watch of the night. The mill seemed filled with sunlight because of him; his crown was studded with uncut jewels, and he was dressed in Chinese brocade. He's like the springtime itself, and no landowner has ever planted a cypress as fine as he is."

Mahuy considered in his heart all he had heard and knew that this was none other than Yazdegerd. He turned to the miller and said, "Leave this assembly immediately and cut the man's head off; if you refuse I'll cut your head off here and now and leave not one member of your family alive." The noblemen gathered there heard his orders and they all seethed with anger; their eyes were filled with tears and everyone spoke vehemently against Mahuy's plan, including his own son.

Yazdegerd Is Killed by the Miller Khosrow

When Mahuy had heard his son out, he turned to the miller and said, "Get on with it; go now, and spill our enemy's blood." The miller heard him but could make no sense of what he was being told. It was the night of the thirtieth day of the month of Khordad, when the miller returned to his mill and the king. Mahuy left the court, his eyes filled with tears, his heart with fury, and sent horsemen after the miller, saying to them, "The crown and earrings, his seal ring and the royal clothes must not be stained with blood; remove his clothes from his body."

The miller wept and his face had turned sallow as he made his way home. He prayed, "O bright Creator, thou who art above the heavens' turning, make this man's soul and body suffer for this evil command he has given me!" His heart was filled with shame and fear as he approached the king; his cheeks were stained with tears, and his mouth was as dry as dust. He came up to the king like someone about to impart a secret in a man's ear and plunged a dagger beneath his ribs. The king sighed at the wound, and his head and crown fell down to the dust, beside the barley bread that lay before him.

> A man who understands the world soon says
> There is no sense or wisdom in its ways:
> If this is how imperial blood is spilled
> And innocents like Yazdegerd are killed,
> The seven spheres grow weary of their roles—
> No longer do they cherish mortal souls.
> The heavens mingle their malevolence
> With kindnesses in ways which make no sense,
> And it is best if you can watch them move
> Untouched by indignation and by love.

The wretched Mahuy's knights saw that the royal tree was felled from the throne and battlefield, and each of them went forward to gaze at his face. They undid the clasp of his purple cloak and removed his crown and torque and golden boots. Then, as they stood again before the king, they spoke at last and said, "May Mahuy's body be like his, weltering in its blood on the ground."

Quickly they took the clothes and jewels to Mahuy and said, "The king knows neither peace nor war now." He ordered that the body be thrown into the river, at night, when men are sleeping. Two callous servants hurried to carry out his command; unaware of its rank, they dragged the bloody body outside and threw it in the mill pond. When day followed night two religious ascetics came into view, and one of them approached the bank. He saw the naked body floating there, and ran horrified back to the monastery door, where he told the other monks what he had seen. "The king is lying naked and drowned in the Zarq mill pond," he said, and monks and priests came running from the monastery doors, crying out in grief for the king. One of them said, "No one has ever seen such an event, or heard of it, not from before the time of Jesus, that a wretched slave, a man of no account, should give a king hospitality and then murder him. May Mahuy be cursed for this! Alas for your head and crown and noble stature, for your heart and knowledge and wisdom! Alas for this scion of Ardeshir, for this young warlike knight! You were alive, healthy, and wise, and now you have taken news to Nushin-Ravan that you who ruled the world and sought out its crowns have been killed with a dagger plunged into your liver, and have been thrown naked into a mill pond."

Four of the monks stripped off their habits and went into the water. They dragged the body of the young king, the descendant of Nushin-Ravan, to dry land, and everyone there, young and old, wept as they did so. In a garden the monks built him a tomb that towered up to the clouds. They dried the dagger wound and treated the body with unguents, pitch, camphor, and musk; then they dressed it in yellow brocade, laid it on muslin, and placed a blue pall over it. Finally, a priest anointed the king's resting place with wine, musk, camphor, and rosewater.

Mahuy Assumes the Throne

A man came to Mahuy and said, "The king of the world is now one with the earth. Byzantine priests and monks have filled the land with mourning for him. Young and old, they went weeping to take his body from the mill pond. They built a great tomb for him in a garden." Evil and shameless, Mahuy said, "Until now, Persia has never been kin to Byzantium." He gave orders that all who had built the tomb or who had mourned for the king be killed, and the area be plundered; this was Mahuy's notion of pleasure and appropriate behavior.

Then he looked about him and saw that in all the world there was no remaining descendant of the royal line. This shepherd's son possessed the king's crown and seal ring, and he longed to rule. He called his confidants to him and told them all that was in his heart. He said to his vizier, "You are an experienced man, and you must know that a day of battle is looming. I have neither wealth, nor name, nor lineage to boast of, and I see that my life is at risk. The name on this seal ring is Yazdegerd's, and my sword is unable to pacify the people. All of the cities of Iran were his to command, but no wise man calls me king, and my seal's authority is not respected by the army. There were other alternatives to the things I did in secret; why did I shed the blood of the king of the world? I spend my nights tormented by anxiety, and God knows the state in which I live." His advisor said, "The deed is done, and the world is full of talk of it. Look to your own affairs, because you have cut the thread of the warp now. He lies in his tomb, beneath the dust, and has the cure for all the poisons that afflicted his soul. Call together men of experience and speak to them sweetly and plausibly. Say, 'The king gave me this crown and seal ring, as marks of authority. He did this because he knew an army of Turks was approaching. He summoned me in the darkness of the night and said, "When the dust of battle rises, who knows who will emerge victorious? Take this crown and seal ring, and it may be that some day they will be of use to you. This is all I have in the world, see that you hide them from the Arabs. Follow my precepts in all you do, and do not give my throne to the enemy." I have this crown as an inheritance from the king, and it is at his command that I sit on the throne.'

In this way you will put a good face on your deception: who will know whether this is the truth or a lie?"

When Mahuy heard his words he said, "Wonderful! You are a true vizier, there is none better!" He summoned the commanders of his army and spoke to them as his vizier had suggested. They knew that what he said was untrue, and that he deserved to have his head cut off for his impudence. One of the champions there said, "This is your business, whether what you say is true or not." Mahuy sat on the royal throne and became ruler of Khorasan by this ruse. He gave grants of land to the nobility, and said, "By virtue of this seal ring I am the world's king." He distributed the world's lands while the stars looked on in astonishment: he gave his elder son Balkh and Herat, and sent armies out in every direction. He promoted evil men, as might be expected of a scoundrel of his character, making criminals governors everywhere, and wise men had to bow their heads and obey them. On all sides, truth was humiliated and lies flourished. When this wretch had gathered together a large enough army and collected sufficient wealth, his heart rejoiced; he gave cash to his troops and planned to fight against Bizhan. He sent soldiers, under the command of an experienced warrior named Garsetun, as an advance guard to Amui. His troops marched on Bokhara and he said, "I must take Samarqand and Chach by the authority of this seal ring and crown, and by the command of Yazdegerd, the world's king, the lord of the seven spheres. I shall be revenged upon Bizhan, since it is he who has brought misfortune on Iran."

Bizhan Fights against Mahuy and Kills Him

News reached Bizhan that Mahuy had seized the imperial throne, sent orders far and wide sealed with the royal insignia, and subdued the countryside. Now he was heading toward the Oxus with an army eager for battle. Bizhan took his head in his hands at this turn of events, and then he summoned his troops to prepare for war. Information came that Mahuy's army had taken Samarqand; they were crossing the Oxus in boats, and the dust sent up by their troops hid the sun. Bizhan led his men out and prepared for battle; when Mahuy saw his opponent's ranks, their armor, helmets, and golden shields, their lances and maces and Chachi axes, his soul seemed to desert his body. Sick at heart, he drew up his troops; the air was obscured with dust, and the earth was invisible beneath the mass of combatants.

When battle was joined Bizhan planned to close in on Mahuy, but Mahuy realized this and, wailing in fear, he fled from the center of his army. Bizhan ordered his ally Barsam to lead men to the flank to cut him off. He said, "Mahuy is afraid of battle. Don't take your eyes off him, he mustn't be allowed to get back to the Oxus." Barsam watched Mahuy's banner; frowning and cursing, he led his men in pursuit of him as far as the sands of the River Farab. There he caught up with the fugitive and urged his horse forward. When they were face to face, instead of striking at him with his sword, Barsam reached out and caught Mahuy by the belt, and threw him easily to the ground. Then he dismounted, tied Mahuy's arms, and flung him on his own horse in front of the saddle. His companions arrived at this moment, and the whole plain was filled with talk of his exploit. They told him, "Don't bother taking him prisoner; you should cut his head off with an axe." Barsam answered, "This is not the way to act, because Bizhan doesn't know I've captured him."

Immediately Bizhan was informed that this vile slave, this ambitious traitor, the regicide Mahuy had been taken prisoner. Overjoyed to hear this, he exulted in his victory and banished care from his mind. A canopy was set up on the soft sand, and Mahuy was quickly brought there. When this sinner saw Bizhan, good sense deserted him; he became senseless with fear and began to scatter sand over his head. Bizhan addressed him, "You lowborn wretch, may no subject ever again act as you have done! Why did you kill our just king, the lord of victory and the throne? From father to son he inherited kingship and was a king himself, the living emblem of Nushin-Ravan." Mahuy said, "From an evil person you should expect nothing but murder and sedition. Cut off my head for the wicked deed I've done, and fling it before this assembly." He was afraid that he would be flayed alive, and that his body would be dragged along, weltering in its blood.

Bizhan knew his secret terror, and he paused a while before answering. Then he said, "I want to cleanse my heart of hatred for you. With this chivalry of yours, this knowledge and understanding and character, you coveted the crown and throne." He cut off Mahuy's hands with his sword and said, "These hands have no equal in crime." Then he cut off his feet so that he couldn't move from the spot. Finally, he gave orders that Mahuy's ears and nose be cut off, and that he be sat on a horse, and left wandering the hot sands till he died of shame. He had a herald go about the camp and announce at each tent, "May those slaves who would kill their king think better of their foolishness; may those who wouldn't give their lives for the king be as Mahuy is, and may they never know glory!" Mahuy had three sons with his army, each with his own crown and throne. There and then a fire was lit, and the father and his three sons were burned in it. None of his family survived, or if they did, anyone who met them drove them away; may the nobility curse this family forever, and hate them for their murder of the king.

After this came the era of Omar, and when he brought the new faith, the pulpit replaced the throne.

After sixty-five years had passed over my head, I toiled ever more diligently and with greater difficulty at my task. I searched out the history of the kings, but my star was a laggard one. Nobles and great men wrote down what I had written without paying me: I watched them from a distance, as if I were a hired servant of theirs. I had nothing from them but their congratulations; my gall bladder was ready to burst with their congratulations! Their purses of hoarded coins remained closed, and my bright heart grew weary at their stinginess. But of the renowned men of my district, Ali Daylami helped me, and that honorable man Hosayn Qotayb never asked for my works for nothing. I received food and clothing, silver and gold from him, and it was he who gave me the will to continue. I never had to worry about paying taxes and was able to wrap myself in my quilt in comfort, and when I reached the age of seventy-one, the heavens humbled themselves before my verses. Now I have brought the story of Yazdegerd to an end, in the month of Sepandormoz, on the day of Ard, and four hundred years have passed since the Hejira of the Prophet.

> I've reached the end of this great history
> And all the land will fill with talk of me:
> I shall not die, these seeds I've sown will save
> My name and reputation from the grave,
> And men of sense and wisdom will proclaim,
> When I have gone, my praises and my fame.

GLOSSARY OF NAMES AND THEIR PRONUNCIATION

The following is a list of the names which appear in the stories included in this volume, together with a brief description of whom or what they designate.

Persian names are pronounced with a more even stress than is common in English, and to an English speaker's ear this often sounds as if the last syllable is being stressed. A slight, extra stress on the last syllable of names will bring the reader closer to a Persian pronunciation.

Persian has two distinct sounds indicated in English by the letter "a." One is a long sound (as in "father") and this has been indicated here by the accent "ā" (e.g., Zāl). The other is a short sound (as in "cat") and this has been indicated by the standard "a" (e.g., Zav). The vowel given as "i" is a long vowel, like the second vowel in "police." The vowel given as "u" is also a long vowel, like the first vowel in "super." "Q" and "gh" are pronounced approximately as a guttural hard "g," far back in the throat. "Zh" is pronounced like the sound represented by the "s" in "pleasure." "Kh" is pronounced like the Scottish "ch" in "loch."

ABBĀS: an Arab warrior who attacks Iran during the reign of Hormozd.

ABUL FAZL: the librarian of the Samanid king Nasr.

ABU BAKR: the successor of the Prophet Mohammad as the leader of the Moslem community.

AFRĀSYĀB: a legendary king of Turan (Transoxiana and central Asia).

AHRIMAN: the evil principle of the universe; the devil.

AHVĀZ: a city in southeastern Iran.

ALĀN: an Iranian tribe from the central Asian steppes.

ALI DAYLAMI: a man who supported Ferdowsi during his writing of the *Shahnameh*.

ALTOUYANEH: the site of a major Sasanian victory over the Romans. It seems likely that the victory referred to is the one that took place near Edessa in 259 C.E., when the Roman emperor Valerian was captured by Shāpur I.

ĀMOL: a city to the south of the Caspian Sea.

ĀMOURIEH: the area between the River Jordan and the Mediterranean.

AMUI: a plain to the north of the River Oxus.

ANDIĀN: an Armenian chieftain.

ĀRASH: an Ashkāniān (Parthian) king.

ARD: the twenty-fifth day of every month in the Zoroastrian calendar.

ARDAVĀN: the last Ashkāniān king, defeated by Ardeshir.

ARDEBIL: a town in northwestern Iran.

ARDESHIR BĀBAKĀN: the founder of the Sāsāniān dynasty. Also Ardeshir, the brother of King Shāpur Z'ul Aktāf, who acts as regent on the death of Shāpur.

ARESTĀLIS: Aristotle.

ĀREZU: the daughter of the jeweler Māhyār; a consort of Bahrām Gur.

ARJASP: a Turāniān prince who fought against Esfandyār.

ARMANI: a Persian warrior.

ARMENIA: the country of the Armenians to the northwest of Iran.

ARZHANG: a legendary Chinese painter.

ASHK: the name of the founder of the Ashkāniān dynasty.

ASHKĀNIĀN: the Parthians; the dynasty that ruled Iran from 247 B.C.E. to 224 C.E., i.e. from the defeat of the Seleucid heirs of Alexander until the advent of the Sāsāniāns.

AVESTĀ: see Zend-Avesta.

ĀYIN-GOSHASP: a scribe at the court of Hormozd.

ĀZĀDEH: a slave belonging to Bahrām Gur.

ĀZĀD-SARV: Nushin-Ravān's envoy, who discovers Bozorjmehr.

ĀZAR: the ninth solar month, and the ninth day of any month, in the Zoroastrian year.

ĀZAR-GOSHASP: the name of a fire-temple in Balkh. Also of a companion of Bahrām Chubineh.

ĀZARM-DOKHT: a Sāsāniān queen who reigned for four months. The sister of Purān-Dokht.

ĀZARMEGAN: the father of Farrokhzad, the chamberlain of Khosrow Parviz.

ĀZAR-PANĀH: apparently the name of a fire-temple, but unattested outside of the *Shahnameh*. According to some mss. the name of a scribe at the court of Nushin-Ravan.

BĀBAK: a ruler of Estakhr; the maternal grandfather of Ardeshir.

BADAKHSHĀN: an area in the northeast of Afghanistan, famous for its remoteness and its rubies.

BĀDĀN-PIRUZ: a supporter of Khosrow Parviz when he is out of favor with his father Hormozd.

BAHMAN: also called Ardeshir: the father and husband of Homāy.

BAHMAN: a son of Ardavān, the last Ashkāniān king.

BAHMAN: a courtier of Khosrow Parviz.

BAHMAN: a winter month, and the second day of every month, in the Zoroastrian calendar.

BAHRĀM: also called Ardavān: the last Ashkāniān king. A descendant of Seyāvash; a cavalry commander under Bahrām Chubineh. Also the name of the twentieth day of each of the Zoroastrian months.

BAHRĀM BAHRĀM: a minor Sāsāniān king.

BAHRĀM BAHRĀMIĀN: a minor Sāsāniān king.

BAHRĀM CHUBINEH: a champion in the service of Hormozd and Khosrow Parviz. He rebels against his monarchs and attempts to seize the throne for himself.

BAHRĀM GUR: a Sāsāniān king: the son of Yazdegerd the Unjust.

BAHRĀM HORMOZD: a minor Sāsāniān king.

BAHRĀM PIRUZ: a nobleman in the service of Bahrām Gur.

BAHRĀM SHĀPUR: a minor Sāsāniān king.

BAHRĀM ĀZAR-MAHĀN: an advisor at the courts of Kesrā Nushin-Ravān and Hormozd.

BALĀSH: a minor Sasanian king.

BALKH: a city in northern Afghanistan.

BĀMYĀN: a valley in northern Afghanistan.

BANDUY: a maternal uncle of King Khosrow Parviz. Also an advisor to Nushin-Ravān.

BARAK: the name of a river and a town in northeastern Afghanistan.

BARĀNUSH: A Roman commander captured by Shāpur I. Also a Roman emperor contemporary with Shāpur Z'ul Aktāf. The historical origin of both figures is probably the emperor Valerian captured by Shāpur I in 259 C.E.

BĀRBAD: a musician who serves King Khosrow Parviz.

BARDA': a town in Azerbaijan.

BARKEH-YE ARDESHIR: a town founded by Ardeshir.

BARSĀM: the son of Bizhan, the governor of Samarqand during the reign of Yazdegerd lll

BARSOM: sacred rods used in Zoroastrian ceremonies.

BEDĀL: a warrior chieftain from Khazar.

BEHZĀD: the father of Mehr-Piruz, a warrior of Bahrām Gur. Also an advisor to Kesrā Nushin-Ravān.

BESTĀM: a town in northern Iran.

BISITUN: a mountain in southwestern Iran.

BITQUN: a vizier of Sekandar. When Sekandar visits Queen Qaydāfeh, he pretends to be Bitqun.

BIVARD: a contender for the crown, after the death of Yazdegerd the Unjust.

BIZHAN: an Ashkāniān ruler. A warrior of Tarkhān. A legendary hero, lover of Manizheh.

BOKHĀRĀ: a city in Transoxiana.

BORZIN: the name of a priest of Zoroaster who built the fire-temple named after him.

BORZUI: a doctor who brings the book *Kalileh and Demneh* from India. Also the name assumed by Bahrām Gur when he visits India in disguise.

BOST: a fortress in Khorāsān.

BOZORJMEHR: meaning "Great Light". The vizier of Kesrā Nushin-Ravān. The modern form of the name is Bozarjomehr.

CHĀCH: a city in Turkestan famous for the bows made there. Chachi is its adjectival form.

CHĀJ: a town near Birjand in eastern Iran.

CTESIPHON: the Sāsāniān capital, on the River Tigris.

DĀRĀ: the son of King Dārāb, defeated by Sekandar.

DĀRĀB: the son of Bahman and Homāy. The father of Dārā and Sekandar.

DARI: a name for the Persian language of eastern Iran and Afghanistan.

DAYLAM: a city in Gilān, to the south of the Caspian Sea.

DELAFRUZ: the name of a thorn-cutter encountered by Bahrām Gur.

DELAFRUZ-E FARROKHPAY: a servant girl who helps Shāpur escape from captivity in Rome.

DELĀRĀY: the wife of Dārā and mother of Roshanak.

ESDRAS: identified with the Hebrew prophet Ezra.

ESFAHAN: a city in central Iran.

ESFANDYĀR: a legendary prince of Iran, and proselytizer for Zoroastrianism. Killed by Rostam.

ESMAIL: a son of Abraham, whose descendants claimed the right to rule in the Yemen at the time of Sekandar.

ESRĀFIL: the angel of death.

ESTAKHR: a city in central Iran.

EUPHRATES: one of the major rivers of Mesopotamia. For many years the de facto border between the Sāsāniān and the Roman empires.

FARĀB: a town on the River Oxus.

FARĀYIN: a supporter of Kesrā Nushin-Ravān against Mazdak.

FARIGIS: the daughter of Afrāsyāb and bride of Seyāvash.

FARROKHZĀD: the chamberlain of Khosrow Parviz. This is apparently a different Farrokhzād from the man who reigned briefly after the death of Queen Āzarm-Dokht.

FARROKHZĀD: the brother of Rostam the son of Hormozd (who leads Yazdegerd III's armies against the Arab invaders).

FĀRS: a central/southern province of Iran. The homeland of the Sāsāniāns.

FARSHIDVARD: a miserly landowner, encountered by Bahrām Gur.

FARYĀN: an Arab king who reigns on the borders of the lands ruled by Queen Qaydāfeh.

FERAYDUN: a legendary Persian king.

FILQUS: Philip of Macedon, the father of Nāhid, and grandfather of Sekandar (Alexander the Great).

FOOR: an Indian prince who fights against Sekandar.

FORUD: one of the sons of Shirin.

GALINUSH: Khosrow Parviz's jailer, after he is imprisoned by his son.

GARSETUN: an ally of Māhuy, the warlord who reigns briefly after the murder of Yazdegerd III.

GERDUI: a counselor to Khosrow Parviz. Brother of Gordyeh and Bahrām Chubineh.

GHASSĀNID: an Arab tribe.

GILĀN: a province to the south of the Caspian Sea.

GOLNĀR: Ardavān's treasurer and Ardeshir's lover.

GORĀZ: lord of the western marches under Khosrow Parviz. After the death of Khosrow Parviz's son Shirui, and then of Shirui's son Ardeshir, Gorāz seizes the throne and reigns for two months.

GORDYEH: the sister of Bahrām Chubineh and of Gerdui. She is briefly the wife of Gostahm, whom she murders, and then of Khosrow Parviz.

GORGĀN: a town in northern Iran.

GORZĀSP: Shāpur's commander of the Persian armies against the Romans.

GOSHASP: the father of Qāren. A warrior present at the death of Yazdegerd the Unjust. The name Bahrām Gur assumes in the house of the jeweler Māhyār.

GOSHTASP: a legendary Persian king, the father of Esfandyār. Perhaps identical with the Achaemenid king, Vishtaspa.

GOSTAHM: a maternal uncle of Khosrow Parviz and a major participant in the struggles for the throne during Khosrow's and his father Hormozd's reigns. Also the name of a Persian warrior during the reigns of Yazdegerd the Unjust and Bahrām Gur.

GUDARZ: an Ashkāniān king. Also, a hero of the poem's legendary section, at the time of the Kayānid kings.

HABASH: the name given collectively to the tribes of Africa.

HAFTVĀD: the father of the girl who finds the "Worm" of Kerman: he rebels against the Sāsāniān king Ardeshir.

HĀMĀVERĀN: Sudābeh's country of origin, usually identified with the Yemen.

HAMDĀN-GOSHASP: a Persian commander under Bahrām Chubineh

HAMEDĀN: a city in western Iran.

HAMZEH: an Arab warrior who attacks Iran during the reign of Hormozd.

HARUM: a town inhabited entirely by women, visited by Sekandar.

HEJĀZ: Western Arabia.

HEJIRA: the flight of the prophet Mohammad from Mecca to Medina in 622 C.E., which marks the beginning of the Moslem calendar.

HERĀT: a city in western Afghanistan.

HOMĀY: the daughter and wife of Bahman; the mother of Dārāb. Also the name of a priest sent as an envoy by the Persian nobility to the emperor of China during the reign of Bahrām Gur.

HORMOZD: a Sāsāniān king; the son of Nushin-Ravān and the father of Khosrow Parviz. A name for Āhura Mazdā, the good principle of the universe. An advisor to Nushin-Ravān.

HOSAYN QOTAYB: a man who supported Ferdowsi during his writing of the *Shahnameh*.

HOSHYĀR: a Persian astrologer.

HUSHANG: a mythical king of Iran.

IRAJ: a mythical prince; the son of Feraydun, he was murdered by his brothers Tur and Salm.

IZAD-GOSHASP: a councilor of Nushin-Ravān, put to death by Hormozd. Also an army commander under Bahrām Chubineh.

JAHROM: a town in southern Iran.

JĀMĀSP: vizier to the legendary kings Lohrāsp and Goshtasp.

JĀNFOROUZ: a warrior in Bahrām Chubineh's army.

JĀNUSHYĀR: an advisor to King Dārā, whom he kills.

JAVĀNUI: a priest sent as an envoy by the Persian nobility to Monzer, the guardian of the young Bahrām Gur.

JAZA': a tyrannical ruler of the Hejāz.

JEDDAH: a coastal town in the Hejāz.

JEZ: Mesopotamia.

JONDESHĀPUR: a city in western Iran.

JORM: a magical site, from which a voice speaks to the mourners of Sekandar.

KA'ABEH: the central Moslem shrine, in Mecca.

KĀBOL: a city in eastern Afghanistan. Kāboli is the adjective.

KAJĀRĀN: a town near the Persian Gulf, in southeastern Iran.

KALBUI: an ally of Rostam (the son of Hormozd) at the battle of Qādesiya.

KALILEH AND DEMNEH: the name of a book of advice cast in the form of animal fables.

KARZEBĀN: a town in Khorāsān.

KĀVIĀNI: an adjective from the name of the mythical blacksmith Kāveh, applied to the banner of the Persian kings.

KĀVUS: a legendary Persian king.

KAYĀNID: the name of the dynasty of the legendary Persian kings, up to the reign of Kay Khosrow.

KAYD: an Indian king.

KAYUMARS: a mythical Persian king.

KEBRUI: a village headman who becomes drunk at the court of Bahrām Gur.

KENĀM-E ASIRĀN: a city built in the reign of Shāpur as a home for Roman prisoners.

KERKH: a town in Mesopotamia.

KESHMIHAN: a city near Marv, in Transoxiana.

KESHVĀD: Gudarz's father; the tribe to which Gudarz belonged.

KESRĀ: see Nushin-Ravān.

KEYD: an Indian sage.

KHANJAST: a supporter of Khosrow Parviz when he is out of favor with his father Hormozd.

KHARRAD: the warrior who captures Ardavān when he is defeated by Ardeshir.

KHATLĀN: the area around Samarqand

KHAZAR: the area to the south and east of the Caspian Sea.

KHAZRAVĀN: a chieftain who fights in the armies of Bahrām Gur.

KHEZR: a Qoranic (and probably pre-Qoranic) figure: in medieval legend the guardian of the waters of immortality.

KHORAD-BORZIN: a confidant of Hormozd. Also, the name of a fire temple.

KHORĀSĀN: the northeastern province of Iran as it was in the Sāsānian period, when its northern boundary was the River Oxus

KHORDĀD: a supporter of Nushin-Ravān against Mazdak. The name of the third month and the sixth day of every month in the Zoroastrian calendar.

KHORRAMĀBĀD: a city built by Shāpur, in western Iran.

KHOSROW: a claimant to the Persian throne after the death of Yazdegerd the Unjust. The name of the miller who kills Yazdegerd III. Also a legendary king.

KHOSROW PARVIZ: a Persian king, the son of Hormozd, father of Shirui, husband of Mariam and Shirin.

KHOTAN: northeastern central Asia.

KHURREH-YE ARDESHIR: a town in Pars, built by King Ardeshir.

KHUZESTĀN: the southeastern province of Iran.

KOHANDEZH: a number of sites in Iran and Transoxiana bear this name, which means "ancient fortress." It is unclear which of them is meant in Ferdowsi's text.

KUFAH: a city in southern Iraq.

KUT: a Byzantine warrior.

LOHRĀSP: a legendary Persian king.

LURIS: a tribal people of western Iran. Ferdowsi claims they were brought from India by Nushin-Ravān.

MĀHAZĀR: a counselor to Nushin-Ravān.

MĀHUY: the governor of Khorāsān in the time of Yazdegerd III; after Yazdegerd's death he proclaims himself king.

MĀHYĀR: a Zoroastrian priest who is

one of the two murderers of King Dārā. Also a jeweler whose daughter Ārezu marries Bahrām Gur.

MAJUJ: *see* Yajuj and Majuj.

MAKRĀN: the southeastern seaboard of Iran.

MALEKEH: the daughter of the Persian princess Nobahār and her Arab abductor Tāyer.

MĀMUN: an Abbasid caliph (reigned 813 C.E. to 833 C.E.).

MANDAL: an Indian king.

MĀNI: a prophet and painter who appeared in the reign of Shāpur.

MANIZHEH: a daughter of king Afrāsyāb of Turan; the lover of Bizhan.

MANUCHEHR: a legendary Persian king.

MARDĀNSHĀH: one of Shirin's sons.

MARDUY: a gardener who befriends the musician Bārbad.

MARGH: a town in northwestern India.

MARIAM: a daughter of the emperor of Byzantium; a wife of Khosrow Parviz; the mother of Shirui.

MARV: a city in northern Khorāsān.

MARVRUD: a river in Khorāsān; also the name of a town situated on the river.

MAYSĀN: a city in Mesopotamia founded by Ardeshir.

MAZDAK: a prophet and social reformer who appeared in the reign of King Qobād, and was opposed by Qobād's son Kesrā Nushin-Ravān.

MEHRBANDĀD: a farmer encountered by Bahrām Gur while Bahrām is out hunting.

MEHR-ĀZĀD: an advisor to Nushin-Ravan

MEHRAK: a rebel who looted King Ardeshir's palace while the king was fighting against Haftvād of Kerman.

MEHRĀN-SETĀD: an envoy sent by Nushin-Ravān to China.

MEHR-BORZIN: a warrior during the reign of Bahrām Gur.

MEHR-HORMOZD: the murderer of Khosrow Parviz

MEHREGĀN: the autumn festival of the Zoroastrian year.

MERUI: an ally of Rostam (the son of Hormozd) at the battle of Qādesiya.

MILĀD: a city in western India.

MONZER: an Arab prince who brings up Bahrām Gur.

MOSHK: one of four sisters, all musicians, whom Bahrām Gur incorporates into his harem.

NĀHID: the daughter of Filqus, wife of Dārāb, and mother of Sekandar.

NAHRAVĀN: a city in Mesopotamia; also a river of undetermined location (the word *ravan* means "flowing," *nahr* "channel").

NĀRVAN: a forested area near the Caspian Sea.

NASIBIN: a town in Mesopotamia, known for its monasteries and Christian population.

NASR: an Arab chieftain of the Hejāz, befriended by Sekandar; also a Sāmānid king.

NASTUD: one of the sons of Shirin.

NASTUH: a servant to King Hormozd.

NAYSHĀPUR: a town in northeastern Iran.

NĀZ: one of four sisters, all musicians, whom Bahrām Gur incorporates into his harem.

NERSI: a Sāsāniān king (Nersi Bahman), the father of the princess Nobahār. Also, the brother of Bahrām Gur, who acts as regent in Bahrām's absence.

NIĀTUS: the brother of the emperor of Byzantine; he is put in charge of the troops the emperor lends to Khosrow Parviz.

NISĀ: a town founded by the Parthians, about halfway between the Caspian Sea and Marv.

NOBAHĀR: the daughter of King Nersi; she is abducted by the Arab chieftain Tāyer and gives birth to a daughter, Malekeh.

NO'MAN: the son of Monzer, Bahrām Gur's Arab guardian.

NOSHĀD: a city built by Dārā.

NOZAR: a legendary Persian king.

NUSHIN-RAVĀN: also called Kesrā: a Sāsāniān king, the son of King Qobad and father of King Hormozd. The modern form of his name, which means "eternal soul," is Anushirvān.

NUSHZĀD: Nushin-Ravān's son, by the daughter of the Roman emperor, who adopts his mother's faith (Christianity) and rebels against his father. Also, the father of Mehrak, a rebel against Ardeshir.

OMAR, IBN AL-KHATTĀB: the second of the caliphs who succeeded the prophet Mohammad; in his reign Iran was invaded by the Arab armies bringing the new religion of Islam.

OXUS: the river that traditionally marked the boundary between Iran and central Asia.

PAHLAVI: the form of Persian spoken before the Arab conquest in the seventh century C.E.

PARMOUDEH: the son of Sāveh-Shāh, leader of the central Asian Turks and the emperor of China.

PARTHIAN: see Ashkāniān.

PASHIN: the son of the legendary king Kay Qobad, and the ancestor of Khosrow, who is placed on the throne by the Persian nobility after the death of Yazdegerd the Unjust.

PAYDĀ-GOSHASP: a warrior chieftain and companion of Bahrām Chubineh.

PIRUZ: the envoy of Rostam (the son of Hormozd), to the Arab armies. Also, a Persian noble who opposes the accession of Bahrām Gur to the throne. Also, a minor Sāsāniān king.

PIRUZ-SHIR: a warrior who reproaches Nushzād when he rebels against his father, King Nushin-Ravān.

PURĀN-DOKHT: a Sāsāniān queen.

QĀDESIYA: the site of a decisive battle between the Sasanian and Arab armies, in 637 C.E.

QAHTĀB: an Arab conqueror of the Hejāz.

QALUN: a Turk who is suborned by Khorad Borzin to kill Bahrām Chubineh.

QANUJ: a city in northern India.

QĀREN: a number of warriors are called this; it was the name of one of the chief families of Sāsāniān Iran.

QAYDĀFEH: the Queen of Andalusia during the time of Sekandar. Also the name of a Roman province.

QAYDRUS: a son of Queen Qaydāfeh.

QAYSIĀN: an Arab tribe.

QAYTUN: the king of Egypt during the time of Sekandar.

QEISAR-NAVĀN: a border area between Roman and Persian territory.

QOBĀD: Another name for Shirui, the son of Khosrow Parviz. Also Kay Qobād, a legendary Persian king. Also a Sasanian king, the father of Nushin-Ravān.

QORĀN: the holy book of Islam.

QOTAYB: an Arab tribe. Also the father of Nasr, a chieftain befriended by Sekandar.

RĀM-BORZIN: a confidant of Kesra Nushin-Ravān and the commander of his armies during Nushzad's rebellion.

RESHNAVĀD: a Persian general during the reign of Homāy.

REY: a city in northern central Iran, to the south of modern Tehran.

ROSHANAK: the daughter of Dārā and wife of Sekandar.

ROSTAM: the greatest champion of the legendary section of the *Shahnameh*.

ROSTAM, THE SON OF HORMOZD: the commander of the Persian armies under Yazdegerd III.

RUDAKI: the tenth-century Persian poet who versified *Kalileh and Demneh*.

RUZBEH: a priest and counselor to Bahrām Gur.

SABAK: the ruler of Jahrom who joins Ardeshir, the founder of the Sāsāniān dynasty, against the remnants of Ashkāniān power.

SA'D, THE SON OF VAQĀS: the commander of the Arab armies that invaded Iran during the reign of Yazdegerd III.

SADEH: a festival of the Zoroastrian calendar.

SALM: one of the sons of the legendary king Feraydun, brother to Tur and Iraj.

SĀM: a supporter of Khosrow Parviz when he is out of favor with his father Hormozd. Also the father of the legendary hero Zāl.

SAMARQAND: a city in Transoxiana.

SARKESH: a musician at the court of Khosrow Parviz.

SĀSĀN: a Persian prince who flees to India and lives there as a shepherd; the ancestor of Ardeshir, the founder of the Sāsāniān dynasty. In the story of Bahman and Homāy, he is Bahman's son; in the story of Dārā, he is Dārā's son.

SĀSĀNIAN: the dynasty that ruled Iran from 224 C.E. to 612 C.E.

SĀVEH SHĀH: a central Asian Turkish leader, also referred to as the emperor of China, who attacks Iran during the reign of King Hormozd.

SAVORG: Sekandar's regent in India.

SEKANDAR: Alexander the Great. The Arabic version of his name was (Al-) Eskandar; Sekandar is Ferdowsi's usual adaptation of this.

SEPANDORMOZ: the twelfth month of the Zoroastrian calendar.

SEPINOUD: an Indian princess who marries Bahrām Gur; the daughter of King Shangal.

SERGIUS: a Byzantine warrior.

SEYĀVASH: a legendary Persian prince, the son of Kay Kāvus.

SHABDIZ: a horse belonging to Bahrām Gur. Also a horse belonging to Khosrow Parviz.

SHABRANG: a horse belonging to Bahrām Gur.

SHĀDEGAN: the garden where Khosrow Parviz's wife, Shirin, answers Shirui's accusations against her.

SHAHD: an unidentified place, and body of water, in eastern Iran.

SHAHRGIR: a warrior who captures Qaydrus, one of the sons of Qaydafeh, the queen of Andalusia. Also a commander in Ardeshir's army.

SHAHRYĀR: one of the sons of Shirin.

SHĀHUY: the son of Haftvād, a warlord who rebels against Ardeshir.

SHANGAL: the king of India during the reign of Bahrām Gur.

SHĀPUR: the name of a number of Sāsāniān kings, the most significant of whom are Shāpur I, the son of Ardeshir, and Shāpur Z'ul-Aktāf.

SHĀPURGERD: a city built by King Shāpur I to accommodate Roman prisoners.

SHAYBĀN: an Arab tribe.

SHEGNĀN: a contender for the Persian throne after the death of Yazdegerd the Unjust.

SHEMĀS: a Christian general who helps Nushzād in his rebellion against his father, King Nushin-Ravān.

SHEMIRĀN: a maternal ancestor of Bahrām Gur.

SHEMR: a warrior whom Bahrām Gur places on the throne of Turān.

SHIRĀN: a supporter of Khosrow Parviz when he is out of favor with his father, Hormozd.

SHIRĀZ: a city in southern Iran.

SHIRIN: a wife of Khosrow Parviz.

SHIRUI: the son of Mariam and Khosrow Parviz; he reigns as king for seven months.

SHIR-ZIL: a supporter of Khosrow Parviz when he is out of favor with his father, Hormozd.

SHO'AYB: an Arab chieftain defeated by Dārāb.

SHO'BEH MOGHAIREH: the Arab envoy to Rostam, the son of Hormozd.

SHURESTĀN: an area near the lands of the Arab king Monzer: the name means "place of bitterness" and is used to refer to a salt desert.

SHUSHTAR: a city in southeastern Iran.

SIMĀ-BORZIN: an advisor of Nushin-Ravān, killed by Nushin-Ravān's son Hormozd.

SIND: a northwestern province of India, now part of Pakistan.

SISANAK: one of four sisters, all musicians, whom Bahrām Gur incorporates into his harem.

SISTĀN: a province of southeastern Iran and southern Afghanistan, lying largely to the east of the modern Persian province of the same name.

SOGHDIA: Transoxiana.

SORUSH: a Zoroastrian angel. Also, an Indian astrologer. Also, the seventeenth day of every Zoroastrian month.

SU: a legendary fountain where it is prophesied that Yazdegerd the Unjust will die.

SURI: the father of Māhuy (the governor of Khorāsān) during the reign of Yazdegerd III.

SUSANAK: one of four sisters, all musicians, whom Bahrām Gur incorporates into his harem.

TABARISTĀN: the area to the south of the Caspian Sea.

TAHMURES: a legendary Persian king.

TARĀZ: a town in Transoxiana.

TARKHĀN: an area in Transoxiana.

TĀYER: an Arab chieftain who attacks Ctesiphon at the beginning of the reign of Shāpur Zu'l-Aktāf and abducts the princess Nobahār.

TAYNUSH: a son of Qaydāfeh, queen of Andalusia. Also, a Roman envoy to the court of Yazdegerd the Unjust.

TIGRIS: the river forming the eastern boundary of Mesopotamia.

TOKHVĀR: a member of the conspiracy to place Shirui on the throne in place of his father Khosrow Parviz.

TOVORG: a brother of the emperor of China, who tries to detain Gordyeh after her bother Bahrām Chubineh is murdered. Gordyeh kills him.

TUR: one of the sons of the legendary king Feraydun, brother to Salm and Iraj.

TURĀN: Transoxiana and central Asia.

TUS: a town in Khorāsān. Also a legendary Persian hero.

VASTUI: a supporter of Khosrow Parviz when he is out of favor with his father Hormozd.

YAJUJ AND MAJUJ: monstrous beings defeated by Sekandar. Identified with Gog and Magog.

YALĀN-SINEH: a warrior and companion of Bahrām Chubineh.

YĀNUS: a younger brother of the Roman emperor captured by Shāpur: he leads an army against Shāpur and is defeated in battle by him.

YAZDEGERD: the name of three Sāsāniān kings; Yazdegerd the Unjust, the father of Bahrām Gur; Yazdegerd II, the son of Bahrām Gur; and Yazdegerd III, a descendant of Nushin-Ravān and the last Sāsāniān king. Also a scribe at the court of Nushin-Ravān.

ZĀBOL: the chief city of the province of Sistān, what was also called Zābolestān, and Zāvolestān.

ZAHHĀK: a legendary demon king, who deposed Jamshid and was deposed by Feryadun.

ZARDHESHT: the chief priest at the opening of the reign of Hormozd.

ZARMEHR: an advisor to Nushin-Ravān.

ZARQ: a village, and also the name of the river, where Yazdegerd was killed.

ZĀVOLESTĀN: see Zābol.

ZEND-AVESTĀ: the sacred text of Zoroastrianism.

❧ A NOTE ON THE TEXT ❧

The translations of the stories in this volume are based mainly on the Persian text of the *Shahnameh* edited by Bertels et. al., (Moscow, 1966–1971).

❧ GUIDE TO THE ILLUSTRATIONS ❧

The following twenty-six pages catalog the *Shahnameh* illustrations selected for the book and provide sources and credits. The list is organized in order of the painting's first appearance in the text and by manuscript and collection, beginning with those images that come from the Shah Tahmasb *Shahnameh* manuscript and going on to images from other collections and manuscripts. Where details have been used to illustrate the text, the appropriate page numbers have been provided. Information such as the name of the painter and the date of the painting have been given wherever available. In some cases, painters are identified simply by a letter (e.g., "Painter A"). These designations refer to specific painters whose works have been identified but whose names remain unknown.

❧ CREDITS AND ACKNOWLEDGMENTS ❧

We are grateful to Abolala Soudavar and the late Prince Sadruddin Aga Khan for generously allowing us to use images from their collections. We would also like to thank William Robinson at Christie's, Deana Cross at the Metropolitan Museum, Mohammad Isa Waley at the British Library, Ben Primer and Don Skemer at the Princeton University Library, Massumeh Farhad at the Freer and Sackler Galleries, Filiz Çagman at the Topkapi Palace Museum, and Lâle Uluç for their assistance in finding and photographing fourteenth- to seventeenth-century *Shahnameh* manuscript illustrations for this book.

We would also like to sincerely thank George Constable for his astute editorial suggestions, Anne Rollins for her sensitive copyediting, Harry Endrulat for proofing the manuscript, Zal Batmanglij for his design suggestions, Rostam Batmanglij for his digital expertise, and Hugh MacDonald for the many tasks he performs at Mage Publishers.

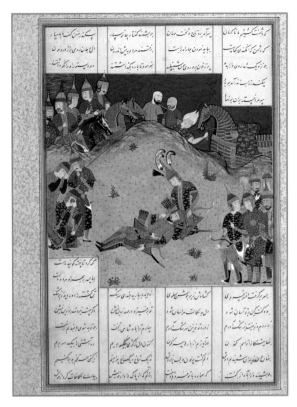

Sekandar Attends the Dying Dara
Painter E c. 1520-30 / folio 486r
Courtesy of private collection.
Details on pages: 42, 43, 45

Ardeshir and Golnar
Painted by Mir Mussavar c. 1520-30 / folio 516v
Courtesy of private collection.
Details on pages: 121, 124-125

Ardeshir's Victory Over Bahman
Painter E c. 1520-30 / folio 519r
Courtesy of private collection.
Details on pages: 131, 132-133, 134, 174

The Story of Haftvad and the Worm
Signed by Dust Mohammad c. 1525-1535 / folio 521v
Courtesy of Collection Prince Sadruddin Aga Khan.
Details on pages: 140-141, 143

Shapur I Meets Mehrak's Daughter
Painted by Aqa Mirak c. 1520-30 / folio 527v
Courtesy of private collection.
Details on pages: 162, 163

Coronation of Shapur
Attributed to Muzaffar Ali c. 1525-30 / folio 538v. The Metropolitan
Museum of Art, Gift of Arthur A. Houghton, Jr., 1970.
(1970.301.59) Photograph © 2003 The Metropolitan Museum of
Art. Details on pages: 178, 179, 183, 190, 191

Caesar Captive before Shapur II
Attributed to Aqa Mirak c. 1525-30 / folio 543r. The Metropolitan
Museum of Art, Gift of Arthur A. Houghton, Jr., 1970.
(1970.301.60) Photograph © 2003 The Metropolitan Museum of Art.
Details on pages: 194-195

The Accession of Ardeshir II
Painter D supervised by Aqa Mirak c. 1520-30 / folio 547r
Courtesy of private collection.
Detail on page: 150

Bahram Gur Takes Azadeh Hunting
Painter C c. 1520-30 / folio 550v
Courtesy of private collection.
Details on pages: 209, 251

Yazdegerd the Unjust and the Water Horse that Killed Him
Painted by Muzaffar Ali c. 1520-30 / folio 553r
Courtesy of private collection.
Details on pages: 218-219

Bahram Gur Negotiates for the Throne
Painted by Aqa Mirak c. 1520-30 / folio 555v
Courtesy of private collection.
Detail on page: 228

Bahram Gur Defeats the Lions and Mounts the Throne
Painter C supervised by Aqa Mirak c. 1520-30 / folio 557v
Courtesy of private collection.
Details on pages: 234-235, 247

Bahram Gur Pins Coupling Wild Asses
Attributed to Mir Seyyed Ali c. 1533-35 / folio 568rv. The Metropolitan
Museum of Art, Gift of Arthur A. Houghton, Jr., 1970. (1970.301.62)
Photograph © 1996 The Metropolitan Museum of Art.
Details on pages: 256-257, 388-389, 552

Bahram Gur Hunts Lions with His Sword
Painter D supervised by Aqa Mirak c. 1520-30 / folio 573r
Courtesy of private collection.
Detail on pages: 240-241

Bahram Gur Slays the Rhino-Wolf
Painted by Abd al Aziz, supervised by Aqa Mirak c. 1533-35 / folio
586r. The Metropolitan Museum of Art, Gift of Arthur A. Houghton,
Jr., 1970. (1970.301.74) Photograph © 1995 The Metropolitan
Museum of Art. Details on pages: 288, 289

Nushin-Ravan Stopped by a Water Course
Painter E, c. 1520-30 / folio 611v
Courtesy of private collection.
Detail on pages: 314-315

Nushin-Ravan Greets the Khaqan's Daughter
Attributed to Dust Mohammad c. 1525-30 / folio 633v. The Metropolitan
Museum of Art, Gift of Arthur A. Houghton, Jr., 1970. (1970.301.70)
Photograph © 2003 The Metropolitan Museum of Art.
Details on pages: 328-329

Nushin-Ravan Responds to Questions from the High Priest
Painted by Mir Mussavar c. 1520-30 / folio 655v
Courtesy of private collection.
Details on pages: 352, 354, 356, and front jacket

Khosrow Parviz Battles at Nahravan
Painted by Aqa Mirak c. 1520-30 / folio 690v
Courtesy of private collection.
Detail on pages: 418-419

The Angel Sorush Rescues Khosrow Parviz
Attributed to Muzaffar Ali c. 1525-30 / folio 708v. The Metropolitan
Museum of Art, Gift of Arthur A. Houghton, Jr., 1970. (1970.301.73)
Photograph © 2003 The Metropolitan Museum of Art.
Details on pages: 202, 434-435, 437, and back jacket

Bahram Chubineh Slays the Lion-Ape
Attributed to Mir Mussavar c. 1530-35 / folio 715v. The Metropolitan
Museum of Art, Gift of Arthur A. Houghton, Jr., 1970. (1970.301.74)
Photograph © 2003 The Metropolitan Museum of Art.
Details on pages: 173, 442-443, 551

Gordyeh Kills Tovorg, the Chinese Emperor's Brother
Painter E c. 1520-30 / folio 721v
Courtesy of private collection.
Detail on pages: 452-453

Barbad Conceals Himself in a Tree
Painted by Mirza Ali c. 1520-30 / folio 731v
Courtesy of private collection.
Detail on page: 473

Assassination of Khosrow Parviz
Attributed to Abd us-Samad c. 1530-35 / folio 742v. The Metropolitan
Museum of Art, Gift of Arthur A. Houghton, Jr., 1970. (1970.301.75)
Photograph © 2001 The Metropolitan Museum of Art.
Details on pages: 482-483, 484

The Coup against the Usurper Goraz
Attributed to Dust Mohammad c. 1525-30 / folio 745v. The Metropolitan Museum of Art, Gift of Arthur A. Houghton, Jr., 1970. (1970.301.76) Photograph © 2003 The Metropolitan Museum of Art. Details on pages: 2, 490-491, 497

Sekandar Sees the Speaking Tree
c. 1335-40. Freer Gallery of Art, Smithsonian Institution, Washington, D.C.: Purchase. F 1938.3. Details on pages: 103, 104-105

Mourning for the Death of Sekandar
c. 1335-40. Freer Gallery of Art, Smithsonian Institution, Washington, D.C.: Purchase. F 1935.23. Detail on pages: 115-116

Nushin-Ravan Rewards Bozorjmehr
c. 1335-40. Freer Gallery of Art, Smithsonian Institution, Washington, D.C.: Purchase. F 1938.3. Detail on pages: 348-349

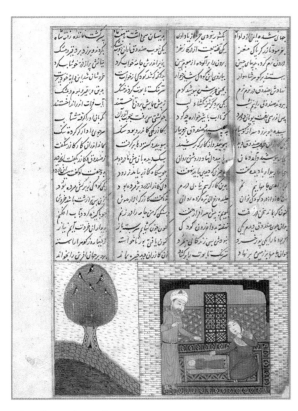

The Fuller Finds Darab
By permission of the British Library (OR 1403 / folio 306r)
Detail on page: 18

The Roman Emperor Has Shapur Sown in an Ass's Skin
By permission of the British Library (OR 1403 / folio 352v)
Detail on pages: 186-187

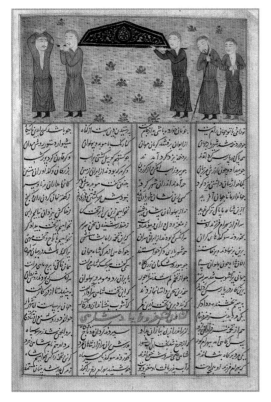

Yazdegerd the Unjust's Burial Procession
By permission of the British Library (OR 1403 / folio 360v)
Detail on page: 221

The Drunk Cobbler's Son Sits upon the Roaring Lion
By permission of the British Library (OR 1403 / folio 368v)
Detail on page: 246

Bozorjmehr Invents the Game of Nard
By permission of the British Library (Add 15531 / folio 3445v)
Details on pages: 335, 336-337

Bahram Gur at Shangal's Court
By permission of the British Library (Add 16761 / folio 389r)
Detail on page: 293

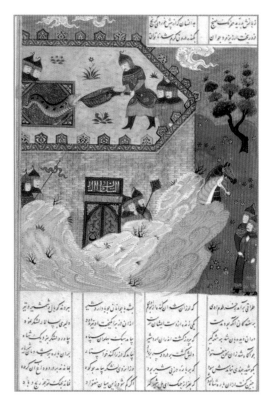

Ardeshir Kills Haftvad's Worm
By permission of the British Library (Add 18188 / folio 336r)
Details on pages: 146, 147

Bahram Gur Hunts with Azadeh
By permission of the British Library (Add 18188 / folio 353r)
Details on pages: 210, 211

Bahram Gur and Lembek the Water Carrier
By permission of the British Library (Add 18188 / folio 358r)
Details on pages: 264, 268

Woman Milks Cow
By permission of the British Library (Add 18188 / folio 368v)
Detail on page: 300

Bahram Wrestles before Shangal
By permission of the British Library (Add 18188 / folio 374v)
Detail on page: 284

Khosrow Parviz Fights Bahram Chubineh
By permission of the British Library (Add 18188/ folio 458v)
Detail on pages: 432-433

Sekandar Marries Roshanak
By permission of the British Library (Add 27257 / folio 326v)
Details on pages: 31, 50

Homay Crowns Darab
By permission of the British Library (Add 27257 / folio 326v)
Details on pages: 14, 25

Sekandar Reaches the Western Sea, and Abyssinia
By permission of the British Library (Add 27257 / folio 337v)
Detail on pages: 88-89

Ardeshir Ferried across the Water
By permission of the British Library (Add 27257 / folio 349v)
Detail on page: 129

Ardeshir Recognizes His Son Shapur
By permission of the British Library (Add 27257 / folio 355v)
Detail on page: 154

Bahram Hunts with Azadeh
By permission of the British Library (Add 27257 / folio 374v)
Details on pages: 204, 222-223, 248

Bahram Hunts
By permission of the British Library (Add 27257 / folio 387r)
Detail on page: 238

Bahram at War
By permission of the British Library (Add 27257 / folio 454v)
Detail on page: 413

Bahram Gur Attacks the Emperor of China
By permission of the British Library (Add 27257 / folio 395r)
Details on pages: 177, 274-275

Bahram Chubineh Fights Saveh Shah
By permission of the British Library (Add 27257 / folio 457r)
Details on pages: 366-367, 379

Khosrow Parviz Meets a Hermit
By permission of the British Library (Add 27257 / folio 488r)
Detail on page: 401

Rostam Son of Hormozd's Battle with Sa'd
By permission of the British Library (Add 27257 / folio 532v)
Detail on pages: 500-501

Qaydafeh Recognizes Sekandar
By permission of the British Library (Ethe 863 / folio 349v)
Detail on page: 77

Kesra Kills Mazdak
By permission of the British Library (Add 1256 / folio 496a)
Detail on page: 309

Barbad Plays for Khosrow
By permission of the British Library (OR. 2256 / folio number 77v)
Detail on page: 470

Homay Crowning Darab
Princeton University Library, Islamic Third Series 310 / folio 279b
Details on pages: 27, 53, 54, 55

Sekandar Kills Dragon
Princeton University Library, Islamic Third Series 310 / folio 296b
Detail on page: 90

Ardeshir Recognizes His Son
Princeton University Library, Islamic Third Series 310 / folio 312a
Details on pages: 156, 157, 159

Bahram Gur Hunts
Princeton University Library, Islamic Third Series 310 / folio 336b
Detail on page: 205

Bahram Chubineh Kills Saveh Shah
Princeton University Library, Islamic Third Series 310 / folio 411b
Details on pages: 375, 377, 380-381

Khosrow Parviz's Army Battles Bahram Chubineh
Princeton University Library, Islamic Third Series 310 / folio 437a
Detail on pages: 428-429

Khosrow Parviz Goes to Shirin
Princeton University Library, Islamic Third Series 310 / folio 452b
Detail on pages: 464-465

Bozorjmehr Discovers the Young Man in Kesra's Harem
Princeton University Library, Garret Collection of
Islamic Manuscripts, 56G / folio 445b

Bahram Chubineh Dies in His Sister Gordyeh's Arms
Princeton University Library, Garret Collection of
Islamic Manuscripts, 56G / folio598a
Details on pages: 447, 449

An Execution
Topkapi Palace Museum, H1478 / folio 268a

Bahram Gur Tramples Azadeh
Topkapi Palace Museum, H1478 / folio 402a
Detail on page: 212

Drunk Cobbler's Son Rides a Lion
Topkapi Palace Museum, H1478 / folio 402a
Detail on pages: 244-245

Khosrow Parviz Visits Shirin
Topkapi Palace Museum, H1478 / folio 359b
Detail on page: 460

Sekandar Listens to the Final Words of Dying Dara
Topkapi Palace Museum, H1485 / folio 382a

Bahram Gur Defeats the Lions and Takes Iranian Crown
Topkapi Palace Museum, H1485 / folio 438b
Detail on page: 232

Bahram Gur Wrestles before Shangal
Topkapi Palace Museum, H1485 / folio 460a
Detail on page: 285

Sekandar Hangs Dara's Murderers
Topkapi Palace Museum, H1499 / folio 339a
Detail on page: 49

Sekandar Kills a Dragon
Topkapi Palace Museum, H1499 / folio 355a
Detail on pages: 92-93

Sekandar Discovers the Talking Tree
Topkapi Palace Museum, H1499 / folio 355b
Detail on page: 106

Bahram Gur, Having Shamed the Lions, Sits on the Iranian Throne
Topkapi Palace Museum, H1499 / folio 392b
Detail on pages: 236-237

Nushin-Ravan Returns
Topkapi Palace Museum, H1499 / folio 433a
Details on pages: 317, 369, 387

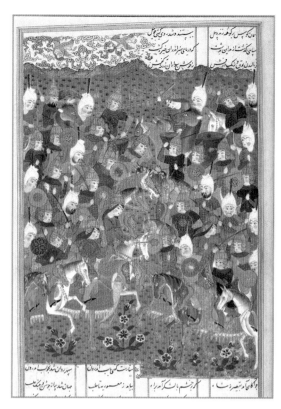

Battle Scene
Topkapi Palace Museum, H1499 / folio 469a
Detail on page: 32

Bahram Chubineh Kills Saveh Shah
Topkapi Palace Museum, H1499 / folio 481a
Details on pages: 382, 384

Khosrow Parviz's Army Battles Bahram Chubineh
Topkapi Palace Museum, H1499 / folio 495b

Bahram Chubineh Kills a Dragon
Topkapi Palace Museum, H1499 / folio 515a

Bizhan Attacks Yazdegerd
Topkapi Palace Museum, H1499 / folio 545a
Detail on pages: 506-507

The Fuller Discovers Darab
Topkapi Palace Museum, H1500 / folio 413a
Detail on page: 16

Qaydafeh Recognizes Sekandar
Topkapi Palace Museum, H1500 / folio 441a
Details on pages: 57, 58, 74

Sekandar Conquers the Country of Sind
Topkapi Palace Museum, H1500 / folio 456a
Details on pages: 63-64, 70

Shapur Battles the Romans
Topkapi Palace Museum, H1500 / folio 490b
Details on pages: 165, 168

Bahram in the Country
Topkapi Palace Museum, H1500 / folio 514b

Kesra Kills Mazdak and His Followers
Topkapi Palace Museum, H1500 / folio 549a
Detail on pages: 310-311

Nushin-Ravan Answers Questions
Topkapi Palace Museum, H1500 / folio 602b

Khosrow Parviz Visits a Monastery
Topkapi Palace Museum, H1500 / folio 642b
Detail on pages: 426-427

Khosrow Parviz Visits Shirin
Topkapi Palace Museum, H1500 / folio 672b
Details on pages: 462-463, 468-469

Battle Scene
Topkapi Palace Museum, H1505 / folio 316a
Details on pages: 318-319, 417

Bahram Gur Hunts with Azadeh
Topkapi Palace Museum, H1506 / folio 412a
Details on pages: 6, 208, 214

Bahram Gur Hunts Ostriches
Topkapi Palace Museum, H1506 / folio 413a
Detail on page: 215

Bahram Gur Kills a Dragon
Topkapi Palace Museum, H1506 / folio 433a
Detail on pages: 290-291

Indian Raja Sends the Game of Chess to Nushin-Ravan
Topkapi Palace Museum, H1506 / folio 481b
Detail on pages: 332-333

Bahram Chubineh Has Parmoudeh Brought to Him
Topkapi Palace Museum, H1506 / folio 511a
Detail on page: 394-395

Sekandar Builds a Wall
Topkapi Palace Museum, H15 1510 / folio 307b
Detail on page: 101

Yazdegerd the Unjust Is Killed by the Waterhorse
Topkapi Palace Museum, H1510 / folio 340a
Detail on page: 220

Sekandar Discovers Yajuj and Majuj
Topkapi Palace Museum, H1511 / folio 182b
Detail on page: 100

Shapur Hunts
Topkapi Palace Museum, H1516 / folio 373b
Detail on page: 160

Bahram Gur Speaks to the Iranians
Topkapi Palace Museum, H1516 / folio 396a
Detail on page: 231

Bahram Chubineh Writes a Letter to Hormozd
Topkapi Palace Museum, H1516 / folio 456b
Details on pages: 259, 330, 487

Battle Scene
Topkapi Palace Museum, H1516 / folio 476a
Detail on page: 360

Khosrow Visits Shirin
Topkapi Palace Museum, H1516 / folio 533a
Detail on page: 466